The Shadow i

Copyright © 2020 Kirsty March All rights reserved

No part of this book may be reproduced, or stored in a retrieval system, or transmitted in any form or by any means, electronic, mechanical, photocopying, recording, or otherwise, without express written permission of the publisher.

ISBN-13: 9798636867845

Cover design by: Christine & Kirsty March

For Sylvander

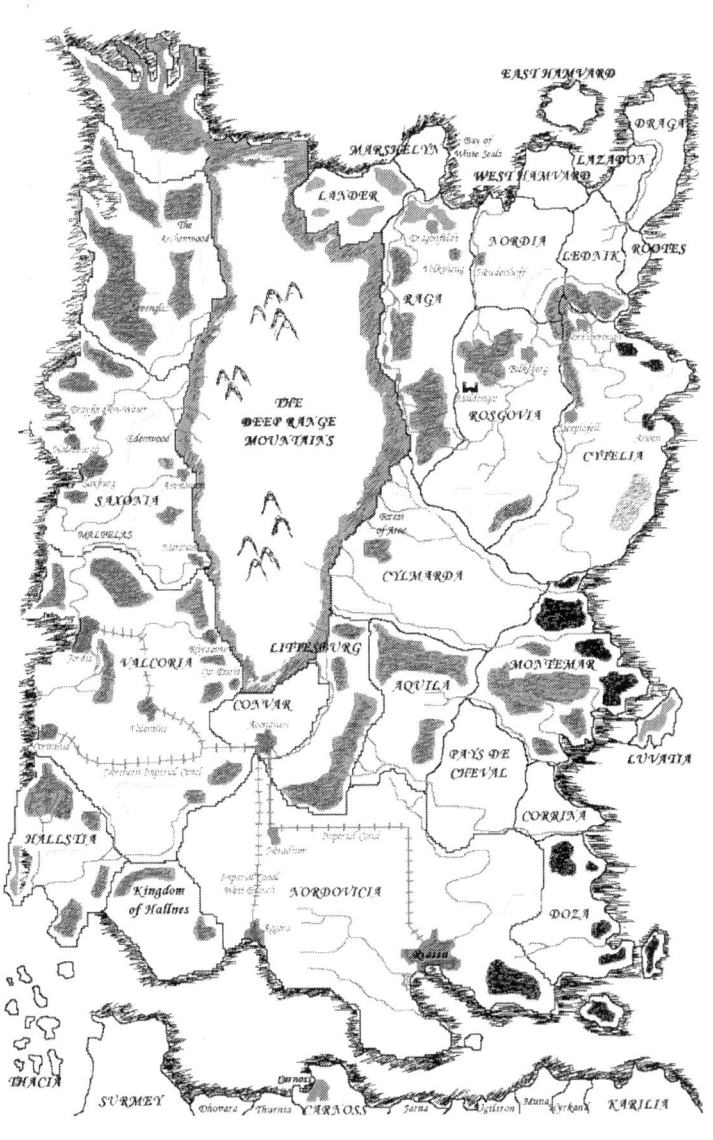

Beasts I

For a brief moment, I hesitated. Indecision is such a human trait.

We all become caught on the hooks of our indecision at one time or another, some more so than others. It is a facet that sets us apart from the beasts. It was a beast that I was facing. It suffered no such indecision but acted on instinct, as I anticipated it would. The snow tiger pounced and I danced aside, throwing the hooked net.

The tiger buried itself in the centre, its impetus thrusting it into the mesh. The trap closed about it and the great animal struggled impotently before it finally lay still, its great chest rising and falling, the snarling subsiding to a threatening rumble. I was not taken in for a moment. I knew, not only because I had been taught and had to repeat it over a thousand times, but also because I had seen first-hand what happens to a man who underestimates the power and the savagery of a beast. I stood my ground.

There was a brief round of clapping and I looked back to the mounted figures. The two guardsmen lowered their crossbows. I looked up into my father's face, his grizzled beard with its white streaks frosted by the cold and snow. He pushed back the sable hat and laughed, clapping his heavy fur gloves together;

"Well taken. Like an old hand."

"Why does Edmund always get to make the catch? Why couldn't I trap the tiger? I know how to do it, father, I wouldn't flinch." Leopold, my half-brother whined, pressing his horse forward between my father and his cousin, the steward, Hildebrand.

"You would not have flinched, I know that, Leopold. You are a Von Tacchim and we do not flinch. Not from anything. But Edmund was ready and you will be soon, but not yet. Come, bring Edmund's tiger and we shall ride home."

The hunting party divided and I watched as four of my father's' hunters prodded at the noble beast until one struck with the point. The great tiger slowly closed its eyes as the poison did its work;

"Put him on the sled. He'll be out for hours", I heard the rough voice of Lancingor. He was one of the men who had prepared me for this moment. A tall, lean man of few words, he was more at home in the wild or with the animals than he was with people. I stamped snow off my boots and then took my knife and standing on one leg at a time, cleaned out the gap between the grips before I remounted my own horse. I got a nod of approval from Finnmeyer and that pleased me too. Of all those who tutored me, Finnmeyer was the one whose opinion I cared about the most. He was servant, companion and friend to my father and had been for as long as I could remember.

Swinging up onto the white mare, I took the reins and turned her head for home. My eldest half-brother, Frederick rode up beside me, "Well caught Edmund. You handled that better than I did on my first solo." He smiled and reached out to slap my shoulder. I grinned back. Frederick would be a good duke when he inherited the title, and I'd be happy to serve him when he did.

The ride home was exhilarating. I galloped ahead with Finnmeyer and Frederick. Leopold tried to keep up but we took the short way down the hill and through the woods, threading through the trees at speed. The three of us flung up snow and laughed as we came crashing out of the pines and back onto the snow bound road. Falkeberg towered above us, its conical towers soaring into the grey-white winter sky.

Ahead, the road wound as it rose, curling like a sleeping serpent about the three levels until it reached the fourth and there, its head became the rampart, its eyes the two arched windows which overlooked the approach from the towers squatting on each side of the road and its jaws the great black Eisentor, the city's main gate. In the cold winter breeze, the pennants on the gatehouse towers fluttered in panic like birds caught upon a vampire-thorn. From where we had pulled up our horses, I tried to make out the coat of arms on the fourth one that flew over the gates. That pole had been empty when we left. With the continual stinging of sleet and the darkening sky, it was hard to see. It had a deep crimson ground with what appeared to be a mailed fist with wings.

"So, he is here."

I turned. My father had caught us up and was sitting astride his black destrier, his breath coming in short icy pants. "What you did there was dangerous, Edmund, Frederick. Leopold might have followed you, been hurt. Life is not a series of games. You, Frederick, will be duke, one day, if you don't knock your head off on a low hanging branch, first."

He frowned, but it was clear that it was not our exuberance that was the cause of his sudden moodiness.

"Lancingor!" He turned his horse and rode back to the sled where the main party came along, behind. "Loose the beast. Let it return to the woods."

"My lord?"

"You heard me. Loose the beast and when it recovers drive it towards its home."

My heart sunk, a little. I had been looking forward to the admiring glances of the young maidens and Viktor's excitement when he came dashing out to see if we had trapped a snow tiger. I looked back at my father. He must have known. He swung in his saddle;

"Now, Edmund. I know you wanted to show him off before you let him run free but you don't know our guest. The Baron would want him as a gift for some barbaric abuse and, as his host, I could not refuse. Better the tiger goes free than be the plaything of a Drachefauste."

"Drachefauste? Here?" I had heard many sounds in Finnmeyer's voice but never this one. It was heavy with a bitter hatred. He almost spat the words as if he had too much contempt to let his mouth speak them. My father nodded. "And we are to make an ally of him for the Empire." No emotion. He spoke softly and flatly. We called it his disguised voice, used when he didn't want us to know what he thought of something. I had practiced and practiced that voice without success. One day, I promised myself, I would master it, too.

"That....an ally?" Finnmeyer swung away. The set of his shoulders spoke louder than words. He did not speak again as we rode home, a dark mask over his usually cheerful features. It was turning into a day of storms and showers as Nan Weiskuchen would say.

There was more to come. Viktor did not come running through the snow to meet us as we rode in at the gates and along the tunnel beneath the great gatehouse. He stood on the palace steps looking uncomfortable in a high collared and starched formal jacket alongside the countess, Francesca De Valdeyez, my father's wife.

She held my youngest half-sibling, Diana, by the hand. To her left, Herlenbrand stood, looking equally uncomfortable in the formal garb of Keeper of the Ducal Seals. His powerful frame, balding head and scarred face looked somehow out of place in anything but armour. A veteran of several imperial wars, he, like my Uncle Raef, was here to remind Drachefauste of our military heritage.

On his right stood the handsome figure of Raef Von Tacchim, Duke of Littesburg, my father's cousin. His light blue and grey uniform of the Littesburg Guard was worked in silver and bore medals from the various battles and wars he had fought for the Empire. Although his dark hair was touched with silvery grey, as were his mustachios, he still looked every bit the hero of Augsbrendel.

He was the man I emulated in my imagination, leading cavalry charges and fighting famous actions. His wavy hair was long, the majority bound by a single band of gold in a plaited queue down his back. He wore his soft, grey leather gloves, one resting upon the fine duelling blade at his side, the other hanging loose. My father leaned towards me and whispered, "put up your hood and stay back with the hunters."

Now my heart was as low as my boots. So, I was not to be presented. I was to be hidden away. A bastard. Son of a concubine.

"Edmund, listen" I heard my father's voice cut through my self-pitying distraction. "I don't want Drachefauste to see you. Just a precaution. I don't want him to mark who you are."

At the time, I didn't understand that. I do, now.

Lord Goran Drachefauste emerged from the gatehouse, where, no doubt, he and his entourage had been waiting to be officially welcomed. If ever there was a man around whom darkness hung, it was this man. He was relatively tall, maybe six feet or just over and overweight so that he gave an impression at once of solidity and of power. Wrapped in the furs of wild animals over gleaming plated and chain mail, the colours he wore were all sombre, even the crimson cloak on his back.

Under one arm, he carried a great helm with a fist crushing a dragonet, its tail writhing from the bottom of the hand, the crushed neck curled back, the head with eyes closed wearing an expression that conveyed agony. He had destroyed the army of Emperor Varilus III and some say he had personally slain the emperor on the field of battle. For nine more long years, Varilus' successor, Prilemus I had tried to conquer and subjugate Raga.

Then he had died, suddenly and a coup placed his cousin upon the pearl throne. Severus VI acted swiftly. The imperial forces were withdrawn. Then, came a peace offering followed by an offer of an alliance. In this, Duke Vasely Von Tacchim was reputed to have acted as an ambassador. Now, he was being entrusted with bringing this man into the fold and taming the beast for his Emperor. But Drachefauste's reputation hung about him like the vile smell of offal. He had butchered his captives, maiming some and leaving them to die in the snow. When the imperial captain, Phenelos, had taken the town of Borumgar, he had turned his main force back and assaulted his own town rather than leave it under a holding siege.

After it fell, he had Phenelos and his lieutenants pinned to the walls, where they died slowly, taunting them each day while the Imperial 3rd Army closed on him. Once it reached the gates, he drove the men of the town out to meet them, calling them traitors for surrendering to Phenelos while he marched his own men away before besieging forces could close.

When the imperial army broke through the small body of defenders that Drachefauste had left to cover the retreat, they found another atrocity awaiting them. Skewered to the doors and walls of houses through the town were the women and children of Borumgar.

Once they were inside the city walls, a group of Drachefauste's Dragon Guard, left behind in scattered hiding places about the town, set flames to the oil-soaked gates and walls. Borumgar became an inferno. Over a thousand imperial troops died in the stampede to escape the hungry flames, the handful of Dragon Guards alongside them - a testament to their fanaticism and Drachefauste's grip upon his elite force.

Shortly after that, the Imperial General, Mandicar Von Ulrich caught up with Drachefauste. He faced another unpleasant surprise.

Drachefauste had trebled his forces by bringing his allies - night trolls and black goblins from the hills, alongside wyverns and other beasts trained for war. Stories were told that Drachefauste had Mandicar dragged before him and put his eyes out with a hot poker before hanging him up in chains and carving him into joints. There were whispered rumours that Raga's ruling class were part troll, and that in battle their wounds healed, their strength was untiring and that they ate parts of those that they slew. Drachefauste supposedly also kept the company of dark mages. If that were true, there were none such visible in his company now.

His Dragon Guards were all huge men, scarred with tattoos upon their arms and faces. Each wore a heavy iron helm studded about the neck and forehead and each carried a double-bladed partisan axe.

It was certainly believable that some of these men were troll or goblin bloods. He had no women with him. The only others in the party were a frail, wiry old man with white beard and pale eyes who was introduced as his chancellor, Uban Trossleg, a name I later learned was well-known in financial circles, and a broad, squat goblin with tusk canines, his ugly squashed looking greenish-black face caused by folds of fat. He used the name of Blorg Skullsmasher. Subtlety is not rated highly in goblin circles.

"Duke Vasely!" Drachefauste's voice was a bearlike growl. He threw his arms about my father and made a great show of crushing him in an embrace, slapping him on the shoulders as if they were brothers in arms. My father smiled but it was not his real smile. He linked arms with this man and steered him to the palace steps, introducing Frederick and Leopold as he walked.

I noticed Finnmeyer had disappeared from the group. Then I saw him, standing in the shadows of the stable, eyes on Drachefauste, glowering. Hatred was written upon his face. I wondered what the baron could have done to so offend the hunter whom I regarded as my friend.

"Where's that lovely concubine of yours? Estella? And your bastard. I heard he's grown into a warlike young buck" roared Drachefauste. From where I stood, I could see the pink flush rise in Lady Francesca's cheeks. Others reacted too, but my father just met his eye and remained as cool as the winter day. "He has duties and Estella is away dealing with business matters for me."

"Oho! You trust a woman to represent you?! The House of Von Tacchim must have grown short of steel if it has to entrust missions to women. Their job should begin and end on their backs... or on all fours, eh?" Drachefauste's laugh was a barking crescendo to this statement and it echoed amongst the gargoyles and carvings that adorned the walls and high points of Falkeberg.

Father's voice was ice tinged, "House Von Tacchim uses steel when it needs. You might remember that, Baron Drachefauste."

Drachefauste raised one eyebrow and just for one moment, the mask rippled, one eye twitched and one fist clenched but then he laughed again, hugely, "Come on, Duke Vasely, introduce me to the lovely countess. And tell her to wear something cut low, tonight. I would like something good to look at over dinner." Lady Francesca flushed deeper and exchanged glances with father but he just shook his head, very slowly from behind the bulk of Drachefauste. They went forward, together.

The formal introductions were made more quietly. Frederick and Leopold moved to flank their mother who looked relieved as they did so. Uncle Herlenbrand managed to smile as he matched the Baron's obviously vice like grip. The others winced, especially mother when he took her wrist to kiss her hand, a rough movement.

It was the act of a man who was sending her a message about what he would do if the chance should ever arise.

Even Raef could not hide a little pain in the handshake but his lip curled into a sneer and Drachefauste, saw that. The exchange in their eyes said enough. Raef's hand went to his sword as the baron stepped back. I knew what he wanted to do. I think there were enough of us willing someone to strike the beast. The baron simply smiled.

"Come through the stable" Finnmeyer's voice was close and half turned. He rested a hand on my shoulder. I hadn't even heard him move closer.

"Why? I'm not afraid of him. I'd trap and kill him just like a rabid tiger."

Finnmeyer smiled although his eyes stayed hard. "I'm sure you would. But this is not the time to show yourself, so come through the stable."

"Why did father speak as if I wasn't here?" I asked, still hurting from being left in the cold.

"Your father is wise. The beast should not be given the scent of one he does not know where to hunt. Edmund, a time may come when you have to go amongst the enemy in disguise. Better they do not know you at all. Better to walk in the shadows unseen and better for your father not to reveal his whole hand."

I tried to understand this but it didn't make complete sense to me. I was going off to study as a bard soon at Lorefast. Father had promised me that I could, as long as I promised to keep practicing my weapons and skills.

That evening, briefed to listen and to pretend to be a squire, I helped serve at the lord's table and poured ale and fortified wines from great jugs. We all wore hoods and tunics in the purple and gold of the house. Once, Drachefauste yelled at me for more ale as I had only half filled his glass. He tried to cuff me but I moved aside too quickly and he sprawled across the table, spilling food and drink in all directions. By the time he had straightened, I had been pulled out of sight and another similar sized squire had been sent to stand there, a nice lad called Ledric.

He took a fist on the side of the head that felled him and I fought back tears. It wasn't anything to do with him. I saw him try to rise and the baron laughing and pointing. I'm glad to say that Lady Francesca, who had purposefully worn a dress with a high collar, rose, made her apologies and left the table there and then. Drachefauste saw her, but he just smiled his feral smile and threw a heavy bone at Ledric. That blow bruised his shoulder, he told me later when I went to ask after him. Ledric stumbled against the wall.

"No steel in them, that's the trouble, Von Tacchim! You need to breed them tougher. Let me show you what I mean"

He signalled to one of his guards standing at the doors and whispered something to him. Two minutes later and a young lad was brought before the table. He looked defiant. His face was swarthy and heavy for a teenager and his build much broader than Ledric. He had a tattoo on his upper left arm but just the one, unlike the heavily marked arms of the Dragon Guards.

"You're training to be in my guards, aren't you, lad?" shouted the baron. The boy nodded. "My lord", his voice had a thick and heavy sound, slightly guttural. Without hesitation, the baron struck him with his fist on the side of the head. The thwack echoed down the hall. The boy staggered slightly and then straightened to stand straight saluting his master; "If I have displeased you, my lord."

"See... that's what a soldier wants to be. You're too soft, Von Tacchim. All of you Imperials. You've been amongst soft courtiers and soft women for too long"

He turned to the boy, "You may go. You may also draw an extra fennet from the captain for taking the blow like a man."

The boy nodded and a grim smile twitched on his features, exposing teeth that seemed oddly canine for a human. Drachefauste turned, slowly to my father; "I could teach that duchess of yours a thing or two about discipline too," he grinned, showing rough and uneven teeth.

Father gave him a long look but refused to answer. The talk died down at the table.

"What's the matter, Duke Vasely?" he pressed.

"Be careful, Drachefauste. An invitation to an alliance only goes so far." My father stood, slowly, twitching aside his cloak. Beneath it, I could see what Drachefauste could see, a pair of long daggers, one white handled, one black. Drachefauste grinned, hugely.

"Sit down. I didn't mean to insult your table," he rumbled, "I just wanted to see if it was true about you. So, you are more than the Emperor's messenger."

I forgot those daggers until many years later, even though, at the time, I meant to ask my father what they meant. In the rush of the event and comings and goings, it went out of my mind. It might have helped me in understanding more had I answered that question then.

After that, the feast proceeded much as any other and the Dragon Guards stopped looking like they expected to have to use their axes. But I had seen them. When father rose to confront Drachefauste, they were not just ready to use them, they wanted to attack.

I stayed out of Drachefauste's way for the remainder of his visit. My father kept the beast skilfully entertained without compromising his own principles and an alliance with Raga was concluded. Under the terms, the Baron became a Duke, granted all the rights and freedoms to rule his domain as he saw fit with a promise of Imperial support should anyone raise arms against him.

The consideration of an electoral position was mentioned, too. In return, Drachefauste finally acknowledged that he was a subject of the empire and that Raga was an imperial fief, owing a small but nevertheless substantial sum in taxes.

So much for the Imperial throne standing by its land holders. No mention was made of the De Maine family who had lost the state when it rebelled. The head of that family had been reduced to a Marquess and given a political post. Such is the way of the rule of pragmatism over the rule of law.

Suffice to say, the peace was short-lived.

Family

"Enough!" Lancingor held up one hand. Frederick and I stepped back, lowering our shields and practice blades. We both opened our helms and stood, panting.

"It is time that I gave the younger ones their lesson in jousting. You both did fine work again today."

We took off the helms and began to walk to the armoury.

"Want to take a ride before we join Finnmeyer for his session, today?" Frederick asked. I smiled, "why not? We could go and see if Ziffer has caught any salmon or trout down by the bridge."

We emerged from the armoury to hear the sound of the tilting mannequin squeaking as it turned on its uneven wheel. Leopold had just ridden by and half struck it, narrowly avoiding being hit in the back of the neck as it swung, whirling a light ball and chain. Viktor rode uncertainly at the target and poked at it with his lance. The mannequin screeched and shook as it turned slowly and Viktor pulled away.

"No, no" Lancingor strode forward, "you don't move the lance at all. You aim and ride through the target, letting the weight of the charge and the set lance do the rest."

He looked up, seeing Frederick and I approaching on our full-size mounts.

"Show him how it should be done, Frederick." Lancingor pointed to the dummy.

Frederick cantered down to the end of the lists. Sitting tall on his horse with his broad shoulders, he looked every inch a knight. Frederick stood over six feet in height with medium length dark hair and a neat beard. Compared to the rest of us he was more muscular in the chest and arms. Wherever he strode, you would see the ladies glancing at him admiringly. He was taller than father.

Leopold was also just over six feet, maybe an inch or so shorter than me but he was leaner and lighter, more like his mother whereas Frederick and Viktor looked much more like my father. I was the only one who differed strongly, my mother having come from the southern states. Diana had long, black hair, more like father but the stature and build of her mother. You could tell that we were all Von Tacchims if you knew your imperial families.

Frederick picked up a spear while on the move, came around and picked up to a full charge, lance set and swinging slightly out as he gauged the target. There was a bang as he struck the shield full on, sending the tilt dummy spinning. Viktor clapped and whooped. Leopold inclined his head to his elder brother.

"Now you, Edmund."

I rode down to the end of the lists and then leaned down and pulled out my crossbow. Coming at a canter,

I turned the horse aside before reaching the target, put a bolt in place and as my horse slowed to a walk, I loosed the quarrel. There was a loud smack and the quarrel tip came out of the back of the stuffed straw head.

"That was not what I had in mind" Lancingor commented dryly. "The crossbow is not a knight's weapon. I do wish old Sergeant Fuchs hadn't taught you that."

"He got his man, though, didn't he?" My father's rich voice came from behind us. We all looked around as he strode down, putting on a pair of gauntlets.

"I'm afraid Finnmeyer's lesson on dirty fighting is off for today" he said to Frederick and I. "However, you boys may wish to join us. There's something you might be interested to see."

We rode out of the gates in a small bunched group. With us, there were four house guard and the chaplain, Brother Elfric. We struck out towards the river and then followed its course, roughly for about five miles or so. Coming around the side of a copse, we saw an old burial mound ahead - not uncommon in the northern lands.

There were tribal people living here for many centuries before the empire established itself. A small group of men looked up as we approached and one, an ageing fellow in a long leather apron raised a hand. I knew him, at once. It was Doctor Hermanns, our historian. He loved nothing more than to teach history when it involved wars and military tactics, but he was also an expert when it came to looking at tools, pots and evidence from places such as this. He could say in an instant what period a thing belonged to and tell you something about the people who made the items, so it was no surprise to find him here. It was much more intriguing that whatever he had found had drawn my father out.

"We have it here, my lord" he said as my father dismounted and handed his reins to one of the guardsmen. Finnmeyer was off his horse in an instant, walking around the site, wary of trouble. Finnmeyer was always like that. His first concern from waking to putting his head down at night, was the safety and security of my father and of the rest of the family. Numerous times over the years, he had insisted on moving us to other rooms or even leaving places altogether and my father never questioned him over it, at least not in public. On two occasions, his wariness had saved us from assassination attempts.

He prowled, signalling for Frederick and I to come and join him. Only once he had checked the perimeter did he remove his black leather helm and mop his brow. I noticed then, perhaps for the first time, that his hair was greying noticeably. I also caught sight of the long scar from his right ear to his throat.

I had always thought of Finnmeyer as our man in the house. He was the one we went to when we thought a decision against us was too harsh or unfair. He was the one who watched over us the way Lancingor watched over my father. Finnmeyer was my father's friend the way Lancingor had been my grandfather's. It was always Finnmeyer who would listen to our accounts and then would give a balanced view. Often, he would side against us, but we would accept that from him because he did not get heated or show any judgement. He always just presented the case back as the other party saw it and would explain why he felt one or other was the right line. Sometimes, he would just listen and make little or no comment.

My father was looking under a large tarpaulin of hemp. I stopped watching Finnmeyer, although I had seen him nod approvingly at me as I continued to circle, also keeping my eyes on our surroundings. He had been teaching me to study a place and to look at it from two points of view. The first was how it could be defended if raiders were to appear on foot or horseback. The second way was to look at how I would attack if I were the raider. I was looking now at the sunken dell we were in and thinking it was a lot easier to attack than to defend.

"Boys. Come and look at this," my father urged. We joined him. Slowly, he lifted the hemp and we saw what had brought him out.

The long stretcher which the men had used to carry out the remains was now explained. It was not a humanoid body that lay beneath the covering. The skeleton was the strangest one I had ever seen. It measured about seven or eight feet in all.

The spine and main length of the body was curved and flexible with a long tail, except that it was heavier and wider and at regular intervals were heavy bone arrangements that looked like they would have protected a soft appendage or organ. The head by comparison, was oversized with horn-like structures that curved back from the forehead. The eye sockets were huge, whereas the mouth, which in a drake would have rows of teeth, narrowed to a small trumpet like opening with no teeth at all.

"What is it?" I asked Doctor Hermanns.

"Well, that is the thing, Lord Edmund, that is the thing, indeed. We don't know what it is. In all my reading and travels, I have never seen anything like this. It is a mystery. It is more bug-like, but nothing I am familiar with. And this is not all.

Why would it be buried with honours by the people who made this mound? This is most certainly from the Post-Rostian stage, probably built by the first men to use iron. They honoured this creature and placed items around it like they did with their own kings and shaman."

"Which is why I had to see it." commented my father, "it gives us a whole series of questions to answer.

This will be something very new in the records, I believe. Doctor Hermann's paper on the find will be kept in the imperial library, I think."

Doctor Hermanns looked down, a little embarrassed and muttered something, but he was clearly pleased with the thought.

"So, what will you do with it now?" Frederick asked.

"Take it back to Falkeberg and study it in more detail. I need to make drawings and to try to determine what the functions of its structures were. I shall indeed write a paper on this, maybe two. There is both the physiology and the archaeology to consider. I am so gratified, your grace, that you came out for just an old man's interests."

"Not at all, Doctor Hermanns. You know that I have always been interested in the past and this is a find of importance. I am sure there is much more to this than simply an interesting creature." My father answered.

"How old is it?" Viktor asked.

"Perhaps earlier than the Eisentor was built, before the first imperial Falkeberg. I should say even before humans settled this area, at all."

"Where did these creatures live?" Leopold gazed about, trying to ascertain if there was some evidence of a settlement, "They must have had towns or something."

"We have yet to find evidence of that, but yes, they must have had settlements. The signs here show they had reached a certain stage in their development." Doctor Hermanns was in his element, now.

Delighted to have so many asking questions, he positively beamed.

"Here is something you boys will like, too." The Doctor fished in a leather satchel and produced a heavy bronze arm ring, encrusted with semi-precious stones. "This was found amongst the offerings. From its richness, I would say that it belonged to a chieftain. Such gifts were given only to those who served a tribal lord faithfully. Somehow, this creature was accorded that status, I believe."

I turned the piece over in my hands. It was ancient, there was no doubt. I had seen such things in our own collection which my father kept in a case in the library. I shook my head and handed it on to Leopold.

"It is a mystery that ought to have a tale or legend woven about it" I said. Frederick laughed. "And you'd write it, given half a chance, wouldn't you? Perhaps one day you when you have completed your study at Lorefast, you can discover the legend and write a lay to match."

I smiled. In the Spring, I would travel to the Bardic and Druidic College on Gwythaor, to learn the formal ways of the old bards.

It was something I wanted to do and my father thought would prove a useful skill for a future ambassador. I would be trained there first. My father had other plans, I knew, but we had not discussed them yet.

The only thing that was decided was that Frederick would train to become duke, of course. Leopold would train as well; in case something should befall Frederick. Viktor would train as a priest and I would become an ambassador.

Leopold took the arm ring and weighed it in his hands. I could see him calculating value. "I wonder if there are more of these buried about in the mounds. We should open them all up. The treasury could always use the income."

Viktor handled the item briefly and handed it back again to Doctor Hermanns, "It would be fascinating to learn more of the races which have gone before us, but not by ripping open sites of interest. It isn't about money, it's about what we can learn."

I smiled at my youngest brother. It wasn't him being naïve. Viktor was motivated by more interesting matters than money and power. He would be a scholar, I was sure. He wanted to be a man of action, I knew, but he was too clumsy and at best only able to reach a basic standard when it came to weapons. Maybe that would improve with age, but I didn't see him that way. When he handled an old book or listened to a tale of the past, his eyes would light up. I loved him for that.

In turn, I thought about my own future.

In truth, I most wanted to ride out like Finnmeyer and to see with eyes like his. But travelling the world and dealing with dangerous situations as a negotiator appealed to me too. I was content.

***

It was nearly another year before I was ready to leave home for Lorefast. During that time, my father was often away. He returned frustrated more often than not. Drachefauste was not proving a model lord in Raga. He had accepted the imperial dukedom, but he refused to return the lands he had seized to the families who owned them. He created new lords and knights from his own followers, and it was rumoured that he was backing barbarian raids on his neighbours. Only Rosgovia was left untouched, for now. My uncles who held land in Raga, complained to my father whenever they visited us. It seemed things were not going to plan.

I was riding out with Finnmeyer on a standard patrol. We paused at the side of the road, looking out from the forest hills towards city gates. I reined in my horse and patted its neck. Everything was silent, except for the birds singing in the trees. Finnmeyer seemed far away in thought.

"Finnmeyer, can I ask you something?"

"Of course."

"That day when Drachefauste visited the city, I remember you speaking about him as if you hated him. Why was that?"

Finnmeyer turned to look at me. I had never seen him look so bleak or so pained. It was as if his expression was a clear sky suddenly darkened by storm clouds. His mouth became a slit and he shook his head. Looking away from me, he replied.

"That is one question I will not answer, my lord. Please do not speak of it, again."

I nodded. "Of course. I understand."

"You don't understand, Edmund, but I cannot speak of it. I will tell you this much, though. Don't trust Drachefauste. He is not a man. He is a beast, a ravenous, evil, rapacious beast. Never turn your back upon him, you understand. Never."

I just nodded mutely. I had known Finnmeyer all my life and I had never heard such bitter hatred in his voice. I didn't know it then but it wouldn't be long till I would cross Drachefauste's path and come to know only too well why Finnmeyer named him as a beast.

Hunters I

The winter passed without further news of Drachefauste, nor did we hunt any more. I began to select items and clothing to go with me on my journey. Gwythaor was far away from the centre of the Empire. Rosgovia was one of the most northerly Dukedoms. Littesburg was much closer but even that was not on the southern coast where the Imperial capital, Riassa, lay. Nonetheless, you could ride from Rosgovia through Cytelia and Cylmarda to Littesburg and from there you could choose a number of ways to get to Nordovicia and eventually the capital. The Nordovician Empire dominated nearly an entire continent. The islands lay to the far west, beyond the Deep Range Mountains beyond the shores of Saxonia, Valcoria and the barbarian lands of Bartragian. To reach Gwythaor meant taking a ship out of Saxburg or Jordis and then a week or more of hard sailing to make landfall.

When the spring thaw came, the rivers ran fast with white water that leapt and rushed over the rocks and stones. Some were so swollen that they burst their banks and flooded the lower land. Traditionally at this time of year, the fishing was good and the villagers went out to repair fences and move their herds back into the woods and the higher pastures.

This year, there was a problem. We had heard rumour during the winter that something had come down and taken cattle and sheep from the fields. Carcasses had been found on the slopes of our wild musk oxen and deer, killed and stripped of their meat. The suspicion was that we had some kind of small giant-blood band up there in the caves. My father said that when spring came properly, he would lead a force up and deal with the issue.

Then he was called away to Riassa to deal with political matters.

"Lancingor will lead a scout force and find out what we are dealing with. The folk of the nearest villages must be warned not to go into the hills until this has been resolved. Finn, Frederick, Finnmeyer, Ledric, Savic, Magdemagus and Tanseval, you will ride to the villages. Travel in pairs and carry the warning." My father looked around at the assembled forces of the household.

"Fulk, you will ready a heavy force to go in if necessary. Send word to Lamorak to prepare a backup in the event it is something more widespread."

Fulk nodded. A swarthy, powerfully built man, Fulk sat squat in his saddle. He always made me think of solidity and dependability. He was like a tower of my father's fortress, a castle amongst his chess pieces. Lamorak was quite the opposite. Much more daring and colourful, he was a knight who moved onto the attack readily.

I smiled. It was good to have a role, even if it was father's way of telling us that we were not to go charging into the hills ourselves.

I rode out with Tanseval. He proved good company. A slim, tall young man, he was in his third year as a squire. That meant he was getting close to taking the trials to knighthood. He was a good singer and we raised our voices and sang as we rode easily along. We passed many folk beginning to tidy up and prepare the fields and patches for seeding and planting. Most stopped to watch and to pass a cheerful word or two. Tanseval seemed to know a lot of them. I made mental notes of those I was introduced to and made a deliberate effort to give thanks when we were offered food and drink. Eventually, we reached the village of Pernad. Pernad had a low wooden stockade which was really designed to keep wolves and such animals out.

It had a well-maintained watchtower on the north-eastern corner, staffed by two villagers with bows at all times. At night, it had a small fire bowl that threw some light on the north fence. Despite that, raiders had crossed the line twice in the last three winters. Small bands of goblins, desperate for food had raided, stealing milk, grain and sheep. There had been some small skirmishes but nothing very serious and, in the end, the villagers had sold food to them in return for semi-precious stones and musk ox pelts.

We delivered the news to the headman and some gathered farmers, but they weren't best pleased. Frederick encountered a similar response when he reached Halvgord.

We gathered back at Falkeberg with our news. Lancingor and Fulk listened to each messenger team in turn. Pernad and Braghen were the two villages nearest to the trouble area. So far, neither had been attacked directly. Braghen was missing two of its men, however, who had gone up onto the higher slopes to cut pine.

Lancingor waited until just Frederick, Leopold and myself remained at the table with Fulk and Finnmeyer. His weather-beaten face looked like old parchment in the half light of the candle flames.

"While you were riding, we went up into The Gallifog."

"And found something, I assume." Finnmeyer leaned forward, intrigued, at once.

"I'd say a giant. One of the rock and cave types, nothing with any real intelligence but dangerous, of course. That's not all. It's not alone. I'd say goblins or worse, bolggoblins. A small group. Bones and bits and pieces all the way through one of the small passes. I have a good idea where the lair is."

"How many men do we take?" Finnmeyer asked, leaning forward like a hound straining at the leash.

"No, Fulk and I will go with an armed band. You take a small party to Pernad and standby. If we run into trouble, I'll sound the horn three times. Lamorak will be heading to Braghen. If we're on his side of the peak, he'll respond quicker."

Finnmeyer nodded, "I'd rather lead one of the groups with you but it makes sense to take Fulk. I will be standing ready."

Lancingor smiled and they exchanged a look of understanding. I knew what it meant. Lancingor was telling Finnmeyer that if he failed, Finnmeyer would have to finish the job. "Thank you, my friend. I know I can always rely on you."

He turned to the three of us, "and you lads are not coming, before you ask. I know you'd do your part but we don't know for sure what we are up against and your father would have my guts for pennants if I let you come along. So, you stay put and that's that."

Needless to say, as soon as Lancingor and Fulk had ridden out, we were nagging Finnmeyer to let us ride out to Pernad with him. He eventually agreed that my father would have ridden into the action if he were here, so it was right that Frederick went and as a scout and warrior in training, I should be fine, too. Leopold started to argue until Frederick told him that he needed someone to sit in the ducal chair while he was away.

Father left it to him and now he was leaving Leopold in charge of the castle and any ducal duties. Leopold had settled himself on the throne before we left and looked pleased at the compromise. Neither of us gave it any more thought. We were thinking how to get beyond Pernad if the opportunity arose.

We thundered into Pernad, causing quite a stir. Finnmeyer wanted the people to see that we were taking the matter seriously. Tanseval and Ledric had come with us, as well as two of Finnmeyer's assistants, Gelf and Max and the scout lieutenant, Jenad, a tall, striking woman and a fine scout. Two of the city guard who were good riders and bowmen made up the rest of the group.

Of course, there would be little to tell if we hadn't been summoned by the frantic blowing of a bass hunting horn about mid-afternoon. We mounted up and sped up the slopes heading for the repeating sound. The echo of the horn was loud enough to bring Lamorak's force as well. We could see them making their way up along a winding trail to the north-east.

Lancingor, Fulk and what was left of their force were wedged tightly in a small defile defending against a horde of goblins. The goblins were armed with an assortment of weapons and most of them sported helmets and shields with various spikes and protrusions. A couple of heavy, seven-foot bolggoblins with axes were up front. The giant lay dead nearby, pierced by a number of arrows and weapons.

We charged in, scattering goblins in all directions. Frederick wielded his axe heroically, carving a path through to Lancingor alongside Tanseval and Finnmeyer.

I held my horse still and used my crossbow to bring down two goblins. Then my inexperience nearly cost me. Swept up in imagining how my father would praise us for our efforts and perhaps make Frederick and myself knights, I was woken from my thoughts by a bolggoblin charging from behind some rocks, wielding a long spear. I panicked, shot wide and then fumbled fearfully with the crossbow, failing to get a bolt in place as he came at me. The only thought I could muster was how much the burning pain of the spear-point would hurt. Then Finnmeyer crashed into the armoured bolggoblin and they both went down.

It was obvious that the bolggoblin was going to recover quicker. It rose and pulled a maul from its belt. Finnmeyer was still on his knees, dazed. Jenad made no mistake though, her arrow found its mark and the bolggoblin went down with a crash. Then she turned her horse and went by, drawing her blade. Finnmeyer raised a hand in thanks and dived back into the fray. I dismounted, drew a sword and followed. Goblins are only four to five feet tall, and although stronger than they look, the reach and height advantage a human has over them makes a difference. I wouldn't have wanted to face a seven-foot, armoured bolggoblin in a hand-to-hand encounter, though. They are quite a different matter.

I took down my first goblin on my own. It was the first time I had actually killed a thinking being hand-to-hand, but I was so pumped up on adrenalin I didn't even pause to think about it until the fight was over.

A short time after I plunged into the thick of it, there was a blowing of horns and Lamorak's force came streaming over the shoulder of the mountain towards us. As the banners broke and the sound of the horses' hooves could be heard thundering, the enemy broke and ran. Goblins may not be that bright but even they know when to back off. The remaining members of the war band scattered into the hills. You may think it brutal but we pursued and slew as many as were able to, to ensure that the tribes did not want to take us on again. The giant's head was mounted on a pike and we marched down via Pernad back to Falkeberg so the people would know we had destroyed the threat to the villages.

When we got back, a crowd of people flocked to see us march through the Eisentor. It was a good feeling to have fought and won my first battle. Of course, it was no more than a small skirmish but at the time, it seemed a grand victory.

Back in the castle, we heard from Harthaldred, my father's steward that Leopold had been busy. He had seen four petitioners, one of which was a case that had been left unsettled days earlier when the judge could not make up his mind what to do.

A rich farmer had died, owing debts. His neighbour, owed five thousand crowns, had seized the farm and the remaining sheep in lieu of payment but there were two smallholders who now were going to go out of business because they had not received so much as a fennet.

They were owed much less and the judge had initially ruled that the farmer who had lost the largest quantity was entitled to take back what he could first. Leopold enquired how much the larger farm made each year and was told his lands could return ten thousand crowns.

The first smallholder made perhaps five hundred and the second less than two hundred. Leopold asked what value the farm and sheep that were seized came to and was told probably two and a half thousand, half the main farmer's owed debt. Leopold then adjudged that the claims should be based on a percentage so since the first two men were owed four hundred and two hundred, they ought to receive at least thirty per cent of what they were owed so the first would get one hundred and sixty odd crowns, the second sixty and the main farmer should have sixteen hundred.

To manage this, the second farm and sheep would have to be sold off. The additional would then also be split three ways. Of course, at this time of year, the sheep would fetch less and the farm wanted repairing so it was unlikely after commission and tax that they would even see that much. Or, he decided, the farmer who stood to gain most from a second farm and all that offered could pay both men in full and keep what he had taken, the payment being split in two, fifty per cent now and the rest in three months' time. The man with the two farms took the point and agreed so the smallholders went away, happy and the farmer satisfied as he had retained what he really wanted.

"Leopold thought of that?" I said, surprised by how good a solution he had found but also that he had the confidence to do it.

"He's got a good head for figures and business." Harthaldred replied, "He'd make a good baron or even duke in peacetime."

Frederick and I exchanged looks and then laughed. We couldn't imagine Leopold as a duke.

My father did not make us knights, of course. He was obviously pleased to hear Finnmeyer and Lancingor's accounts of how well we acquitted ourselves but was not pleased that we were there at all, even as part of a relief force. However, he accepted both men's point that we had to do what was expected of us and at his age, he was already fighting beside his father. Tanseval was made a full knight immediately after, passing his trial with ease. Leopold was congratulated heartily for his sense in dealing with the petitioners and showing what a duke ought to be doing. We understood what he was telling us but Frederick and I would always prefer to be in the action than sitting in dusty halls.

***

I was just finishing my packing when my father dropped in to see me. He sat down on the end of my bed and stared at me for a few moments. It might have seemed disconcerting to some but he always liked to read us just as he did his companions.

"Are you certain that you want this?" he asked.

I nodded, "only there are other avenues, for you, Edmund. You have good skills and you'll make a fine soldier. Finnmeyer would like to train you as a scout.

One of these days, he'll be too old to do what he does and the family will need a man who can lead ranging patrols, keeping the villages safe and tracking down our enemies. Lancingor would like you as captain of archers and I could teach you the skills of an ambassador without you having to travel halfway across the world."

I was slightly taken aback. We had not discussed alternatives to my journey to Lorefast. He watched the emotions and thoughts flicker across my face and in turn, I watched his expression. It is not easy, I am told, to let a child go, to fly from the nest and take its own course, but I was excited at the chance to travel so I answered without giving him real consideration.

"I have looked forward to the day I leave for Gwythaor. I want to explore the islands, become the first Von Tacchim to get to know them all well. More than that, I want to learn the ways of bards and diplomats who use their voices as a power. I have written many small ditties, enjoyed singing and learning to play instruments.

I have imagined being able to charm a group with a song so they hang on my words, to write poetry that expresses how I feel and have it critiqued. Most of all, I have imagined being able to speak a few words with such force that even Drachefauste would step back daunted."

My father's brow creased, slightly at the mention of that name.

"I think Drachefauste is so beyond the emotions of normal men that he would not notice such wiles and they would have no effect on his heart or soul. I know I promised and so it shall be. But Edmund, this opportunity is not for you to simply enjoy yourself. It has to have a purpose. We need your strengths and this is designed to add to them, enhance your ability to lead and to negotiate. At the end of it, we are your family and like all the rest of us, you must serve the family, first."

"I know that. And I will return, a sharper weapon than before. I will keep up my practice with sword and bow, my riding and movement. They say the elven folk are some of the best swordsmen and archers in the world. Perhaps I shall have them teach me their ways."

"Perhaps you will." He reached out and messed my hair for the last time, "You'll be a man full grown when you return. I hope that you will find some wisdom to bring back to us, the gods know, we could use it sometimes. I fear that this war will go on like a wound that will not heal, letting blood year after year without any decisive end. I think, too, that you will fight for us again when you return. I just hope that it does not cost us too dearly but we cannot let Drachefauste seize any more of our lands. What he took in Raga, I can live with. I know your uncles wanted him stopped there but that would have brought open war. If we continue to skirmish here and there over small parcels of land and possessions, that we can sustain."

"And what if he grows greedy and wishes to swallow Rosgovia and who knows what else?" I asked, picking a few more items from my drawers to pack, "what then?"

"Then we will have war, of course. But I am sure that if he invaded, the Empire and other dukes would come to our aid. Nobody wants to see a precedent set by allowing such a creature to start conquering land after land. Cylmarda and Cytelia would be concerned. And we would draw forces from Littesburg which would lessen the Emperor's armies. He needs forces to fight Surmey, Carnoss and Karilia. He cannot afford us to start pulling our troops off to fight wars within the Imperial borders."

"And what if the beast has allies? He might be stronger than you think."

"He is too new to the Empire and untrained in diplomacy. His allies, if he has any, will be barbarians and tribes who think they ought to have something more than they have. They will not be popular with the Imperial dukedoms. No, I think he will isolate himself if he starts a war with us or any other dukedom in future."

"I hope you are right, father." I sat beside him. He placed a hand on my shoulder.

"You're a fine son, Edmund. If Frederick had turned out to be less capable, I would have broken tradition and named you as my successor. I am grateful I have so many fine sons. I just wish I could have had more time to ride with you all, hunt with you and join in when you were learning your weapons, but duty must always come first."

"You did when you could." I replied and squeezed his arm. "I always knew you had many important tasks. I have always been proud that you're my father."

"Wouldn't you rather have had your Uncle Raef?"

"No. I think it's great to have a famous duellist uncle, but you were always the best."

There was a day to come when I would recall those words.

Stones I

Leaving Rosgovia, I travelled south-westwards, stopping at the oldest walled city of Acondium and then by the Imperial Northern Canal to Jordis. Acondium greatly impressed me. It has a slumbering magnificence, reflecting its past history as the original imperial capital.

The city is still the seat of one of the ecclesiastical electors, with buildings that date back to the time of the Fondlanians and the ancient races. And there is a wonderful atmosphere around the great water market and the regal buildings that became the university. Jordis was also impressive by comparison to the much more functional towns of my own country.

A sprawling port on the south-western coast of Valcoria, it is smelly, bustling and cosmopolitan. I had never seen so many different races mingling in one street as on the Street of Bazaars, the thoroughfare that leads to the great square. It was almost as impressive as Acondium with its soaring buildings of white and black marble. It was in Jordis that I said farewell to Finnmeyer and the honour guard that had seen me this far. Finnmeyer was wearing a hardened black scale doublet over softer leather, his favourite bow on his back and a short sword on his belt. He stroked his black beard, momentarily and then straightened to his full six and something feet, the light catching his craggy features so that his blue eyes seemed like two gems in a rough wedge of stone.

"Remember lad, it's how a man lives and dies that matters. Your actions remain as the evidence of your life, their consequences sometimes forgotten but at other times echoing long after you have departed this world. You may never be a lord or lead an army but that doesn't mean that you don't have an important role to play in the events of the empire and its surrounding lands. Always be ready. Keep up your practices with weapons and skills, study tactics of the great leaders and when you listen to tales about them, try to evaluate what they did well and when they went wrong. And take care of yourself. Next time you're home, we'll catch another snow tiger and this time you can bring it back for all to see."

His face softened and the eyes crinkled into a smile. We shook hands. Finnmeyer put a hand on my shoulder. He looked like he had more to say but he merely nodded and turned away. I knew he was still troubled by the alliance with Drachefauste but try as I had done, I could not draw him out on the subject. I raised a hand and saw him turn and do the same. Then, they were gone and I was alone for the first time.

I departed Jordis on an elven trader bound for Gwythaor. It was docking at Orsiliath and from there, I'd take a river trader, a wherry or similar to Warvane. I'd never sailed on an elven ship before. It was a revelation for me. Elves are not a common race in the Imperial lands. There are a few of course, and I had seen elven hunters coming to barter over furs and other items. The elves on the ship, "Windsong" were very serious.

They sang, but the songs were all of legend and rather sombre. They worked with a quiet efficiency, each member of the crew seeming to know their place at any time.

There was none of the good-humoured jibing or the yelling of orders that you would expect on a human vessel. No one ever seemed to raise their voice. Bells rang and jobs were changed. The vessel cut through the waves so lightly that you hardly felt the swell. I recalled that the elves were the first race to create fleets and taught men to sail. Watching them at work, you could see a thousand years and more of refinements in the way they handled a vessel.

In Orsiliath, I simply bade them farewell and departed the ship. There was no camaraderie or shouts of well-wishes. I felt rather sad and lonely, then. For the first time, I realised how far from home and how utterly alone I was. My father still had some influence here but House Vas-Coburg ruled Gwythaor. The extent of the Von Tacchim presence was an embassy in Warvane. The Ducal Isles were recently established at this time, representing the westernmost border of the Nordovician Empire. The throne in Riassa depended upon the fairly autonomous lords to rule, protect and provide tax from the islands. Left alone with the power to build their own armies, the seeds of rebellion were sown. They lay dormant for now upon these rich islands, awaiting the right circumstances.

And so, by what Myneus the Navigator would have described as "By divers routes withe many a winding and a twisting", I reached Warvane and saw, for the first time, the beauty of the nearby woods.

They rose to the hill at the centre where the Lorefast Stone Circle stood as it had since perhaps the dawn of time. It was here that I was bound.

As advised by my father, I took rooms at a local inn rather than request shelter in Lorefast's tree village. After a slice of hot game pie with vegetables and bread, a pint of dark ale and a pipe of cherry wood tobacco, I felt a lot better.

The Boar at Bay Inn had an interesting clientele. I studied them over my pint and tried to take in the faces for future use. I was particularly intrigued by a young rat-catcher who seemed to be a lot more than just that as he advised groups of younger lads who were obviously impressed by the silver coins he produced to pay for food and beer.

When an elder man tried to give him a clip around the ear for cheek, he just slid away from the blow with a laugh and a wink.

There was another man who intrigued me, there. He stood out because he was so different in manner and dress. He wore a long coat made primarily, from a strange hide with strands of the soft coat of some beast in a ring around the collar, the cuffs and the upper arms.

The coat had an odd smell, too. Beneath this, he wore a light jacket in deep crimson and gold with a chainmail layer from collar to just below the heart. It had chainmail at the waist, also, to keep it hanging straight. Under the jacket, he had a plain tunic of midnight blue the same colour as his leggings.

A dagger was slipped through a band towards the top of one of his long black boots. The dagger was curved as was his blade, a well-fashioned scimitar. He sat, one leg crossed over the other, watching everyone. He had deep olive brown skin with a thin moustache and a small, short goatee. Upon his head, he wore a deep blue turban with a small cluster of garnets in a brooch pinned to it. It was rare to see such folk in the north. It seemed even rarer to find one seated in this tavern, apparently unbothered by any of its patrons or, indeed, by anything.

Finding me watching him, a smile touched his lips and he raised his stoneware tankard. Another incongruity, it seemed. Most of the southern folk that I had seen, rarely touched alcohol and then, only very strong spirits. This man was drinking beer. I was drawn to take a seat nearer him;

"Your pardon, good sir," I said. "I did not mean to offend by staring at you."

"No offence taken." His voice was rich. You might call it creamy; it was smooth and unhurried. The twinkle of humour remained. "You are new, here, yes?"

"I am not from these parts, so we have something in common, my young friend" he continued.

I smiled. I couldn't help it. There was just something likeable about him. "I am Edmund Von Tacchim." I offered my hand which he took. His grip was quite firm despite the elegance of his slim, long fingered hands.

"Kharr. You might wish to be careful, Edmund Von Tacchim. Some may realise that you have lord's blood in you and think you might make a good ransom. I would adopt a suitable adventuring name while you are here"

"I'm bound for Lorefast, to study, as a bard" I told him. He inclined his head.

"A worthy profession. Nevertheless, a name less liable to attract attention would serve you. You are a long way from home, no? Which branch would you be from?"

He pondered, momentarily "Not Littesburg. You'd be wearing one of those ridiculous grey and blue jackets with golden buttons and already attracting the wrong kind of attention. Convar, perhaps, or maybe... Rosgovia."

I started wondering if he might be some spy or agent but he seemed to be just curious and again, I decided I could trust him.

"I was born in Rosgovia. My father is...."

"Shhh. Best not speak of your father, here. There are ears that you do not see. You are obviously the son of a small noble sent to make something of yourself and that is good."

"Yes, yes of course. That's it, sir. How do you know so much about them?"

"You could say that I am a well-travelled man." He smiled, again, "would you like another drink? The inn here is not a wonderful place to spend time thinking or indeed sleeping but it does serve a very good ale."

I nodded and smiled, a little uncertain and then added "please, yes, that's very good of you." We had one more ale, together and I learned that he came from the borderlands of The Ephiniate Kingdom of Surmey. He was indeed a traveller. He had seen so many states that it was more a case of where he had not been.

In turn, I explained why I felt that learning the skills of a bard at Lorefast would enable me to open doors as both ambassador and spy. I wandered Warvane for an hour or two after that. That was how I found myself in an alleyway in Cheapside, having taken a wrong turn. I say a wrong turn because I had found a large, bulky man looming behind me who had the look of a brigand written all over him just as the weaselly looking individual who stepped out ahead, holding a long knife, looked like a cutpurse. You could have placed them with any crowd of peasants and picked them out as the thief and the thug. I'm sure you know what I mean. Anyway, there they were.

I wasn't a defenceless young man, even in those days. I spun, kicked the thug between the legs, slipped by one grabbing hand and caught only a clipping blow to my shoulder from the club. I might have taken care of these two but then two companions appeared, drawing knives.

"Bugger kicked me in the bollocks!" the thug pointed at me. "Do 'im boys!"

At that moment, a fifth figure loomed behind these two, took both of them by the scruff and crashed their heads together, kicking the pair to the ground. The metallic hiss of a scimitar being drawn was heard as he stepped over them. I parried the weasel's knife and opened his arm from wrist to elbow with my own.

"Bloody 'ell, it's Kharr" the thug yelled. That was enough. They all took off down the alley, the weasel trying to wrap something round his arm as he ran. Two of them stumbled, still dazed from the bang on the head.

"Having trouble with the local wildlife, my friend?" The laconic voice was still edged with humour. I turned and offered my hand again.

"Once again, I owe you, sir."

He shook it. "I really suggest that you do something about finding that name. I did warn you that the thieves guild will be a lot less interested in a common student than they will be in the son of one who might be able to afford a ransom or have wealth of his own."

I nodded. An idea was coming to me. If I could not be my father's son, then how about Finnmeyer's son. He was no noble and I admired him greatly.

"Finn" I said "how does that sound?"

"Not a bad start, my friend. It should serve"

"No, better, Black Finn" And there it was. Meyer meant black in the islander tongue. Finn-Meyer. Black Finn.

"Ah, now that, I like. It has a certain suggestion of roguishness or danger about it. I approve. Come, Black Finn, let's walk."

Shadows I

Thus, I became Black Finn, wayfarer, bard, adventurer or soldier of fortune depending on the company and place. Naively, I thought I could portray those roles. It took many years, much blood and no small amount of agony before I could say for true that I could claim all those titles. For now though, I was content.

My friendship with Kharr grew. We drank together now and again and he invited me along on one or two less than above board missions. Kharr wasn't against using his skills to earn some decent coin. When one thieves guild wished to send another a "message", they liked to hire contractors and Kharr was available. Having picked up the hire, he talked up his expenses and I went along as a 'second pair of eyes'.

This particular night's work involved a warehouse on the old canalway. The thieves guild were going to receive a shipment of smuggled tobaccos, drugs and spices. Our instructions were to take out the fence and his men, destroy the shipment and make sure the dealers got the impression that selling to this guild was liable to land them in trouble.

"The first principle of a job like this" Kharr said, as we sat at a table in The Red Wyvern Inn outside Stokemarch, enjoying a long ale, "is to get to know the opposition.

We want to find out how many there are, how well armed they are, whether they have any routines and what jobs they do when it comes to the business they're in. To assist in this, I have procured a small narrow boat and a lighter full of Dharingian tea."

I nearly spluttered into my beer, "That must have cost a fortune. How will you get the money back?"

"You misunderstand me. When I say I procured, I mean that I relieved a smuggler of the items a couple of nights ago and stashed them down the river in a convenient cove."

I simply gaped. Kharr watched me and then gave a short laugh.

"You should not let your mouth hang open, my friend. You might attract the unwanted attention of a Zoafran Desert Bee that is seeking a place to nest."

I shook myself out of my stupor; "I wasn't…it's just that I didn't expect you to have begun the job without any help."

"Oh, it wasn't a difficult task. I didn't need any assistance. There were only three of them."

My brows knitted, "A risk, nonetheless, surely?"

Kharr shrugged and waved a hand vaguely.

"As I was saying. I have procured some items to provide us with a cover. Tonight, you and I shall become smugglers seeking a sale.

When they reach an agreement with us, we will bring in the boat and help them unload the lighter. Hopefully, this guild wants repeat business and they won't try to kill us to avoid having to pay up."

I have to say that I didn't like the sound of this overly much. Kharr, however, was plainly unperturbed by the possibility.

"Having established ourselves as smugglers, we won't seem out of place wandering about the wharf area and we should be able to observe our quarry with ease. In fact, we may even get them to tell us all we wish to know."

I nodded. I could see what he had in mind but, inexperienced in such matters, I didn't grasp the full plan. However, this adventurer that I had come to think of as a friend was so plainly confident, I couldn't see what could go wrong.

Sometime after darkness had fallen and most men were either drinking, away home or on the night shift in one of the warehouses, we slipped downriver and found the hidden boats. It took us about three or four hours of toil to get the small barge and its towed cargo to within a short distance of Redler's Wharf, after which we took a short rest.

Redler's Wharf was and still is a rather run-down place known for its somewhat dubious commerce and cheap markets. It is the main canal port for Stokemarch, centre of an agricultural area that produces wool, grain and orchard fruit.

The wharf had wooden piers and bollards for tying up, a couple of decrepit wooden and iron cranes and a cobbled rectangle surrounded by warehouses and workshops. During the day, come the sounds and smells of tar and pitch, scorched metal and leatherwork. One warehouse had a series of spinning frames where sad looking middle-aged and elderly women come, each day, working from first light until dusk to turn raw wool into garments and bales.

We had to make contact with a man known as Scroper Farlane. Scroper was, apparently, the boss ganghand for the men who 'ran things'. Scroper turned out to be pretty easy to find. As we walked into the warehouse area, three men were kicking someone who was writhing about, begging them to stop. A large man with a shaved head and tattoo on each upper arm stood back, a club held loosely in his hand. He watched us approaching the warehouse, which we had been told was the one to start at.

"Yeah? Can I help you?" he growled out as we reached the doors.

"We have business with a Mr Farlane", Kharr said with an impeccable south-coast accent.

"Oh yeah? Do I know yer?"

"I doubt it. We have had to, um…shift our operation to a new location after some local trouble"

"What yer got?"

"Dharingian Tea. A lighter full of best leaf"

"Oh yeah. How best?"

"I have a sample if you care to."

The big man planted a kick in the ribs of the unfortunate on the ground, "Get out of here, scumbag and don't go causing trouble, again, right?"

The whimpering man got to his knees, retrieved a fallen cap, made some obsequious promises and limped off. The big man turned his complete attention to us.

"Let's have a looksee."

Kharr brought out a fine pouch and handed it to him. He uncapped it and sniffed.

"Orright.. I'm interested. How much are we talking?"

Kharr entered into negotiation. In the end, he sold at a shorter price than we would have wanted if we had paid for the stuff and this seemed to satisfy Farlane. When business was concluded, we noted we were being scrutinised by a well-dressed fellow who stood on a balcony entrance to the warehouse.

"When can you ship in?"

"Oh, tonight" said Kharr. "The sooner the better."

"Ain't going to have all yer money by then" Farlane said with another growl.

"That's fine, Mr Farlane. I will trust you to pay up. After all, we are intending to do more business, here."

"What else do yer handle, then?"

"Wine, spices, whatever comes into my hands from my business associates. Let's say that they do a little privateering in neutral waters."

"Pirates, yer mean."

"I dislike the term" Kharr said with a slight smile.

"Alright... tonight it is. You'll have to help with the unloading. I ain't going to find that many extra hands at this short notice."

"Of course. That's not a problem."

"Your talkative friend going to help, is he?"

Kharr just glanced my way. "Oh, he's just part of my insurance policy."

I did my best to play the part, just giving the big man a smile and let my hands drift to the knives at my side, twitching the cloak aside to show heavy throwing daggers.

"I get the point." Farlane used his growl and stuck his jaw out. "So you have an assassin on your books as well as pirate friends, but don't think that cuts any ice, here."

"Rest assured, Mr Farlane, I wasn't thinking of you or your operation for one moment."

The bald man made a noise that sounded dismissive, "Just as well."

He took another long look at me, though.

Looking back, I think that may have been the first time I felt comfortable with the idea of being an assassin.

It took a long time to unload the lighter. I was aching in just about every joint by the time we were done.

"Is there an inn with rooms, here?" enquired Kharr, when the gangers had finished counting, weighing and checking the tea.

"The Old Duck is alright but a bit rough. Or there's the Cock and Anchor in Stokemarch itself.

"The Old Duck will do fine" said Kharr

"Just up the lane, there" offered another ganger. "Ask for Molly Moll. She'll tuck you in at night if you're good to her, too."

Kharr bowed, slightly. "She sounds my kind of landlady."

"She's the landlady's daughter" growled Farlane, "the landlady is Butter Milly. She's a big lass too. Better not let her catch you with her daughter, neither."

I was a little uncertain where this was all leading but Kharr set off with purpose and I followed quietly behind.

"Always best to stay in with the locals, don't you think?"

"I'm not sure" I said.

"How many of them did you count at the warehouse?"

I thought. "There was Farlane and the three that stayed during the negotiations, Wall, Tumps and Garner and that other one who kept shouting swear words. Oh, and the fellow who came and went when you were talking about prices, or was it two? And the man watching us…"

"It was two." Kharr nodded. "And there were at least three others in the warehouse, Stone, Bellows and Coles. I heard them all called by name. Plus, the man who checked the weights who looked like a priest or mage."

I added up, "twelve, then?"

"Indeed. So, call it thirteen to fifteen to be sure."

I looked puzzled.

"Always overestimate the enemy. Now, who was on guard?"

"Farlane and Garner, I suppose. They didn't do much to help."

"And at least two of the men inside the warehouse."

"Oh, right. Couldn't one of the three you heard called by name be the one who did the weights check?"

"Perhaps but the three were called roughly by Farlane whereas he was nothing but polite to his weights and measures man. I'd guess Mr Weights is higher up in the organisation than Farlane."

I nodded, keeping note. Kharr knew the way it all worked, of course. He had done it all before, whereas I was eager to learn.

"So, do you think the man watching was the overall boss?"

"I think he may well be in charge here. The real boss of this group will be back in Warvane or wherever this guild has their headquarters."

"I thought we were taking down a fence and his men here in Stokemarch"

"Oh, we are. But this one's a smallish cog in the wheel of the operation and for future reference, it would be good to know who we are really up against."

"On that, Kharr" I said, concerned; "I know you're experienced, but fifteen men is a tall order for the two of us."

"Then we'll have to use guile, my young friend", Kharr grinned and patted my arm; "You should learn to worry less and spend the time thinking how it will be done."

The Old Duck proved to be a rowdy, smelly inn where bar brawls were a regular feature of the evening and everyone had an opinion.

I saw, swiftly, why Kharr had chosen to stay here and not a more comfortable well-provisioned place. The gangers soon swelled the numbers and Farlane was in for a while, presumably off his shift of duty. As the ale flowed and money was won and lost in card games, the talk ran on and became looser.

We learned that Mr Weights and Measures was the city boss' financial man and went by the name of Hodengragger. We also learned that the warehouse and the operation were run by Jenner and Saul and that these two were considered dangerous enough that tones were lowered when anything was said about them. Farlane reported to Jenner, and Jenner to Saul. One of the two was usually there. Jenner had left for the day sometime after we had seen Farlane, so Saul was currently the on-duty leader.

He must have been the man in black who was observing us from the balcony. In all, through careful prompting, we discovered there were twelve but only ten of them were there after about mid-afternoon and of those, only five were on duty overnight unless extra hands were needed. Saul was the man who talked to the real boss. His name did not come up. An important shipment was arriving at midnight on the following day, and we found out. Farlane and his men would be heading back from their usual drink at the inn to see to it.

The following night, we joined Farlane and his crew in the bar, avoiding drinking ourselves but generously buying rounds and making sure they had more than enough. Our very good healths were toasted several times before they staggered out.

"I would guess that they're heading back to take on night duties," Kharr said, in a confidentially low voice.

"Shall we hit them during the unloading?" I asked, trying to think tactically.

"Sounds a good plan to me. There will be a little disorder as it is. With three of them having drunk too much to be useful, we should be able to create quite a stir. And, although Farlane held back, his senses will be dulled too. Which means only this Saul fellow will be in good shape of the five on night duty."

We got into position, hiding behind stacks of old crates and waited.

Just before midnight, there was a smell of smoke accompanied by creaking and a large black barge came into view. At first, it was just a darkness on the glimmering water, the smoke from its tin capped chimney writing a scrawl across the face of the moon. It crept forward, noises of protest coming from the lighter that it was towing. Slowly, slowly, it reached the shore and rested against the wharf with a soft bump.

Then, the scene changed to a frenetic one. Men appeared from hatches and tripped lightly along the narrow walkways. I counted three, although one went back down to the stern where I assumed he set about anchoring and tying. Scroper Farlane and his team emerged from the warehouse. A slim man in black followed at a slight distance.

I guessed he must be Saul.

A fourth man appeared out of the barge quarters. He doffed his cap, "Mr Saul, sir. A pleasure, as always. And Mr Farlane, of course."

"Is it all here as agreed?" Saul spoke, for the first time. His voice had a precise meter. His clipped accent was central states, imperial territories.

"Of course, sir. What do you think I am? I don't never welch on a deal."

Farlane grumbled something low under his breath but Saul, who had moved up to the group, just reached a hand out to hold him back.

"That's not what I'd heard, Grover. After all, you're selling to us now and you always used to sell to the Ringers."

The little man wiped his nose with his jacket sleeve and whined.

"Now, now, Mr Saul, sir, that's 'ardly fair now, is it? I delivered on the last lot just like I said.

And it weren't my fault what happened with the Ringers, neither. I'd still be doing business with them too if that Mr Joffrell hadn't taken over. What him and that new lot are doing…"

I never found out what Mr Joffrell and the new lot were doing that Grover didn't like because Kharr tapped my arm and stood up, drawing his bow. His arrow took Saul just below the ribs and sent the slim man stumbling to the ground. My crossbow bolt was aimed at Farlane. He grunted as it punched into his side but he didn't go down.

"Treachery! Treachery!" shouted Grover; "back on the boat! Get back on the boat!"

I took in the situation. Grover's three men were busy unloading the goods and were not at all ready for a fight. Grover scuttled for cover.

Tumps and Garner, who had been with Farlane, looked around stupidly, probably befuddled by drink. What was unexpected was the two additional men in scale with crossbows who came sprinting from the warehouse at Saul's shout. He had obviously decided to put in some extra insurance in the event of treachery from Grover.

I picked up the second crossbow and levelled it as the two men slowed and looked for targets. My shot hit the first under the chin and he tumbled back with a slight whimper. Kharr shot Grover in the leg, sending him sprawling. Kharr had flung his bow aside and was moving forward with blades in hand while I was still taking stock.

Seeing the second newcomer aiming at Kharr, I charged, hurling one dagger and then the other. The first clattered off the man's bow but put him off and he shot wide.

The second took him in the chest and he staggered back. Kharr went between Tumps and Garner, slicing with his sword and long, curved dagger. They made noises of pain, one falling one way, the other stumbling in the opposite direction. Then Farlane hit Kharr with a swing of his club, the pain of doing so making him grunt. Kharr took an additional bruising blow on the upraised dagger arm, as I drove my blade into Farlane's chest. This time, he fell over.

We turned on the three men from Grover's barge. The fence, Grover, was dragging himself into the barge cockpit. His three men looked at us agog. One charged forward, waving a short sword.

The second fumbled and drew a dagger but the third turned tail and jumped onto the barge. Kharr stepped aside and neatly disarmed the charging fellow by taking half his hand off. He fell past us. I whipped up my daggers and on one knee, threw a spinning shot that hit the second man in the head just as he raised his arm to hurl at us. I rushed him as he stumbled, passing Garner, his tunic soaked with blood. I struck him across the back of the head, putting him out of his misery.

Kharr advanced on the fallen Tumps to make sure of him. Grover's man tried to draw his sword and I saw the fear in his eyes as he tugged at it, vainly. I couldn't afford to be generous. I thrust my blade approximately where his heart should be. He made hardly any noise as I pulled it free, falling in a heap at my feet.

"Stop the barge!" yelled Kharr.

I turned to acknowledge him and let out a warning shout. Saul had risen from behind my friend. Before I could act, he drove his dagger through Kharr's back. The point punched out of his chest and Kharr went down on his knees. I knew the blow had killed him before he went over sideways.

"Nooooo!" I heard myself yelling as I charged at him. Saul drew a short blade but my impetus bowled him over and I came down on top of him. I rammed the other dagger I had picked up into his chest and twisted. He screamed. Then I cut his throat with a swift movement and stood up, panting.

I knew Kharr would have wanted me to finish what we started. I sprinted for the barge and jumped.

Landing heavily, I crashed into the bargeman at the tiller, bowling him over. Grover limped out with a club while I was recovering, but he was no fighter. I raised my sword and used it to block his wrist so he dropped the club. The bargeman and I struggled.

Ducking my shoulder, I shoved him over the edge into the water. Grover started to try to offer a deal but I was still full of fury. I slashed his face with the dagger and he put his hands over his torn nose, sobbing. It spared him seeing the blade thrust that killed him.

I turned and threw a rope to the one in the water who grabbed it, eagerly.

I pulled him in. It was only as he started to haul himself up that he realised my intention, too late. I slit his throat neatly, pushing him back into the water.

He floated away on the tide, turning slowly as the canal carried him off in its cold arms. I threw the anchor line to shore and hauled to pull the barge back to the edge.

"I was sure you could handle it on your own. Nice job" said a familiar voice, behind me.

I spun, blades coming up. Kharr put up his hands, palms turned outwards to me

"I surrender, partner."

"But I saw you go down!"

"He missed my vitals…"

"The dagger went through you"

"Under my arm," he nodded. I pulled it off him when I fell. Thought it best."

"No, I saw you."

Kharr touched the side of his nose "If you think you know something, best keep it to yourself. Of course, if you aren't pleased that I made it, you can always put that sword through my chest and keep all the proceeds for yourself."

I dropped my blades and hugged my friend, "I thought you were…."

"Yeah, I know. Sorry kid."

And that was pretty much that, really.

We left the bodies in a neat row along the wharf, leaving a bonfire in progress that destroyed most of the tobacco and other drugs, the majority of which seemed to be black leaf of some type.

We stuffed a few pouches with tobacco and spices for our own use and a little extra profit, of course. After that, we just sailed down river on the first narrow boat, towing an empty lighter and stashed it at anchor outside Warvane because, as Kharr pointed out, "You never know when you'll want a thing."

Circles

"The fae are not easily found by mortals. They linger in dew drops and starlight, which their immortal souls are attracted to. One does not generally find them so much as come upon them. Even that is rarely by any but their own desire. They are unpredictable at best. Their magic is old, nearly as old as any and the most powerful merely have to think for it to be so. Our advice to all students is always to let them be. Some chosen folk will learn much more of their minds and powers. There are one or two amongst our order at any time that interest them."

I was listening intently to Malderin Evensong. His knowledge of the fae folk both dark and light, was a matter of common knowledge amongst the students of Lorefast.

"How can a fae be slain, then?"

I turned my head to look at the student who had asked that question. He was a tall, burly young man with messy chestnut hair and dark brown eyes. He had taken on the name Cedarwood. Malderin also regarded him with a question in his face, studying the young druid for several moments before he answered. "The fae are immortal, not invulnerable. There are probably many ways that they can be slain. Why the question?" The elder's gaze alighted upon the druid, from beneath frowning brows.

"I read somewhere that they hate iron and will even be cruel to those who carry it. The reason suggested was that they are burned or even slain by iron."

Cedarwood didn't even pause. If he noticed the deepening frown, then it didn't put him off from his pursuit of the subject.

I felt a slight admiration for him. It is not an easy thing to do, to put a master to question or to follow a question when there are warning signs that it is a subject to be dropped. Malderin inclined his head.

"It is true that iron is said to poison the fae. It is also said that the power of their domains is affected by our actions and by the encroachment of places of worship whether circle or temple. Although Lorefast is visited by the fae and we have the friendship of some of the wildfolk, they do not enter the boundary of the circle itself. So, my advice if treading paths that might lead into fae domains is to leave iron items, particularly weapons and armour, behind.

"Does that answer your questions, Cedarwood? I would just say again - do not meddle in the ways of the fae. They do not think as we do and are given to chaos. "

It wasn't until some years past that I remembered this particular lecture and the question that Cedarwood had posed. There had been a motive behind it but it was not to become evident until a long time later when I returned to Lorefast after being away. At the time, every question merely seemed like scholarly interest and I was fascinated by the answers to nearly all of them.

Lorefast is unique, as far as I know. The centre of the village is built around an ancient stone circle supposedly constructed by the first elven druids. A circular path runs around the lawns from which paths radiate out. Northwest is the tree village, a sprawling community of tree houses, huts and teepees where the majority of the inhabitants and students live.

On the perimeter of the village stand three long halls of oak and beech. One is the Harpers Hall, where the bards give performances and where there are rooms for individual tuition. Many beautiful old instruments reside here.

The second building is the Village Lodge, the administrative centre of the college. The third is the library. The outside of the library is eye-catching with its carvings and ornate arches but inside is where the treasures can be found. Rows upon rows of book shelves soar with walkways that reach to their towering heights. There are reading areas with carved tables and archives of old scrolls kept in dry air rooms. It is said that some of the texts in that library are thousands of years old.

Northeast lies the ranger fort, a wooden construction with a single watch tower and stables.

The Rangers of Lorefast travel the land with the duke's blessing and authority to bring justice and to hunt down evil and malignant creatures that blight the beauty of the isle.

If one walks West from the village centre, the path leads through open wood to a quiet dell where it is said that sprites and other fae creatures live in peace with the neighbouring village. To the east, the woods grow thick but the trail leads to the coastal way and eventually to the sea. South-West lies Warvane, to the South, the lakeside trail and eventually Alborough and to the South-East, the elder woods of Larrelorn where the centaurs and dryads reside.

At first, life amongst the folk of Lorefast was easy paced and pleasant. I attended group sessions on bardic skills and theory.

My tutorials were with Malderin Evensong. He would have two or three of us work with him for a couple of hours, his undivided attention on just those students. Malderin was typical of the Lorefast masters. His age was hard to place although he was obviously old, even for a half-elf. He was lean and tall with a long wispy grey beard and clever hands that could fashion things as well as music from harps and pipes. His straight hair was silver with some black streaks, worn loose and long, reaching well below his shoulders. He always wore a robe, usually green or buff, decorated with runic symbols along the hems and cuffs. He walked using a staff although he did not need it and he continually wore a silver chain attached to some device that he kept hidden under his robe.

I also attended the general sessions on forest lore, druidic beliefs, mythology and any other classes I could fit in that interested me.

Within the college, bards and druids were divided into coteries. These were a mix of students, headed by one of the masters or mistresses of the council.

Members were moved from one to another each term, allowing new joiners to come in and for those with particular interests or skills to be matched up with the most suitable coterie or master. I was initially placed with Malderin Evensong in his coterie, Moondancers. When I joined, there were six coteries, each of five bards or druids with a master or mistress at its head. The college had only just opened its doors to outsiders four or five years ago, so most of my fellow students were still forest folk and elven.

I had made two friends within my coterie. Caladril was a lean, young elven bard with short dark hair and a preference for blues and greys. He wore a slim sword on his belt and turned out to be an expert fencer, quick and clever. He liked to dance when he sang and spent many hours studying old lays.

The other was Campion, a half elf who always favoured Autumnal shades of russet, gold and brown. He was good with a lute and lap harp but also skilled with flutes and fifes. He was a good bowman too and often he, I and Caladril would range on the outskirts of the woods, finding particular shaped marks on trees to use as targets. Eventually, we started making our own and hanging them from branches until we had enough to walk or run through, firing arrows to see who could get the most on target.

It was after one of these outings, having volunteered to collect up the arrows, that a low voice called on me to halt on my way up the trail towards Lorefast. My first reaction was that I had met bandits intent on robbing me. It was just past twilight and seemed the kind of time that such folk might be abroad. I slid into cover and took my crossbow in hand.

"Who's there?" I called, cautiously.

"This is Gatebrand Jeffery Cullen. I will know who passes into Lorefast, for such is my charge."

It was one of those formal answers and the voice was well intoned. Almost certainly elven. I put the crossbow back and stepped out but kept a hand on one sword.

"Show yourself, then, Jeffery Cullen. I am Black Finn, a student at the college. I do not show trust willingly, especially to those who hide in the brush with weapons."

As I spoke, I scanned the bushes ahead as best I could.

A figure stepped from beside the gates with an elven bow in hand. "You may approach", the voice was not male, this time. I walked forward and by the light of the lanterns on the gates, I could see a lithe female elf in greens. Then, a tall elf in brown with tumbling golden-brown hair stepped from my flank.

"I am Jeffery Cullen and this is Amnuvar" he said. "Your name is not known to us, Black Finn but I have checked the rolls and you are listed there. My apologies if you were taken aback but nobody nor any creature shall pass the hedges and bounds of the inner village without the say so of the gatebrands."

"I was not aware that the village was guarded although, thinking about it, it would have to be."

"Look north along the line of the hedge and up into the trees, Black Finn and tell me what you see."

I looked where he pointed. I could just make out a soft, silvery light.

"Perhaps one or two elf lanterns."

"Whereas I can see a platform upon which two of my brethren sit with bows on their laps, watching the woodlands. There are similar points all around the village. Occasionally, even Lorefast is subjected to attacks."

I smiled, "I am glad to know that I am less likely to be assassinated in my sleep."

"One should not joke about such matters, Black Finn. Assassins go as they will and some may even be good enough to get past a gatebrand."

"I am glad to hear you admit that," I said, offering my hand. "I have met a number of folk who believe they are as near perfect as is possible."

"Nobody is infallible. I am sure you know this, Black Finn."

"Only too well." I replied, walking by.

***

It was early Summer and we had just completed a class on shaping our own musical instruments. Master Anvarth Elthirien had led this. He had suggested that everyone choose one instrument to begin with, ideally something relatively simple. He had shown us how to fashion the soundbox of a lute from choosing the wood through to the first steps towards making the body of the instrument.

In our coterie, Morwen Danydd was the most advanced and she already had the skills. She was carving the decoration into a lap harp that she had been working on for many weeks.

Caladril was making a lute with a long neck, whereas I decided I would begin with something easier and went for a simple flute.

We emerged blinking from the workshop into the blazing sunlight of an early Summer afternoon.

Some others were gathering on one of the lawns near the great stones. Caladril and I wandered across. I noticed Campion and nodded to him with a smile. He responded and pointed at his harp with a question on his face. I shrugged. I wasn't sure what he meant.

"Who will go next?" Master Malderin said, looking around. "Perhaps you, Rhynnadel."

The willow-like Rhynnadel rose and gave a slight bow to the group. Her silver-blonde hair fell straight, emphasising its beautiful weight and length, falling nearly to her waist. She bound it so that it was pulled together with a small ponytail just at the end, adjusted her silver circlet and looked up at the trees. Then, without any instrument or starting note, her voice soared to a great height, plummeted and rushed away in tumbling phrases, jumping and dancing. I could not follow the elven phrases but her voice was so pure and wondrous to listen to that we were all enraptured. Finally, it slowed, repeating a soft phrase and then died down to a quiet last note.

There was applause that grew as we all awoke and joined in.

"I have not completed it all, but that is the majority of it." she said, in the common tongue.

"It describes the river perfectly." Malderin nodded, "a very fine piece to enter for the competition, this year, I think."

"Thank you Master Malderin. I did intend it for such."

"Then you need to work on the late middle and end parts" Meranissia commented, "it is a fine piece but you must not let it seem that you lose interest when it starts to wind slowly in the plains or finally spreads into an estuary and enters the sea. There is still much to find in it, there. Some thought perhaps to the teeming life?"

Rhynnadel bowed again, "my thanks for your thoughts, Mistress. I shall spend some time studying the later phase and give your words much thought."

"Harsh," I whispered to Campion and Caladril.

"Not really" Caladril replied, "a competition piece must be as perfect as possible. It was unfinished as Rhynnadel said."

"Now who might we hear from next? Gwayne, what about you?"

He stood and balanced his lap harp on one upraised knee.

"My compositions are only beginnings. I shall seem dull after such a performance." Gwayne said with a smile.

"Come now, Master Gwayne, we all know you have a good voice. Let us hear how you progress." Meranissia coaxed. Gwayne gave a short bow and struck the harp. The sound was at once clear and rang out around the glade where we sat. He began to sing and indeed, he also possessed a fine clear voice, tenor with enough weight to add power as needed. His song was a descriptive one about a summer dawn.

There was polite clapping from most of the audience. "I intend to add more to the start and perhaps a couple more verses after the third." Gwayne said, having broken off quite suddenly at the end of his song.

"It is shaping well." Malderin nodded. "I like some phrases better than others, but you have a sense of it."

"It has a human ring to it." Meranissia added, "not unpleasant but heavy-handed."

"I felt it," Shantarra commented, "I imagined the moment that Gwayne was providing. I think it was better than heavy-handed, mistress. You are too critical."

"I merely seek to guide, Shantarra." said Meranissia sharply.

"It would not make a competition form, perhaps the mistress means" Shaan Borath weighed in, his expression was unreadable. He made me feel uncomfortable.

"I didn't suggest it would be anything like that good." Gwayne started to stumble, "it's just a song."

"And as such, it does fine." Shaan added, "Perhaps that is the difference."

Meranissia inclined her head towards the elf with the short blond hair, "indeed so, Shaan. I was not being overly critical, Gwayne. If one is happy to compose songs, that is fine. But eventually, one must endeavour to work on something which has more impact."

"Why?" I asked, annoyed slightly by this superiority. "Why can one not be satisfied in the enjoyment of simpler music and songs?"

Meranissia laughed, softly although not unkindly. "We seek to improve our art, Black Finn. If one does not try to lift the level of one's work, then we make no progress and take on no challenges."

"And you'd just be an ordinary troubadour or minstrel whose place would be entertaining at an inn or some foolish lord's court." Shaan added, more cuttingly.

"It depends what each person seeks, here." Malderin interjected, holding up one hand. "Not everyone enters the song competition. Not everyone wishes to study music and verse from an intellectual standpoint. The shared love of the arts, particularly words and music is what brings us together. I give great thanks that we do not all try to write the same song."

"So, are we going to hear something from you, Black Finn?" asked Shaan, pushing.

"I am only a beginner and would be far too heavy-handed for this group." I replied, fixing him with a look.

"I'd like to hear something human" Shantarra said, with a smile that I returned. I didn't mind being teased and I knew she was having a dig at Shaan and Meranissia. I picked up my lute and resting it on one knee, I began to play something I was writing. I broke off half way through a verse.

"That is as far as it goes at present." I said when the smattering of applause ceased. "It is drawn from one of the legends of King Athol I and his ancient kingdom of Nordland."

"Sir Varrent the Black and the fair lady, Eleanor" Gwayne nodded.

"As you said, it is both human in style and quite simple" Shaan commented, "although nicely executed."

"You have a decent voice" Meranissia said, "you must also think eventually, on something more challenging but it is a nice lightweight piece."

And so, we went on for a while before I got up and walked away. Gwayne followed me.

As we left the group, I became aware of a man watching me from the shadows, where he was leaning against a beech tree. I looked him over, briefly. He was inclined to weight, of medium height with the biggest and most exaggerated mustachios that I had ever seen. His loose shirt was white with laced collar and cuffs, his trews brown and tucked into high boots where he had dagger sheaths. The most striking piece of apparel was a wide sash belt in blazing orange. Into this was tucked a short blade and he wore a falchion. A mandolin rested against the tree. He looked a most unlikely student for Lorefast.

"I rather liked both your pieces." He said, as we approached. He held out a hand. "Marcabru at your service."

I inclined my head and shook his hand. "Black Finn at yours."

"Gwayne."

"So, Marcabru," I said, smiling, "can you use that mandolin? Why abstain from joining us?"

"Ah, I am no student. I am visiting because I am interested in Lorefast's work. I like to seek new story and song subjects in the library and besides, I was visiting an old friend."

"But you play and presumably sing." Gwayne indicated towards the mandolin.

"I am a troubadour and sometimes minstrel, yes. I play for money and to entertain. I don't believe some of your students or masters would approve of my music."

"Try us." I urged.

With a big grin, Marcabru gave a deep bow and picked up the mandolin. "Feel free to join in if you think of something" he suggested, "It's something we do when we play at the inns."

Marcabru began, with a smile. His style was simple and easy, yet he played with great skill.

Once we'd picked up the beat, Gwayne and I joined in, playing parts that harmonised with the mandolin of the troubadour. In turn, I and then Gwayne improvised verses.

Marcabru finished with a flourish, giving us both a nod so we could play our final notes in time. There was some laughter and clapping from an impromptu audience that had gathered in the trees around us.

"That's my preference for a song." Marcabru grinned at us. "I like the elven epic tales and the technical pieces well enough but you can't beat a good old inn song."

"Marcabru. I thought that was your voice." One of the group stepped through. She was a human woman quite unremarkable to look at, dressed in a dull brown skirt and boots and soft green waistcoat. Her brown hair was tied rather roughly into a ponytail and she carried a quarterstaff in one hand. I discovered over our long friendship that she was anything but unremarkable and she would become the firmest of all friends with the woman I chose to love.

"Ylloelae, I heard you were in the village so I dropped by to pay a visit as well as to listen for some new tunes." Her and Marcabru embraced, briefly.

"These are two new friends I have made. Black Finn, there and this is Gwayne." He waved at us. I bowed elegantly and kissed her hand.

"My lady."

"I'm no lady" she laughed, "as you will find out. I'd rather you didn't refer to me as such. I'm not one of your soft noblewomen."

"Nonetheless" Gwayne bowed deeply and courteously, "Lady Ylloelae it will be. I have seen you here before, have I not?"

"Quite possibly. I come and go. I study healing and Lorefast gives me access not only to some fascinating texts but also some practical lessons in herbal and other remedies. I am thinking about requesting a tree house here. The peace suits me and I think it would make a better home than an inn."

"Surely that does not mean that you would be leaving our group?" Marcabru said, sadly.

"No, no but I would visit rather than live there. Besides, we are all spreading out as our travels and responsibilities take us further afield. You yourself are there less often than you were."

We reached a fireplace where there was food being cooked for the evening meals. Soon we were sat around with hot meats and bread, chatting as we sipped mead or wine. The Lorefast vineyards produce some wonderful golden wines. I was tasting their 'Spring Wine' now, something I would have a long love affair with as my favourite of drinks.

"So, you two have known each other a long time?" I asked.

"A couple of years." Ylloelae nodded, "I was introduced by another friend and soon got to know the group of adventurers that Marcabru frequents. We have shared one or two interesting times."

"Ylloelae is our healer. Without her, we would have come off much worse than we have." Marcabru added.

"And what of you, Black Finn. That's an adventurer's name, rather than a bard. What's your story?"

"I am training here as part of my duty to my family. I am not really an adventurer although I think I would rather be that than a student. I am more comfortable with a bow or sword in my hand than a lute."

"Your manner and speech sound like those of a noble family." Ylloelae commented, "I think you are of that stock."

"My lady is correct." I smiled, "I am from a noble family who hold lands within the empire."

Gwayne smiled. He knew, of course.

"And you, my lord Gwayne are one of the duke of Gwythaor's sons, if I am not mistaken?" she added.

"You seem to have the advantage." Gwayne said, "I know nothing of you but you have placed us swiftly."

"I heard that you were studying in the village. Combined with your manner and speech and that you are with another young nobleman, it wasn't difficult to guess that you were that Gwayne."

"What is your background?" I asked her.

"Oh, I'm from ordinary peasant stock. My parents were farmers. I had the gift so was sent to study when I could be spared. I learned some spells and some methods, got on well with my letters and so when I was old enough, the local temple sponsored my entry to a college in the city.

I hated the town and I hated the way it was all so formal so I gave it up and headed home but while I was away, war had come to my land and plague had followed. I reached my mother before she died, but there was nothing I could do for her. So, I packed what I needed and set off on the road, intending to bring healing and help where it was needed, especially where war had destroyed communities."

"An admirable aim." Gwayne nodded, "I hope you will stay a while in Lorefast. There is much to learn here but also there is peace to be found in one's heart."

"I thank you, my lord but I will find my heart's ease where I will."

"Now let me guess. You are a noble on the run after having an affair with the queen or princess of some far-flung realm?" I joked with Marcabru.

"Merchant's son who was a ship's captain in the trade fleet until we lost everything after the ships were sunk in a sea battle we had no place in. I left home when I was nineteen and have been a footloose troubadour and adventurer since. I like inns and women and swordplay. What can I say?"

I laughed. "It sounds like a great life."

We parted and went our separate ways to our rooms but after that Marcabru and Ylloelae joined our group, regularly. It seemed Ylloelae also knew Jeffery, the Gatebrand so, after a while, he also started to eat and talk with us when his duties allowed.

***

One afternoon after lessons, Campion, Caladril and I were taking a walk through the woods looking to bring back a couple of wood grouse for supper when we heard a scream followed by shouting and sword play. The three of us headed directly for the sound.

As we burst into a clearing, we saw Jeffery backed up against the brambles trying to hold off two men with falchions. Two more lay on the ground. One was the ranger, Farlow whom I knew in passing. The other was unknown.

Drawing our own swords, we joined the contest. Four against two turned the fight around immediately and in a few moments, we had one down with a wound in the shoulder and arm and the other surrendering with several cuts.

"Thanks" said Jeffery. He nursed his own right arm where it had been sliced while Campion bound it, swiftly. Caladril knelt by Farlow and then shook his head, "Farlow's dead."

Jeffery nodded and added, "There are two more of these men. They kidnapped the daughter of a local merchant. Farlow couldn't find any other rangers so asked me to join him. The gatebrands work closely with the rangers. We were pursuing the kidnappers when these three ambushed us. Farlow got one but he was hit twice. Two of them went for me while the other two dragged her off."

"Then we'd better get after them." I said, eager to leap into an adventure.

"I have some skills in tracking." Jeffery ventured, "what about any of you?"

"I can read some of the movement of people and animals" Campion replied.

We set off. As it was, the passage of two men, dragging an unwilling captive was pretty easy to follow even for someone with no skill in woodcraft. The trail led us out onto the main road and in the direction of an inn, The Four Hogsheads. Jeffery was able to ascertain that we were on the road to Alborough and Wolfsgate. As we approached, Ylloelae and Marcabru appeared from some bushes just off the trail.

"I'm glad to see you four. Some men were dragging a young woman along the road and have gone into the inn. I doubled back and fetched Marcabru." Ylloelae explained.

"We were also on their trail lady healer," Jeffery bowed slightly.

"Oh, I hope I haven't given anything away." She replied.

"I'm sure you haven't" Jeffery smiled, "but we would be glad of your help if you wish to join us."

We approached from different sides. Caladril and I went around to the rear door. Ylloelae, Marcabru and Jeffery went to the front door, while Campion set down to watch the side door into the vegetable garden and yard with a bow ready. Being overbold and enthusiastic, I put a boot to the rear door and went in, sword drawn.

Let me council you, should you be inclined to think the same about the potential imprudence of crashing in pretending to be a drunken client or slipping in unseen and having a cautious look around, the latter would be the better choice.

I suppose I had expected there to be a few ordinary patrons but about a dozen men swung around as I blundered in. The girl and another who looked very similar were tied to chairs in a smaller room that I could see into. By the sound of things, there had been an argument going on between the barman and the others over how they were going to conceal the girls. I just caught the tail end of that as the barman was angrily shouting "and what do I say, then? I'm sorry but you can't use the snug because we've got hostages tied up in there? Perhaps you'd like me to say it's being re-decorated!" The argument ceased abruptly as I came flying in and stumbled over the raised step.

The barman picked up a cudgel. The rest already appeared to be armed as various knives, short swords and clubs appeared in their hands. They moved in.

I was fast enough to disarm the first with a feint and a thrust which cut his wrist and lower arm causing him to jerk back, his club falling to the inn floor. I went for a second who backed up, letting two others get around on my flank. One blow struck me on the shoulder, deadening my left arm and the second caught me on the side of the head, sending me reeling. That might have been it for the adventures of Black Finn but for the entry of the others.

Having seen that we were so outnumbered, Caladril had not leapt in but paused, let one man come at him whom he wounded in the shoulder and then dodged around the bar. As the group gathered about me, he gave a great shout. It was a bardic skill that I had heard about but it was the first time I had seen it in use. The effect was like a ripple of sound that made your head seem thick and heavy and then the main wave hit and the majority went from slight confusion to collapsing to their knees, stunned.

Jeffery, Marcabru and Ylloelae then followed in, Jeffery and Ylloelae laying about them in fine style with staves while Marcabru backed off a couple of men with his swordplay. The dozen suddenly looked too few as Caladril came leaping in shouting which brought Campion crashing through the side entrance in time to put an arrow in the barman who had just gone for an axe to replace his cudgel and take a swing at Caladril from behind. I was up fairly quickly although my head was still ringing. I don't think I did a lot but we prevailed without any serious wounds and by the time I was fully with it, Ylloelae was healing two of the men we had put down. That's when I questioned her, first about it.

"Ylloelae, shouldn't you see to Caladril's wounded arm or the nick I took in the leg which is still bleeding before you care for them? Personally, I'd let them die. They don't deserve any particular kindness and I doubt that they'll escape the Duke's prison for this."

Ylloelae looked up and smiled, gently. "I know you find this hard to understand but in the creator's eyes we are all his children. Some make mistakes but that does not mean we do not forgive them or succour them when they are hurt or upset. Healing is a path to forgiveness and forgiveness offers men a second chance to turn around their lives and do better deeds. These wounds are serious and the two men I am seeing to might indeed die if left to bleed. Yours and Caladril's wounds are minor. I will deal with them, later. Campion has gone to fetch the militia. I wouldn't want them to seize these men and drag them off as they are. They would certainly perish, then."

"One or more of these men murdered Farlow, a ranger doing his duty." I replied, crossly.

"And they will pay, but in a courtroom and because they will have to live with what they have done, today. It is not your job to be judge and executioner. The rangers bring men to justice."

"Often, good sister" interjected Jeffery, "that does mean killing them rather than bringing them anywhere."

"But not when unneeded?"

"No, generally, they are brought back to answer before a justice, that is true."

"And until justice is served and even after, were I asked to help, I would ministrate to those in pain and sick. The creator does not judge his children in the same way."

"It's no good arguing with her." Marcabru grinned, "We've many of us had this discussion. Our lady healer remains firm in her commitment that where she is not forced to kill, she will not do so."

Later on, that evening, back at Old Tom's in Warvane's market place, we sat and drank, talking of our plans and hopes. I spent just over a year studying under the wonderfully talented elders and journeymen of Lorefast. I learned much about heroic tales, care of instruments and use of the voice arts. It was the only time in my life that I genuinely felt carefree. Alas, that was to be short-lived.

Two life changing events came in quick succession. Firstly, Gwayne's elder brother was killed by a wild boar while out hunting. There were three days of mourning across the country. Flags were lowered and a tournament was held in his honour at which all the knights wore black. Gwayne was not only grieving at losing a brother with whom he got on so well, but that he would have to depart from full time study at Lorefast. He was now heir to the ducal throne and as such, would have to be groomed for that role instead of one as an ambassador with a knack for music and verse.

The second event was the outbreak of war back home. At first, it was just a border war but then it spread. At first, Drachefauste was only implicated, I understood from my father's letters. The man was proving impossible to develop into a model lord and now there were three barbarian tribes harassing our lands and those of the neighbours in the north. Only Drachefauste's demesne was untouched. He claimed it was the fear of his reputation and that of his men. Then Drachefauste moved openly against the two neighbouring states and placed a large garrison just north of our own border. He seized Marshelyn. Within days, he had subjugated the small state and its Earl had vanished. Then, he invaded Nordia. Under our agreement, that was tantamount to declaring war on Rosgovia.

Perhaps, Drachefauste thought we would not come in but dither and try diplomacy to solve things. In that, he was wrong. My father had made a promise and despatched forces under Fulk, at once. I wondered if I would get to fight against his famed Dragon Guard. My skills with sword and bow had improved greatly since leaving home. With Kharr's help and with the challenges laid on by Gwayne and his friends, I had learned to ride better, to joust, fight on horseback with axe and sword, improved my skills with long, cross and short bows, throw a dagger with real accuracy, hold off a man with a quarterstaff and understand tactics for using horse and foot, properly.

I was just helping Gwayne pack away the figures from the war games table where we had spent a few hours recreating an old battle between the early Imperial army and the Karilian Guard.

"I shall miss our songs and stories around the fire at Lorefast" Gwayne said, grimacing, slightly.

"Perhaps there will be time, again, one day" I suggested, hopefully.

"You could always come to the ducal court"

"I could, but then I would have to give up my studies and would never be a good enough bard to play in public"

"That's not true." He smiled "You're better than most ordinary court bards, already. Your tales are always full of fun or adventure."

I sighed.

"If only all tales ended so well."

Gwayne turned to regard me with a serious air.

"There was bad news in that letter you received, then?"

"Yes. I have been recalled to my home. There's a war that seems to be spreading on our borders, so my father has called us home to council."

"I'm sorry. Will you be coming back?"

"To be honest, I don't know. The hint in my father's writing suggests that my training will be moved on to something more immediately useful to the family. I'm not sure what he had planned after I completed my first qualification, here. I don't imagine my father will want me engaging in the war, at least not until we are forced to fight for our own land. But who can say? Whatever will be will be."

"Philosophy now?" Gwayne managed a smile. I grinned.

"That's more your field, talking and theorising. I'm a man of action."

I ducked as he aimed a friendly clip at my head.

"We'll see, one of these days. I don't intend to sit on the ducal throne and do nothing. My father has avoided becoming embroiled in just about everything happening. Perhaps I will now learn why or perhaps I'll prove a less wise duke and pitch in."

"Be careful, my friend" I said, becoming more serious, "politics are safer than war."

"War is just another form of political negotiation", he grinned, again.

"Nonetheless. Gwythaor profits from being considered a peaceful neutral with no military ambition."

"And ripe to be plucked. I don't intend to wait for one of the militaristic states to add us to their list of conquests. I'd rather cede from the Empire and take our chances alone."

I nodded, "There has been much rumour about the islands breaking with the Imperial Throne but the empire would strike swiftly and with great fury. I wouldn't underestimate the ability of the Emperor even if Riassa is a long way off. There will come a time but it is not now."

"Now you sound like my father" Gwayne's eyes sparkled with humour, but there was a truth in the tenor of his voice.

"Then maybe you need to understand his reasoning" I replied, wondering why I could give that advice to others but never take it myself.

"Maybe." Gwayne fell quiet and we continued packing away.

Stones II

A few days later, we parted, Gwayne to begin an intensive period of coaching in Warvane while I took a merchant cog to Jordis and from there, a fast warship on which I managed to arrange a passage. That would get me to Riassa from where I would head northwards.

Riassa was far bigger than I had imagined. It sprawled all around a great recessed bay, protected from the worst of the weather by two peninsulas to the east and west. Northwards, it extended all the way to the Zovnian Marshes. I was overwhelmed by the vastness, the hundreds of ships moving in and out of the many harbours and an even larger number riding the waves at anchor.

As we neared the trading port, I could see teeming market places filled with people going about their daily business. The riot of colour, the range of sounds and scents and the noise assaulted my senses. I stood, open-mouthed just trying to somehow take it in. I had thought Acondium was impressive. Beside Riassa's waterfront, Acondium looked like a village hamlet. My ship had been faster than expected, so I was glad to have a few days spare to explore.

The deputy master of the ship I was travelling on put a hand on my shoulder

"First time in Riassa, lad?"

"It is."

"Quite a sight, isn't it?"

I nodded, attempting to gather my thoughts. While I was still trying to assimilate all the information from my senses, the lateens came down and we were immersed in the noise of the dock and seafront market place. I dimly heard the sounds of the crew going about their final duties. The warmth, smells and physical proximity to so many people wrapped me in a new and more intimate invasion. I stepped ashore in a daze, vaguely waving away the first urchins and street traders who thrust wares before me. They offered me services at best prices, places to stay and places to find women after my voyage. I was moving like one who has inhaled black lotus and floats out of his body, aware of all that is going on but disconnected from it.

"I said, you must be Edmund."

The urgency in the voice and the light touch on my shoulder awakened me from my reverie. I turned to regard the man who was speaking. He was small, wiry and much older than me. Tufts of grey above and around his ears were all that remained of his hair. His face was lined and worn like old leather; his hands bony but his eyes were full of humour. I smiled.

"Yes, I'm Edmund. To whom do I have the honour of addressing?"

"No honour, young sir. I'm just Baslos, your father's shipping clerk and trading agent. He asked me to meet you and make sure you were comfortable for the night as you have a long journey ahead, I suppose. If you follow me, I'll take you to my villa where you can rest. My wife is a good cook, plain but good. I'm sure she'll want to make sure you get a proper meal. Oh, and watch your pockets. The thief masters are always putting more of their ragamuffins on the street, especially here in the Seamarket. Come on."

He pushed aside a lad holding mangos up for our inspection and moved purposefully up the cobbled street away from the port. It was only after I had gone some way that I realised I had never thanked the master of the ship. I looked back.

The milling crowds had swallowed my companions on the trip. I shook my head. I would try and remember to put that right, later. For now, Baslos was pressing on too quickly to turn back and have any hope of catching him, again. I shrugged and followed him, hauling my carry bag up on my shoulder.

"I was hoping to see some of the city," I said, catching up to the stiff looking back of the hurrying clerk.

"Not sure that would be wise, sir" he stopped and turned to look me over.

"I'm sure you can handle yourself but with the Emperor so ill and the talk of civil war, any young noble, especially one who comes from a family that's involved is liable to be pressurised, maybe taken hostage or worse, killed even. Factions are busy recruiting and disposing of those who won't join them. They say the Brotherhood of Executioners have not been so busy in years."

"The Brotherhood of Executioners?" I furrowed my brows, questioningly.

"The Assassins Guild", Baslos said, in a manner of voice that suggested I should know that.

"There is a guild for assassins here?"

"There is a guild for everything" he smiled thinly, but his manner softened. "I forget sometimes that so many people have no exposure to a big city like this. There is more than one, probably. There are certainly at least two or three Thieves Guilds. There are even guilds for sell-swords, these days."

I nodded and made a mental note. The idea of an assassin's guild intrigued me.

"It's exactly those sorts of organisations that are accepting money from the faction leaders to deal with the captains, gentry and nobility who are on the other side. The guilds don't care. They'll accept jobs from all sides and kill anyone, provided they get paid enough."

We went on up the street. I started imagining eyes watching us, taking note of me - the stranger that Baslos had been sent to meet. I patted my blade reassuringly. Let them come. I might not have been a city dweller nor know their ways but I'd learned a few things about fighting, brawling and surviving. I smiled and looked about with a new eye. Let them look. Let them see I didn't care if they looked, either.

***

"So, then I kicked his legs out from under him and he falls on the first guy."

We all laughed. Encouraged by the reception to his tale, Rill went on loudly. We had all been drinking and telling tall stories for a while.

"I'd have got away if I hadn't been so busy admiring my handiwork that I stepped on the anchor chain and went over backwards right on top of the heavy, Munz. Well, he lifts me right up onto his shoulders, spins me around and the next thing, I'm flying right over the other two, over the rail and into the water. And by the brothers, it was cold."

I'd been in Riassa for a few days now and, during a visit or two to the drinking establishments on the harbourside, I'd fallen in with an interesting bunch.

Rill claimed to work for a 'guild' and was coy about what it did. A rogue who obviously went from stealing to adventuring, he was no more than a year or two older than me. He was lightly built with dark curly hair, a pencil thin moustache and favoured leather waistcoats over his white shirts.

Tu'Lon, by comparison, was short, thickset and had the dark skin of the tribal peoples from Tropicania. He claimed to be a priest but he invoked Merlos, the god of gamblers, not that he seemed to be blessing his priest with any luck recently. Tu'Lon was a man of good humour though, and a fine drinking companion.

The other man at the table was Coyle Mavern, a self-confessed failed wizard's apprentice who could conjure up the odd thing and seemed pretty good at sleight-of-hand tricks. Coyle was similar in appearance to Rill but a little stronger in frame, a little taller and wore no moustache. As we were laughing, a newcomer pulled up a chair, uninvited. He was a thickset man, perhaps four or five years older than the rest of us, with a neat black beard and long hair. A gold earring and a diamond studded ring showed he had some wealth at his disposal.

"Klavon," Coyle sat up straight, "fancy seeing you here. Gentlemen, this is Klavon; mercenary, pirate and the finest jewel thief that I know… in fact the only jewel thief that I know."

"Hush," the man's voice hissed with menace. "Don't draw so much attention."

The mood at the table sobered. Rill was giving this man a strange look. I started to pay more attention. It looked like there were things I needed to know about him.

"Klavon" Tu'Lon nodded in an uncomfortable way.

"I'm looking for some likely lads who can handle themselves to help me with an important job."

Four faces stopped smiling, and leaned in closer to listen.

"Go on, Klavon" Coyle said, softly. "You know we're likely to be interested."

"If you lads want to earn some decent coin and add to your reputations, come and see me tomorrow evening at the back of the harbourmaster's office, an hour after sunset. Bring your weapons. You may need them."

He nodded twice and then rose.

"Good to see you as well" he said, loudly. "Might see you around again before I head off."

I watched him go. He had a soft tread and there was menace in it just as there was in his posture and eyes. I noted the polished handle of the throwing knife that peeped from a boot holster and the longer slightly curved blade on his belt.

"You know this guy?" I said to Coyle.

"You're probably the only one who doesn't," Rill said in a guarded way.

"He's trouble, but he does get some plum jobs", Coyle added.

"He's in with the biggest thieves guild in Riassa" Rill said with a definite note of dislike, "They're trying to force any thieves to join and pay dues or end up face down in a wastewater ditch. I don't trust him."

"I didn't say I trusted him" Coyle protested, with a grin. "I just said he gets some well-paid work and he does pay on time. I've done a couple of things for him and his associates, before."

I was interested. The idea of getting to know someone with connections to the shadowy guilds excited me. It would be a little different to be in with such men and women.

"I'm interested" I said, "especially if it pays well." The rest of the group believed I was just another young mercenary making my way.

"I'd be in. I could use the money, to be honest" Tu'Lon added, as he sat back and looked around at the rest of us.

"Yeah, I'd do it" Coyle said, and offered his hand to the two of us.

Rill glowered slightly and then shrugged. "Fine. You can only die once, right?" His grin nearly returned and he drank up what remained in his clay cup.

"Count me in." He rose.

"Where you going?" asked Tu'Lon.

"For a piss and then home. Much as I have enjoyed your company gents, I suddenly don't feel like laughing any more this evening."

The following day, I met the group behind the Harbourmaster's office as planned. I had taken some time deciding what I would wear for such a job as this.

Eventually, I had settled on the armour that I had had made for some of the undertakings that Kharr and I had engaged in. I looked it over. A hardened black leather jerkin including a guard brace, with metal studding down to the ribs for added protection. Over my tunic, I buckled leather couters and wrist guards. I opted for gloves that could be used for climbing, and I left the leather greaves and cuisses behind. They were good for extended combat, but made the legs a little too inflexible for running and climbing, in my opinion. The helm was half open, offering cheekbones and upper nose some cover without restricting my view.

Next, I selected my favourite weapons. I had become accustomed to having three or four weighted throwing knives about my person. If nothing else, you can always cause confusion and slow pursuit with a missile or two. I had read that lesson many years ago, in my father's library.

I chose a short falchion, so I could cut or stab in restricted space, and a small, round buckler to wear on my left wrist. The falchion, I buckled on my right hip. Then, I turned to my other weapons and decided on a short, compound light-crossbow. It didn't have a long range but was good and easy to use for short punch shots. It had an easily operable lever, which drew the string back into reload position. I put a small case on low down on my left thigh to carry half a dozen short bolts with heavy heads that could puncture armour and one heavy blunt. I felt a little encumbered by the time I was done but after walking a way, I settled comfortably enough into the equipment I had chosen.

"Looks like we're the first to arrive" commented Coyle, from the deep shadows. I hadn't even seen him on my approach.

"Can you teach me to lurk like that?" I asked. "I didn't even see you. It's quite a skill."

He grinned and slapped my shoulder, "It'd be a pleasure. Just don't ever use it on me, though."

Coyle didn't look like any kind of wizard, failed or otherwise. He had a soft leather hauberk and a selection of weapons not unlike my own. His helm was soft leather and cut back from the face and ears. A bandolier held a number of vials and small bags, which I assumed, held spell components. A moment or two later, Rill slipped around the corner and put his back against the wall. He had a dark hooded cloak over a soft helm, similar leather jerkin to Coyle and assorted knives and blades hanging from his belt and in his boot sheaths.

"I'm sure I was being followed." he stated. "If this is a set-up, I'll carve my name in Klavon's heart, so help me."

Coyle and I drew our blades. The tension increased as we waited.

A stranger rounded the corner, dressed not unlike Coyle and Rill but in black leather and carrying a short bow. His skin was dark and his head shaven, maybe a southern barbarian or Carnossian. He put his hands up to show he had no other weapons drawn.

"Friends, please. I'm with you. Klavon asked me along. The name's Barnabus."

"Klavon didn't say anything about you" Rill growled.

"A small oversight", Klavon himself stepped out from the opposite corner to Barnabus. "Are we all here?"

"We are now." A patch of darkness seemed to move and then became Tu'Lon.

"Impressive" Klavon commented, "a spell or an item?"

Tu'Lon ignored the question, "I wanted to be sure it was a safe meeting so I decided I would remain hidden in case you needed some back up" he said. Coyle grinned.

"I'm glad to see we all understand one another" Klavon commented, dryly.

"Now, to business. Time is short and so are the hours of darkness. There is a merchant arriving on a secret visit to the harbour, tonight. He will have at least two well-armed guards. He'll be carrying money, which you're welcome to, but more importantly, he will be wearing a large gold signet ring and brooch with the arms of the guild.

They are both decorated with a sizeable garnet, so should be easy to identify. Our job is to take these without killing or wounding the man. Hopefully, an efficient hold up will do the trick and we can be away."

He produced a bag of black masks that covered all but our mouths.

"Best not to be recognised" he said, handing them around.

"Once we have the two pieces and any money we take, we leave. We meet back at the inn, tomorrow night. Lie low for the day. The militia and the guilds may make enquiries and it is imperative that nobody is caught. Once the deal is done, it will be safe again. My guild will take the jewellery to the merchant guild as proof of what we can do. That is why it is important that the merchant himself is not harmed."

"So why employ us to do a job that the guild could organise?"

"Because if you fail, you need to be people who aren't known as members and, more importantly, there are complications that you will be able to overcome but that a guild heavy wouldn't have a clue about. The first is that there will be two carriages.

The merchant's one needs to be identified and targeted. The other must not be touched in any way. They will look exactly the same when they come through those gates. Secondly, the merchant has a ring that allows him to become invisible. I assume that one of you can cast something to counter that."

At this Tu'Lon and Coyle both nodded. "Good. To get into the inner mercantile dock, we have to climb over a wall. There's a watchtower so it's a job for those who can be stealthy. Finally, I wanted to see you in action. I am thinking about future jobs where I need contractors. Do well here and you may find it lucrative longer term.

Now, I have calculated the best place to cross the wall. Once we are inside the mercantile harbour, we want to watch the gates and then move, probably in two groups, down to the quay. We take the merchant before he gets on board the ship where his meeting is to take place. Any questions?"

Rill, who had been looking doubtful, throughout was first to speak, "Shouldn't we assign out the tasks? Someone has to hang back to deal with the extra guards, assuming there are any and someone else should check to make sure there are no others still in or with the coach. And what if the attack on the merchant arouses the ship crew and we end up with twenty seamen rushing in to join the fray?"

"I'm interested in how we know which carriage is which", Tu'Lon added.

"I can probably deal with that" Coyle nodded.

"Shall we?" Klavon waved towards a white walled area some distance from the office.

"I can't wait" muttered Rill under his breath. Coyle flashed him a grin and patted my shoulder.

"Come on then. Let's see what's in store."

I grinned too, but inside, my heart was pounding. I was wondering what my father would make of it if his son were to be caught in an assault and robbery, dressed like a thief and in the company of the same.

Getting over the wall was relatively easy. Lines were thrown and we were over in under a minute. The only moment of any trepidation was on reaching the top where the guard tower could potentially see you.

But the position was in deep shadow and the tower guard was likely looking out towards the main road. The lanterns in the tower never moved throughout. I dropped lightly over the wall and almost slid down the other side, gripping the rope with my feet. Once in the yard, I was against the wall with the others in a moment.

"Easy, isn't it?" Klavon grinned at me. "Nice ropework, by the way. You learn that at a guild?"

"No," I said truthfully. "On the job, I suppose you'd say."

Barnabus and Tu'Lon were last over. Barnabus lowered Tu'Lon down slowly before hooking something on the line and sliding down. He used his boots to slow the descent a little and hit the floor with a soft thud, bouncing off the rope and moving onto one knee, short bow ready. I liked that move better than mine. He scoured the yard and roadway.

"Whoever is paying the watchman should ask for his money back" Barnabus commented.

"I reckon he's asleep up there."

Klavon chuckled, softly. "He'll get into hot water later, when news of our escapade gets back. Let's hope it's not one of our contracts."

"The guild has guard duty contracts?" I asked, somewhat incredulously.

"Oh yes. They're a good bet to get anything back that is lost, after all. More to the point, if the guild is guarding, they aren't likely to be stealing from you, are they?"

Rill made a disapproving noise. Klavon gave him a dark look. The history between them was evident without any words having to be spoken. I was a little concerned how that might end. I liked Rill but beside Klavon, he looked like a beginner.

Klavon had style and self-assurance. From what I'd seen of his climb and the way he handled himself, he had good reason. My musings were interrupted by the sound of the gates opening to the north of our position and then two carriages rattling across the paving slabs towards us.

We moved back into the deep shadow as they went by. In the first, I could see a man in rich apparel accompanied by two armoured companions. The driver was in scale and had a crossbow beside him. The second carriage contained two smaller cloaked and hooded figures. The first carriage bore right, heading straight towards the quayside. The second veered left and went down the narrower street that led towards storehouses and the eastern end of the harbour.

"Alright, that makes it easy," Klavon said, softly, "let's pick up our target and get this done."

We spread out, leaving enough of a gap for each to fight without impeding the next. Moving with silent strides, we closed the gap and went into cover just as the first carriage drew up. The driver climbed down.

"Now, while we're on the blind side of them," hissed Coyle. We broke cover and ran towards the carriage. Two capstans and a low wall lay between the disembarking men and us. We spread wider as we ran in.

"Put up your weapons!" shouted Coyle.

"Step out where we can see you!" Rill added.

For a moment, it all looked like we were in complete control as the three armoured men moved into view with the merchant behind them. But only a moment. I must have sensed it because I got that sinking feeling in the pit of my stomach and started to raise my crossbow as I saw them react.

The coach driver jerked his crossbow up and loosed a bolt. that missed Coyle by some way. My bolt took him in the chest and Rill's throwing knife hit him in the right wrist.

He was spinning and falling as the other two armoured types, both wearing heavier chain hauberks with surcoats, moved sideways to gain partial cover. In unison, they dropped to one knee and let fly with their crossbows.

The supposed merchant was right with them but far from staying out of it, he was yelling out power words. That's how it went very wrong.

We were ready for trained fighting men, but someone using magic was unexpected. Coyle yelled something and there was a flash which jolted the two men at arms. Tu'Lon, coming in from the left flank, flung a dagger which bounced off the plate pauldron on the left-hand man's shoulder.

Then one of their bolts winged Rill's right leg and the other narrowly missed me as I dived behind the low wall. An inky patch of dark shadow engulfed the coach and our three remaining opponents. Tu'Lon cursed softly and nodded to Coyle who was now crouched behind a capstan

"I'll do it. You hit them with something."

Tu'Lon leapt up, pointed and shouted out some arcane phrase. There was a flicker of light and colour.

The darkness vanished, revealing one of the men on top of the coach and one underneath it lying on his belly, both with crossbows ready while the 'merchant' was casting a spell over the fallen driver well under the cover of the coach.

Rill dashed forwards. He stumbled as a bolt ripped past his ankle, regained his balance and flung a knife up at the man on top of the carriage.

I tried to give him cover by sending a bolt low so it skittered along the paving towards the prone soldier. Coyle stood and flung out a hand, yelling out some words.

There was another flash and a blast, which sent up a cloud of dust and fragments. The man on the top of the coach was lifted into the air and crashed down out of sight with a cry and a heavy thud.

Then Tu'Lon was casting again and so was Coyle. A blast under the coach from Coyle forced the prone soldier to crawl backwards, leaving his crossbow as he covered his face and moaned out. The recovering driver half rose and seemed to freeze on the spot as Tu'Lon's spell struck him.

At that moment, we had the upper hand but the noise and the flashes had attracted the crew of the ship where the meeting was due to take place.

On the ship, I could see movement and what looked like a bunch of well-armed seamen assembling on deck. Down the gangplank came a single man dressed in scale who drew two swords and came at us.

It was only then that it occurred to me that neither Klavon nor Barnabus had actually done anything. I looked around. They were not anywhere in sight. At that point, things took a turn for the even worse.

Rill had disappeared down the side of the coach in the shadows. He tried to come swiftly in on the newcomer's flank with a thrust designed to put him out of the action.

There was a flicker of blades and I saw Rill recoiling, blood forming a patch around his shoulder and upper right arm. The second blade put him down. Coyle leapt up with a shout to hurl a blast at Rill's assailant. The man staggered, but then there was a flash like lightning right amongst us.

The so-called merchant had emerged from cover. Coyle was flung back in a twitching heap. Tu'Lon raced to his side and I came up to give them cover, firing a heavy bolt that made the swordsman duck aside. I moved to help Tu'Lon drag Coyle into cover but there was another flash and smell of ozone.

I only recall being on my back alongside the other two, twitching uncontrollably. You know what it feels like when you get a bang on the end of the elbow that sends a shock through your arm? Imagine that feeling all over your body and add to that your muscles reacting involuntarily as if you are jerking about like a puppet on strings. That's how it felt.

The swordsman moved towards us with a dark look, and all I could think about was how angry my father would be. That is when I noticed the swordsman had six fingers in each black leather glove. Rill moaned and tried to crawl towards us. The man looked round with a satisfied smile and carried on towards the three of us. Pity, I thought, that my adventuring had to end so soon. I tried to reach for a weapon but my arms wouldn't work.

"Leave them be!"

Barnabus shouted out from somewhere nearby. The swordsman turned, flexed his neck muscles and glanced back at the 'merchant' who was also moving towards us, pausing only to free one of his men from Tu'Lon's spell.

"I've got the princess here," Klavon's voice was low and menacing, "I'm sure we wouldn't want any misunderstandings."

The man from the carriage stepped back a pace. His cloak unfurled in the wind to reveal the robes of a priest beneath. I knew he was no merchant, but it seemed we had engaged with a priest-mage and presumably quite a senior one. By now, men from the ship, in livery and dressed like guards or marines, were all around.

"Sevenhands" he spoke the name softly. The swordsman shrugged and walked backwards until he was beside the priest. Then, he sheathed both blades.

"What do you want?" The priest sounded irritated.

"We will take the princess. She will be returned unharmed but you will have to request her release from the guild. The guild will take the credit for her return. The details of how and where she was taken will remain unknown. You and your master will see to this. Next time, perhaps you will be more willing to enter a discussion instead of mistreating our …ambassador."

The priest started to say something and then bit back on whatever was about to come out. His expression, even in the low light, was of barely concealed fury.

"If she is harmed, mistreated, even inconvenienced by bad behaviour or uncomfortable surroundings, your guild will never stop paying."

"I can assure you she will be well looked after. Providing you do as I have said. The word must be out that the guild has it in hand and is looking after matters. We will be listening on the streets. Now order your dogs off."

With an irritated wave of his arm, the priest gestured and the soldiers dropped back. The warrior called Sevenhands scowled but turned his back and stalked away, the ranks parting to let him pass.

Between Tu'Lon and myself, we hauled Rill up and supported him. Klavon emerged with a woman, her hands loosely bound behind her.

"You surely didn't think that dressing her as the maid would fool me, good priest?"

We backed down, steadily. There were still a lot of crossbows pointed in our direction.

It seemed to take a very long time but eventually, we left the complex and turned back into the city. Klavon loosed the woman's bonds and apologised profusely for the inconvenience. I heard her voice briefly, rich, dark and low.

"Oh, I didn't mind. It's all rather an adventure. I enjoyed seeing Cavallari and his master being inconvenienced. I shall trust you to keep to your word, as will Annalena."

An open carriage came up from a dark side-street. Klavon ushered the lady into it politely and with an elegant bow.

"Milady." He waited until she was seated, "I wish to assure you of our loyalty and good intentions towards you and your family. We would serve you well, over the years to come. You will only ever have to ask. All we seek in return is that we are allowed to continue as we have done since time immemorial and are not subjected to any further persecution by the high temple."

"I cannot assure you of that, master thief, but I can tell you that my father is as sick of their interference in the state as you are of their presence upon the streets."

And then the carriage was away. Four hooded individuals came out of the side street to join Klavon and Barnabus. Klavon turned to us;

"A good night's work."

"You bastard. You hung us out to dry as a decoy," Rill spat the words out. Blood and spittle dribbled down his chin.

"Now, now. Everything was under control. Of course, had you been members of the guild, you'd have known the whole plan."

"He's right. You played us, Klavon. That was ill done." Coyle glared at the man.

I shrugged, "It worked, though."

Klavon laughed and slapped my shoulder. "Yes it did, my young friend, and all of you are alive. I didn't bargain on Rill trying to best Sevenhands. I thought you'd all hang back and they'd stay at bay, exchanging shots. Unfortunate that anyone got hurt but no serious harm done."

"Count me out of any future schemes you may have." Tu'Lon's face wore a dark scowl.

"Thanet", Klavon spoke to a blond man amongst the four. He grinned and fished some large bags from a hidden belt.

"For your inconvenience. Perhaps this will help ease your moods and your debts."

The blond fellow offered them. Tu'Lon scowled and then took his. Coyle likewise. Rill spat.

"I don't want your filthy coin."

"Yes, you do," Coyle said and took a second bag. I accepted the one offered to me.

"We always pay our debts. Think about it. You might make good profits working as contractors for the guild. There is going to be action, a war on the streets to bring the independents into line. I suggest you choose the winning side and the one that will pay best. Good evening, gentlemen."

With which, Klavon, the four hooded fellows and Barnabus all left, Barnabus with a shrug that looked like half an apology to us.

"Bastard" Rill muttered. "One of these days, I'm going to spit him."

"But not today" commented Coyle. "I say we drink on the strength of some of his coin."

I nodded. I had learned a new lesson.

Beasts II

From Riassa, I journeyed home, mainly by horse. It was a long journey and involved numerous stops, some in comfortable inns and some off the roadside on hard, cold and stony ground. I made a point of taking an indirect route through Littesburg.

Stopping with my cousins was the high point of the journey. For a few days, we just enjoyed ourselves around the estate. Rupert was a year younger than me, Rudolf another five or so. Emmelina who was three years younger than me, was as feisty as her brothers and just as ready to race a horse or go hunting. The other two, Raphael and Raoul, at six and eight years younger weren't allowed to join in all our activities but both wanted to hunt with us and demonstrate what they had already learned with a duelling epee.

I was able to see my uncle, Raef, again and hear his views on politics and war. My uncle saw the border troubles as a pre-cursor to something much more far reaching. His view was that new nobility who felt excluded from the inner circle at court were preparing for a war that would change everything.

Being young and full of ideas of adventure, I found the idea quite exciting. I rather relished the idea of leading troops and fighting great battles. Wisdom comes with age and bitter experience.

After leaving my cousins behind, I travelled through Aquila. I was surprised to find much preparation for war and found I was treated with some suspicion in the towns.

It seemed the local lords in that territory were certainly expecting the coming conflict that Raef had talked of.

Cylmarda was quieter. A large and sparsely populated dukedom, its towns and villages seemed to sleep at ease. Perhaps being neither close to the capital nor to the borders, Cylmarda's farming country remained in blissful ignorance. Cytelia, too, was quiet.

I entered the main city, Anoen, once the Imperial Capital long before Acondium took that position and back when Riassa was just a fishing port.

Anoen was a beautiful city, then, all in white stone with delicate spires and shapely temples, every plaza possessing a fountain or statuary; every archway and gate named with some relief stone sculpture to provide a theme linked to the name. The tale was told that Anoen was built, originally, by elves in the days when they had an empire of their own.

Whatever the truth, it was undoubtedly the most beautiful city I had ever beheld, I could certainly believe it was the work of elven folk. The curves in the walls and the narrow walkways with their coloured paving looked the work of fine hands and imaginations beyond the ideas of normal men. Cytelia seemed quite unprepared, yet I heard rumour in Anoen of several lords who were raising small armies.

The lack of suspicion or questions about their motives appalled me. Riassans would not have shown so much naivety. I was almost glad to leave. Although I enjoyed the city itself, it almost hurt to see how unprepared they were and to imagine what might befall the many artists and musicians and appreciative young folk who seemed to frequent the plazas.   At last, I crossed the border into Rosgovia and was soon met by a patrol of my father's outriders. At least it was evident we were not about to be caught sleeping while the enemy were mobilising.

Captain Janed was in command. She rode up and saluted with a tight smile, "Lord Edmund. It's good to have you home. Your father needs every fighting arm he can muster for what lies ahead. You were always a good rider. Perhaps you will join the scouts?"

I smiled at Janed. She was not a beautiful woman but she was striking; tall, powerful with long legs and a great mane of flowing brown hair.

Her brother, Ferad had been killed while scouting on just his third assignment. When she had told her father and the captain at that time, that she wanted to replace her brother, they had both laughed.

But Janed was a determined girl. She learned and she fought her way up until she had proved that not only was she the best scout but she could handle most of them in a fight, too. Her nose had been broken and reset twice and she had a scar on her forehead where she had just avoided a blade that opened a head wound rather than slaying her outright.

Now she was commander of the Rosgovian scout regiment and one of my father's trusted officers. She had taught me some of what I knew. I would happily have joined her on patrols but I doubted it was my father's intention.

"Perhaps so." I said, "I have learned a great deal on my travels. I might even give your men a decent outing with bow and sword, now."

"Any time you wish to see how much you have improved," she said with a smile and patted her sword, "I am happy to give you another lesson. I'm sure it won't be as painful as the last one." She gave a barking laugh but her eyes twinkled with humour.

I chuckled, too. She was referring to when I was twelve and had been sent for a few days to learn survival skills. I thought I'd be clever so I hid a load of expensive foodstuffs and some wine in my kit and smuggled it into camp. Everything was going well until I lost some of it in a card game, Janed spotted one of her men with certain items and tracked them back to me. Suffice to say she removed my stash and I had cause to remember the aftermath when she overcame my attempts to escape with some choice items.

Janed insisted in sending an escort of two men with me as far as the bridge at Ruenna. Finnmeyer was waiting for me as I crossed. He looked concerned. Fear rose inside as I read his face. I knew something was wrong and that each step my horse took, brought me closer to finding out what it was

"Finnmeyer, it's good to see you." It sounded forced. He nodded. He paused only a moment,

"Your mother was sent on a diplomatic mission to try to negotiate with two of the Hamvard chieftains on the northern border but we got word that Drachefauste is on his way to the same meeting. I fear for your mother, Edmund. He would love to capture her. It would be another symbol of your father's impotence in dealing with him. I sent two riders to intercept her but they didn't return. Your father won't send a force. He says it would be too provocative. I thought you should hear it from me rather than find out when you got home."

I nodded, trying to take it in. I couldn't imagine why my mother would have been dispatched on such a mission. She was a concubine and manager of domestic staff not a diplomat. I wasn't going to abandon her to fate's chance, especially when it involved the beast.

"How far behind are we?"

"A day, maybe day and a half, but she has a sled and was travelling slowly. We should catch her before she reaches the border if we go today. I'd go alone but I need someone to watch my back, especially if those two scouts have already been ambushed. It may be they are with her and everything is fine, but I would have expected word back."

We began to ride together, turning onto the northbound road.

"You sent two scouts?" I was still trying to assimilate the position at home and had little or no information to go on.

"Your father made me commander of scouts. Janed is my deputy now. He said a war is coming and wanted to make some changes. Frederick is a captain and Viktor has come back home, too and tried to join the fighting clerics. Leopold is dealing with administration and the duchess has been back and forth to Riassa working diplomacy on our behalf there. Everyone has a role, these days."

"I don't understand why father doesn't call out Drachefauste and then arrange for Uncle Raef to stand for him in the duel."

"Drachefauste wouldn't be such a fool as to face your uncle directly. Even the emperor calls on Raef to fight his duels against those he challenges. Your uncle has been killing men in duels of honour for ten years. Nobody in his or her right mind would take him on in a one to one formal contest. No, somehow, we have to prove Drachefauste is involved in treason and then get a licence to bring him down any way we can. He and his allies are stronger than they were a year or two ago, though. Drachefauste has allies amongst the barbarians, as well."

"Uncle Raef has a good deal to say on that, too. He told me that Drachefauste has allies among the Kralian and Bartragian tribes and at least one baron from one of Cytelia, or Cylmarda."

"I expect your uncle will have an interesting conversation with your father, when he arrives, then. We had word this morning that he is going to visit. Maybe speaking to you made him think it was time he found out what the feeling is in Rosgovia. Anyway, your uncle Pellinore is also coming. Raef will have Rupert with him so we will have quite a house full. The duchess has been fussing since the letters arrived."

I smiled. I could imagine she would be working the household up into a frenzy.

"I'm glad Uncle Raef is going to speak to father. If anyone can make a difference to his position, it's him."

"Remember that Raef is only your father's cousin. He probably pays more attention to his brothers. I would say your uncle, Pellinore, is the more outspoken. He and Adhils are involved in decisions about the family too, remember.

Their lands may be small but they are your father's brothers. Adhils will put his view more quietly but don't think that he lacks influence. He is an adroit politician and closer to the imperial court than any of them. If Herlenbrand and Hildebrand come, too, then you'll certainly hear blunt speaking. Herlenbrand by rights could have succeeded in Littesburg as the eldest if he hadn't been the son of a concubine as you are."

I nodded, reflecting, briefly, on that. Uncle Herlenbrand had always had a soft spot for me. He was a brusque, physical kind of man who despised cowardice and loved hunting. He would liven things up, for certain.

His younger brother, Hildebrand was a real extrovert and someone you usually heard before you saw. Their sister, my aunt Hildegarde was no less formidable, either. I had heard her tick off the whole group when they came in after hunting once. She cowed even my father and uncles.

This council of brothers and cousins could only mean war was close. It was rare to have one family visit us but all the heads of the households meant serious matters were to be debated. Once again, a thrill went through me and I had visions of galloping at the head of a charge as we swept down on Drachefauste's infantry. Defeat never crossed my mind.

We tired the horses all too soon but made our way into Sligartt where we changed to new animals. There was no question even asked by the garrison commander, Uri Benecci.

As soon as Finnmeyer approached, he was out of his office, snapping a salute and ordering men to take our existing beasts away to be drenched, rested and fed. We thanked Uri and set off again. We tired before the horses, and after walking a short time, we made a temporary camp amongst some trees.

The snow was heavy on the ground outside the main towns. Moonlight sparkled on continuous white, broken only in places by animal tracks. As darkness fell, animals and night birds hunted while others crept into shelters as we now did. The wind was icy and we had few blankets and a paltry fire that wavered and went out several times. By morning, we were cold, stiff and glad to be away again after the briefest breaking of our fasts.

Soon after leaving the main road from Sligartt, we picked up the trail of sleds travelling by the direct but more winding route from Falkeberg. Heartened, we sped on.

As we came over a ridge, we found the first bodies. One of Finnmeyer's riders lay sprawled on the ground where he must have fallen from his horse, blood staining the snow. He had been worried by small animals overnight which made the scene more unpleasant for us both.

He had died from the effect of three arrows that had struck him in various places, two in the back, one probably puncturing a lung. A little further on was a dead archer in furs and cloak who looked like a barbarian scout.

He must have been ridden down as he tried to escape. The barbarians had merely marked his body with some stones, perhaps indicating they were going to return or were still present. He had been struck on the forehead by a descending sword blow and it had split his skull.

We moved on, cautiously but still mounted, Finnmeyer with horse bow ready and me with a loaded short crossbow in my right hand. The second rider was down in the dell. He had been struck by javelins or long spears; pulled from his horse by the look of the marks and then butchered.

Tracks led away north-west and we followed these but the sleds turned north while the other tracks split north-west and north-east. The north-east trail was made by heavy boots and a force of footmen that I guessed were dragon guards heading back to some outpost. That was bad news but at least meant we did not have to face the entire force.

"Sleds?" I asked.

"I think so" Finnmeyer rode on, steadily, signalling for me to hang back as he ascended the next ridge.

"Damn!" I heard him swear under his breath and rode up to join him. Below, one sled track headed away north-eastwards.

Two overturned and smashed sleds lay in the next dell and scattered about them, the bodies of five men and a woman. My mother's guards and one of her maidservants had died, here.

The slaying blows had been dealt with heavy bladed weapons, probably axes or polearms. I pictured Drachefauste's elite guards and nodded grimly, "These weren't killed by barbarians. They were killed by beasts in the guise of men. Drachefauste's Dragon Guard."

"Quite likely and if that is so, we shall have to be even more careful if we are to try to steal your mother back from them. I am sure they have her and are heading for Drachefauste's fortress in Guislor. They can't be far ahead. These men died maybe an hour or so ago. They are still slightly warm. We'll have to come back and bury them. We need to catch the sled."

"What's your plan?" I asked.

Finnmeyer shook his head. "I don't know. I need to see what we are up against." He stroked his short black beard, his face lined with thought and concern.

We set off, again. It wasn't long before we found more death waiting for us. Eight barbarians, similarly dressed to the dead archer lay scattered. Axe blows had killed them too. It looked like there had been a falling out. From the weapons and the blood on their blades, they had at least wounded some of Drachefauste's men.

"Let us hope the odds have reduced enough for two determined men to snatch away the beast's prize." Again, Finnmeyer's voice was harsh and his eyes as hard as black basalt.

"Finnmeyer" I needed to know. He looked across at me "What did Drachefauste do to you that you hate him so much?"

His eyes flickered and then he shook his head.

"It doesn't matter. This isn't the time for revenge. We have to get your mother safely away. One day, maybe. Maybe."

His voice tailed off. His face was gaunt and expression far away. I nodded, mutely. We rounded a wood and started down a slope through the trees. Then we saw them. There were two sleds. One was carrying packs and something else covered by several large blankets.

It was being pulled by huge dogs which were being guided by a single Dragon Guard on a large, heavy-looking horse. The other was carrying my mother and being driven by a squat goblin in mail. Riding beside the sled, going slowly, was Drachefauste. The other four tramped on foot, two behind the sleds, two ahead. Seven enemies in all, including the beast. I wondered. Could two of us handle so many.

If Kharr had been here, I would have said yes, without hesitation, but these were not just bandits or thieves. I pulled my horse up.

Finnmeyer took the lead, "We have to go on foot. The horses will hinder the weapons we can use and give us away, into the bargain."

We dismounted and I put on the hard helm that I had bought in Riassa, taking my longer-range crossbow, the knives and falchion, a long dagger and the short crossbow slung on my back. It was a little heavy going but we moved up on them, steadily. They had to travel maybe five miles to reach the border. We needed to stop them before that.

"We'll have to try to pick them off and hope Drachefauste doesn't kill your mother and ride off. I don't think he will, though. He wants to parade his prize far too much for that. I'll take the Dragon Guard on the rear right of the sled and then try for the left. Can you get the horseman? "

"I think so. But if he threatens my mother, we have to move in if we have time and otherwise back off and try to break her out of his fortress."

"That might not be so easy." Finnmeyer's face was grim as he tested his horse bow. We moved apart, going quickly through the trees. I waited for his signal and we both went into cover from which we could loose arrows. I gave him a thumbs up sign. He raised one arm and then we came up to full height with bows in hand.

His first shot was inch perfect. It took the guard in the side of the head and he went down in the snow.

My bolt struck the horseman in the side and he leaned over with a grunt. I saw Drachefauste swing in his saddle, realise he was being ambushed and watched him slide quickly to the ground and use the second sled as cover.

Meanwhile, Finnmeyer had taken a second shot. The other rear guard was struck in the shoulder as he started to move off.

The horseman slowly fell out of his saddle so I targeted the running guard and put a bolt in his chest. He spilled over backwards. The goblin cracked his whip and mother's sled began to gather pace.

I couldn't let him escape. I ran after it despite Finnmeyer's warning shout. Behind me, I heard weapon play as Finnmeyer must have moved in on one of the other two dragon guards. I raised my crossbow and took the most important shot in my life to date.

The goblin pitched into the snow, the dogs ran on, briefly and the sled stopped. My mother was rising and getting down even as I realised I had hesitated too long. I started to draw the Falchion but the beast was faster.

I felt a terrible pain and heard a crunch as his swinging mace took me in the right shoulder. My bow shattered and I flew backwards into the cold snow. He wiped spittle from his mouth and growled. I saw him move forward and knew I couldn't defend myself.

There was a shout and Drachefauste looked up as Finnmeyer came flying in, short sword poised as he made an all-out flèche attack. The beast twisted so the blade ripped through his tunic and tore the scale armour beneath, leaving a bloody rent where the edge had scored his side.

Off balance, Finnmeyer tried desperately to dodge the inevitable counter-attack. The mace clipped his left arm and he spun slightly but Drachefauste's lunge to finish him missed. Finnmeyer had been sent stumbling in a circular direction by the first blow and Drachefauste failed to anticipate that. I saw the remaining Dragon Guard loom up and tried to shout, but the pain was too great and all that came out was a hoarse whisper.

The huge guard raised his partisan to strike and then, inexplicably pitched forward into the snow. Inexplicable for a moment, at least.

As he fell, he revealed my mother, standing behind him with a bloody dagger. Finnmeyer's sword punched home and the beast crouched low, left hand favouring the wound. A crimson patch spread across his tunic and he lowered his head.

I tried to look around. My mother nodded to Finnmeyer and he advanced, raising his sword. Some sixth sense told me it was not over, yet. This time I did manage to shout. A shrill scream burst from my lips but it was too late. The beast exploded from the position he was in, mace swinging like a club. It lifted Finnmeyer off his feet and he flew back into the snow like a rag doll tossed carelessly by a petulant child.

In the same movement, Drachefauste reached my mother, grabbed her upraised arm and twisted the dagger from her grasp. Dropping the mace, he slapped her across the face so hard, she spun and went down on her knees.

I tried desperately to get up as the beast advanced, slowly, wiping blood from around his mouth. He recovered and balanced the mace as he spoke to my mother.

"Ah, Estella, I'm going to enjoy you even more than I thought. I do like a spirited bitch and you haven't disappointed me." He turned his attention to me, "As for you, you did well. It was a good fight but now it's time to make an end."

"No!" my mother screamed out and rushed at him hitting him furiously with both fists. Drachefauste, turned and caught her, pushed her backwards so she sat down hard in the snow.

"Oh, so…now why would you care so much?" He looked from her to me and back again.

"Of course. The same darker skin, the black hair. He's your bastard, isn't he? I remember thinking that I didn't see him when we met to write our alliance."

The word alliance was laced with irony. He started laughing "Oh, he must be such an embarrassment to the duke. Shame about your servant too, I know how much he meant to you,"

I knew Finnmeyer was dead but when Drachefauste said "meant", it brought it home. I felt my eyes sting with tears. Drachefauste was laughing, heartily.

"Do you know what, bastard. I'm going to let you live. Only because having to rescue you and have you back but not his lovely concubine will increase Duke Vasely's embarrassment and shame. Who knows, perhaps he will blame you and put you to death, but if I know him, he'll be too soft to do anything at all."

Drachefauste pulled my mother to the sled and bound her hands. Then, he walked back and kicked the fallen dragon guard. To my surprise, the man grunted. Drachefauste dragged him to his feet.

"Get up you fool! You aren't that bad"

The man slouched away. The wound in his back was no longer bleeding. Drachefauste walked out of my view. When he returned, he was supporting the guard that Finnmeyer had taken with his sword.

I noticed that the horseman was now crawling around. He got a kick, too. Within a few minutes, Drachefauste had four dragon guards again. Only the one Finnmeyer had hit in the head was left in the snow along with the goblin.

"Unfortunate. Snorda is dead" the horseman reported.

"Leave them!" Drachefauste shouted as the guards started to lift the dead bodies of their two comrades. "They failed. Let the wolves feed on their carcasses"

Drachefauste rode back as they started off again.

"Bold try lad, but pointless. If we meet again, I will kill you. Tell your…tell the duke that he won't get her back by assaulting my fortress, although I invite him to try any time he wants to get a bloody nose. Hah!"

He turned and rode away. I shivered. I was still lying in cold, wet snow, my shoulder and right arm smashed so bone poked from my flesh. I tried desperately to turn over and crawl. I must have passed out and it would have ended there.

Sleep and then cold death beckoned but I woke again with a start, shivering in darkness. There were animals moving about. I was still in agony, but somehow, I forced myself to my knees and stumbled across to Finnmeyer's body.

A coyote made off as I approached, but it was with three others and they continued to circle, watching with hungry eyes. I knelt beside Finnmeyer and fumbled with my good hand until I found his small flask. I knew he always carried spirits in cold weather. I managed to get the cork out with my teeth and swigged.

It was hot and heady after having no food for a day. I breathed in and then stoppered it, again, putting it roughly into a pocket. I rose but my legs gave way and I fell back down beside my friend and mentor.

Tears welled up as I knelt looking around at the scene of my failure. We should have got help. We would have won if we had others with us. Finnmeyer would still be alive. I bowed my head and breathed in, hard, trying to get control and to find the strength to move. I remember rising, stumbling towards the trail and then I fell. The snow was thin. I could feel the rasp and bite of the loose gravel beneath.

I tried so hard not to close my eyes.

Friends I

I would have died in the cold snow beside Finnmeyer if Raef Von Littesburg had not come to visit. As soon as he heard we had gone, he set off with some of his men and tracked us down. He followed our trail to Sligartt, where he talked to Uri Benucci. Raef and his men were re-supplied with horses as we had been and, having considered our likely options, made the same decision as we had, coming down through the open woods to the trail where he found us.

Finnmeyer was buried with full honours a few days after we got back home. I stood, heart full of anguish and the weight of responsibility to right the wrongs done to Finnmeyer and my mother by Drachefauste. At first, my hatred rose in me like bile and I could think only of revenge. But the days went by and the pain became a dull ache. I recovered slowly from my wound but I was back in the yard, practicing as soon as I was allowed. Slowly, I learned to fight effectively with my undamaged left hand.

My father stayed away from me. I know he had been at my bedside when I first arrived home, but it seemed he did not wish to speak to me, thereafter. I wondered where Frederick and Leopold had gone.

Only Viktor came to visit when I was lying abed. He was cheerful but evasive. After several days I found out that my other brothers had left for Littesburg. Most of the cousins and uncles had departed after the council.

My father wanted my brothers' training finished properly, and there were opportunities to fight and command with the Littesburg regiment in the service of the empire. We were one of the families providing men to fight in the troubled Kingdom of Hallnes.

Uncle Raef visited often and told me I was a young fool on every occasion. The way he said it, I knew he would have done the same thing himself. He started to join the practice sessions and taught me how to turn a useful left hand into a really good sword arm.

Within three weeks, I was beating men who had been able to handle me with ease when I first tried fighting wrong-handed. My right arm gradually became usable, although sore, but as the weeks went by it became obvious that it would never be as strong, again. From that time, I became a primarily left-hander with the blade. It's something I rarely even think about now, even though I still use the crossbow with a right-handed stance.

The moment I was up and about I went seeking my father, of course. I wanted to know what he intended to do about my mother's abduction. Having forced my way into his planning room, I began an argument with him over his whole attitude towards Drachefauste. I could see he was hurting too, but I was less caring of his feelings than my own, as we often are in our youth. He tried to explain how my mother knew that Drachefauste would attend the same meeting she was going to and how it presented an opportunity. I wouldn't listen to his rationale right down to the moment he flared up, himself.

"It wasn't my idea; it was your mothers! I told her I didn't like the plan but she insisted and you should know how pig-headed she can be when she gets an idea in her head."

"Why would my mother want to go and negotiate anything with Drachefauste, what utter nonsense. You don't really expect me to believe that do you?"

"Negotiate? Negotiation wasn't the plan. She went to kill him. Your mother is one of the most highly trained imperial assassins in the Empire."

My mouth fell open.

"Yes, that's surprised you, hasn't it? If you'd learn to listen more Edmund, you'd make a worthy Duke yourself, one day. The negotiation was a cover.

Estella knew that Drachefauste would want to capture her and parade her as a prize. What easier way to assassinate a pig like that than when he has you in a bedchamber and thinks he is going to have his way? I told her he wasn't an ordinary man and I hated the plan but she has executed powerful men before.

Then you and Finnmeyer showed up and forced her into a position where she had to make a choice. Now she is far more vulnerable. The fact she was able and ready to stab one of his guards will have alerted Drachefauste that she could be more dangerous than he had considered."

My father sighed.

"Finnmeyer should have trusted me. Nearly twenty years, he served me loyally. This was unexpected. He shouldn't have gone after her and he shouldn't have involved you, either."

"Perhaps you should have trusted him" I retorted angrily, "If you'd told him what the plan was, he would have understood and would have consulted you on what to do if things went wrong. It's your fault for leaving him out of it."

"No, Edmund. It's the job of men like Finnmeyer and any others who serve a house to do as they are asked. They should come in private to question any decision they do not understand, not to take matters into their own hands.

I loved him too. I feel his loss, deeply. He was my friend as well. Before you were even born, he was my friend. Do you think I don't want to rush out there with an army and rip Drachefauste's fortress down brick by brick?"

My father sighed. I didn't know what to say. I wanted to jump in and defend Finnmeyer but at the same time, I saw I had misjudged the situation. My anger was abated. I fought to keep back tears.

"And now your mother is in danger. I knew I should have forbidden her." He slapped a fist into his other hand, pacing back and fore.

"So, what are you going to do?"

I asked, trying to steady my voice.

"Negotiate", he said, quietly. "Negotiate her release because all Drachefauste wants is a public display that places him as the stronger one. Let him have that. The score can be settled, later. There are more important matters afoot."

But I could not sleep. I hadn't been able to since that night. So, I trained. I trained and in secret, I trained even more, practicing knife throwing, crossbow shots on the move, leaping, climbing, anything I might need. In my head, a fanciful rescue plan was forming. I just needed some small assistance.

If only Kharr were here. We'd go in and get her out. I sent letters asking him to come. I also despatched letters to Rill, Coyle and Tu'Lon, giving details to a servant who was to contact Baslos on my behalf on where and how to find them. I even sent letters to Gwythaor but learned later that Ylloelae and Marcabru had moved on and had not received my request whilst Jeffery had gone to train with the rangers, giving up his post as a Gatebrand.

Days went by and became weeks. The negotiation proceeded slowly and with little sign of progress. Obviously, my mother had not enacted her plan to slay Drachefauste, which worried me.

I grew frustrated, knowing I was not yet up to putting my own plan into action. And then, one bright, frosty morning as I crunched through crusty snow in the outer courtyard, I saw a lean horse being escorted through the gates and on its back, a familiar figure all hooded and cloaked against the cold lifted an arm to wave a greeting.

"Coyle! It's good to see you." I ran up as he dismounted. We embraced, briefly.

"You never told us you were the son of a Duke or that you had a home like this. I always imagined you were some buccaneer or mercenary's son. When I received your letter, I came at once. Rill and Tu'lon are on their way. They decided to go as far as they could by sea and then take a protected route overland rather than riding. I told them I'd get here ahead of them. I did get here ahead of them, didn't I?"

"You did. By the gods, I'm glad to see you. Come on in. You must want to rest"

"Actually, I'd like a shot of something strong and some food. You can tell me what the mission is and the background, too."

"Of course. But don't mention any mission to my father or his men. This is between us. As far as anyone knows, you're an old Riassan friend visiting because you heard I had been wounded."

"You were wounded?"

"Yes, I should have died but the man who did it thought it would hurt more to leave me alive. I messed things up, Coyle."

"Hm, well, we've all done that. And now you're going to have a crack at him without your father's knowledge, is that it?"

"Not exactly. I'm going to rescue my mother from his fortress."

"Sweet Nanyala, you don't do anything by halves, do you?"

I grinned.

"And now you three are going to be with me, I know it can be done, too."

"I hope there's some reward for all of this."

"Oh, there will be. My father is beside himself with grief and worrying what is happening to her as a prisoner even though he is being assured she is fine during negotiations for her release. I happen to know the bastard that has her better than my father does. He'll kill or maim her before he hands her back. We don't have a lot of time left, either."

Rill and Tu'Lon arrived the next day. They brought a man called Merik with them, who I had not met. He had apparently taken my place in the group, providing some blade, bow and general combat skills.

Merik struck me at once as having a similar background to myself. For one thing, he looked familiar. He wouldn't have looked out of place in a Riassan noble house. He had a strong jaw, dark well-groomed hair and beard, stood a little over medium height, powerfully framed but muscular. He was well spoken as well. My only disappointment, now, was that I had heard no word from Kharr.

For a few days, I showed my friends around the city of Falkeberg and introduced them to some of the family's most loyal retainers, and Frederick. While I was working on a plan to get my mother back, I thought it a good idea to keep up the appearance that my friends were visiting and there was nothing more to their presence. We frequented the taverns on numerous occasions. It was on one such evening that I finally got them to tell more of their pasts.

"It was pretty unexpected, you turning out to be the son of a grand duke, Finn." Rill grinned as Coyle brought the subject up, again. "We had discussed you a few times and decided there was definitely something more to your background than you were saying. Something about your manner and ease amongst different social groups. We put you down as the son of a diplomat or maybe a rich merchant."

"I didn't realise it was so obvious" I replied, slightly downhearted, "I always thought I'd remained neutral enough in accent and style of speech to be harder to read."

"Nah," said Rill, "you sound a bit posh and you know too many words. You have a way of speaking that sounds more like some people'd write. You know, like a bard or one of them storytellers that do it all in rhyme."

"Well since you know my story, now, how about you share yours. We never finished the discussion about backgrounds, last time. I seem to remember that I ended up telling the stories and you four just sat and drank."

There was some laughter. "I think we had the best idea" Coyle grinned, but fair's fair, I suppose. Go on Rill, you were going next."

Rill sat back, sipped his beer and began. "We had a pretty tough upbringing, me and my brothers and sisters. Never knew my dad. Mum said he was some sort of guildsman who travelled. I had three brothers and two sisters.

My eldest brother died when he was nine and then mum went too, during a bad outbreak of plague. The rest of us survived it but we had been sold into the possession of the Pawnbrokers and Moneylenders guild by then and we were owned by a man called Calhoun.

Calhoun wasn't a kind man. He gave us very little to buy food and clothes, although we were to work for him as soon as we were old enough. He was supposed to do more but he was mean and bad-tempered. He beat us all and made us live in a hovel that was little more than a shed on his land. He sold my brothers within a year or so which seemed to please him. So then there was just me, Jemima and Katie.

Jemima pretty much brought us up and Katie chipped in as soon as she was old enough. I was just three when my mum went and seven when Calhoun sold my two brothers.

He loaned me out to help a wife and her husband look after the wife's sick mother. The husband was never around. He was a sea trader of some sort. When he came home, he was nice; generous to a young lad with the odd gift of a bit of chocolate or fine food from far off climes. Once he even gave me a bit of tobacco which I tried smoking later and once I'd stopped choking, sold on to some older boys for a couple of silver, which was the most money I'd had.

The wife treated me like a low servant and scalded me often. She said I was clumsy and good for nothing, a waste and such things. I would cop a clip about the head if I wasn't quick enough, too.

But as I got older, she came around slowly until we had a kind of agreement that she would only rant at me when she was upset by something and then forget it the next day like it had never happened. She would try to make it up, though, giving me some clothes or leftovers, the odd few coins. They weren't that well off between her husband's visits, but never short, either.

One day I went home and found Katie in floods of tears. Calhoun had taken Jemima away and said she wouldn't be coming back. So, then it was just us. I broke into Calhoun's house that night.

I had become quite good at finding ways into places, by then. I found Jemima's dress, all ripped, chucked in a scuttle to be burned. I sat in the dark, there, wondering what had become of her. It was more than a month before I got word where she was to be found. I visited her and we exchanged news.

She was different, her hair all brushed and she had red lips and rouge, a pretty dress and shoes. She talked oddly to me as if I was below her now. She was a maid servant in a big house. I didn't go and see her more than a couple of times after that. She seemed more distant each time.

Later I found out what Calhoun had done when he ripped her dress off and that went on my list to be dealt with, too. I guessed, too, that Jemima was not just serving at the table where she was working and that's why she was so prettily dressed.

Anyway, two years later, the old lady I was helping look after died and the goodwife, Catherine, was beside herself. I was upset, too. I'd got to know the family and it was the nearest thing I had to my own.

As well as that, it meant I wasn't needed any longer. I was nearly sixteen and found myself comforting Catherine who leaned heavily on me for the next two days and talked about things I could still do so that I didn't have to leave.

On the third night after the old lady died, Catherine took my hand and led me upstairs to her darkened room. She undressed me and helped me undress her. She laid me gently down and mounted me. She wasn't a beautiful woman but it seemed wonderful to me and she seemed incredibly grateful.

I left the house soon after. Calhoun wanted to find me a new job and I went along to see a couple of prospective employers, neither of whom I liked the look of.

That's when I bought a dagger in a back-street inn near the docks. A week before he sold Katie off and placed me elsewhere, I caught up with him in a back street as he weaved his way home, drunk as so often and I put the dagger in his chest.

I told him that was for Jemima. I stabbed him several more times before he stopped struggling and then I slit his throat from ear to ear and left him. I took his purse and hidden money belt but I tossed them in the river all bar a few silvers. It would be too obvious if I suddenly had money and my supposed benefactor was dead.

 The new appointee was a sounder gentleman who found Katie proper employment as a housekeeper and I was sent off to the Merchant's guild to train as a clerk.

Not long after, I fell in with some other young men who had a need for an extra hand on some jobs they had to do. I started out as a lookout but soon progressed by virtue of breaking and entering a few places with them and eventually stabbing a rival thief in a fight.

That got me into the Thieves Guild and being a clerk became what I did for cover during the day. I transferred to a master who was part of the guild so I could work less hours and start later, leaving me fresh and ready for the night operations which he was really responsible for."

Rill drank off the remainder of his beer and went to get another. I nodded, "Okay, so Rill had a tough life, compared to me. What about the rest of you?"

"I remember," Tu'Lon begun, "how proud my parents were when the village shaman agreed to take me as one of his disciples. I was never very taken with the gods but I liked the stories and I knew them all. I was much more interested in the influence over men exercised by the shaman of the villages.

At first, I studied everything with a serious manner but as I grew older, I realised that there was power which existed in itself if you knew how to tap it.

I was fifteen when we had one of the longest dry spells in living memory. The rivers became little more than a trickle of water through soft mud, the ponds and pools dried up. Our shaman taught me and the others how to divine for water so that we could establish a new deeper well. It meant that the village had enough to survive the summer.

It might have been that pressure on water and food resources or just the movement of packs and tribes but the Leonids came that year. Leonids are the most powerful of the savannah tribes. They are half man, half lion and as big as the centaurs of the northern forests. At first, they competed with us for prey but when the herds grew slim, they switched to attacking the villages. Raid after raid was made, usually at night time. The hunters went out and tried to retaliate but the Leonid packs were stronger and the fighting made them worse.

One night, they came in what must have been a whole tribe rather than one pride.

They tore through the village, slaying men, women and children without discrimination. My father fell in the first of the fighting.

I was too late to save him or my master who flung every spell that he had to help our warriors before he was torn down. Most of the Leonids were driven off or slain but our warriors had fallen almost to a man. A small pack of them came prowling around, intent on finishing whoever was left.

I sheltered my mother and sisters in the ruins of the meeting hut, using my powers to bring darkness and to counter detection by laying down false scent and other misleading enchantments but they closed in, slowly, circling ever closer, growling softly and calling to one another.

It was then that I turned in truth to the gods and prayed to Tergaron to protect the home, to Orus the hunter to take my side, to Kedro to grant us his blessing and even to Merlos to bring me a gambler's luck. I promised them that if they saved my family, I would serve them faithfully from that day onwards.

Perhaps they really did hear me, who knows? The gods or whatever you call them are fickle, that I can tell you. Just as the Leonids poised to move in and tear us to pieces, a herd of Hybsilopes galloped through, using bows on the rest of the Leonid group. They must have been tracking the pack who were hunting us.

That scattered the Leonids and before they could reform, the warriors who had been called from the three villages nearby arrived with our scouts who had run for help. I emerged in time to fling what battle magic remained to me and saw the Leonids slain or chased off. Of course, I had made a promise so I could not stay. What was left of our village amounted to a handful of people so they joined and became part of the larger community to the north.

As for me, I set out for the city to join the temple and serve as I had promised. I won't say that I have always been the most faithful servant nor obeyed every tenet as laid down by the temple elders but I have paid my dues and served my gods in my own way and I think they know that. I just wish Merlos would be more forgiving and hand his poor supplicant the best dice rolls and hands of cards more often."

"Unlike the two of you," Coyle began, indicating Tu'Lon and Rill, "I never knew my mother. The first I really remember; I was on the road with my father. He was a tinker. He did whatever jobs he could get wherever he stopped.

I never understood why he didn't stick in one place for long until I was old enough to realise why we had to leave villages in a hurry in the middle of the night. At least when that happened, he always had coin for food and drink and often a sack full of interesting items that he had been 'given' by his grateful and generous employers. By the time I was eight, I was assisting by getting into places and opening up doors or windows so my father could grab what looked valuable.

Just thinking back reminds me of the mix of fear and excitement in running from places, sometimes being pursued or being in a house when someone came back in. On a handful of occasions, I found there were people in the house and had to escape before I was spotted. I can't even count how many times I have had to outrun guard dogs.

Anyway, one day we broke into this shop in a sleepy little village. It was midsummer, just after noon with hardly a soul around. The workshop at the back was dark and the shop had a *closed for lunch* sign hanging on the door handle. I went in through an open skylight at the back and found myself in the strangest workshop I had ever seen.

There were glass jars and bottles with what looked like body parts and strange creatures floating inside, powders of many colours, dried plants, seeds in smaller jars, strange coloured liquids and many odd ornaments, items and cupboards. I felt a knot of fear taking hold of my stomach as I gazed about me. I had expected a craftsman's tools and part-finished work.

As I tried to slip through the narrow aisles between racks of items, seeking a doorway, I saw human heads with dull, lifeless eyes floating ahead of me in even larger jars. I remember swallowing hard, wondering if I'd be looking out at the workshop, my soul captured by the sorcerer whose home I had obviously entered. I panicked and ran back to the skylight, climbed up and banged on it, shouting for my father to get me out but he had gone on around the side of the house, somewhere, presumably to the door I was supposed to open. I can still remember becoming quite frantic as I searched about for something to use to climb back up.

There was nothing at hand and so I stood there, sucking in the air as I took deep breaths and tried to remember what my father had taught me about keeping a cool head when you were in a tight corner. I became very calm and went purposefully off down the room, looking for a gap that led to a doorway.

It didn't take me long, once I set to it. There was a door as I'd expected, in a side wall. I could see an arched opening ahead into the main body of the shop. It seemed like shadows moved out there and I became very wary, anticipating the presence of the owner.

It was when I laid my hand on the door that I received my worst fright. There was a sudden screaming and whispering around me and I felt a gathering air movement like a wind building. I put my shoulder to the door and stumbled out into the light even as it seemed like cold hands reached for me. I ran to my father and clung to him.

"Hey fella, what's up?" he said, giving me his usual lopsided grin, like an apology for what we did together. I blurted out a stream of garbled explanation. "Whoa, whoa there. You said it's a what? A mage's shop. Nah, can't be. It's supposed to be a herbalist's place you know, selling stuff that's supposed to help heal you, make you better, make women like you, that kind of thing. I expect you just let your imagination run away with you. What you saw were just mushrooms and plants and bark and dyes, not magical stuff at all. Look."

He laid his hand on the door. I couldn't see past him but I saw the effect on him as he opened it. His hair seemed to stand on end as he slammed it shut and staggered back, pale as death.

"Come on" he muttered, "we're getting out of here."

We didn't run but we set off up the road towards our next destination at a good pace. We didn't stop until we reached a crossroads outside the village where an old man sat on a large stone. He was hooded and cloaked, gripping a strange staff with a twisted pattern and markings on it. He looked up and we saw bright, sharp eyes regarding us. Under the hood was an aged face with a hoary beard and whitening hair;

"It is ill conceived to enter the sanctum of a magus without his or her permission."

My father started. I just stood open mouthed with that awful feeling where your feet are rooted to the spot in fear.

"Come here, lad. I need to remove the invisible mark from you or it will find you as soon as nightfall comes and, well, let me remove the mark. You don't want to know more."

"Go on, Seamus," my father urged, "I'm sorry, sir. We didn't know it was the house of a true wizard. We thought it was a charlatan's place so we would just be taking from one who himself was taking from the people, like" my father begun.

The old man held up a hand and my father fell silent although whether it was his choice, I cannot say to this day. The old man stood, slowly and reached out a hand which he placed upon my head. He spoke words which were an undoing of a summoning and binding. Of course, I didn't know that, then but I listened and was greatly taken with the sound of them. He lifted his hand.

"It is done" he said and the turned to my father, "how much for the boy?"

For the third time that day, I felt panic rise inside. What would the mage do with me? Would he dismember me and put bits of me in jars? My father scratched his head. I didn't like the way he did it, at all, "well now... he's my flesh and blood. I don't think I can just sell him away like a trinket, you know."

The mage considered, "but you would sell him for the right price?"

My father scratched his head a second time. I was about to say I didn't want to be sold when the mage added, "he'd be better off with me. You'll only get him caught and then he'll lose a hand or worse, maybe he'll hang.

With me, he will learn the ways of magic and make something of himself. He has the gift. I have felt it on him. That's why he was able to resist the summoning and escape the door, although he didn't realise it."

My mouth hung open, dumbfounded. There was some haggling but for sure, my father took the coin and I became a mage's apprentice. That night, I had a dark dream which I will not repeat.

Some years on, when I had learned something of the dark magic practice, I realised that the mage removed the mark from me but when my father opened the door and saw whatever he saw, he must have been marked as well."

Coyle drank a deep draught and wiped his mouth, "I never got on that well with structured study. Almost as soon as I had learned enough to read a scroll or tome and get something from it, I left the village behind. My master wasn't that bothered. He always said I was a poor learner and by then, he had two more apprentices who were much more attentive. Most of my spells are self-taught, usually stolen from one source or another. I do well enough, though."

There was a short pause while we all contemplated the tales and supped before we all looked to Merik. He put down his tankard heavily and scowled.

"I've no tale to tell, certainly not now when it wastes good drinking time" he growled.

"Oh, come on now, Merik. You must have some stories." Coyle grinned.

"You heard me. Bugger off" Having delivered this dismissal, Merik picked up his tankard, drained off the remaining beer and got up. He set off for the bar where he remained for some time.

"Looks like that's a no, then" Rill wiped his mouth with his sleeve and tucked into some more of the cheese and bread that was spread across the table.

"Ever heard the story of the one-eyed virgin, the drunken priest and the son of the nobleman?"

There was a volley of bread and some cheese, too which sent Rill ducking under the table, "alright, alright, I was just kidding"

Cages I

Over the three weeks since my friends had arrived, we had studied what plans I had managed to lay my hands on showing Drachefauste's castle and surrounding area. Raga had once been an imperial possession and it was imperial architects who designed the fortress, which Drachefauste now called his own. Dragonfeldt had become the chief stronghold of the Drachefauste clan since they defeated the imperial army. By the end of the third week, we knew how we were going to do it and I had added one more to our little conspiracy. Janed had been around a lot, recently. She had watched me and my friends and one night, had knocked on my door. By the time she left, she had got the plan out of me and added herself to the team. She wanted revenge for Finnmeyer, too. I think she also wanted to watch over me. I sighed when she left. I knew what I yearned for, but if she noticed, she didn't show it.

When Kharr arrived, the group was complete and my confidence grew. We waited until the weather turned bright and dry before setting out. Not even the most desperate adventurer would willingly take on the blizzards and freezing winds of the northern wastelands.

At first, we made good progress. We avoided Sligartt and opted instead to head for Mahlenfelz first. This took us off the direct route but that was intentional. I was wary that we might be followed and our progress reported upon. Mahlenfelz was a much more natural town to visit to take in fine architecture and the arts. It was also famed for its beers. We paused there, for a day and then left under cover of darkness.

Sometime before dawn, when the sky was beginning to turn from blue-black to a dull grey, I heard something crunching, heavily and repetitively in the snow ahead of us and held up a hand. Throwing the reins over a low hanging branch, I left my mount and crept forward. A moment later, Janed joined me to my right and Rill to my left. The others organised the horses behind us. We could hear the sound of heavy boots in the snow and some low voices. As we looked down from the bank where the woods led to open fields, we could see ten heavily cloaked figures. Eight of them carried pikes with plain, round shields slung on their backs and nondescript helmets on their heads. The other two stood out even under fur cloaks. They both carried big partisan axes and had the shaped helms of Drachefauste's elite Dragon Guard. We had run into a border patrol.

I glanced to Janed and signalled that we should go back. She nodded. I did the same to Rill. We slipped through the trees to rejoin the others.

"We should let them go by" Tu'Lon suggested.

"They'll see us for miles across those fields. We'll have to wait for a long time." Janed said. "I'd rather we took them out than that."

"There's a risk" Merik countered. "If one was to get away, we'd be in danger of being exposed."

"Merik's probably right" Coyle nodded, "although I don't like the idea of waiting until well after its light and then crossing the open fields."

"Darkness is our best cover. That's how we planned the route" I said, firmly.

"Yeah, we don't want to be out in the open in sunlight" Rill added.

We all looked at Kharr. He was checking the string on his horse bow with care.

"It is obvious we will vote for fighting" he said, waving one hand, "and that is well because ten dead guards can be buried in snow by daylight. Seven riders don't vanish so easily. We need to get down into the valley beyond and ride along that during the day. If there is a foot patrol along this border section, then there will be a mounted patrol, as well.

"Then we should agree how we do it" Merik nodded at Kharr's logic.

"We ride out and use our advantage of being mounted to outmanoeuvre them, going down both flanks and using bows." Janed said.

"That should work but I have another suggestion" I countered.

"If two of us emerge from the woods looking like we might be scouts or spies, pretend to see the guards for the first time, shout and run, I bet that they will give chase. We set a couple of traps and take the pursuers out in the woods. The combat will be hidden from view, that way. Less chance of someone seeing what happened and reporting it on."

"I like that approach" Kharr nodded to me. "We should still have two or three riders holding back so that if some chase and others move off away from the woods, the riders can go after those in the open."

"I like the plan, too" Janed said with a smile, "I'll be a rider"

"And I" said Kharr.

"You should be the third, Finn. You can ride and use a bow." Tu'Lon said.

"Merik has a long spear if it comes to riding a man down" I said.

"I'll be third rider then," Merik nodded once again, "it makes sense."

"So, Rill and I will set traps. Coyle, you and Tu'Lon will have to be the decoys. Are you alright with that?"

"No problem for me but Tu'Lon he could lose some weight."

"Hoy" Tu'Lon shoved Coyle in a friendly manner. "I'm fine over a short distance. I used to walk and run everywhere back in my village days."

"And it shows how long ago that was" said Coyle with a cheeky smile as he ducked away.

"Give us a few minutes to set a couple of trip wires and a rope net and you can get on with it." I said. Rill and I set to work. We picked a reasonably open natural path down which the two could lure the guards.

Making an improvised net with tangling weights took longer but lanterns hung on four corners and woven rope coils soon produced something. We moved forward as our two decoys set off. We picked a second spot behind our trap point to haul back a sapling and tie it, adding some spikes nailed to the branches that would swing down when the rope was cut.

"You wait here." I said. "When the rope trap comes down, it'll probably only get the first guards through. If any run back to get help, you cut the rope, and they get a face full of tree."

Rill grinned. "Sounds good, Finn. And I can throw knives from here."

The three riders set off in an arc to let them out of the woods just ahead of the point where we thought the guards would be when Coyle and Tu'Lon appeared. I trailed Coyle and Tu'Lon so that I could keep watch on what did happen and make a decision on changing plans.

The plan worked as it was supposed to. So often, something comes along and ruins the best thought out approaches but not this time. The guard leader sent six of his men careering after Coyle and Tu'Lon, four getting crossbows off their backs which lost them ground at once. The first two tried to run into the trees with their pikes and got tangled. Instead of dropping them, they tried to hack and pull to force their way through the thicket.

It was not an impressive performance. It wasn't until the Dragon guard leader bawled at them that they thought to drop their pikes and draw falchions instead. By that time, the four crossbowmen had passed them by and were trying to close and get a shot off. Coyle and Tu'Lon passed the trap point, leaping over the wire in the same way that they had been bounding along. One went behind a tree and the other dived behind bushes. The crossbow bolts struck undergrowth harmlessly.

The four reloaded their bows and walked forward. At this point, the original two guards caught up, rushed into the back of their colleagues and the six stumbled forwards in poor order.

As the first two hit the tripwire, they staggered. The net came down and four of the six got caught up in it. They didn't go down but it had them in a mess. The other two just stood looking stupidly at what had happened. I hit one of those with a crossbow bolt right in the face of the helm below the noseguard.

He went backwards like he had been struck with a giant club. The other looked around just as Rill's first dagger took him in the back. Then Coyle and Tu'Lon jumped out and hurled knives as well. The four men struggling with the rope net were getting themselves free but we closed in on all corners and with the advantage, made short work of them.

"Pity. I was hoping to see how the sprung tree trap would work" Rill said.

We moved swiftly on to see what had become of the four guards in the open. It seemed they had fared little better. When the riders emerged behind them, they had tried rushing forward with pikes and axes. Janed had put an arrow in one and Kharr the same, which slowed them.

Then Merik had used his long spear to skewer one of the two Dragon Guards. The leader stood, turning around, seemingly unable to decide who to go for first, so Kharr and Janed shot him twice before Merik ran him through with a spear.

The first Dragon Guard got up, still wounded but recovering fast. Merik got down from his horse and levelled his spear. Kharr rode up, leapt down where the second guard had fallen and took off his head. When Merik lopped off the first dragon guard's right hand, still holding his falchion, Kharr did the same. Janed, meanwhile, picked off one of the wounded guards and then rode by and put her blade in the second as he broke for the woods. By the time we arrived, there was only the account of the contest to be heard.

The action proved that the one thing that Dragon Guards couldn't do well was think quickly. In fact, it seemed Drachefauste had bred out any notion of using initiative. On the one hand, it made them loyal unquestioning servants. On the other, it might yet prove to be their greatest weakness.

***

We were riding into the outer city under the great Dragon Gate within four days of leaving home, posing as mercenaries looking to join the swelling ranks of Drachefauste's army. That is to say, five of us rode in. Janed would enter with a handcart, pretending to be a farm lass trading some basic goods in three days' time and Kharr would arrive as a clerk for a foreign merchant wanting to open trade negotiations with Raga, now it was part of the empire.

I had expected some kind of check or questioning at the gates, but we were stopped just briefly. Obviously, Drachefauste was not expecting trouble or if he was, he was supremely confident about the security of his inner citadel. In some respects, my father's refusal to respond, immediately, had paid dividends. I imagine that Drachefauste had expected something but as the weeks went by and negotiation continued, rather publicly and with nothing but suggested threats in the hints dropped by both sides, it looked less and less likely that our family would commit to any real action.

I had heard my father argue, before, that a long delay is often one of your best weapons as it gets through the guard of those who grow complacent. For two days we just ate, drank, brawled and gambled our way around some taverns frequented by soldiers and mercenaries. If we were being watched, we reckoned they would soon grow bored and put us down as what we claimed to be. On the third night, we took a wander under the walls of the inner city and spent some time observing the high citadel above.

Next day, Janed joined us during a drinking bout, pretending to be picked up by Merik. I was jealous that she chose him and not me, even though it was just for show. She kissed him full on the mouth; how I would have savoured that kiss. It reminded me, painfully, that I was still younger than most of my father's servants and most of my friends.

That night, six shadowy beings crossed a wall when the sentries were at their furthest point. Six figures stole across a quiet residential square above the smells and noise of the outer city and into the quiet of the upper city. Many of the houses here were quite large and some appeared to have functions, being workshops for finery and specialist trades. We climbed a bell tower attached to a small temple and used the vantage point to carry out observations, two of us working while four rested. Sometime before dawn, we melted back into the throngs in the lower city and found an inn where we rested a while. Kharr joined us the following day and we discussed our plans.

Getting as far as the gates of the inner citadel would be easy enough but entry into that fortress involved a high degree of risk. We could not afford to be picked up on the way in. One failed attempt would cause the guard to tighten and be a lot more alert. If we were going in, it had to be once and the way in had to be flawless. We debated numerous options that might work until finally, I hit on an idea.

"What if we went in and concealed ourselves in a workshop then gradually worked nearer the gates over the course of a couple of days? The armour forge is very close under the walls of the citadel. If we could get that far, we might even be able to cross from the forge roof to the tower ramparts and climb the last twenty feet."

Tu'Lon looked thoughtful, Rill's face was blank but he nodded. Merik just waved a hand as if to say it wasn't up to him. Janed looked closer at the plan we had sketched.

"The risk of being spotted on a twenty-foot climb to the main gatehouse is too high but the idea of starting close by works well. Are there not better places?"

"I think Finn may be onto something" Kharr sat back and contemplated. "When we were trying to get into Quolorn Vadith, we launched our assault from a stable that had carelessly been built against the fortress wall and using its roof as cover, mined the wall by ripping through the back and attacking the stone, having brought the quicklime and other equipment with us over the course of a day or two. Now, we don't want to go mining a wall and causing a collapse, good diversion though that might be."

"A diversion would be useful, though and if it were on a scale large enough to attract attention," Coyle began.

"It would cause the security to double or quadruple and send men running in all directions," I finished, "which would make it twice as hard."

"Not necessarily," Janed answered, "in the confusion, a couple of guards might very well end up in the cell area or even move prisoners to avoid them being taken back by Duke Vasely's assault."

"I like that plan." Merik nodded approval. Janed smiled at him. My insides churned. I was jealous, of course. If he was bedding her really, he would be doing everything I always dreamed of. She was moving on while I was daydreaming.

"Mining a wall is a serious business!"

"But is possible" Kharr added.

"With some magical assistance, it ought to be possible to create a very believable assault by a unit of elite Rosgovian guards. If one team was doing that, the other could be going in." Coyle observed.

"That would be me" I said.

"And me" Kharr added.

"Make that the three of us" Janed said.

"Two is enough" Kharr said firmly.

One half of me wanted Janed to come. "Perhaps Janed and I as it's proper that we should undertake that risk. You are good friends. I don't wish to put you in more danger than you already will be."

"I think it might be better..." Kharr began.

"No, Edmund's right. It should be the two of us." Janed gave me a look and my heart soared, momentarily. One day, I promised myself.

"What would I be doing?" Rill asked, "I'd imagined I would go in, given my skills in opening doors."

"Rill has a point" Tu'Lon nodded. Coyle also nodded.

"I'm sure," I began.

"They are right my young friend" Kharr said, firmly and with a nod, "It might be better, in fact, if Rill and I went but it is your mission so."

I sighed, softly.

"Fine. Rill and I will go in. Who will cover our exit?"

"That would be me and Merik" said Tu'Lon. "You'll want some magical backup."

"The others will join us to provide covering archery as soon as they have retired from the diversion."

"I will be creating a nice troop of illusionary soldiers" Coyle explained, "but we'll need some real people in amongst them to loose real arrows and knock a few people down so they make the ruse more believable."

"As well as the diversion, our group will mine the wall of the forge thus leaving an exit for Finn and Rill" Kharr explained, drawing rapidly in the dirt with a stick.

That night, we got down as far as a silversmith's workshop where we stowed in the ceiling void. We rested, through the day, listening to the sounds of workmen beneath us.

The next night, we split up and went for our positions. Rill and I would come from the forge chimney where we would be perched like gargoyles, hidden amongst the chimneystacks.

The signal would be a flare of fire going up on the west side of the citadel. As darkness fell, I could feel the adrenalin beginning to pump as Rill and I made our way across the slate roof.

We were soon hidden amongst the chimneys of the weapons forge. The signal seemed a long time in coming and when it did, I was stiff from crouching in the same spot.

Rill and I waited, watching the guards on the wall cross. We had estimated that gave us twenty-eight seconds to get to the parapet so we set about the climb with intent. I swung over the parapet first and got set with a crossbow.

I dropped the first guard while he still had his back to me. Rill moved in on the second with a knife while I went to check that the first wouldn't be getting up. We took their tabards, helms and pole arms. Then we ran. Down the steps, we went, to the lower rampart, along that, down a tower, through an arch. We were unchallenged by the two men stationed at the archway who just raised a hand as we went by and then finally, we were across the quadrangle towards the disturbance being created by our friends.

At that point, we changed direction and went up the stairs of one of the inner towers, across a short parapet to a gatehouse and inside. Leaving pole arms leaning against the doorway, we drew swords and moved on. Now, we were just one wing, a descent and a few twists and turns from where we believed the dungeons would be. That assumed my mother was being held in the cells, of course. We pelted along the corridor of an inner wing until a figure appeared ahead of us. A guardsman at an inner doorway had stepped out. He was a young Dragon Guard.

"Where are you going in such a hurry?" he asked. It was not a suspicious question. He seemed genuinely concerned.

"Looks like the Rosgovians have come for their woman. She'll have to be moved and extra men are wanted to cover and get an ambush ready when they break through."

"We were told they'll think she's in the cells, if they do come" the man ventured.

"Not necessarily" I replied, trying to think quickly as to how to extract the information we needed. I knew we must be on the right trail in some respect or he surely would have said something about where we were going. "They may have inside information. They only have to find out that the Baron…" I let it trail off and sort of inclined my head.

"Oh, she's still in the chamber near his, so he can amuse himself."

"Of course," I said.

"But the Dragon Guard will see to any intruders who get near the Baron."

"Yes," I replied "but we're to set up some archery positions to hit out at any intruders who come at the stairs."

I gambled. The Baron's quarters were somewhere in this or the next wing and would surely be on the upper level. His courtroom was in the next wing on the first floor above the huge kitchens and guardrooms.

"Besides which," I added, "if we can drive them into the great hall, we can finish it, there."

"Of course. I'm just surprised I've been left here and not called over to hold the stairways from the hall to his quarters."

"Maybe it was an oversight. I'd say you could come with us but you'd better not leave your post until you're told. You know what he's like."

I emphasised "he's". I was sure there would be at least one tough sergeant in the guards.

The Dragon Guard smiled, grimly. "Oh yes. I wouldn't step six inches from the post until I get word. I expect I'll see you over there, later. Where do you two usually work, by the way?"

"Town and outer ramparts. Usually night duties."

He nodded and opened the doors with a heavy key off a ring.

"Better get going" he said.

"Thanks." We went past. I turned and regretfully put my sword through him. Having seen a Dragon Guard recover, previously, I took his head off with two more blows and dropped it into a large plant pot. Hopefully, that would deter him from getting up, again.

Picking up our pace, we headed for the upper level using the next stairs and then pounded along as swiftly as we could. A couple of women looked out of doors as we went by and then ducked straight back in. I don't know who they were but it wasn't until we reached the end of this wing that we came to a door which could be opened from the inside but was obviously latched shut.

I pointed and Rill nodded.

"Probably a guard on the other side" I whispered.

He nodded again.

"Be ready to take him, but be careful. We could walk out right into the middle of something"

I swung the door open. Sure enough, there was a Dragon Guard on duty. We had reached the highest landing above the grand hall. Across it must be the apartments of the Baron. Six Dragon Guards, one of clear commanding rank, looked at us as we burst through.

"Dead Dragon Guard at the other end of the wing" I shouted, breathlessly.

"Intruders. About five of them going that way." Rill pointed back towards where we had come from.

"Right. You two stay here and guard this landing. Dragon Guards, with me."

They trooped off, taking the door guard with them. I grinned at Rill.

"How about that for a stroke of fortune?"

"I swear, you are charmed" he grinned back.

"No, Dragon Guards are just stupid. Right. Let's find her."

We moved across the landing. I watched the stairs with a crossbow ready. Rill picked the lock. There was a satisfying clunk and he turned the ring. The door opened onto a narrow, dark corridor with similar polished and crafted doors, three on each side. We could make out a pair of double doors at the far end. I took out the parchment and consulted the map. I guessed they were the doors to the grand staircase from which the Baron would descend on state occasions.

"This has to be it."

We began working along the corridor, checking the doors. All six were locked. There was nothing for it. Softly, I called mother's name at the doors. One of them brought a muffled response.

Rill went to work with his tools, his nimble fingers making quick work of the lock. I noted that he had improved his skills since we last met. He grinned and we burst through the door, expecting guards. My mother was chained by her wrists, in a standing position. She was wearing a silk robe and little else. She looked pale and haggard. I levered the plates out of the wood, tearing them free with the blade of a short sword. Rill watched the door. That set her free but she still had cuffs and length of chain. She stood, stunned and just looked at us.

"Mother" I hugged her. She let me, arms hanging limply at her side.

"Edmund?" she sounded somehow frail, like an old woman.

"Yes. Come on, mother. We have to leave, now!"

"Edmund?" she still stood, eyes far away.

"What has that bastard done to you?" I hissed.

"Finn. We have to go, and I mean now" Rill beckoned.

I ran the chains out of the cuffs as quickly as I could but the second length that connected the two cuffs was going to need serious attention and we didn't have time.

My mother was going to have to come with the chain between her wrists. It was loose enough that she could move her arms all the way to her sides anyway. I pulled her and she stepped slowly forward, stumbled and nearly went down. I shook my head and bent, lifted her onto my shoulder and followed Rill from the door. She didn't struggle but just lay there like a dead thing.

"Which way?" Rill asked.

"Onto the landing and then stairs to the roof. If we can use the roofs, we can get all the way around to the battlements on the outer left flank of the fortress and go over from there. I hope you've got plenty of line and some hooks."

He nodded. "I have but if they get archers along the walls, we'll be soft targets for them."

We ran as best we could. The landing was still empty but we had to wait while Rill picked the lock of the doors to the stairs that led up into the bell tower and onto the roof.

The climb would have been easy, but we had to lash my mother like a parcel and haul her up because she was still unable or unwilling to move. It seemed to take a very long time. I wondered whether the others were moving around regularly, giving the impression that there were a lot more men involved in the attack. I was very surprised that Drachefauste had left my mother unguarded. It was almost as if he didn't care or had baited a trap.

We reached the roof, finally and pulled mother up onto it. I rested against a stone dragon, panting and soaked in sweat.

My mother had freed herself from the rope we had used to keep her in a tight bundle, stood up and began to walk like she was asleep, towards the edge of the roof.

"Mother, stop!" I forced my aching limbs up and grabbed her. She started to scream. Down below, in the quadrangle, I saw Dragon Guards look up and point. Then I saw Drachefauste. I cursed. If I had been able to use my crossbow, I could have taken a shot at that ugly face. He led the guards at a run up the steps and started to work his way to the roof in pursuit.

"If she's going to make it more difficult, Finn, we may have to leave her. She's going to get us both killed."

"I'm not leaving her, Rill!"

"Well I'm not dying pointlessly. You're my friend, Finn but this rescue is going wrong."

We dragged my mother across the rooftops. Now she resisted us and screamed, kicked and beat at us with her fists. In the end, I tied her hands and slung her on my back, again. Progress was too slow. We hadn't reached the arm of the parapet that joined this inner section to the outer wall when Dragon Guards burst from two hatchways. They couldn't quite cut us off but we had to hustle, now.

We reached the parapet just ahead of them.

"Take my mother" I yelled at Rill and shoved her at him. He grabbed her and dragged her towards the walkway of the outer wall. I drew my blades and stood my ground. The narrowness of the parapet allowed only one to pass. While I stood, they had to come through me.

The first Dragon Guardsman came charging, bull style, head down, shield up and weapon swinging. I kicked his shield and that threw him off balance. The partisan swung him further away and I slammed my falchion down on his neck right at the join of helm and gorget. He crashed down onto his side, obstructing the second man who stepped back. I thrust across the falling body and put my point through his front.

He grunted and went down on his knees. I shuffled backwards, chancing a glance at Rill. He was hooking in lines and letting them down.

He was sitting on my mother who was struggling and screaming abuse. A third Dragon Guard went for me but his swing was short. I caught the partisan as he brought it back, using the falchion to push it wide, and stabbed in the eye of his partially closed helm with my short blade.

Blood gushed and he went stumbling back. I followed through and stabbed again, deep into the left lung area before retreating further along the parapet.

He staggered and then there was a panicked cry as he stepped over the edge of the parapet. He fell onto one of the very steep-angled roofs on either side, slid and dropped into the darkness.

There was a heavy crash as he hit something in the courtyard below. I hoped it was very fatal. To my dismay, a number of Dragon Guards were loading heavy crossbows and more guards were appearing who had short bows in hand.

Drachefauste stepped forward and gave a slow, ironic clap,

"A good effort, again. Your devotion is touching, bastard. What is your name?"

"Black Finn," I spat, "you'd better remember it"

"Why would I need to do that? I said if we met again that I'd kill you."

My mother got free of Rill and came at me, beating at me, ineffectually with her fists. I slapped her and she started to cry.

"Do you like what I have done with her? I have taught her a few lessons and now the poor thing seems to have become devoted in the way a bitch does when her master kicks her often and rewards her occasionally."

"You bastard."

It sounded pointless and I wished I had not said it. Drachefauste just laughed.

"Leave me and go" my mother said, suddenly. She stood with fists clenched at her side,

"You can't beat him. He will eat the world. You are wasting your time and dying for nothing." The words came out in a stream. She sounded so pathetic and so unlike my mother. She looked like she had truly given up, too.

Drachefauste laughed, heartily.

"You know what? You can take her. I spare you a second time, boy. Take her back to her duke and tell him she has been properly house-trained. I did enjoy her. I shall look forward, tell him, to teaching his countess some manners, too. This one spat and fought like the little bitch she is. I expect Lady Francesca to obey like a lady."

He gave another short and heavy laugh.

"Go on boy, run away. Guards!"

He lifted a hand and turned away. I might have tried a dagger but I knew it would not be enough. His contempt towards the danger we posed was written in the way he gave us his back and went down the steps laughing. The guards drew off more warily. Rill stared open-mouthed.

"I can't believe we got out of that" he said.

"We didn't. That was the point he was making. He could have killed me this time and last time. He doesn't want her any more. He's just using us as his messenger boys instead of sending his own people with her."

I looked down where my mother had now fallen to her knees, sobbing.

"Don't leave me" she was whispering and holding hands out to Drachefauste. I shook my head. Nothing had prepared me for this. I had thought she would run into my arms and then we'd escape together fighting our way out, if necessary.

But now, she didn't even look like my mother and she certainly didn't look like a woman who could ever have been an assassin. She came dumbly when we led her away. We spiralled slowly down the lines, using the walls to work a descent. When Rill got down, I lowered my mother with her hands and feet lashed comfortably but firmly with some rope and delivered her to Rill, below.

We were standing on the wrong side of a moat that faced down a steep slope. The slope, in turn, ended in a sheer drop to the lower city. The swim was cold and muddy and the descent we did make, in the end was slow and laborious because my mother would not help us although, thankfully she no longer resisted us, either.

Once in the outer city, we used a cart to exit, dressed as guardsmen, one driving, the other with crossbow scanning the road as if we were carrying something of importance. We were not stopped. We made the rendezvous point before dawn. The others appeared from various places where they were concealed. I looked around at the faces of my comrades, some smeared with soot stains, some blood where they had obviously met opposition.

"Where's Janed?" I asked, fear knotting in my stomach. I couldn't stand the idea of the beast laying his hands on her. If she had been captured, we would have to go back, this very night. Kharr looked down. So did Coyle. Merik grimaced and shook his head. It was Tu'Lon that spoke, his voice soft and level, like he was comforting one of his flock.

"I'm sorry, my friend. She didn't make it. She died instantly. She felt no pain. We had to leave her or else we would have lost more."

I looked at my mother, silent and broken, her eyes just watching me and I walked away, numb and cold.

I watched dawn break, alone with my thoughts.

Friends II

Horses champed and nickered, mail and tack jingled as we emerged out of the cold and swirling mist. And then a golden glow rose over the shadowy peaks to the east and almost at once, the mist lifted. The five of us, wrapped in heavy hooded cloaks on five horses laden with equipment emerged into a deep valley where snow-capped peaks pierced a blue sky, securing it to the ceiling of the world.

Kharr had travelled on ahead to take my mother home. For some reason, she seemed more at ease with him than the rest of us. Meanwhile, we decided to follow up on a lead about Drachefauste - something that might let us strike a meaningful blow against him.

Somewhere high above, a bird of prey called and was answered across the divide by the harsher calls of ravens. Disturbed from their ledges by the intruder, they took to the wing, two black witches in ragged gowns moving faster than the high clouds that now lazed on the wind.

We were riding northwards seeking a ruined fortress or something similar, a place mentioned in verse, no more than a legend until recently.

It took on much more significance when a map fell into our hands. This had come by chance, courtesy of a little night work in one of the summer mansions. If the legend matched up, then this offered a little added spice over merely being a possible source of adventure.

It was rumoured to have something to do with the beginnings of the family that became the Drachefauste clan. If so, it would feel good to somehow tread upon such beginnings; and who knows, maybe take something that belonged to his ancestors or better, expose some dark secrets about his bloodline.

We had only ridden down the throat of the valley a short way before Coyle pointed and we all looked where he was indicating. "Griffons," he exclaimed, "remember what the doggerel on the map says – locked in the ice beneath the sister peaks there will you find the prize, look first for the twisted horn and where the griffon flies."

I smiled; hearing Coyle bring that up. Verse and other written clues would usually be my domain but it seemed this one had caught everybody's imagination. "And there must be the twisted horn" I pointed to the left. Opposite the mountain where the griffons circled high, as we rode forward, again, one strange peak came into view, indeed appearing to be twisted by forces unknown and savage. It reminded me of the horn of a mountain ibex.

"Then we can't be far from the road that leads to the gate" added Merik, also quoting part of a phrase on the map.

We rounded a bend and standing clearly before us were two peaks of almost exactly equal height. Even at distance, we could see a winding ramp-like road that led upwards around the mountain base and at its height, arrived at a stone structure which jutted from the cleft between the two peaks.

As the sun caught it, we could see the glint of metal. "That glittering must be the gates of silvered bronze" I said. "It looks like we've found it, then" Merik sounded pleased. "I was doubtful when we first found the map. I wasn't sure it existed and even if it did, I thought it might have been robbed long ago and we would find a vague ruin. The gates still being there is a good sign."

"It may well have been visited already," I added, "I did suggest that. But we won't ever know if we don't take a look. It's an adventure even if there is nothing but old bones and rusted mail to be seen."

"Let's hope that isn't all," Rill said with a grin, "I like to turn a profit and there are always jobs that pay in town where we don't have to freeze our bollocks off or risk being lunch for ravenous griffons."

"If you get eaten, I will pray for your soul." Tu'lon kept a completely straight face, although his eyes crinkled in humour.

"That's not re-assuring" Rill answered.

We turned our mounts onto the winding ramp and began to climb upwards, steadily.

"Talking of ravenous griffons, we've got company. They must have smelled the horses." I pointed with one hand while reaching for the leather pocket that held my crossbow.

I pulled on two clasps and it unrolled. I slid from the saddle, pulling my horse down with an urgent order. It knelt and I used it to steady the bow across as I kneeled, inserted a heavy bolt and checked the sight and trigger.

The other horses started to turn about and nicker in panic as they detected the approach. Griffons love horse flesh. This was going to need more than a little persuasion to see off their attention.

There were three of the great beasts now, stooping with wings outstretched like oversized eagles, their heavy bodies hanging beneath, rear claws ready to snatch and heads lowered to keep watch on their intended prey. Tu'Lon raised a hand and spoke some words.

A soft glow surrounded the group and the horses seemed to grow calmer. Rill was busy trying to control his horse but as soon as it calmed, he was out of the saddle and yanking a short bow from a roll at the rear of the saddle. Merik remained seated, bringing a shield up and taking a long spear from out of its buckled loops which he brought up like a lance. Tu'Lon was quick to dismount, sheltering behind the horses while Coyle swung down, lightly and went around behind the line.

The griffons bore in, beginning to speed up as they trimmed their wings and began their attacking stoop.

My bolt buried itself in the head of the first, low down where the feathers were thick about the throat.

The beast shuddered but kept coming. Tu'Lon called to Lammas, his battle god and flung one hand out. There was a roar of wind and we all felt as if we were filled with a bold energy, any fear or even trepidation falling away.

Coyle sent two short blasts of energy at the lead beast which screamed out but, despite the slight smoke on impact, showed no real sign of being hurt. Griffons are tough beasts, I learned.

The first descended in a rush and Merik spurred his horse into a lunging canter. The lance struck out, piercing the griffon's neck right through. It pulled away, ripping the long spear from Merik's grasp.

His griffon was shaking its head and tearing at the lance with its claws as it alighted clumsily amongst the rocks on the trail above us. It went into a frenzy, ripping, roaring and lashing its tail but the spear would not come free until finally it broke it off with a claw, tearing its own neck even more and causing it to stagger around as blood poured from the great gash it had made.

Meanwhile, the second griffon struck Tu'Lon's horse and lifted it into the air, the horse whinnying and thrashing in a panic as its hooves left the ground.

The third came for Rill's mount but he and Coyle flung daggers as it got in closer, the knives thudding into its face and neck along with my second bolt which hit it in the chest.

The griffin veered right, pulling away from the direction of these strikes. As it did, Merik charged up the trail and caught it with his second spear. The lance made a crunching sound as it smashed bone, entering through the lower ribs.

As the griffon kept pulling away, Merik leaned back, letting the lance rip free but the tip broke off before it could. The damage was done, however. The third griffon plummeted over the edge of the rampway and fell to its ruin on the rocks far below. I raced up the trail on foot to find the beast that was still thrashing and tearing at the broken lance.

It cowered back and then lifted its head, to screech out a challenge. I approached carefully and placed a heavy bolt on my bow coated with a paralysing poison. I aimed at the fleshy area around one eye and loosed the shot. The bolt thudded home and the beast flung itself backwards.

Still clinging to life, it tried to rush me, claws and tail flailing but I was watchful and skipped aside. I backed off, blades now in hand, the griffon drew itself up and with a last effort, charged again, kicking up dust and rock. I rolled as one claw ripped at my shoulders and one at my face.

It reared above me but it couldn't see me and shuddered heavily as it stood up on its hind legs. The griffon crashed down, rolled onto its side, eyes half closed and finally lay, twitching. The poison had taken effect. I moved up to it and pulled the lance free. When it didn't jerk, I knew it was out. I took what was left of the lance and drove the point through its heart. The griffon that had taken Tu'Lon's horse was a distant speck heading back towards its mountain lair.

We considered the matter briefly and decided one horse for two griffons wasn't a bad exchange. Tu'Lon rode with Rill and we went on up the trail, eventually reaching a wide courtyard with overgrown shrubs just before nightfall. Thirty-foot-high fence gates towered above us. Through the bars, we could see another overgrown courtyard and then beyond that, double wooden arched doors some twelve to fifteen feet high that led into the mountain.

We stood nervous watches that night, expecting that something might issue from those great metal gates or beasts from the mountains would be drawn by our small camp fire but it was not so.

The night passed without incident and morning rose slowly and lazily from his bed, stretching grey clad arms across the sky in the form of low cloud accompanied by a steady, chill breeze.

We checked the horses and repacked the blankets and other camp gear before arming up. By this time, we were all complaining about the cold. We stood and inspected the gates and what we could see of beyond. Since nothing was moving, other than a few small mountain birds, we pushed on the partly open gates.

They swung slowly open, as easy to move as they must have been when they were first installed. I marvelled, inwardly at this. The smooth manner in which they moved and the way they eased to a halt suggested engineering of great skill.

I would have said they were dwarven or elven fashioned but if legends were true, neither of those races would have made these gates. I had met trolls in dark places and they were far too stupid, goblins too lazy and slapdash and giants not given to engineering as much as decorative handiwork.

It was the first question which hung over the mountain fastness. Birds flew up from the bushes as we approached and startled us into drawing weapons. We stood closer for a few moments. When nothing else appeared, we cut away the vines and creepers that obscured the great doors and pushed on those. They did not give as the gates had done.

We regarded the oak doors with some concern. They were far too thick to hack through, besides which, they were beautifully worked with carvings of mountains and a rising sun, flying beasts and birds, plants and clouds all in slight relief layered and shaped with great care.

Rill and I consulted over the lock and began to work. It was not that hard to understand but must have required a large and complex key which needed us to work together with different picks to simulate.

When it clunked heavily, we both breathed a sigh of relief. We pushed again. The doors gave slowly but were still held. We could just make out a loose and rusty bolt. Putting our weight to the doors, we heaved.

The bolt made a screeching sound and began to give more. I took out a small hacksaw from my pack and after a lot of hard work from each in turn, we cut far enough through that a good heave caused it to snap with a final protest of twisted metal, followed by a sharp clang as it sprang apart and fell to the stone floor beyond the doors.

We waited, holding our breath, for some response but there was nothing but a deep silence following this assault on the security of the place. We pushed the doors open. Unlike the gates, they grated across the floor, picking up stones and detritus that had littered the flags behind them.

The whole area was lit by a golden glow from orbs on poles that ran along the walls at regular intervals and a cluster of four placed almost centrally. We saw the first body, then.

A twisted skull on the end of a heavy backbone and rib cage lay looking backwards towards the door as if its owner had fallen and their last action had been to turn their head around and tip it back at an impossible angle to watch what was happening at their gates.

The dead being still had a rusted metal breastplate, that must have once been fine armour. A broken lance lay nearby, fashioned of the same metal, its tip broken off, perhaps in an enemy struck before the guardian or indeed, the raider was overcome in combat.

The helmet also lay at hand, a strangely designed piece with a long, curved crest, fanned cheekbone guards and jutting protection for the jaw. It opened in one piece apart from a visor of criss cross gauze that must have made vision easier than a closed helm.

Presumably it had been a lot stronger than it looked, now, in thin rusted and smashed form, half twisted off the helm where it was riveted. Its owner must have stood seven or more feet in height. Another shattered skeleton of the same type lay near an archway to the right.

Ahead, another archway opened onto wide stairs going down. The same gold glow lit the stairs. There were other weapon pieces and bones about the place but no sign that there had been more than these two who fell here in whatever battle took place long ago. They can't have been adventurers. I concluded they were gate guardians of some type and had refused to abandon their posts. What this also told me was that the attackers must have sacked the place, already. It seemed unlikely that we would find anything here but dust and a story to piece together.

Cautiously, I moved towards the broad stairway, using the archway to cover my movement. Rill did the same on the other side of the arch and we both looked around, scanning the steps.

Two more bodies lay sprawled on the steps. One was much the same as the two we had seen, already. The other was entirely different, a squatter, heavier frame with a heavy skull. This warrior had been carrying a round shield of leather with a thin layer of iron now rusted and flaked away, leaving what was left of the decayed and slashed leather.

One skeletal hand rested on a long, ruined axe. We moved down, Coyle and Merik covering us from the landing behind.

"Goblin blood I'd guess" I whispered. "But very heavy. One of the mountain races, maybe a cross blood tribe. The size of the hands and head are out of proportion to the body. That's usually the sign of a half blood."

In my head I was back in the past, witnessing the scene of the conflict. A band of raiders, many more in number than the strange incumbents burst through the doors and rush the guards. There is a brief and brutal combat before the horde pour down the stairs, some turning right through the archway on the upper level that Tu'Lon and Coyle had gone to look at. Seeing Coyle at the head of the stairs, I guessed they had found nothing of real interest, there. Beyond the stairs, we could now see another hall. Here, many more skeletons were scattered about.

We moved ahead, slipping into the hall but this, too, was lit by the same magical lanterns so there was little shadow to conceal our approach.

The others came up behind us. I checked the fallen. There were six of the tall beings and over twenty of the goblin like ones. The hall offered two archways left and right which were dark and one pair of oak doors of some ten feet in height ahead of us.

Small alcoves had stone plinths about three feet in height but whatever had rested upon them had gone long ago. There was a scatter of small shards in places, fine crystal in white, black and clear shades. It looked like the raiders had smashed them in a frenzy, presumably seeing no value in them.

"What did you find through the archway upstairs?" I asked Coyle, quietly.

"A fountain that was no longer running and about thirty dead goblin types with eight of the tall beings. Looks like there was quite a fight, there. One of the tall ones was wearing some kind of robe or similar and carrying a metal rod which was melted and twisted out of shape."

I nodded, "interesting place."

Coyle grinned, "If you like that kind of thing. Personally, I'd prefer to have found coin scattered about."

I laughed, softly. Merik came up on my shoulder, "I suggest that you and Coyle check the right arch, Finn. Rill and I check the second and Tu'Lon, you stay central ready to react with some covering magic if anything happens. Also, you get the job of watching the doors."

"Oh thanks. Just leave the priest to be devoured by the creature behind the double doors. That's no problem, at all."

There was more soft laughter. We split and inspected the archways. The right archway led into a long corridor that soon faded from view, being unlit. At the near end, there were a few more scattered bodies and a lot of detritus that proved to be pot shards and smashed statuettes.

I dug a small bullseye lantern from my pack and lit it, opening the eye very slowly as we moved down the corridor. It was as well I did because just then a large dust louse ran out and just as it headed away from us something came from above, snatching it up with long tentacles. There was a crunching sound and we both looked up to see a creature like an octopus attached to the ceiling by a flexible sucker with four barbed tentacles that it had used to grab its prey and a horned beak, which it was currently using to do the crunching. It looked quite capable of doing the same to a human.

If the beast was aware of us, it hadn't made any move to attack, so we stood still, waiting. Evidently, the giant dust louse was a good meal because the creature pulled its tentacles in and shortened the sucker until it was tucked hard against the ceiling in a purple and blue tinted ball. I dimmed the lantern and slipped past, reaching the end of the corridor, which ended in another archway off which was a globe shaped room from which three other arches led into short corridors. I returned to Coyle who was still keeping a wary eye on the thing on the roof.

"More arches and corridors," I reported, "but nothing moving that I could see."

Coyle nodded at the creature, "What do you want to do about that?"

I considered, "Nothing unless we are going that way. It may ignore us if we leave it be."

We backtracked to find the others waiting at the entrance to the left archway. "Empty corridor leading to empty rooms other than skeletons and a scatter of worthless and ruined belongings."

Merik shook his head. "It's not looking that positive, so far."

I explained what we had seen, "Probably the same layout I imagine but we could take a further look. My opinion is leave it until later. At the moment, we have a watchman at our backs, potentially."

Nobody disagreed so we turned our attention to the doors. These opened without any effort and we stood, weapons ready at the entrance to a huge hall. This was lit by a soft light from a hundred or more tiny globes that clung to the rafters and cornices. At the far end, it was dominated by a stone dais on which stood a great carved wooden throne with two smaller seats slightly in front of this to the left and right. Two sets of low steps rose from the floor, which was of marble or similar polished slabs. Whether it was some property of the wood or something produced by it rotting away, I couldn't tell, but a strange, sweet smell hung in the air.

Skeletons were piled all over the room. In the centre, there was an octagonal table that could take about sixteen or maybe twenty-four seats although most of the seats that had stood there seemed to have been broken into so much rubble and dust. There were skeletal remains even on the table itself.

We spread out. I went around the left wall, checking everything. Rill went around the right. Tu'Lon and Coyle began casting small enchantments to search for anything magically hidden or unusual.

It was quite slow and painstaking but when Rill got behind the thrones on the dais, he gave a shout. "I've found a panel here!"

We all left our checks and came over to see. Rill was busy feeling around. There was a click and the panel shifted upwards, a section of the dais folded down into steps and two more panels slid apart to offer a doorway. Rill lifted his lantern and the light reached into the darkness beyond the new archway. Stale air mixed with odours of various types drifted out. We waited, wary against the possibility of poisons being used to protect whatever we had found. Once the stuffiness and smell resided, we moved in, Rill and I taking a lead.

We found ourselves on a mezzanine with a low balcony of stone overlooking a half circular hall below.

Spiral steps led down from the centre of the mezzanine into the lower hall.

The mezzanine was relatively bare apart from some finely worked statues and two animals like bears carved from a dark wood and inlaid with gold and silver.

None of those items were going to be removable. The half circular hall looked a lot more interesting. There were several chests, a collection of ceramics and crystal but dominating the hall was a semi-circular raised plinth with two centrally placed horns of metal that glowed with power and attached to each, seemingly held in place by the energy around the metallic protrusions, a long sword, the right one having a great red gem gripped by a golden hand as its pommel and the left one a blue gem on the palm of a clawed hand.

The right sword was of dark metal, the left of a blueish-white with a sheen that closer inspection proved to be frozen droplets of water.

I looked to Tu'Lon and Coyle, "time you two used enchantments to check for any traps or enchantments on the steps or between us and the treasure." Coyle nodded and spoke a short set of phrases, bringing out a small rod tipped with a clear piece of quartz.

He held this in front of him, swinging it right and left in an arc as he walked ahead. Tu'Lon called upon Bathsheba, the cat god for help in seeing the way ahead clearly and without impediment. He seemed perturbed by something and started a new prayer while we headed for the chests and other items. Merik went straight for the plinth and stood inspecting the two blades. I was similarly tempted but thought to help the others first, checking the chests for spring clip traps that might plunge a poisoned needle into a finger or thumb.

Coyle was also checking each item, re-casting his spell and pointing the rod at them. As he approached one chest, he jumped back as the crystal swirled with red as if it had filled with blood. As he did so, the chest seemed to reform into a shapeless creature, one long tentacle snaking out to wrap itself about Coyle's waist, another long limb ending in an outsized claw rising to swipe at me and where the chest lid had been, a gaping maw full of spectacularly sharp teeth now gnashed and slavered.

How long the creature must have lain dormant here I could not even guess but it seemed the wait had made it ravenously hungry. It hauled on Coyle who panicked and let fly with a blast that missed it and knocked Rill off his feet so he fell over a chest, smashed a large pot and brought a second down on him, raining him in shards, some of which went in his eyes and mouth.

Tu'Lon, distracted by his long prayer, looked up and shook his head, halting his current call. He drew a long-handled mace and pointed, shouting for Orus to give us the strength and speed of the hunter.

I managed to dive aside as the shearing talons ripped, tearing my leather jack from shoulder to elbow but failing to reach my flesh. Merik took two strides and pulled on the right-hand sword. With a battle cry, he spun and flung himself towards the creature.

The sword flared with fire so he brought it down in an arc of flame and sliced right through the tentacle that was holding Coyle.

The ragged remains drew in but the creature put out a new limb with a heavy spiked end which it swung at Merik. He was speaking in a language none of us knew as he met the attack head on, blocking the blow and thrusting the sword into the tooth-filled maw.

There was a flash of flame, an acrid cloud of evil smelling smoke that made us retch and the creature flopped down into a rapidly oozing mess of something that looked like melted toffee.

Merik stepped back and leaned, momentarily on the blade then raised it in front of him and turned slowly, looking around as if he expected another attack. "That's some blade" muttered Coyle.

"What happened?" Rill finished brushing bits off himself and rubbing his eyes, which were now bloodshot. He stood up. "Bloody hells alight. What did you do to it?"

Everyone looked at the other blade. Behind me, I could hear Tu'Lon praying to Akanaten.

"Go on Finn," said Merik, "you're the logical choice to take the other sword."

I stepped towards the plinth. Something just held me back for a moment as I regarded the sword with its ice touched blade.

"Stop!" Tu'Lon yelled and I withdrew my hand, "It's a trap. The two blades will force the holders to fight until one destroys the other."

Merik raised his blade and pointed it towards me "Draw the other blade, Finn. Now, do it!"

I stepped back, aghast, as the point of the sword hovered before me. Coyle raised a hand. Tu'Lon spoke a soft prayer to Kenubis and golden light enveloped us.

Merik started and the blade lowered, "Damn. That was far too close. The sword was speaking in my mind. It says its name is Clave and I can never set it aside unless I fight and defeat the ice blade, Reive. It has agreed to fight with me as long as it can share in the death of a living creature often enough to rebuild and keep its strength."

He put a belt clip on the hilts and swung the blade over one shoulder. "I'll find a way to carry it so I only have to use the blade when necessary" he added, as soon as his hand had left the hilt.

"That was strange. I was still Merik but I was also Clave. He is old, very old and powerful. They were living beings once, he and this Reive."

"You say you cannot throw the blade away" Tu'Lon said "I am sorry. I read the curse too late to warn you not to touch either sword. By itself, it is no more dangerous than you have seen and maybe you will learn to control it, in time. Together, they seek only to completely destroy the other, however many lives that takes. Neither of you would have survived, I think and then the blades would have tried to force us to take them in turn, probably strengthened by drinking your life forces, first."

"Charming" Rill said, "I vote we take all the normal booty and get out of here. This whole place gives me a bad feeling."

In the end, we found enough in the room to increase our own personal wealth. Tu'Lon took a bigger share of the treasure to compensate him and so, in the end, we left, happy. The only question mark that hung over the expedition, for me, was in what way had what we saw there, related in any way to Drachefauste's ancestry. That puzzle remained and I wanted to one day uncover more about the events that had led to the slaughter of the strange mountain dwellers whose palace we had become the first living beings to walk since the day of its fall.

Beasts III

My father seemed to withdraw from everything after we returned my mother to Falkeberg and the failure of the family meeting. At first, he praised my friends very publicly while challenging me angrily in private over the danger we had all placed ourselves in. I would not stand down on this. I berated him for his failures, accusing him of being weak, unable to read his enemy and, ultimately incompetent in a way that endangered the family. I said he should stand down as duke and let one of his brothers conduct the war. It was obvious, I went on, that he lacked the strength or skill to match Drachefauste.

When I stalked from his room, I was still full of anger. He spoke little during my tirade except to say, cuttingly, that I was not to return to Lorefast but would be travelling to Car Duris to commence my real training. I would then be able to serve the family properly, if I was capable. He added that he found my attitude to be the biggest disappointment of all and that he had thought so much more of me.

So, we parted on poor terms. Merik decided to accept a commission which my father offered. He would become a Lieutenant in the guards.

My father tried to persuade Kharr to take over Janed's position and suggested that Lancingor would find quarters and roles for Tu'Lon and Coyle, too.

But Kharr wanted to return to Gwythaor while the others were bound for Riassa and their usual haunts. I remained in Rosgovia, for a short time. Thus, when we finally had the opportunity to face Drachefauste, openly, I was with our forces, under Raef Von Littesburg, our finest leader.

***

It was a pale dawn full of shivers and pennants snapping in a chill edged wind when we finally rode to meet him. Horses shuffled and champed as the lines drew out. We had the slight advantage of the higher ground; the slopes almost bare of trees and scrub whilst our enemy laboured a little through the heavier ground in the valley where the beginnings of brooks encouraged heavy tufts of grass and some rushes to grow.

Drachefauste had brought a force of largely barbarian tribes from the borderlands and steppes. Some, like the Irellani and the Rag-Dari were old enemies. The black raven flew above their advancing host. They had brought some cavalry although the vast majority of their force fought on foot. The Rag-Dari chieftain, Verridan the Red, was there with his house guard and his berserkers. The guard had ravens on a red ground on their shields. In the centre, Drachefauste's iron and Dragon Guards dominated.

I allowed myself a grim smile. I would be pitched in against them with our own elite guards under Fulk of Cylmar.

The heavy horse, which Frederick would lead himself, would be tight on our left flank. On the right flank, the grey and blue of Littesburg horse showed as Raef manoeuvred our forces to match what he was seeing.

The barbarians were chanting and clashing their shields as they approached. Some waved long handled weapons in the air. Although our lines stirred, there was no sign of fear amongst the waiting men. Behind our line, men started to load the few ballistae that we had brought with us. Raef sent two small units of light cavalry around the rear into reserve.

Most of the troops with us were Nordian. We had come to their aid when Drachefauste marched on Nordia rather than on Rosgovia. We didn't have forces from Pellinore or Adhils. Both had retired to Littesburg after the strategic conference and both seemed reluctant to follow my father's lead any further.

I watched everything from a distance, like someone appreciating a great work of art. I felt removed from the reality that we were finally facing Drachefauste.

At issue, I should explain, was the town of Neudenhoff. Many of the people of that fine city had already made their decision and were leaving in trains of wagons, bundled high with their possessions and offspring.

The deprivations and the sack of three other towns had set rumour at work on the backstreets. The difference here was that we were defending from outside. The town had closed its gates. It stood on the Nordian border at the head of the Veron Pass. It was, as had been mentioned at a number of tactical meetings, a key settlement since one could not afford to ignore it and it provided the holder access to Hamvard, Rosgovia, Raga and the river which went out into the Bay of White Seals.

In the previous cases, when we had gone to Nordia's aid against barbarian raids, we had been welcomed and the townspeople had fought alongside us, but Nuedenhoff's actions had forced us into a more open conflict.

I doubted there would be butchery, here. Drachefauste would be keen to demonstrate his magnanimity to those who turned their backs upon their own nobility. Thus, we stood, beyond the walls but no less ready to defend them than in the previous cases. There was another difference today. The previous settlements had fallen despite the efforts of localised armies to hold them. This was the first time we had assembled a full fighting force commanded by experienced men where the trained soldiers outnumbered the conscripts.

In the distance, I could see people peering over the battlements, presumably straining their eyes to see what was unfolding in the valley below them. I shook my head and muttered something defamatory. They reminded me of crows, waiting to pick the flesh off the bodies of the fallen.

Below us, Drachefauste was pushing through the ranks of his Dragon Guards. I could see his helm with its metal dragon and the way that the ranks shied away were a clear indication it was their lord and not one of his four or five counterpart dupes.

He emerged, a banner bearer and one of his captains a step or two behind him. He breathed deeply and looked about with the air of a predator that senses its prey is within easy reach. He was measuring the battlefield, pacing it like the executioner upon the gallows. After a moment, he stopped his stride and stood leaning on a great axe. His voice carried even in the breeze. It was harsh and deep, "You do not all have to die, today," he began, "I offer you an alternative. You can seize the fools who lead you and hand them over to me. Lay down your arms and leave the field as free men."

He punched his axe into the air and his guards cheered and yowled. The barbarians joined in this derisive taunt. Drachefauste half turned to his force and lifted both arms then faced us once more.

I looked left and saw my uncle, head lifted seeming to scent the air before he rode forward. Raef's voice was fine and contrasted with the rough brutishness of Drachefauste's tones.

"I challenge you, to stand forth as your own champion Drachefauste and to face me in single combat. If you win, we will retire from the field. If I win, you will retreat no less than ten miles and give up this town to us."

He paused and waited. Drachefauste hefted his axe into the air a second time. "To the death, then" he yelled. His forces burst into another round of yammering and jeering.

I wanted to shake my head but Raef was the victor of a hundred such combats, a duellist called upon by the Emperor himself when such matters needed to be resolved. I knew, at once, he would accept. I also knew that should he kill Drachefauste, the enemy would still attack.

"Fine. To the death, then, Drachefauste." He removed his grey and blue jacket with its gold epaulettes and strode forward. Drachefauste looked back and I imagined him grinning within the half mask of the helm that protected it.

Raef walked along to Frederick, "You are in command while I am facing Drachefauste. If he wins, don't let them take my body. And if I win, cover my retreat as I have no doubt his dogs will seek to do their worst. But if he does win, you are to give up the field, do you understand? I am giving my word and we, unlike that pig, keep our word."

Frederick nodded, "I will order my horse down to cover you when you have the beast on a spit, uncle."

Raef gave a smile, but I saw the hard look in his eyes. He drew his favourite blade and looked it over then replaced it, pulled on a heavy gauntlet and fetched a small buckler from the ranks. This done, he walked proudly down the slope to where Drachefauste waited, leaning on his axe.

We cheered and clapped but I felt a cold shadow fall upon my heart. I would not begrudge my uncle the kill. If it could not be my blade then Raef or Finnmeyer would have been the men I wanted to bring Drachefauste to his knees, and the latter had fallen already to his hand.

They stood facing one another. Drachefauste looked huge in his bronzed plated armour beside the lithe, slight figure of my uncle. Raef bowed to the beast and said something. The beast turned to his men and raised his axe, shaking it at them and they howled and cheered, growled and clashed their shields with blood lust. We responded, raising a great cheer, calling out Raef's name.

The two stood off. Drachefauste made the first move, rushing in, axe swinging in a scything sweep that made my heart miss a beat. But Raef was not cowed, a veteran of such encounters. He danced aside and his blade made a small movement. There was a brief lull, as the two men moved apart, but from where we stood it was clear that it was the beast who had come off worse from the encounter. We applauded.

The enemy howled for retribution. Drachefauste circled and then tried to get in close. His shoulder came up and he attempted to club Raef with one fist while hefting the axe with the other.

Again, Raef slid away from the blow and his blade pierced the outstretched arm of his opponent. Blood sprayed as he ripped it free and waited, point ready, poised like a matador controlling the show. The bull wasn't about to put its head down, though.

Drachefauste seemed to move slowly but his leg lashed out in a swift motion. Raef stumbled. The enemy sensed victory and yowled again as the beast swept down, axe coming in at an arc that would cleave Raef in two.

But my uncle had found his balance and although his own slashing riposte went wide, he was well clear of the blow that had been meant for him. He moved like a dancing master, showing up a clumsy pupil.

Three times, he picked at Drachefauste. A stabbing strike to the shoulder, a cut across the right arm and then a strike that pierced the beast's left knee and at last, Drachefauste gave voice to his hurt, sounding his pain across the field. The baying of his men fell silent as he sank to one knee.

I am certain I was not alone in silently urging Raef to finish him while he was down but my uncle was far too honourable to do what the beast would have done without hesitation. "Get up. Get up and let's finish this."

Raef circled Drachefauste. Drachefauste rose, slowly. The double handed long axe lay discarded on the ground, now.

He pulled a single-handed axe from his belt, hefted his shield and came at Raef again. Buckler met shield with a clang that echoed across the battlefield. Raef stumbled back but as Drachefauste rushed in, Raef's poise returned at once and he slid aside.

His blade pierced Drachefauste's thigh, again and more blood flowed. Again, we cheered. Raef stepped in and used the blade edge, a slicing cut, opening Drachefauste's right arm to the elbow.

The axe shaved him and ripped his cloak as he spun away, but a further blow to Drachefauste's side had the beast on the ground for a second time, blood dripping thickly from his wounds.

"Surrender damn you!" yelled Raef. "Enough of this slow death".

Drachefauste started to laugh. Raef was taken aback and circled closer. "Come on, get up and die like a man."

The laughter choked and Drachefauste spat a gobbet of blood. He coughed. Raef moved a few steps closer, hefting the blade. "Come on, do it," I muttered. Drachefauste half rose, gathering what strength he had left, he rushed Raef, swinging the axe in a wide arc but Raef was unperturbed, a master in one to one combat. He leant back, letting the axe pass by, placing his sword so Drachefauste took the point in his chest. He went down with a crash, rolled over and lay still, blood dribbling from his mouth.

There was a huge cheer from our side. The opposition remained silent. They did not even let out a single mournful cry.

But they did not leave the field, just lowered their pennants to stand normally and waited. In the meantime, we were raising our fists and shouting defiance, whooping and congratulating Raef.

The first couple of men to him were patting him on the back when I saw the beast twitch. I had been staring at his body and wishing it had been me that had slain him. At least Finnmeyer had been avenged.

What would he have made of seeing Raef spit the beast like the creature he was? I frowned and wiped my eyes, trying to get a better look. Drachefauste moved an arm, reaching out until his hand found the haft of his bloodied axe.

I started to scream and shout, pointing, but the noise from our ranks was so great that I could not make Raef hear. He was walking between the two forces, raising his arms and invoking our troops to keep celebrating. Then his eyes met mine and he saw me. He started to turn but it was too late.

Drachefauste rose in a rush that must have been driven by pure willpower and muscle. He flung the axe. I saw it whirl end over end as it flew at Raef.

He began to spin and raise his blade but the weapon came far too quickly. It struck with a sickening thud. to the back of my uncle's head, sending him flying forwards. He hit the ground and rolled over on his back.

His once handsome face was shattered, one eye a bloody sunburst from the lifeless pupil. Drachefauste snatched up his great axe and brandished it above his head in both hands, facing his army. A huge baying cheer went up and they raised and waved weapons in salute. He began to turn back towards Raef.

"Frederick!" I shouted. "We don't let him take Raef's head. We don't, do you hear?"

Frederick gagged. He nodded and straightened in the saddle, taking a few steps forward on his horse. I could hold it no longer. "Charge!!!" I yelled. The bellow was way beyond my normal shout and it had the effect I wanted.

As I ran forward, drawing my falchion, the men around me came too. We rushed down the hill. Drachefauste looked stunned. We had finally surprised the beast by doing something he would have done but we had always seemed too honourable to even consider.

We crashed into the iron legion and barbarians who had just begun to respond, throwing them back. Our cavalry struck hard. Drachefauste met the charge, taking the entire head off a horse and spilling the first of Frederick's men onto the floor.

I was desperate to reach the beast and kill him, myself. I rammed my shield into the teeth of the first of the Dragon Guard and took him down with a blow to the back. Ripping my sword free, I made for the beast only to find my way blocked, again by another iron clad hulk of a man. I met his hack with my shield and cut him to the wrist, causing him to snatch back his arm.

I looked into the face of my enemy and momentarily paused. I recognised that face. In a flicker, I recalled where. He had been the boy that Drachefauste punched in the head on that fateful night when the beast first crossed our threshold.

He had been used to demonstrate how tough his people were. Now, in the heat of battle, his wrist sinews cut half through, there was doubt, even fear in those staring eyes. He was chewing something, but even with the narcotic fuelled aggression, there was still animal fear so palpable, you could smell it on him.

He made a vain effort to grip the axe and swing it again but my shield was in the crook of his arm, preventing him from bending it enough to strike while my blade bit into his side. I drove it down with hateful anger so it pierced his bowels and then pulled it free.

He looked down at the blood welling from his stomach and then his sphincter muscle loosened too much. He slumped, stinking and beaten, an animal driven to savage fury only to sacrifice itself on the blade of the enemy.

I kicked him in the head and tried again to reach the man I wanted to slay, but then Frederick and his cavalry were amongst us and I watched as my brother's axe split Drachefauste's helm with a ringing clang. The beast fell on his face. I stepped back, anger nearly spent, breathing hard.

In a final rally, the Dragon Guard closed about their fallen icon, pushing Frederick and his men back.

Making a shield wall, they cut their way through the lighter skirmishers who were closing about their forces and retreated, Drachefauste carried on the shoulders of four of his guard. With the Dragon Guard departed from the field, the remaining barbarians broke and scattered.

I regretted, later, that we had not given pursuit. Drachefauste would not die, it seemed. Within two weeks, we heard he was back in the field, harrying our forces in the north. He really must have troll blood as the stories suggested or some such to have such powers of regeneration. Any normal man would have fallen that day.

I stood, spattered in blood amongst the Dragon Guards and barbarians that my troop and I had slain. Fulk came over and patted me on the shoulder.

"You wielded a mighty blade, today especially for such a young man. They'll remember you, Edmund and hopefully, they'll fear you a little, too. Raef would have been pleased with this victory even if we did ignore his request for nicety over giving up the field."

"We can't win unless we learn to be as hard and as ruthless as the enemy."

"I know that lad. It's your father that you have to convince"

There were celebrations and a feast that night but they left me cold and frustrated. My anger was for Raef's loss, and while I understood people wanting to enjoy the victory, I could not escape my heavy heart.

I had lost both the men who I had wanted to be from the time I was young. I knew that the war was not yet at an end and there would be more loss before we were done.

I could hear Leopold boasting loudly to the countess. She had arrived with an entourage, although my father was absent and it was she who sat in the main chair at the head of the high table now. I rose clutching my goblet and walked along the front of the dais until I was standing face to face with Leopold. My half-brother looked up and the words died on his lips.

"What do you know about war?" I asked, my tone vitriolic. Leopold paled and the countess looked aghast. Frederick swung round from his conversation but before he could intervene, I continued

"This is war" I lifted my cloak to reveal the spreading red patch where my wound was weeping. "It's about pain and loss, destruction and hatred. We fight because we have to. There is nothing magnificent about it, but then you wouldn't know since all you have ever done is ride in to celebrate once the battle is over. We lost our best soldier today!"

I banged down the goblet, spraying droplets of wine over he, the countess and Frederick. I span and marched down the steps between the tables as I headed out of the hall. Adhils nodded grim approval but the silence on the upper tables was palpable. Frederick rose and followed, "Edmund!"

"Why do you follow him?" asked Leopold, "let him go."

"You fool." Frederick turned on Leopold who flushed, red. "He's right. You know nothing. He will be our next Raef, that's why I listen to him and that's why he's right." I didn't stop walking even though Frederick's words did make me feel better.

Herlenbrand had also followed and he checked me at the door. He put a hand on my arm, "Edmund, wait a moment lad. I know you feel bitter and maybe it does seem wrong but the people need to celebrate. Nobody is forgetting Raef but do you think he'd want us all moping about or holding a wake? Come back to the table. You and Leopold need to set aside these quarrels. He's still young and has much to learn about politics and war. One day you'll have to work with him and for him in various capacities."

I drew away but without any anger and bowed slightly to my father's cousin. "That may be so, cousin, but as we stand, I cannot imagine ever working for Leopold, so perhaps our paths lie in different directions. Frederick will be the one to be duke, thank the gods. If Leopold had been first in line, I would have left by now."

"Family loyalty and ties are more important than anything, Edmund. Be careful before you consider turning your back on your own blood." I nodded but continued on. Frederick caught me in the corridor.

"I know he's an annoying little prick sometimes, Ed, but you should come back. That is, when you've had that wound looked at properly. You're bleeding again."

"Are you asking me or ordering me to return?" I asked, a trace of annoyance returning to my voice.

"Asking," Frederick laid a hand on my shoulder, "as your brother and your friend."

"One day, you will be my duke," I said, evenly, "you should get used to making it an order." I turned and walked away. I hadn't stopped in the infirmary for more than a few minutes when we returned from the field, earlier. There were so many men with worse wounds and more needs than I had. It was much quieter, now. I looked in and at once, one of the nurse healers came across.

"You are hurt?" She asked, softly, her eyes sympathetic. I met them and saw pain and experience etched there beneath her calm demeanour. I nodded and let the anger flow from me. "Yes sister," I said, "I am hurt. I have a weeping wound but it is my heart that is wounded more seriously."

She gave a soft smile and touched me lightly on the shoulder. "We all continue to weep inside for those we lose. Narva bring peace to your heart, young man. In the meantime, I shall do what little I can to ministrate to your physical wounds."

Shadows II

A dull smog had settled over the eastern docks. Even breathing deeply made you feel grimy. You spend so much of your life waiting. I was waiting now, loitering against a dock wall in Acondium. I was smoking a pipe and trying my best to look like an itinerant seaman and not like an assassin waiting for a contact with a job to be done.

It was my second term at the Guild in Car Duris and this was a co-operative assignment. The first term had been simple enough, even with the distraction of war continuing back in my homelands. I had learned all the basic skills, some of which, I already had an advantage in, compared to other students. I had certainly benefited from years of accomplished teaching in the skills of arms, riding, bow and tactics.

Drachefauste had soon recovered from his wounds but his unexpected defeat seemed to have to have made him more cautious for a while. The campaign season was short in the northern states and it appeared that a relative stalemate had been reached. Frederick led well with able men to support and advise him. My markings on the map in my room showed that we were conceding ground, albeit gradually.

At this rate, there would need to be a major victory or a siege where the beast was thrown back or we would start to lose major towns. My father had forbidden the other commanders to give me any place in their ranks so I had little choice but to concentrate on my studies.

I just hoped that my skills would be put to use soon. I had been sent to learn the skills of assassins and spies at the Guild of Stealth and Shadows. My hopes of becoming a bard of Lorefast had been dashed by the war. Now, I would become a much darker force to be used by the family. I would be a pair of eyes in dark places and carry out their wishes.

The previous week, I had been assigned to a team of five, oft referred to by our tutors as a pentagon. Each pentagon member knew only the other four and the masters who were training them.

In time, one would be selected as leader and would get to know four other pentagon leaders, thus making it possible for five pentagons to operate in a coordinated manner if such a thing were needed. As a result, you would never know any others in your guild unless it occurred by accident or in a time of extreme need where such conventions were broken.

In the meantime, tonight's task was here in Acondium, some twenty-five miles from our base. It was a mission we had to complete in pairs.

We would begin on receipt of a note, and a bronze token from an unknown source - the sign that we had taken on a contract. The contact would only approach when he or she felt we had satisfied the first criteria of not drawing any potential attention to the exchange.

We had three possible drop points, one before midnight, one on the stroke or just after and then a third at any time between then and an hour before dawn. The earlier we picked up the task, the less pressure there would be to get it done.

The deadline was dawn by which time we had to check in with the master who was monitoring our progress, and hand in our tokens as the sign that the task was complete. We would then be told to return to Car Duris. Marks would be awarded for how we had progressed and what we had achieved. I intended to pick up at the first point and as early as possible.

I had sent my mission partner, Jen, to the second point, dressed as a gypsy selling charms and small crafted items. She was to find something to eat and then sit and look tired on a stone bench at the edge of the square. It would put her in place to receive if I failed to make the first drop work.

I caught the sound of a cough and a stick on the cobbles. I glanced up at the old man approaching and I had to make an effort to appear outwardly calm. Typical, I thought, that the contact would look like an old seafarer. He had a grizzled beard, lank white-grey hair and looked the worse for wear. As he got nearer, I could smell him. He couldn't have bathed for days or even weeks. He nodded affably enough. "Evenin' laddie." The accent was northern, perhaps Valcorian or Saxonian in origin. I inclined my head. "Evening to you, also." I thickened a Rosgovian accent, sticking to something I knew well. "Spare a coin or two for an old sea dog what's fallen on 'ard times?"

I nearly laughed. He was such a caricature of the drifters you could see in every city, the flotsam and jetsam washing to and fro with no direction until they eventually washed up dead on the shore of their own lives in some back alley, where they had died of the cold and lack of proper food in their bellies. I dipped into a concealed pouch and brought out a handful of coins. I decided I could probably reclaim the expense of playing out my part on the mission later so I gave him a silver crown. "Get a proper meal and a drink" I said.

The old fellow's eyes lit up; "Why that's right generous of 'ee laddie, blessings of Aulsuuli on you and your ship... right generous, aye"

He began to shuffle off. I felt a little disappointed. I thought I had executed the part well enough. I nearly asked him if he didn't have anything for me but then it occurred to me that this would be part of the test so I leaned back on the wall and puffed on my pipe. I just nodded his way with a smile. "Take care old timer" He raised a hand and continued, unsteadily along, leaving an authentic whiff of alcohol and stale urine.

Heavy footsteps rang out. I looked up just as a mail-clad city guard loomed up literally in my face. He stuck out his jaw and pretty much started yelling. "What the pig's arse do you think you're doing? Encouraging beggars and tramps, that's what. And anyway, what're you loitering about here for? Up to no good, I'll warrant. Come on, let's hear it and it better be good or we're taking a walk to the barracks to go through your stuff and see if you can afford a fine or two. I'm sure we'll find something we can get you on."

I wasn't used to being spoken to like this, back then and nearly gave him a piece of my mind. Then, I remembered I was just supposed to be an ordinary seaman and the old man would probably be observing how I dealt with this unexpected turn. I glanced about and saw the old seaman hurrying away from the confrontation.

The guard had a sergeant's rank badge. "I am begging your pardon, captain" I began, putting on an accent, "I only just arriving and have to be shipping out in the morning. I am just wanting a smoke and maybe have a think about my girl and what to do there when I get back," I shrugged, "if I am doing wrong thing, I am sorry. I am not being paid much monies and how am I bringing my girl something nice? Ah, I am not understanding things I am thinking."

"Yeah? Well you had enough "monies" to give an old beggar coins so you can't be that hard up."

"Excuse. In the fishing village from what I come, it is always giving old seamen help that we are expected. He was probably once being like me. I'm not knowing this hard up."

"Yeah, he probably was. Stupid and likely to find himself in hot water." He still looked angry.

"No, we are sailing northways in the morning. It will be very cold water, I am thinking."

"Don't try to be funny with me, son."

"Excuse. I am not making a joke already." I was starting to sweat a little. This was not going well.

"Let's see what money you've got on yer." He pushed me, slightly. I lifted both hands, not giving him any reason to accuse me of assault. I dug in an outer pocket, this time taking out a handful of mixed coin all of it pretty poor.

"That it?" he asked.

"Is a lot of monies, no?"

"Alright put it away. Bloody foreigners" he fumed. He looked me over and I waited.

"Have tobacco. You want?"

"You trying to bribe me?" his pugnacious ire resurfaced in an instant.

"Excuse. Is meaning, this bribe?"

"Never mind" he rapped. He looked around. I hoped he wasn't considering violence if he saw nobody looking. I let one hand drop to rest on a partially hidden dagger so that I could bring it to bear swiftly. I didn't want to have to hide a guard's body as part of the night's work, but I might have to if this went much further. Meanwhile, the guard's features changed completely. The belligerent face pulled back and became amused, concentrating on my face; "Before midnight I usually drink at the Lucky Mermaid."

I was staggered. These were the code words for the first exchange. I paused for a moment, considering if he had seized the real contact.

I had been so sure it was the old seaman. It looked like I had blown a silver crown for nothing; "Isn't that the inn with the ghost of a cabin boy?" I replied, although still using the accent.

"No, it's the inn with the cellar where an emperor once hid."

I nodded, "A tale of daring."

He palmed a half scroll of parchment into my hand, and a metal token; "You'll need this to keep out of trouble, boy" he said in his guard's voice as a drunk drifted in our direction, talking to the night. I slipped both up a sleeve in a quick movement.

"Thank you for your help, captain," I said, "a stranger often is wanting some directions also." He grunted, nodded and headed off into the night. I breathed in and out, again, sucking the night air deeply even though it had the flavour of coal tar and smoked leather. I put a hand to my head. It was as well that it was dark or he could have seen how much I had been sweating.

I walked away at an even pace, heading for the spot where Jen and I had pre-arranged our next meeting. I knew she would be watching it regularly for my arrival.

Pausing beneath a pair of lanterns outside the Silversmith's Guild, I unrolled the half scroll and read the instructions "Sometime before midnight, the crew of the Caravello, Nyslinder will come ashore and head for an inn, leaving just the captain or first officer on board.

Your task is to kill this individual, leaving the enclosed token pinned to the cabin wall or other suitable place where it is clearly on show. You will search the officers' quarters, seeking a letter bearing an imperial style seal depicting a griffon passant.

Your task is to deliver this to your handler by dawn. If you are discovered and the guard is called out or you are pursued and need assistance you will lose marks. Failure to complete the assassination or retrieve the letter will lead to a failed mark."

I checked the "enclosed" and found a silk hand and twisted dagger symbol with a heavy pin. I knew that one. It meant that the target had betrayed their employer or was otherwise involved in unsanctioned corruption. Obviously, the officers were in it together, if not the whole crew. This was serving a warning.

I reached the edge of the square and made for the side street with the old statue on the corner. I saw Jen sitting on a stone bench near the central monument and inclined my head, slightly. She rose and disappeared off into an inn. I waited.

Only a few minutes passed before Jen appeared again, slipping down the side street to join me, still putting her hair into a high ponytail. The gypsy garb had gone, replaced by brown leathers. I couldn't help giving her an appraising look and she blushed.

Professionalism, I told myself and shook my head. I decided to retain my disguise. A seaman on dockside worked, after all. Jen threw on a hooded cloak. Like two shadows that were looking for their bodies, we drifted along the dock in the deepest darkness, checking the trading vessels that were tied up along the quay.

"Forgotten where your ship is?" I started at the voice. I thought we had stayed under cover on our approach. My hand fingered my long dagger. Jen stopped beside me but I put a hand on her arm to stay her weapon. A neat, little man stepped from what must have been an old filled in doorway in the dock wall so that the quay lanterns just revealed him enough to see him if you stood close. He smiled and continued, "Which is your ship, anyway?"

"The Angry Rose, over in the east docks." I used my Rosgovian accent

"A barge man, are you?"

"She's a wherry" I said in pretence of being slightly angered by the idea of a barge. The man smiled again. There was a sharp, observant intelligence behind the smiling face and I could see he was unconvinced by this charade. I wondered who he was and how he fitted into the night's work. "And your lady friend? She's no barge or wherry girl, is she?"

"I didn't ask. I was looking for a ship with no lights and an empty cabin if you know what I mean."

He gave a short laugh, "Aye, I understand. When you've been at sea for months or even years, you won't even care what they look like, friend."

It was my turn to laugh, now. I decided to take a chance "We both know none of us here are seamen nor here to take the fresh, sea air" I said. I extended a black gauntleted hand "Black Finn." He hesitated just for a moment and then took my hand in a steely grip, "Jaef". I nodded, "This is Jen." Jen twitched her hood aside and smiled, nervously. "Your job wouldn't involve the Golden Queen would it?" he asked.

"No, it wouldn't."

"That's fine, then. But do me a favour. Move along and do what you must do without arousing attention. I don't want to find my work complicated by a couple of incompetent youngsters out for a quick killing."

I frowned. "We'd like to go unobserved, too."

"I'm sure you would."

"Then we'll say goodnight and fair travels, Jaef."

"And to you, Black Finn" he nodded. I noticed, then, the matching hilts of his daggers, semi-precious stone of some type with a dark swirling pattern.

He wore a signet ring with the same stone as its centre. So, he wasn't concerned about those who knew him recognising him by his style. He was a small man, yet I sensed a danger in him that would be unwise to put to the test.

"You told him our names. I can't believe you did that." Jen rounded on me when we were out of earshot.

"He's clearly in the same line of business, maybe even in our guild. If I'm any judge, he's not only more advanced than us but would have no trouble finding out who we are and other information we might rather keep concealed anyway. Better not even to tempt him. We may meet again one day, perhaps on the same side, perhaps as enemies. It's good to know who is who."

"I still don't think you should give names out."

"They aren't our real names, remember."

"They are our working names."

I shook my head, "I'm not worried Jen."

She raised her voice and it became more shrill, "Well I am, and next time you want to tell a stranger, you stick to giving your name. I'll decide if I give mine."

"Fine" I said, and went back to concentrating on the task.

"I didn't mean--" she began. I cut her off. "Let's stick to the job. There's our target."

She fell quiet. I could feel her behind me, though whether she was sulking or sorry, I wasn't going to say any more.

I sighed, inwardly. This was not the best way if I wanted to get closer to Jen but then, such things were discouraged. Better we kept it to a business relationship, I told myself. We split and took positions, observing the caravello deck for any activity.

A cabin light burned brightly. It must be a large lantern, I guessed, possibly more than one. The deck was unoccupied and lay silent and inviting. "I'll go first" I whispered. She mumbled a response. "You keep watch" I added.

I stepped gingerly onto the gangplank which creaked. I shook my head and stepped off again. I walked along the quayside and eventually borrowed a long plank that ran over to the deck of a ketch, "Let's hope they don't come back" I said, putting this on top of the original so one braced the other. I tried the new walkway and found it more to my satisfaction.

I ran across, lightly, inspecting the deck and then going around the side of the deckhouse where the light blazed out. The lantern would make the night outside seem darker and deeper. If anyone looked out, they would have difficulty seeing through the reflection from the light within.

I waited for Jen to join me. "There's one door and although we could try a porthole window or even enter from above with a little work, either would probably alert whoever is in there. It looks like they are going to know we are here, pretty soon anyway, so we may as well use the door. Do you want to take the lead or would you like me to?"

Jen considered, before replying "I'd like to." She cocked a light one-handed crossbow, picking a short bolt with three barbs. Carefully, she fetched out a wide vial, un-stopped it and dipped the bolt into this, turning it slowly so that the viscous liquid clung to the barbs. When they were coated, she put the bolt in place with her gloved hand, returning the vial to the pouch. She nodded to me.

"If you kick the door in, I'll rush the cabin and, hopefully, put a bolt in his vitals or in the head. If you can follow up with your knives, that'll just make sure, in case I miss or he survives longer than expected."

"That sounds fine," I replied, drawing two weighted throwing daggers, "on a count of three, then -- one, two, three!" I put a boot to the outer door. It swung in, surprisingly easily and Jen slid through the gap like a cat through a crack in the dairy doorway.

There was a second open door beyond this small reception which obviously led to the officer's cabin or quarters.

The lights were showing from there. I stumbled over something as I went in and realised there was a failed trip wire.

As I came upright, I saw a shadow move behind the door that Jen was going through. "Jen!" I shouted. She started to react, twisting away from the blow that clubbed her to the ground as a burly man, who had been waiting behind the cabin door, came into view. He had a long wooden truncheon.

He saw me, "There's two of them" he shouted, rushing at me. I saw a little woman, slimmer than Jen in a purple basque top, tight fitting black trews and knee-high boots move forward. She had a rapier in one hand. Her salt and pepper hair was tied back in a ponytail by a colourful purple and silver patterned scarf.

Her hard face was lined with experience, her overly heavy use of decoration to emphasise her eyes and lips giving her that look of a woman who is refusing to admit her youth has left her. "Now you'll die, you little bitch!" she hissed and went for Jen with the rapier.

Jen screamed and huddled into a helpless ball. It wasn't what I expected of her, nor was it helpful. I made a snap choice. My first dagger hit the female captain right between the middle of her forehead and the bridge of the nose, smashing it out of shape so it gushed blood. She toppled over, backwards, the rapier thrust expended uselessly in mid-air.

Jen must have realised at that point that she was still alive and despite the buzzing head, lunged for the big man's legs, grabbing the left one desperately.

Nevertheless, it saved me from a more direct hit as I had chosen to cast instead of defending myself. The club numbed my right arm and sent me off balance. He came after me, swiping at me again, but I swapped the dagger from right to left hand and ducked aside. Jen got both his legs at the knees and he teetered.

He used the handle of the club to bang her head down onto the floor with a clunk that made me wince, but it did buy me time. I put the dagger in his chest and as he yelled out and tried to straighten, I went past him, grabbed Jen's fallen hand crossbow, steadied the bolt and turned in a single motion.

He was already swinging around, so as a result I found myself pointing it into his face almost at point blank range. I pulled the trigger and the quarrel pierced his throat. He dropped the club and clawed at it. I pulled my dagger from his chest and plunged it downwards into his right knee, which made him grunt in agony and fall to the floor, quarrel half hanging from his torn throat. He gurgled, face turning red. I used my boot to strike at his neck and he sprawled, quite dead at my feet.

I reached down and pulled Jen up. She leaned on me, her voice controlled but furious, "They knew we were coming."

"So it seems," I replied and nodded, "must have been a leak somewhere. It can't have been part of the test. They seemed to only be expecting one of us as well. My guess is that the crew may well be back at any moment."

She nodded and squeezed my hand, "I would have been killed if you hadn't gone for that sea-bitch. I owe you Finn."

"That's what we are here to do for each other" I answered, as matter-of-factly as I could. "Is that all we're together for?" she asked. I was about to answer that when the sound of distant voices reached us.

"Come on, we have to get out of here."

We entered the cabin and searched rapidly through the sea chests, turning up fifteen silver coins, two silver concubines and the letter. We shared the coins out and smashed out a porthole, cleaning the glass away altogether with a sharp-edged tool. Feet sounded quayside close by, "Damn! Too quick. Get out of the porthole Jen."

"What about you?"

"Just go and take the letter. When you get onto the quay, run. Don't look back"

She started to say something but I was boosting her up and out, "Just run. Promise me".

I arranged the captain on her chaise longue, left the big man lying where he was and pinned the silk hand above her head with her own dagger. As the outer deckhouse door opened, I dived into the captain's wardrobe and sank back amongst her heavily perfumed dresses, jackets and blouses, trying desperately not to sneeze or sniff as the overbearing scent got up my nose.

Angry voices sounded, yelling about the captain and Mal. Then someone shouted, "There goes that bastard assassin. He's running off down the quay. After him boys!" Feet rushed out again and more clattered off the deck. I left the wardrobe. One man was watching his colleagues from the deckhouse door. The rest had gone after Jen.

The pursuit sounded drunken and noisy. I took the watchman from behind and sent him over the side in a single swift movement that carried me out onto the deck. I leapt onto the adjacent boat, slipped onto the quayside and ran towards the pursuers then up a gangplank two ships along where a brig stood quiet with no one on the deck. Hearing their floundering colleague shouting for assistance, some of the crew came running back. I leaned out over the side of the brig, "Hoy there. What's up?"

"The captain's been assassinated!" shouted one man.

"What? You're kidding. Damn fine woman. Anything I can do to help?"

"They're after the assassin, right now." He pointed. I drew my falchion and came down the gangplank of the brig, "Come on then" I said. Leaving the others to haul the fallen man from the harbour, the rest of us ran after the chasing group.

We caught up with them, looking left and right along the warehouse way. "This bloke's come to help" puffed the seaman beside me, "he knew the captain." I lashed my sword in the air, "Come on, let's get the bastard. We'll split up. First one to see him, yell as loud as you can and we'll come running."

We went three ways, two groups turning left and right and one going out of the gates onto the main street. I sprinted after Jen, having seen her go left with two crewmen rapidly falling behind. She half turned and loosed a bolt not even realising who was chasing her. When I caught up to her a bit more I shouted, "Jen, it's me!"

"How the hell did you manage to join up with them?" she shouted, still running. "I'll explain later. Come on, I'll boost you over the wall at the end, there. Chuck me a rope to follow." We reached the wall. I looked back. The two pursuers were yelling and waving weapons. Others appeared in the distance. I bent, took Jen's left foot in my hands making a step and shoved upwards. She hauled herself to the top of the wall and went over, dropping a rope off so her weight would brace it as she fell. I took hold, got a gripped climbing boot in place and half ran as I scrabbled up the wall, swung over and dropped beside her.

I found Jen standing against the wall with her dagger wavering. I heard a low growl. Two huge black mastiff dogs were baring their teeth as they approached. They didn't seem pleased to see us.

"Nice doggy," I ventured. We dived off behind a standing wagon and ran like all the devils from hell were on our tails.

Cages II

There was an investigation after Jen and I had reported to Master Shadow. That was a daunting moment for us both. It was the first time we had met a master, directly. He sat behind a higher table on a dais, hooded and covered by darkness, although a candle burned beside him so he could make notes with a quill. He spoke little, asking a few pointed questions in a half whisper from beneath the deep cowl. It was like talking to a ghost.

Eventually, after what seemed like an age, he placed the quill in the long, decorative inkpot which was shaped like a lily. "Your account is more than satisfactory. You did well, last night. You have taken a first and important step on the road to becoming more than initiates." When we rose to leave, we noticed that two other figures were sitting behind Master Shadow and had been listening to our account from the outset. Later we found out that they were Masters Black and Grey.

Needless to say, nothing was discovered but we knew that someone had tried to ensure we were 'turned over' as they say on the streets.

I personally suspected "Lady Wanda", one of the new pentagon members, and one who stood to gain most from our failing. Her false name was clearly based on her real status. I guessed that she was here, as I was, to train for the benefit of a noble house where she would play the part of an ambassador's wife or ducal relative who was really there as their travelling assassin.

It didn't occur to me then that she could be the longer, political reach of another noble house trying to eliminate a rival at source or some other agent acting against the interests of the guild.

The rest of the term was spent on technique and simpler missions. I got to know the others in the pentagon. Jen was a reliable partner, as was Verity, who was better at sleight-of-hand and with locks than weapons. Wanda was a planner, although she could handle a weapon and certainly did not lack anything in athleticism. Zeth was that rare beast, an assassin-mage, giving him the advantage of supplementing or enhancing his abilities with small enchantments or glamours. As such, he was the outstanding performer amongst the five of us.

Unfortunately, Zeth had a tendency to brag, his bombastic nature coupled with inconsistency. As a result, he was as often in the bad books, but his humour and happy manner made him a decent companion.

We got along and I soon learned that he was to serve a guild master in Riassa once his training was complete. Jen was being sponsored by a rich mistress, a high priestess of one of the powerful temples to whom she had promised ten years of service.

After that, Jen would have her freedom to become a freelancer or pursue some other interest. Verity had started as an apprentice to a mage, but having proved to lack what it took to handle magic, he would now return offering a different option to his master.

He expected to grow rich and eventually intended to become independent. Wanda admitted that she was affiliated to "a great house of the Empire" but would not say more. As for me, I claimed to be the bastard of a minor lord who wanted an assassin as an option, given his forces were meagre and his servants small in number. Wanda looked down on all of us and that was fine with me.

I returned home in late Autumn. The campaign season was about done and my father had called in the armies, sending Frederick and Pellinore out with forces to reinforce key cities while Adhils watched the northern border, with Fulk patrolling to the east. My father retained a force at Falkenberg while Herlenbrand held another close by in Fort Schlader. It was good to hear that his brothers had now answered the banner call. Almost at once, my father called me in to speak with him.

"Edmund, how go your studies?"

"Well father. I have been commended this term and will move up to regular live mission training in Spring."

"Already? Then you will change pentagon, I expect."

"No, the whole pentagon is to go together. The masters seem very keen that we should stay together as we have some high performers."

"So, you have become the leader?"

"That is undecided, as yet."

"I had expected that you would be placed under an experienced man or woman so you could learn about best methods. A group of untrained recruits allowed to continue on their own develop bad habits."

I felt slightly annoyed at this. After all, what would he know about it, the son of a grand duke, who became a grand duke? I had always respected my father in politics and in war but now he was in my environment and speaking with his usual authority.

"The masters are there to provide guidance and they haven't picked me up on any "bad habits" yet", I answered, slightly acerbically.

"Well and good then," he frowned and seemed to consider for a while, letting the silence deepen. I remembered the teachings of Master Black, "Only a fool fills the silence when there is nothing for him to say."

So, I remained silent and waited, watching my father. After a moment of thought, he picked up a sealed envelope.

"I need you to undertake a mission for me."

My heartbeat increased. I stayed outwardly calm but inside I was excited at the prospect. It would be the first opportunity to show I could be the man I was being trained to be.

"Are you sure you are up to taking on something on your own?"

I weighed this up, "Tell me more about the job and I can judge if I have the skills to manage it alone or not."

He nodded, eyes on me, presumably testing if I was mentally ready. He seemed to like this answer and smiled, slightly. He held the envelope out to me. "This letter needs to reach a particular contact and none other. On receipt, the man who has to get this will ask you to perform a mission. You must then judge how you will achieve it and whether you need help. Whatever happens, the task will have to be executed under a veil of secrecy."

I nodded. "Who is the contact?"

"He is the Chief Librarian of the Imperial Palace and his name is Waldegrave De Villiers. He is usually to be found among his books but also has a chamber in the palace."

"A librarian?" I said with barely concealed disgust. My heart sank. I thought it was going to be someone important. The job would probably be taking some illicit book to a noblewoman or collecting one that had been borrowed for too long. I had hoped for something more than this. My father gave me one of his sterner looks, which meant he thought I was being stupid and had missed the point.

"This is not any librarian. This is the Imperial Librarian," he said, softly, "one of the five closest advisors to the throne and one of the select few who run the Empire. And that, needless to say, is not information to share with anyone else."

I fell silent, went to say something and then stopped myself. So, this was a secret worth knowing. It was clear that the machinery of this complex state was even more obtuse than I had imagined.

"So, it is imperative that the letter is handed directly to him and nobody else," my father continued. I inclined my head, "I understand that."

"Be careful Edmund. There will be eyes that mark your approach and watch where you go afterwards."

"I will do my best to confound them then. I have had some training in the technique during the last term."

"I'm sure that you have, but you may need to improvise more. Don't forget, there will be seasoned professionals working for the interested parties."

Once again, I became silent. His words suggested a far greater threat than merely being followed or watched. "They would assault a courier about his duty?"

"Without any compunction."

I nodded softly. "Then I will have to avoid being marked as anything other than a person of no interest."

"Everyone who enters the Imperial court is of interest, even the lowliest manservant."

"I understand, so the action that I have seemingly been sent to perform should not draw interest in me personally."

"Then you succeed in staying outside their circle for another day, yes."

"Now I see why most houses use their ambassadors to deliver messages. They, at least, cannot be targeted so carelessly."

"Indeed. It is unfortunate, however, that to send in an ambassador announces your business to the watchers, the rumourmongers and everyone else involved."

I tucked the letter into an inside hidden pocket.

"Talk to Commodore Savlin. He will ensure that you get as far as the main port of Riassa. From there, you are on your own."

***

Arriving back in Riassa felt like coming back to a place I knew well, not home but a familiar hunting ground or place of play. I disembarked dressed as a plain soldier and went to find Coyle, Rill and Tu'Lon. It was not a difficult first task. We drank and caught up on news, "Damn shame about your mother" said Tu'Lon after a while, "When we got her out of there, I was hopeful that she'd recover in time."

The others nodded in turn. Coyle added, "that Drachefauste fellow wants a real lesson before you rip his guts out. One of these days, we'll go with you and do him over a treat."

"Aye," added Rill, "and take bits of him as souvenirs."

I felt the sadness dogging me again. Since the rescue, my mother had to be fed and dressed. She hardly spoke two words in any given day. She was getting worse and looked constantly sick. I bitterly regretted the ill-judged rescue attempt by Finnmeyer and I. It had cost Finnmeyer and Janed their lives and my mother her sanity.

I sighed and sat back. Tu'Lon patted my shoulder. "Being in your position is harder than being in ours at the moment, I know, but remember you've always got your friends and we'll always be here for you when you need us. We'll be there the day you need to face Drachefauste and that's a promise."

I wish to this day he hadn't made that promise. You should always be careful what promises you make. The further out from the time when they are to be discharged, the harder it is to foresee what might prevent you from keeping them. The real problem is, as I am doing now, those who receive a promise do not tend to forget it.

***

To enter the imperial court, I decided upon an unusual course of action. I would pose as a lawyer's clerk trying to serve a writ on someone for debt owed or another common complaint towards the classes who walked those halls.

It might attract some ribald comment but probably no interest. I worked my hair well with dye until it was blond, shaved my beard off, put my hair into a pigtail and added some bogus fair-gold fluff to my chin to cultivate the illusion of early youth.

A simple scroll of parchment with a wax blob in the right place and I had my writ to add to the authenticity of the role. I worked on the still warm wax to create the impression of a seal in the style of a guild coat of arms. My costume was obtained from a proper outfitter. "My usual day dress is so shabby," I complained, "my master does not cover my expenses and I can't go into the imperial court in such clothes. I wish to make my way."

The clothier nodded and made the right sympathetic noises whilst fitting me for a hired clerk at law's outfit and overcharging me for the job when he was done. I had to return it the next day or lose my deposit, as well. I tipped assiduously and with an air of finding this awkward, but presumably something I had been instructed to do. I then set off for my chambers to put the whole thing together.

I had chosen my target with some care. Count Maurice De Gaulvais was a known womaniser, libertine and extravagant dresser. He was a man who had many reasons for clerks at law to be serving him with writs, an occurrence so commonplace that he probably wouldn't recall the incidents for which he was being sued.

Since he always ignored them anyway, unless his patron twisted his arm pretty hard, it was a good bet that the latest complaint against him would attract little interest. I also knew that, although he was officially at court, he had left on the previous evening to follow up an invite to stay up country at the home of the Duc de Lanois while the duke was away but his lovely wife was not. I knew he had received the invitation because I had written it myself on scented paper and slipped it into his carriage while he was conferring with some young nobleman outside the Seven Dragons in West Square.

I had seen the count's carriage rattle by on the road to Calendrez about two hours later.

Making my way to the court, I chose the route from the inns of court and walked hurriedly with an air of assured authority which might accompany a young man who was trying to make an impression on a job where he felt he had the right.

At the outer doors of the Grand Reception, I paused while the guards checked my general papers, most carefully forged from some authentic, stolen ones, since returned to their owner. When I mentioned what I had come for, I saw them exchange knowing grins. I had guessed, rightly, that it was not uncommon for the court to receive visiting complainants against the man.

"You can enter the hallway and take the left staircase to the Hall of Appellants. You should be able to find whichever clerk is covering the count's business, today."

"But I have to hand him the writ, directly" I said, seemingly flustered and more than worried by this.

"Nobody ever hands a nobleman anything like that, lad. Your master will know that. You give it to the clerk who has the count on his day list and then you leave. If you are offered tea, water or juice, you may stay and drink. If you are very lucky you may get to have a conversation with somebody who will remember you. Don't go anywhere else, don't try any doors unless directed to them, avoid staring at the ladies of court or speaking to anyone above your station. Best speak only if spoken to, in fact."

"But how do I find out who is the count's clerk?"

"You wait for someone to notice you and ask your business, of course."

I looked more flustered, mopped my brow twice and fiddled with my pigtail. Inwardly I chuckled at my own performance.

"Well get on with it." one of the guards said, and held the door open.

I stepped inside and looked around. Footsteps rang on marble floors, people bustled and conversations drifted from all directions and levels as the business of court life unfolded.

The babbling cloud of voices was occasionally pierced by one distinctive or raised voice. I scanned the options open to me while proceeding generally towards the hall that I ought to be seeking.

There were a multiplicity of doors and other exits offered through archways or up flights of stairs from the great vaulted hall that was referred to as The Grand Reception. Ahead, at the far end, were four grand staircases, one turning right and one left, while two went straight up onto a landing that carried on into the distance past statuary that would have looked equally at home in a square or plaza.

The staircase that I should take opened onto a balcony where more doors were available, as well as another stairway to a higher level. Beneath the staircases, two archways right and left and a pair of double doors offered alternatives that added to the bewildering number of choices and, from my point of view, to the potential danger if I chose badly. I decided that there would be no way to check every possible direction if you were escaping or entering out of hours and trying to avoid discovery.

I knew that the library was not joined directly to The Hall of Appellants but that it was to the left, in the west wing of the palace. I decided with so many watching eyes and bustling people, I would at least start by taking the correct exit from this place. I turned left and apologising to those that I had to dodge or make way for, headed up the shallow stairway to the double doors opposite where they reached the balcony. These stood open, revealing a long hallway filled with groups of conversing people in various manners of dress, the most common of which were similar to my own. It was even noisier than the reception hall.

I started to shuffle and push my way across the hall.

As I supposed, since nobody knew my business and my costume marked me out as a lowly legal clerk, I didn't even attract passing interest from anyone other than to complain that I was obstructing them. There were two staircases at the far end of this hall, one turning right and one left, with two doors between them at this level. All of them were guarded. I needed to go up another floor to proceed more easily according to my original plan.

I noticed that occasionally, a group of gowned men would go up the stairs, continuing loud conversations on the balcony as they headed off somewhere else. When this happened, there were usually a group of younger men trailing in their wake with papers and books, presumably the clerks of these grandees.

The guards did not stop these groups so it seemed that they were not only known, but their presence served as a pass for those who were with them. That decided my next course of action. I gravitated to the edge of a group with two such gentlemen and waited, nodding occasionally as if I was paying attention to instructions. Sure enough, after some minutes of legal argument and negotiation, they headed for the stairs, apparently to find a room where they could sit down and beat out the detail of an agreement. I got amongst their clerks and paid close attention to my papers as we reached the guards.

The guards barely glanced in my direction as we went by, a party of at least seven following the two in their gowns and soft hats.

We exited into a long gallery down which the leaders swept while the rest of us were drawn in their wake. I stayed on at the end of the group. On we went through another set of double doors into a wide corridor. I stayed with them until they finally threw open a pair of doors and turned right. I broke away at the last moment to continue on down the corridor. I was alone, now, with a fake scroll in one hand and little else to use as an excuse for being in this area of the palace.

Nevertheless, I went on with a confident air as if on some business and, passing a couple of men coming the other way, was greeted with affable nods to which I bowed my head and doffed my cap.

It was as if my mere presence on this floor elevated me to a more significant level than my garb suggested. I came to a T-junction, took a left, slid along a new corridor that I had entered as quickly as I could and looked around the corner of the next junction. This emerged onto a balcony along a large gallery. There was another opposite.

If I had remembered the map well enough, this was a grand hall of portraits which meant that the upper library lay off the opposite balcony, with the main doors below off the hall itself.

The issue for me, now, was that to reach the opposite balcony would mean descending to the hall and this had a number of guards on various doors.

Making my way along the balcony, I leaned out and could see the library doors, beautifully carved with bas-relief wooden motifs above and the scrolled working with old imperial lettering proclaiming a motto that unfurled along the top of the doors, "To learn is to live in this world but to understand those which have gone before." The doors were guarded by armoured men.

I scanned the balcony. There was no other way to the library other than the staircase down to the hall below. I tried to think what would happen if I went back, and if there was a bridging corridor elsewhere.

I knew that it was possible to access the far side via another higher floor, but that was where many nobles and dignitaries had their quarters. Such private rooms would be guarded and the corridors patrolled. There would be no excuse for being up there. I had to solve the issue by staying on one of the first three floors and find a way to work my way past the guards. I sighed, inwardly. It seemed less than likely that I could proceed any further. Performing some feat of acrobatics to cross the divide would not only be seen but was bound to bring guards in their droves upon me.

There was a polite cough at my right elbow. I started. I am normally so careful to stay aware but my long, pondering indecision had taken me away so that I hadn't noticed the soft footfall of an approaching stranger.

I found myself looking at a very senior looking man in a powdered wig, dark blue jacket finely brocaded in gold thread and wearing a deep gold sash with matching ribbon about his neck on which hung a key and something that looked like a medal or amulet.

His heavy face with its hanging jowls was creased with lines of experience. His eyes crinkled with humour deep beneath the impressive jutting brow;

"Contemplating, young fellow?" he asked, although it was more of a statement than a question. "Not an easy prospect to get to where you are going with so many checkpoints and so many small-minded and obstinate sentries, is it?"

I was slightly taken aback. He was so calm and matter-of-fact. I could have been a desperate assassin or anarchist, armed to the teeth for all he knew, whereas he was an old, overweight and, as far as I could see, unarmed man. I gulped slightly and nodded.

"So, is it the library that you wished to get to or one of the chambers off the long gallery?" I doubt it was the kitchens, guardroom or armoury."

"The library." I blurted. It was very hard to conceal it from this man and I felt he would know if I lied.

He nodded, softly. "Difficult to represent your master's business isn't it? I remember it all too well. You'd better follow me."

And so saying, he set off for the stairs. I followed in something of a daze. He descended at an even pace with me just following on his coattails.

He breezed past the guards at the foot of the stairs, crossed the hall to the library doors where two guards straightened at his approach. He pushed them open in an expansive gesture.

"Welcome to the Imperial Library" he smiled over his shoulder, continuing on his course and, when I was through, closed the doors behind us.

I looked around in awe at the vast, vaulted hall. It had two balconies high above, running around the whole of the roughly lozenge shaped hall and towering bookcases in walls, forming deep, shadowy canyons, informal avenues, open-sided stadiums and squares surrounded by high buildings with just alleyways between, all consisting of stones of many colours upon which were elegant traceries in gold, black and other shades, some angled, some scrolled.

My companion waved a pudgy hand on which he wore two expensive looking rings. "Over a hundred thousand books and manuscripts reside here and no man has ever read or even viewed every one."

He looked about, "not even my friend, our inestimable librarian."

And so saying, he gave a slight bow, with a humorous smile towards another man dressed similarly but by contrast, leaner, taller and less showy. He was wearing a pair of golden pince-nez on his rudder-like nose and a longer wig than my companion that seemed to have lost one or two of its curls, with the result that some locks hung rather limply below his shoulder and down his back.

"I have a young man here who I believe may be seeking enlightenment in your domain." His voice was even more laced with humour.

He turned to me. "I shall leave you with our excellent chief librarian. Remember me to your father, my young friend."

I bowed, flushing slightly as I did not have any idea to whom I should refer.

"Thank you, Lord Treasurer," the librarian's voice was quite thin and reedy, especially beside the hale, gourmandic tones of my companion. I tried not to gape.

The Lord Treasurer gave me a slight bow and sailed out of the library much as he had entered it, nodding to the guards as he went.

"He has an excellent eye for faces which, sadly, I do not share. You will have to tell me who he is, your father." The Librarian turned his full attention to me.

I was really taken aback by this. How did they know I wasn't a threat? If they were truly men of power, why did they not have their own shield guards and followers at their heels. I took a grip on myself and bowed deeply with a flourish.

"Edmund Von Tacchim, son of Grand Duke Vasely." I intoned, in the formal manner.

"Ah yes," he clapped one hand on the book he was grasping, "of course. I should have seen it at once. A Von Tacchim. Now you say it, it is obvious even to me although out of an unusual line. The darker skin, Father's eyes but not overall build or face. I assume your hair colour is not really blond?"

"Black." I inclined my head.

"Black and fine, the curls from your father but not the texture. Your mother must be…I know, of course, the Duke's chief concubine. Ah, such a woman. How is your beautiful mother?"

My face dropped and I hung my head, slightly. When I looked up, I noted a tinge of sadness in his eyes, perhaps at seeing the effect of his question or because he suspected the answer.

"She is unwell, my lord."

"Such a pity." He sighed and the sound of it suggested the weight of great burdens which he had to bear.

"Remember me to her" he said, softly and turned away.

He adjusted his pince-nez and peered at me more closely, leaning forward a little like a heron that is considering whether it will lunge for a particular fish or not.

"A Von Tacchim, eh? And with no appointment?"

"No my lord. I thought it best not to make one and thus announce that we had business."

"Like your father, cautious," he remarked, "so what is your business here, today, young man?"

"I am seeking Lord Waldegrave De Villiers. Am I right in assuming that I have found him?"

"You have."

"Then I have something for you" I said and handed him the envelope with my father's seal upon it.

He took it with a slightest of bows, produced a small letter knife from one of his many pockets and opened it with elaborate care. Adjusting his pince nez, once again, he studied the contents, accompanying his reading with a number of humming noises. At length, he looked over the letter at me and once more, the pince nez shifted on his long nose so that he could see my expression more clearly.

"Know what's in here, do you?"

"I do not, my lord, no."

"Yet your father makes promises on your behalf. Does that worry you?"

"Should it, my lord?"

"With some fathers I would say it should but with yours, I am certain he maintains his almost legendary care and gives a balanced assessment."

I waited, hands behind my back in a stance I had been taught was appropriate when awaiting further instruction.

"I'm sorry. I cannot help your father in this. You must tell him that the Emperor warned him not to let it turn to war. It is out of our hands, now."

I tried to remain as bland-faced as I could in the face of such high matters of state.

"I'm sorry" he muttered, "I wish there was some way but the issue was decided many weeks ago. You may tell him that he will receive recompense for what he must give up, but we are in desperate times with enemies at the door to the north, south, east and if rumour proves true, the west as well.

In such times, extraordinary warlords are in need. He had an easy choice to make but allowed his feelings to override his judgement. It is done." The last words were spoken with a finality that left me in no doubt. He folded the letter, carefully and then tore it into strips which he put into the fire, poking the coals and wood with a poker to ensure that no evidence was left un-charred.

"You have nothing for me to do?" I asked, softly.

"Only to return to your father with my message. I will not commit it to writing. We have debated, agonised, argued but in the end, agreed that our original judgement was correct. There is nothing more to be said on the subject not even if your father, himself, came to petition. Please make that very clear to him. It is over."

Burdens II

I knew my father would be disappointed with the response from the Imperial Court. Had I understood the consequences of that decision and if I had understood the game that was being played out, I would have stayed in Riassa. Had I known anything, I would have taken action to shift the pieces on the board, somehow, but I did not.

When I returned to give him the librarian's message, my father listened to my account almost in silence, asking only a couple of questions about those I had seen and how the court appeared. When I told him how final the words had been and how he had said that the Emperor's mind was made up, my father grew strangely still, clearly lost in thought.

After pondering for some time, while I stood and waited, he seemed to come to a decision and rose from his chair. "There are things that I have put off which I have been considering for a long time." He spoke softly, "It will mean changes." He looked up at me and his eyes seemed to be close to tears.

"You are a good and worthy son, Edmund. In many ways, you might have made a better duke in these troubled times than any of your brothers."

I felt a slight chill go through me. I wondered what he was going to ask me to do. Was this when I would be asked to sacrifice myself for the family, perhaps?

"Will you fetch your brothers, please?"

I stood for a moment or two before the request sank in. When I left the room, I realised my legs were unsteady.

I had to wake Viktor. Frederick was on the West Tower, looking far away. After I had explained the request, we went down the long winding stair together. We found Leopold playing cards with some of his friends amongst the younger knights.

When we were all assembled, my father took a box from his drawer. It was of fine, carved wood with gold corner brackets, gold keyhole and edging. Taking a key from beneath his black silk tunic, he unlocked it and took out a scroll, three signet rings, a seal and finally a brooch with a deep purple gemstone set in a gold mount with eagle wings that extended upwards from the main brooch in two finely worked leaves of gold.

He looked along the line of items with a grave expression.

"My sons," he opened his arms wide and made a motion of embracing us all. For a second time that evening, a chill passed through me. "I must leave our lands and travel abroad. There are many people that I must see and even more conversations that I must have. I cannot be the duke when I must go quietly, often unseen between courts and castles, camps and temples. I am sorry that such burdens must fall upon you all while you are all still so young, but there is now no other way."

He handed the scroll, the seal and the first signet ring to Frederick. "Tomorrow, I will announce that I am stepping down because of illness. I will declare you as Duke and head of the family, Frederick. Here are the ducal ring and seal with the Orders of The Constitution which you should affirm in a short ceremony, before dusk on the morrow. Then, I will leave. I hope to see you again in this life but nothing is ever that certain."

He gave the second ring to Leopold. "This ring shows that you speak with the power of a duke, also, for it is the old ducal ring of Govia Minor and proves that you are the successor to your brother, should fate overtake him. Bear this with gravity, Leopold. Your brothers, your family and your status will need you to grow up faster. Never must the two of you occupy the same field of battle again, nor the same castle outpost, no, not even the same city while we are so embroiled in a state of war.

Today, I have heard what I have feared for some time. We are alone in this and nobody will stop what has been set in motion, lest it is one of us or Drachefauste who fall. There was never meant to be a war between us and Drachefauste but although he has precipitated this, the Empire intends to back him and not us. If we are to win, it will be standing alone and outnumbered."

He handed the third ring to Viktor. "This ring will identify you as being neutral in war and admit you to any temple. I want you to go at once to Saxburg to see the Cardinal, there. The Boharts have no love for the Empire. They will shelter you."

Viktor stirred. "But I don't want to go. I want to fight, too" Frederick put a hand on his shoulder. "We all know you're as brave as any of us, Viktor," he said, warmly. Viktor looked up and smiled, grasping Frederick's arm and squeezing it.

"And you will do as you are told," my father responded, "I will not be the duke who presided over the end of his line and that is always one possible outcome. If the rest of us fail, it falls to you to re-establish and continue the name of this house.

"Besides," added Frederick, softly, "if father had not already ordered it, sending you to safety would have been my first act as duke-elect."

My father inclined his head in approval and we fell quiet again. He handed the brooch to me. "As for you Edmund, you will return to Car Duris and complete your training. Your brothers will have need of your talents. This brooch announces you as an ambassador of our house. It will open many doors that you could not pass, otherwise. Use it with care. Thereafter, I expect you to serve your duke with distinction and to do his bidding in all matters."

Frederick and I exchanged glances and I smiled, "Of course father." I inclined my head.

***

So was the die cast. The announcement caused some shock and not a little rumour and consternation but within a few days, Frederick was putting together his army to face Drachefauste across the Zeiger river, once more. Being used to seeing him in this role, everyone treated him as duke quickly enough. Leopold was surly and kept asking why father could not tell us where he would be going and what it was that he intended. I rode out with Viktor, travelling with him as far as Jordis before we parted.

"Remember," I said, pressing a black silk rose into his hand, "if you need me, send this and I will come."

He wept when we parted. I don't think he had ever been so far from home, and now, but for a couple of servants and a single shield-guard, he was alone.

I knew how he felt. I remembered how it was to turn away from everyone you had known and go on by yourself to some far-off place. It no longer bothered me. In fact, if anything, I felt a strange air of confidence surrounded me when I walked alone. I waved as he turned to look back one last time.

I decided to go to Jordis to send letters to Gwythaor and find out what news had come in and out of the port, recently.

Using one of my father's contacts, I was able to get an introduction to someone from the Thieves Guild there.

I paid him to let me know of any interesting people who had come in or out over the last week. I heard that Kharr had been through although he had gone on again.

I was delighted to also hear that Marcabru was in town again. Listening for his mandolin around the inns, I soon found him and we sat down to catch up on news.

It turned out that he was with a group who intended to take a look at the ancient halls and palaces of Caramoss, beneath the mountains. It was rumoured that the gateway was just outside Car Duris, so we would be travelling the same road. Legend said that an ancient race built a great complex under the mountains. Caramoss was their fortress and chief palace. If rumour was true, although beasts and other creatures unknown to most lurked there, so also were fabulous treasures to be found.

I was introduced to the group he travelled with. The first was a small, dapper man, who favoured grey. He wore two duelling blades and several daggers about his body. His name was Sihlus.

The second was a slim young woman with not dissimilar skin shades and black hair to Kharr. She was wearing purple robes gathered up to give her freedom to move. She had a belt of daggers and a short bow but carried a slim staff with a blade on the end and one edge. She was called Zira.

The third was an elderly man, Philomus, a tall, slim individual with grey, long hair, heavy hooked nose and long fingered hands. He wore several rings which looked expensive. His robes were mid-blue and he had a long dark blue cloak over these. Clutched in one hand he had a staff of blackened iron with a small crucible at one end, the heel being shod in silver and with a curved spike. On his belt were a number of pouches, waterskins and a single long dagger, but most interesting, a set of odd-looking keys of crystal.

The final member of the group wore weather worn clothing, old leather armour and a lot of worn knives and weapons, but was clearly experienced and had an easy engaging manner. Slim, with dark hair and neat moustache, he went by the name of Gustav.

The five of us had a pleasant journey to Car Duris, where we were parted with an open invitation for me to join them on their expeditions at any time. I suspected that they had guessed more about my background and purposes by the time we arrived.

Despite the good company, when I remembered the events of the last few days, I once more felt the burden that accompanied the sinking feeling, within. If I ever understood the expression "with a heavy heart", it was now.

***

Letters were waiting for me at the guild in Car Duis. There was an update on progress in the war from Frederick. There had been two indecisive battles before Nordia's army was shattered and we had to withdraw into Rosgovia. Vome had been killed, which saddened me. I had never got to know him well, but I knew he had been a loyal member of the house entrusted with many missions over the years.

The second letter was from Viktor. He was making good progress and was going to transfer to a fighting order based in West Saxonia. He had got to know one of the younger Boharts well but talked a lot about the leader of his fighting group, a man called Hornric. I was glad that he had settled in and seemed, also, to have found someone to look to as a leader who might guide him.

The next letter was from my sister, Diana. She was going to be married to Robert of Convar. Her letter sounded excited and happy. I knew Robert by reputation. About five or more years her senior, he had a reputation as a clever soldier and politician. It was a good match and the Convar family were allies. Robert was a cousin to Gwayne, so I hoped we would all end up at the wedding together.

Finally, there was a letter from Leopold. I expect he had been told to write as well, whether he wanted to or not.

His notes were about general procedures and comings and goings at the ducal court but I enjoyed hearing about those things, too and smiled when he mentioned that Nan Weiskuchen had been given a special 80th birthday celebration where all the family who were there made much of her. I imagined that must have made her very happy even if she would have said "Away with the lot of you. You're all as soft as puddings" and some of her other choice phrases.

Arriving on the tail of these small moments of joy was news I had been dreading. A formal letter signed by Leopold but that read as if it had been written for him, informed me of the death of my mother by her own hand. It was not unexpected but still felt like a dagger to my heart.

I put the letters carefully into a small pack and hid it in my room. I didn't want anyone reading those and finding out more about me than I wanted them to know.

I threw myself back into my training, glad for the distraction. Our new group was put through its paces in small exercises. My hand-to-hand fighting, unarmed fighting and armed combat improved markedly. I got better at throwing knives and my crossbow work sharpened up. Most of all, I began to really work on moving silently, hiding and climbing. The range of skills we had to practice over and over again was turning us into dangerous individuals and potentially, a deadly team.

Shadows III

It seemed strange to be back at the guild, so far removed from the war. I understood my father's view because my future effectiveness would be heavily influenced by what I was learning. At the same time, I felt I was being sent from my brother's side when he most needed a lieutenant that he could rely upon. Of course, there were my father's brothers and we had plenty of other good captains and leaders who could fight the war, but I felt that I had something extra to offer. My map still showed that we were losing ground, but slower. Frederick and Fulk had won a battle at Hertzfeldt, denying the river crossing and Adhils had retaken Urlenzag. Drachefauste would be forced to attempt another crossing of the Zeiger soon and that engagement would likely take place in the open field.

I had explored much of Car Duris by now. It wasn't a vast city like Riassa or even as large as Acondium, but it held a significant position.

The city was built on a huge plateau of black basalt rock, surrounded on three sides by a moat of lava. The constantly flowing lava from a volcano to the northwest had been harnessed long ago and forced along a great channel that provided the city with a unique defence. One bridge only spanned the smoking red-hot river to the east and west, with two bridges to the south, the Gate Bridge and the Fortress Bridge.

The Fortress Bridge lay nearly at the south-western corner of the plateau and led to the gates of a fortress of the same black stone as that which the city stood upon.

This was held by the Guild Mercantile whose mercenary forces were the only real force in the city. The Gate Bridge was more centrally placed, crossing to a wide plaza before the huge gates of the city. All of Car Duris lay within a curtain wall carved from the basalt along which parapets and towers were placed, some owned and run by particular guilds.

The city was governed by a Burghemeister, the most senior guildsman who lived along with the other members of the council, at the Exchequer Palace. That building had once been home to the family who originally held Car Duris. Now, it was one of the few free cities of the Empire, owing no allegiance but to the Pearl Throne and, so most said, then only second to its many Guilds.

The city was a maze of streets and squares, plazas and alleys. It had grown up in an unplanned way through the ages. The most important and richest quarters were involved with trade and money. The key guild houses could be found in those places. The most impoverished were little more than a collection of shacks and hovels, leaning together in chaotic groups.

This was going to be a critical term for me. I had been integrated into a pentagon in the second term but now, another term on, one of us would have to lead it. It was clear that Jen wasn't the one so that left Lady Wanda or me.

Wanda was at least ten years my senior and though that gave her more experience, it was holding her back on the practical side as she was neither as physically fit as the other members of the group nor as keen to throw herself into the more demanding trials.

She was playing for leader and majoring on the skills a more accomplished diplomat and court operator would use over talents suited for insurgency missions.

So, it was we found ourselves on the roofs above Pelongra Plaza with Wanda responsible for delivering on the mission objectives. This was her chance to shine and we had been briefed that we would all be under observation and each member was expected to completely back the team leader and to do their best to deliver. Any attempt to undermine or sabotage the mission would end in summary dismissal from the guild. My role as deputy was to offer alternatives or challenge plans that I felt were ill-thought out. Ultimately though, as with the rest of the team, I must follow the final decision of the leader.

We waited now while Zeth and Verity climbed from the back alley. I was already forward, running observation on the potential routes across the plaza into the private gardens of the Exchequer Palace. Wanda was eyeing us all in a cool, appraising manner, as if she wasn't sure of any of us.

I slipped back across the roof and reported.

"There are rotating guards on the main gate so that it is never out of view and I am pretty sure there are two more in sentry boxes just beyond, so going over the gate or wall at the front is out.

The route around to the town hall and then via back alley onto the wall would expose us as soon as we were going along the top of the wall, regardless of how low we stayed. That leaves two ways in. One is to go back down, get into the sewer and thread our way across and come up once we are under the palace grounds. The other is to go across the south end of the plaza and then get into the public gardens, crossing the east wall into the palace grounds. We would still have to risk exposure when we went onto the top of the wall but that would be a brief moment before each dropped into the grounds on the other side."

Wanda considered and I continued, "I recommend the sewers. Less appealing but we have time and it would offer the best cover."

Wanda pulled a face. "I was going to go via the alley along the side of the town hall. It offers plenty of shadow and is the quickest route, besides which, we don't have to be seen in the plaza at all which reduces the chance of being reported after the event."

"That's true," I conceded, "but the risk is still high. It means being on the wall either individually or in a line for several seconds longer and in full view of the guards if they look that way."

Wanda made a tut sound and looked at the others. Jen fiddled with something on her belt and then looked up. "I'd go with the sewers."

Wanda gave another tut as if to say that was expected. Zeth shrugged. "It's your call Wanda."

Verity inclined his head. "Happy whichever way you want to do it. I quite like using the public gardens. The gates will be closed so there should be nobody there. We don't even know if the sewers will provide a route so we'd be guessing."

Wanda stood up and leaned against the small tower. "I don't fancy the sewers for exactly that reason. I like the town hall route as it gets us in behind the guards but fine, the public gardens is a good compromise."

I nodded softly. "It is your call, of course. We need to get up and over the wall quickly, then. Jen is the quickest. If she takes the line over and secures it, the rest of us can get up and swing over the top without having to pause on the wall in view. What do you think?"

Wanda pondered, again. "I think it would be better if you go first. If there are any guards or anyone out of view on the other side, you're the best at neutralising them silently."

Jen scowled but said nothing.

"As you wish," I said, "although Jen is just as good if not better."

Jen glanced at me and the scowl became a slight smile. "No, you first." Wanda was firm. "Jen brings up the rear and recovers the line. Once over, we split into two groups. Finn, you take Verity and get up onto the garden balcony where you set up cover for us if we need it on the way out. I will take Zeth and Jen and go in as planned via the window above the balcony, into the long gallery and from there. The way should be clear to use the east corridor to access the state room and the prize."

I went to disagree again but decided better of it. I was a logical choice to cover but Verity was the best on locks.

"Let's get to it." Zeth hissed, "I'm getting cold waiting around while you two debate plans."

"That's why they are the chosen leaders." Jen grinned.

"Yeah, well I can just go with it, do you know what I mean?"

"Not really, no." Jen's retort was heavy with sarcasm, "lack of a plan--" she began.

"--Yeah, yeah, I know. I've heard Master Shadow say it often enough, thanks." Zeth made a face.

"Are you two done?" Wanda snapped. "Let's move before we grow old up here."

"That's what I was saying," Zeth grinned and set off.

We went down the side of the building and one by one, crossed the end of the plaza in the moonlight. If anyone noted our passing, they didn't show any interest. Two to three minutes later, we were hidden in the deep shadows cast by the east wall of the public gardens. The line went up and over and I followed it, rapidly. I dropped softly over the wall, looked about and, choosing a bush for cover, tugging three times on the line. The others followed.

That was the easy part. Five shadows drifted across the public gardens, using trees and bushes to cover their approach to the east wall of the palace gardens. We paused and then I went up the wall to look over.

There was plenty of cover. I spun the line sinker over the wall and listened for the soft thud as it hit the grass. Securing it, I climbed, swinging up and over the wall in a fluid motion, presenting no real profile to distant eyes, a momentary darkness perhaps and then, if they blinked and looked again, nothing. I was hidden behind a mature shrub inside the palace grounds. Now I looked about with care. Guards were evident in the sentry boxes but they did not seem alert, probably half asleep in the soft glow of small braziers. I waited, listening. I couldn't hear a patrol mounted or on foot. I gave three quick tugs. Verity joined me. "Anything?" he whispered.

"No. Not a sign. You signal them over while I watch. If I tap your shoulder, signal to stop."

He nodded, so I crept forward. It was too easy. I knew there were patrols in the grounds. I'd studied the place in the expectation it would be an assignment at some stage. There ought to be two teams with a dog. I spotted one, coming around the corner in a leisurely manner. They would pass about thirty to forty feet from the garden wall. They stopped, stood and talked. There was a flare of light and the smell of tobacco. They continued on. The dog started to pull a little but they forced it to turn and go left through a gate into the main grounds. The garden was safe, again. The others joined us one by one.

"There are two teams of two guards with a dog that each patrol the inner walls." I said. "One pair just entered the garden through the north gate and then left through that gate," I pointed, into the main grounds. "They may return through the lower gate but we'll be behind them, then. The other team come around in the opposite direction. Be careful. The dogs will see you, hear you or smell you long before the guards spot you."

"Are you done giving briefings?" Zeth asked.

Wanda looked irritated. "I decide if we need to pause and talk about guards, Finn, but thanks anyway. Noted. Now let's get on with it, shall we?"

We moved off. The team split in two. I concentrated on the objective that I had been given. Leading off, I went from the gate into the main grounds, heading for a large tree with a trunk that could hide more than one person. I scanned the grounds and signalled. Verity slipped across the gap and crouched beside me.

"There's no cover after those bushes on the edge of the formal garden," he said, pointing, "how does she intend us to get up a balcony right at the front of the house without any cover?"

I grinned, "Sometimes, cover isn't as obvious as it looks. Wanda wants this to go well. She isn't trying to make it difficult. Her team have to come out that way even if they approach from the dining hall side. Come on, the guard and dog have just gone behind the west wing."

We ran for the shrubs along the upper wall of a sunken formal garden and dived into cover. I took a knife and sliced the bark of a zubia. "Rub this on your leggings and tunic. It gives off a strong sap smell that will mask our odour from the dogs."

Verity did as he was told. "Where did you pick that up? I don't recall it in any of the lessons on using salves and oils."

"Back home," I said, "from a good friend." I paused. Finnmeyer had shown me that years ago when I was a boy and we were playing hide and seek with the others. Leopold had brought a beagle pup out with him when it was his turn to catch us. Clever, but cheating. Finnmeyer, who was pretending to watch casually, had seen me go behind a water butt and slipped over with a cut piece of bark he had apparently been whittling. I never forgot. I had used the sap of that bush a few times over the years.

"Now," I said softly, "see that low stone wall on the other side between the house and the formal garden? You go for that and lie down behind it. Nobody can see you from any angle unless they were on the narrow path with you. The guards and dogs can look across the grounds from as close as in the garden itself and you'd be invisible. Similarly, anyone looking out of even the ground floor window would simply look right over you. You go first. I'll cover you."

Verity met my eyes and nodded. He ran, jumped softly and disappeared. The guards came around the east side of the house and walked right along the edge of the formal garden, talking. I stayed put in the middle of the bush, happily safe in the heavy scent of zubia. I saw Jen pause and grow still. She was in the open but close to a bush. She crouched and then was flat using the contours of the lawns. The guards went on by. I breathed again.

I went lightly across the formal garden and joined Verity. I then rose, gave Jen a thumbs up as she made it to the shadows of the east buttress.

The curtains were drawn across the windows of the out-curved hall. I looked up at the balcony. It was quiet. There were no doors or windows open to it or overlooking it, that I could see. I hefted the hooked line up and dragged on it until I felt it impact and dig in. Hopefully, it had bitten into the brick of the lower balcony wall.

I looked around one more time and then I was a spider going up the vertical wall, until I slid across the stone balcony rail and dropped backwards onto the balcony so I was looking out towards the grounds. I rose, slowly and took a long look. From here, I had a view of the whole grounds. Nearly a full one hundred and eighty degrees from the front of the house were in my view, bar where the curving jut of this hall and the two towers obscured patches from me.

I couldn't see Wanda's team. I assumed they were hidden in one of those blind spots. It's where I would have been if I were her. I waited until one pair of guards went around the west end of the house and the others headed, with their backs to it, towards the far gates and sentry boxes. I tossed a handful of small stones towards the east tower. I saw a face pop out and look. I signalled. Thumbs up from Jen. The three began their ascent to the upper balcony from the east edge of the hall. I watched as they clung to the palace walls, urging them, silently, to hurry. They had time, but Zeth was slow and held the other two back. Eventually, they made it. I relaxed and spent a few minutes on my bow, readying for action if needed. Verity suddenly crouched out of sight, back to the balcony. He was trembling.

"I don't like this, Finn. This is a really stupid idea. I think we were supposed to decline. I know there is one mission in each term that you are supposed to identify as suicidal. We'll never get out again. Look towards the west gate."

I looked around. There was a detachment of soldiers heading for the house. They didn't hurry so I wasn't worried that they knew we were there. It was bad luck, though. I couldn't signal Wanda if all three of them had gone in and I couldn't risk climbing up to find out. "Verity" I hissed. He stayed where he was, "We have to stop them piling out and over the parapet into full view."

"How?"

"You watch the grounds. I'll watch the balcony and if I see any of them, I'll loose a shot up towards them. Hopefully, they'll duck and take cover then stop long enough to see the danger."

There was a hiss from above as Zeth came skidding out clearly, not under any kind of control. I tried to catch his eye but he was too busy talking back to the others who must be behind him. I loosed a bolt over his head. Then, he looked down and I waved frantically for him to get down. He half ducked and then got up again to give me a quizzical look. I pointed outwards. He shrugged and said something to someone behind him. A line came over and the next thing, Zeth was sliding down to our balcony with a statuette in one hand and a stupid grin on his face.

"Get down you idiot," I whispered as loudly as I could.

"It's alright, it was easy, look." He waved the statuette and dropped onto our balcony. I shoved him to his knees with some force. "We've got company." I said, holding him by a pinch grip to the shoulder until he started to show some sign of pain.

"Can't you follow a simple signal?" Wanda peered over. "Didn't you see that company of soldiers?"

I sighed, "Why do you think I had to use a bolt to get Zeth to pay attention and wave at him."

"I didn't understand what you meant"

Verity cut in "What? This doesn't mean get down and a bolt doesn't either? You could have got us all killed."

"Ok, clear to come down." I hissed.

Wanda and Jen sailed down the line and we tried to shake it free. The line stayed put. "Leave it," Wanda snapped, "nobody should spot that in the dark."

"That was much too close for comfort" I commented. "What in the gods were you doing, Zeth? You came out onto the balcony like you were being chased. You can't have known if it was safe even without the unexpected troop arrival."

"I suppose he expected to get a straightforward signal from you." Wanda replied, acerbically.

"He got one," I came back hotly, "or didn't you notice? Next time one of the group puts us all in danger, maybe the bolt will be aimed at them not over them."

"Shall we move on?" Enquired Jen, with sarcastic sweetness.

"Yes, I think we should." Wanda moved and looked over the balcony edge. "When the patrol has gone by. The far pair are heading away from us so there must be another close by, if they haven't stopped their patrol because of the arrival of the troops."

We waited in silence as seconds became minutes. Verity started to fret, shifting uncomfortably. "What's keeping them?" He asked to nobody in particular. "We can't stay up here all night." He added a moment or two later. "Wanda?"

Wanda scowled. "One of us will have to go down and take a look. Finn looks like a job for you to me."

"Fine." I said curtly and took another look. I went around to the east edge and looked over again. With a slight sigh, I hooked a line on the balcony lintel and went over, going down backwards so I could walk down the wall as needed. I moved swiftly and signalled for them to pull the line up. I headed for the bushes beside the path and crouched, heart pounding. I could have been exposed in open air if the guards had come around the corner at the time I was descending.

Our plan had been ill conceived in my view with too many risks involved. This wasn't just a burglary from a townhouse.

As well as the guard patrols and the gate guards, there was a standing garrison and now, an additional unit, any of whom may come outside at any moment.

The guards had still not appeared. I had to move and find out where they were. The other pair had nearly reached the end of the West wing and would soon go around the back of the house. I slid to the wall of the house where the slightly sunken path was relatively well concealed by the shrubs all the way around. They would be on the other side of the low formal hedge from me and from the larger shrubs that marked the next flower border. I hoped the deep shadow would hide me. The dog would be the issue if the bark sap had worn off. I couldn't be sure but there was nothing for it now.

I edged along the path to the rear corner of the east wing and peered around. The guards were nearly on top of me as they came along, chatting with two soldiers. Four more stood smoking about ten yards away. They must have stopped and chatted for some time and now were moving only because the other patrol was up on them. I ducked back, my heart making a leap as well as pounding hard. I flattened myself against the wall and slid down into a crouch. The guards came around the end of the building and passed by, too busy talking. The dog turned its head and sniffed but got pulled and trotted on, seemingly unconcerned. I breathed again. The question now was whether the second team followed hard on their heels or waited, given that they were supposed to be spaced well apart. I chanced a look around the corner, again. The second team had stopped and were smoking and talking with the group of off duty soldiers. That was well and good but they could restart their patrol at any time.

I signalled to Wanda. The rest of the group came down into the shrubs and I explained the situation.

"You took a chance calling us down. I'm not happy with that decision." She snapped.

"You know, Wanda, I think we have some things to discuss back at base but not now.

And it's your call on whether we move or wait for the next patrol because one way or another, we can't stay in these bushes too much longer. The chances are increasing by the minute that someone realises there are balcony doors open and a line hanging over the upper balcony."

Wanda nodded. "We go now. One by one for the trees down there," she pointed towards the east wall. "I'll lead this time." She went, sprinting lightly across the gap between house and the irregularly planted trees.

"I'll bring the rear up." I said.

Verity went, then Zeth. Jen was about to when I pulled her back down. The guards had rounded the corner. We crouched behind the shrubs, waiting. They went by slowly, talking about the arrival of another troop before morning. I rose.

"Okay, go quickly."

Jen ran. I waited until she was half way and followed. I felt a lot better when we reached the trees and got our backs against one each, facing the wall we were going to get across to make our escape from the place.

Wanda pointed to three or four pine bushes and moved again. We followed. Now we were in good cover. The wall was just about thirty feet, through a shrub line that grew pretty much against it then up and over and we would be back in the public gardens.

"Finn, you go first and take the line."

I nodded. "We could do it more quickly and go over three and then two, taking three lines over and leaving one. Or we could go along the line of the bushes here and go back out via the palace garden."

"We could," said Wanda, "but we only have two lines left and one at a time will draw less attention."

"As you wish." I exchanged glances with Jen. I took a last look and moved swiftly to the wall, securing the line around the stem of a shrub where it branched. Climbing the wall with the assistance of the greenery, I got over easily and had the line secured on the far side in a few seconds. I shrugged my crossbow back into place, drew a throwing knife and scanned around. We had dropped over at the rear of the public gardens by the north gates. The gardens were clear as far as I could see. There was a tug of weight on the line and I braced, using my weight to help keep it tight. There were shouts in the distance.

Verity came over. "We've got company if we don't get out quickly. Another troop suddenly came in and some soldiers came from the garden area to meet them, they spotted us and started shouting. I think they have bows."

I could hear shouting and movement as feet clattered on stone.

"Some of the troop are heading for the gates just north of us. They'll be at the garden gates and here in thirty seconds. Come on!" I urged as Wanda came over.

"We don't have any time left." Jen swung over nearly beside Wanda. She had climbed the wall without the line. She dropped beside me.

"Why is Zeth bringing up the rear?"

There was a flash and much cursing.

"That's why," said Wanda firmly. "He suggested it and just set off a blinding flash spell. It may dissuade them, knowing we have magic ability."

As she spoke, the line tugged and Zeth reached the top of the wall. He grinned and stood up full length, the statuette in his hand. He whooped in triumph, waving the statuette at the pursuers.

"Get down you stupid..."

The sound of shafts whirring cut through Wanda's angry yell. The bolts thudded home.

For a moment, Zeth stood, choking. Blood welled from his mouth, turning the celebration into a gurgle.

The statuette fell from his hand and smashed with a tinkle of pottery on our side. Zeth tottered and before we could grab him, pitched off the wall into the palace grounds. I was pretty sure he was dead when he hit the ground. There were three quarrels in his chest and stomach and one had pierced the side of his neck.

Jen picked up the ruins of the statuette. Wanda stood open mouthed and white faced. "Gods! What has he done?"

The boots were heading our way, now and there were hands at the gates.

"Come on, now!" I pulled at them, "We have to leave him and we have to get out of the south gates before we get cut off. Come on!"

The others galvanised as I moved off and we ran for our lives, pursuers behind and probably coming across to cut off our escape from the gardens, as well. We burst from the gates, half-flattened a drunk who was weaving past and, leaving him in the gutter, sprinted full pelt across the plaza.

***

"A pity that such a priceless piece should get broken." Commented Master Grey in his dry way. "It is fortunate that Zeth was dead when they took him. At least they will find out nothing. Master Black will ensure that he is identified as a drifting adventurer who has been around the town for some time. Losing a member of a pentagon is always unfortunate. Have you had time to reflect on what went wrong?"

He looked at us, in turn.

"It was Finn's fault. He was supposed to watch the guards. He didn't warn us properly about there being soldiers and then he led us over the wall when it obviously wasn't secure."

I said nothing but my scowl probably said as much as an immediate denial.

"What utter crap," Jen responded. "you went against every good idea Finn had. He warned you about going in and you ignored him which made it hard enough and then you ignored the route he suggested and the idea of using multiple lines."

"And it was your decision to send me in first on every occasion, Wanda" I added, in a measured tone. "But all those things would have worked if you had kept control of Zeth. I gave you warning when he came skittering onto the upper balcony all pumped up with the excitement of the job. You failed to reprimand him or to keep him under your thumb."

Wanda started to give a retort but the master held up one hand, "I'd like to hear what Verity has to say."

He turned his eye on Verity who shrank slightly. "I...I'm not sure really master"

"A report, Verity. The way you saw it."

"Um, okay. Finn was sent first and Wanda didn't want to hear what he had to say because she was in charge. But I don't think it was her fault. It was Zeth being stupid. We would have got away with the statuette and all been home if he hadn't danced on the wall making gestures at the guards. Although Finn was right about the best route. Wanda didn't want to go via the sewers because of the smell and the shit, not because we didn't have a known way in. We have maps of every passageway here. I've seen them."

Wanda flushed red and spluttered something about us not following her lead properly and me challenging her, constantly.

"Wanda was unlucky," Jen added.

I inclined my head. "And if I made it hard by questioning you Wanda, it was only intended as the role of the second."

"I didn't make you second!" she snapped, still red faced.

"No. I did." Master Grey spoke quietly. "Alright, we have lost one of our order and you may wish to pause and mourn or at least reflect on how such things happen. There will be others, Wanda. Over the years, you will sometimes find you have no choice but to sacrifice one for the good of all or you lose someone unexpectedly. However, in this case, I find your command wanting. Retaining discipline is key to success. Listening, making best use of the team and sometimes asking them all what they think is good practice.

Finn will get his chance on the next mission and we will see how he gets on with you questioning him. You had better give some thought between you to who will be the new fifth. There is no point in us returning the statuette as was intended. Last night's mission was a failure. You will each write a report, please, analysing each aspect and hand it to me by supper tomorrow. We will go through the mission as a class exercise in a few days and look at the alternative choices, consider how we might have approached it and whether there were better options that you all failed to think about. This lesson will be insightful and should be easier to assimilate as it had a real consequence. I think you will find it a useful learning exercise."

Friends III

If you choose to hide in a wet ditch, about three in the morning when there is a thick, clinging fog, you do have a tendency to suddenly wake up and notice how cold and damp you are. I woke to the uncomfortable feeling of soaked and chilled legs where I had sunk into a particularly boggy patch while asleep. I must have rolled out of the blanket that I had wrapped about myself some hours earlier when I had come off watch. We have been given a few days reprieve after the last mission, though I was now swiftly regretting how I had chosen to spend them.

With no starlight getting through, it was pitch black. I opened my bullseye lantern just a fraction. "Hey," a hissing whisper came from above, "that's bright in this darkness."

I sighed, "The fog is too thick for anyone to see a bonfire through it never mind a lantern. I can't even see the shape of the fortress from here."

Rill came down the slope, carefully. "Shit, you're soaked"

"I know," I said, "I noticed."

There was a groan from near at hand, "Will you two keep it down. I was asleep... I think."

Coyle sat up and rubbed a hand through his curls. "Ugh, the water has soaked through my blanket. Whose idea was it to hide down here? We could have stayed at an inn and come across country tomorrow and have been outside by nightfall. Why do we have to sleep in a brook? We're not frogs." He stood up and wiped mud off one hand. "Delightful."

Merik got up silently and came to join us. "With this fog, we could easily move in closer and find a more comfortable hiding place. The chances of meeting a patrol are slim and being seen, even slimmer."

"I'd welcome that" Coyle nodded.

We all looked round at Tu'Lon. He was snoring loudly. "Looks like someone doesn't mind lying in stagnant water. There's always one" Merik commented. I poked Tu'Lon with a foot.

Tu'Lon shot up "What? Are we under attack?!" He looked around at all of us, "What?"

"Get up, we're leaving." I said.

"I was comfortable" he complained, rolling his blanket. It was dry.

We all looked aghast, "How is it we are all soaked and you are dry as a bone and comfortable?" Tu'Lon gave us a slight grin, "Prayer" he said, packing the blanket, "prayer and good deeds. Your Gods would reward you, too, if you ever paid them any respect."

We gave him doubtful looks. "You mean you cast a spell to keep yourself comfortable and neglected to mention that you could have done the same for the rest of us?" I said, tone slightly sardonic.

"You wouldn't have got up to do guard duty" he countered, with a grin.

"Remind me later to do something by way of special thanks for our priest" I said.

We moved around, getting ready to leave, complaining about being stiff, cold and wet. Tu'Lon didn't look at all repentant though.

We went softly into the fog, Rill and I with bows, Coyle and Tu'Lon next, with Merik bringing up the rear, sword and shield at the ready. We heard horses at one point and muffled voices to our right but other than that we saw nothing and heard little as we worked our way towards our goal. Eventually, a grey shape rose out of the fog and we knew we had reached the fortress of Maldengar.

Drachefauste had taken this key castle about six months ago and was using it as a base as his invasion of Rosgovia pressed on, swallowing land from the neighbouring dukedoms as he devoured all in his path with his customary greed and ambition.

The difference between an army attacking, which would almost certainly have failed and we five was that I knew a secret way into the castle shown to me long ago by my Uncle Adhils. Furthermore, I had played over the years in and out of every passage, garden and tower of the fortress. I knew it nearly as well as my own home. I knew where Drachefauste would have his rooms, where he would probably post guards and how to get across the main hall to the main noble quarters without being seen or heard by anyone in the hall or at its doors. I had planned the whole thing with great care.

When I was done and had checked it, I had taken my friends through my plan until they too could repeat back our route, the escape points and the sentry points that would be most dangerous.

We had hatched the idea of going after Drachefauste while I was on a trip to Riassa. If we could lop off the head, we surmised, the body would die. The lack of organisation and initiative without Drachefauste would enable us to turn the tide of the war. Once splits started between the barbarian tribes, without a leader strong enough to hold them together, we saw them splintering, following their own interests or just returning home.

The fortress had an outer wall with watchtowers then a moat and an inner wall. I led the group down into a ditch that was overgrown with bushes.

Brambles and other thorny material arched out over it, hiding the course from view right up to the wall where nobody had been diligent enough to cut it away.

After all, an army was hardly going to try to march through the briers so it had been left like a bit of extra defence. That was a mistake that I would correct, if we ever got our lands back. We ducked under bushes and crawled along until we were against the wall.

"I didn't think we could get any wetter," commented Rill, "unless you'd have us swim the moat"

I grinned to myself in the fog. "How did you know?"

He groaned. Rill was no swimmer and neither were Merik or Tu'Lon. I took out a rough knife and worked on the edge of the small grate through which the overflow from the moat ran down the watercourse and out through the wall. It came out with a slight hiss and clink. I waited, silently. We all seemed to be holding our breath but the sound would have been so soft that we were the only ones to hear it.

I ducked half under the water and squeezed through the gap. Getting my head above water, I looked around. Beyond the wall on this side, the ditch continued between huts and stores used by the waggoneers and wheelwrights, smiths and coopers. I stood up. The others followed, reluctantly, I guessed from the wait.

"Lovely," Rill added, as he surfaced, "ditch water, no doubt with added excrement"

"Only if you saw something floating" I said, with a grin.

"Thanks Finn," Merik joined us, "that makes it seem so much better."

"Needs must, first rule of the assassin. Never refuse an entry point for the sake of a little foul-smelling waste. It all washes off, later. That's what the moat is for."

Rill gave a slight cough. "Seems clean enough water to me," Coyle said as he came up, last. "It is" I said, "just run off from the moat."

I beckoned, 'follow me'. We went along the back of the tanner's pits behind the fence that kept them from the hay barn. The gap between the buildings was just enough to slide through one by one. From there, a side door opened into a barn full of wagon equipment and hay racks. We ghosted through to the far door and I opened it, carefully.

Looking up the gap between the barn and the smithy, we had to pass behind a sentry point where steps went up to the battlements above. That was easy enough, but now we had to move through the potentially occupied smithy. If it was our own people enslaved by the invaders, we could pass by with their blessings. Otherwise, we'd need an excuse. We went in, talking about equipment and walked straight past the smiths who were busy at work and, from the looks, didn't care much for us. They were a mix of people I recognised and new faces so I kept to the shadows and we inspected the weapons rack, briefly before leaving, still talking as if we owned the place.

Now we could go around behind a washroom where the castle laundry was addressed. From this, there was a drainage overflow that went into the moat.

This is where we got to use my local knowledge. I stamped twice on what looked like an ordinary flagstone behind the laundry and watched my companions' reactions as it slowly turned, revealing narrow steps down into a damp passage. We went down, pulled the handle inside and closed the entrance after ourselves. The passage suffered from a badly dripping ceiling caused by the moat above. The brickwork was not perfectly sealed. We passed beneath it, under the walls and courtyards and arrived at a set of carved stone steps that led into a small chapel just outside the keep.

I went first again. The trapdoor that I used came up behind the altar so I stayed low and opened it with great care. This wasn't a good time to stand up and find yourself facing a congregation or even a few people at prayer. I crawled out, staying behind the altar and peered as cautiously as possible around the edge. The chapel looked dark. I stood and looked around. The others followed me.

As I slipped into the private room used by the priests to robe and get ready for services, there was a sound and a door closed, as a priest came in from the courtyard. He turned. I put a finger to my lips. I gave a sigh of relief as he turned and I recognised him as Father Thiery, one of the chaplains from my youth. I stepped into the light,

"Father Thiery" I said softly, "nobody must know we are here."

"Edmund?" he moved forward and shook my hands in his, "Has your father come with an army? Will they relieve the fortress?" I looked down "No, I'm sorry, Father. The army is far away and my father is further. Frederick is duke until such time as he returns."

He frowned, "And you realise who will suffer if you do something and leave the barbarians in control. You should leave, Edmund. If you kill any of his men, Drachefauste will put ten times our number to the sword."

"Not if we kill Drachefauste, himself." I said.

"Assassination," he tutted, "I would not have thought it to be the way of your family, Edmund." He sighed. "That war should make such creatures of us all and drive us to such measures."

"Yes Father, that is true," I sighed, "but sometimes cutting off the head is the only way to kill the beast."

He bowed his head, then and spoke softly, "I cannot let you endanger my flock. If you will not leave, I fear I may have to hand you in."

"I'm sorry you feel that way, Father." Tu'Lon stepped out of the shadow.

"I'd hate to kill a priest, especially one you know, Finn," added Rill, "but he isn't leaving the room."

Thiery lifted his arms, "Do what you must. What is one more victim of this conflict?"

"I'm sorry Father," I said, "but we must tie you up. We cannot afford to be discovered and it might be better that it looks like you were taken unawares."

We gagged and tied the poor man and then put him into a closet, barring the door with a chair. I regretted it but we could not do otherwise. Besides, I hadn't prayed in a long time so I didn't feel I was going to be in much more trouble with the gods for one more act of blasphemy or sedition.

From the chapel, it was easy to get into the keep, as the chapel lay below the battlements so only someone leaning over would see anyone on the roof and you could easily put a plank or use ropes to access one of the windows of the east tower unseen.

It was a flaw that I had exploited in the past to avoid being found outside the keep late at night. We took a bench top from the chapel and used it to get up onto the roof via the bell tower. Laying the bench top between the roof edge and the window ledge, we were able to let the sentry patrol go by and then in turn, run across, squeeze through the tower window and drop into the stairwell unnoticed.

Now came the first sentry point that might be an issue. We had to either go down and across a hallway past the two sentries at the door which joined the tower to the central keep rooms or we had to go up, enter the library ante-room and then cross the library and records chamber. The library itself was a mezzanine opening onto a long hallway where there could be sentries patrolling, increasing our chances of being seen.

I listened at the door to the library ante-room, trying to decide if it was quiet, suggesting the door between the small chamber and the main library was closed. After a few moments, I was content and we went in. What I had not expected was to find two sentries standing on the door to the upper library, looking very shocked at the sudden entry of a group of armed intruders.

I thought, in the circumstances, that I reacted swiftly. Drawing a short blade, I rushed the first and before he could get his polearm sorted out, I had taken him and as he was falling on his knees, kicked him swiftly in the head to stop him yelling out. Coyle hit the second with a flash bolt that sent him reeling and then Rill finished him with a knife.

We stood back. "Hm. that could be difficult to explain if anyone happens to come along to change duties." Merik pointed out. "We'll have to stash these two somewhere" The options on somewhere were slim so we ended up shoving them into the one cupboard in the room and taking all the leather-bound registers and other documents out and heaping them against one wall.

"Why were they guarding an old records room off a library anyway?" Tu'Lon asked the question on everyone's mind.

"We have to find out," I said, "maybe Drachefauste is in there or something."

I tried the door into the library but it was locked. Rill set about it with a lock pick set, ears straining for the sound of clicks. It took only a minute or so. I moved forward and pushed on the door gently, as I peered in. What I saw beyond was a bigger surprise than the guards. All the book cases had been cleared. The whole mezzanine was dominated by a single piece of furniture, an outsized chaise-longue type creation but a massive one with about ten pairs of legs.

Filling this was something that looked like a huge semi-opaque white grub. The head tapered to a definite snout, above which sat two great black pools for eyes. The eyes gave the impression of a sense of extreme intelligence. The rear of the creature split into two sections that curled upwards, with wiry protrusions that curled back on themselves like two coiled whips. Along the lower abdomen, it had a row of six muscular openings, equally spaced about two feet apart. By the look of them, I guessed they were either for egg laying or reproductive use, perhaps both.

There was a strangely stimulating smell like vanilla that hung heavily in the air. I really had no idea what to make of this so I closed the door again and explained what I had seen to the others.

"Anyone make any sense of that?" I finished.

There was a silence, "Finn, do you remember when we raided that old palace in the mountains?" Tu'Lon was thoughtful, "Didn't we find a similar piece of furniture rather rotted away with a similar odour?" I cast my mind back and nodded. I recalled it very well.

It had been a short expedition into the mountains. I had hoped to find something, some clue as to Drachefauste's source of power or at least some explanation of where his people came from so suddenly that they could dominate the other tribes, seize Raga and now defeat our armies despite our better tactics.

"I do remember, yes. But I am not certain what to do next. This is unexpected and puts an obstruction in our path. I suppose we could kill it and move on but that could be passing up some chance to do a lot more damage to Drachefauste's plans. It must have some value to be kept here and I think there were guards down below in the hallway, too. In a fortress where no trouble is expected, that's pretty serious."

We pondered in silence. As we did so, Tu'Lon seemed to go into a reverie. At first, I thought he was praying but then I heard the voice in my head, just after he started and he spoke, "It wants us to come in and talk with it."

A slow and strangely sophisticated voice, speaking in deep feminine tones that were both somehow languorous and seductive came into my head. I can recall how it felt, vividly and how we all talked about what we had experienced later.

I wanted to resist because I was sure this was a twisted trick to draw us into harm's way. Yet we all moved as one and were on the mezzanine, looking into those dark eyes before we had even realised we had moved.

There were guards below. There were guards on this level too but they seemed oblivious of us, all walking in a dream and never looking our way. "Do not be afraid of your enemies. They will not see or hear you" the voice reassured us. The being shifted, slightly on the long chaise.

"You are right, dark skinned one. I am a prisoner, here, taken long ago by your terms, from my people, my poor people whom they butchered like hornets falling upon hapless hive guards before we became so much more."

It must have been able to hear my thoughts. "Yes, one who sings, I was what they were seeking, to birth their armies." Projected into my mind was an impression of beings growing inside her white-opaque body, her own blood and digestion nourishing them with a milk-like honey.

"With my milk, they receive some wisdom, longevity but most of all, regeneration of wounds and immunity to sickness of any sort known to us. For generations, I have been their brood slave, producing armies of their kind. I have suffered the pain of birthing them alone and with no hope.

They started by using human females but although they did birth a new generation, they found that they had gained weaknesses so they came for me. I can only breed males or so I have let them believe.

I could make another like me if I chose to, but I could not subject another to what I have suffered. They are still breeding females from humans, pretending that the girls are high born so they can marry them off for gain.

The current leader of these people is worse than his three predecessors. Before, it was just for their armies, but he has turned the breeding into an industry to fuel his ambitions. Without me, they would soon lose their powers to recover from wounds and some of their strength, too." The voice paused.

We were all transfixed, looking sympathetically at this strange looking creature, so far from our own and yet, mentally seeming so close. We could intensely feel its pain and suffering. When a being uses its mind to speak, the words and images carry emotion and imagery that is far stronger than the spoken word.

As we stood, considering what to do, my mind wandered even further back. I recalled the day when I rode out with my father, Finnmeyer and Frederick to see something discovered in a burial mound. The pieces fell into place. This was the tribe mother to an ancient race of people who had once been widespread. All we had seen were fragments of the history of their end. Drachefauste's ancestors had discovered the power that came from the brood mother and had slaughtered the rest of her people to capture her and maybe others like her, before that.

They had forced their strongest to breed with her and so produced a new race. That was why the Dragon Guard were such an effective fighting force. With no illness, abnormal strength and more than anything, the power to regenerate, they were physically superior to the rest of us.

"We could take you with us," I said desperately, "get you out of here. We came to kill Drachefauste, but saving you is much more important"

The voice answered, again, slowly and sadly. "Look at me. You would struggle to carry me even if you could somehow walk out of here untouched.

I cannot bend the minds of those I birthed. The minds of those about us now, all bred from ordinary stock, I can handle. No, that is not an option, even though I would give much to see the mountains again before I die. Please, end this for me. End it quickly and leave me to my rest.

As for your enemy, he is not within the fortress. He left several days ago."

Merik nodded sadly and drew Clave from his back, "Clave, will you do this quickly, without pain and leave the soul of this creature untouched?" The sword flared into life, flame licking the blade, hungrily. He stepped forward, "May your maker forgive me." He lifted the sword high.

"My thanks will live on within you." The dark eyes seemed even rounder and sadder, "Remember me to my people should you ever find any that survived."

Clave swept down and severed her head cleanly. There was a strange flicker and the opaqueness faded so she was just white. A few moments later, her body changed to grey and then gradually went black. The odd vanilla odour was replaced by a bitter stench.

As the guards woke from their trance state, we were already running down the stairs and back to the chapel roof. There was consternation eventually but they couldn't remember seeing who did it or where they had gone of course. Her last blow against her captors must have been to erase minutes of their memories.

Knowing Drachefauste was not in the fortress made the retreat a sensible course of action. We had struck a blow, albeit not the one we came for. Drachefauste would not breed any more of his elite and we had put an end to the extreme suffering of another being. We got to our horses and as we rode southwards, we were already planning how to strike at Drachefauste when the next opportunity arose.

Burdens III

After the loss of Zeth, we had been over the mission again and for a while, the failure hung over us like a shadow. But we had to move on, we all knew that. A new fifth was brought in, a young man called Cody. Zeth had actually spotted him originally and mentioned he thought he was a sharp young man. He was put through a few tests but he excelled at everything. He was nodded in and confirmed by our master a few days later. We were put through a lot of training but no real missions for a while.

***

We had been sent off to Riassa with orders to report to the guild house, where we would receive a few days training in some dirty fighting techniques and take part in a small competition with a Riassan coterie. We were also told to relax in between, enjoy the city life and to leave our doubts and any grief or guilt behind.

Only Wanda and I had been to Riassa previously. The others seemed to find it quite overwhelming. I was a little surprised. I had assumed that some of them would have been through the capital or maybe had even come from a family here.

The guild welcomed us and then put us out into a fine inn where we had our own rooms.

I heard during that visit that Klavon had been confirmed as a senior journeyman within the Thieves and Assassins Guild at Riassa. He was definitely a rising star. I didn't have cause to cross his path, this time.

Learning the finer skills to get the upper hand in a brawl or bar fight was fun. Better still was the way we defeated the Riassan team in knife throwing, lock picking, traversing without touching the ground and problem solving, giving us an overall victory by a good margin. We were told we all had five days off and then there would be a final briefing on some new tools and how to make them, for those interested in such skills.

At first, I knocked about with the group for a day or two and introduced them to my friends. Wanda seemed quite taken with Merik especially and tried to seduce him. He was on a break after his contract with our family had been completed, but confided he was considering a second. When Merik did not respond in the way she hoped, she led Coyle upstairs when it came time to turn in for the night. I was thus very surprised when she turned up at my door a day later, in the early hours, her kirtle unlaced. I didn't want to offend her but I had no intention of getting embroiled with a woman who I felt was going to be a poisoned ivy that I may have to deal with one day. I flattered her, flirted with her and finally steered her back to her own room. It wasn't long before there was another soft knock on my door. I groaned, inwardly and slipped out of bed, again, throwing on a silk gown. "Wanda, I already..." The warm body of a young woman pushed past and closed the door. It was Jen.

"Why did you think I was Wanda?" I didn't answer for a moment, "I don't know. I just had a feeling she was putting herself about this week." Jen gave me a disbelieving look and I decided the truth would be better. "Alright, she already visited and I sent her back to her room. I thought she had decided to come back for a second try."

Jen shook her head, "Bitch," she said "I confessed to her that I had been thinking about getting closer with you. I suppose she thought it'd be fun to be in your bed when I knocked on your door."

Jen then moved very close. She was wearing a light, short shift belted loosely at the waist. "I know you said we should always stay professional, but I have always seen how you look at me, how you cover for me and... well, Finn, you know..." and she put her arms about my neck.

We slept until late to avoid everyone else finding out. I regret I didn't call a halt then, while it was just a one-night dalliance. I let it drift for months afterwards, on and off with no intention of staying with Jen after we were done but without finding the heart to tell her so. But that was later.

***

I had set myself a little task for my own amusement and to see how much I had improved at what I did. I was going to enter the Imperial Court again and see if I could find my way to the library.

I wanted to ask the Imperial Librarian why Drachefauste was being backed. I wanted to know why the Emperor had made up his mind that Drachefauste was going to be allowed to take our lands, leaving us with no help from any of our allies, all warned off by a decree from high. Drachefauste, on the other hand, was getting money and gathering more forces all the time. Only our fortitude and luck in battle would turn the war in our favour, now.

The latest reports I had were of Frederick falling back, consolidating, hitting out at targets to slow the beast's advance but being unable to stop his advance. He wrote to me that he just wanted one chance to get Drachefauste onto the field again where he could try to cut him off from his main forces and finish him. Without the beast, there would be no war. He had no viable successor and he was the driving force behind the conflict.

Pellinore had returned to Littesburg to reinforce his land and gather a new army. Fulk and Adhils were wounded and the old warhorse, Vorne De Haille was dead. Lancingor was now captain of the ducal guard, in his place.

I stood considering how to approach the court this time. I could re-adopt my disguise as a legal clerk but I fancied something of a change. I had the emblem that would admit me as an ambassador hidden on me. I could use that. I preferred to get in first and then use the powers of ambassador only once I was past the large number of watchers.

One of the costumes that I had managed to collect on my travels was that of a cardinal's chaplain. Given the importance of the High Cardinal and the general propensity of guards and other officials to keep their hands-off churchmen, I decided I would breeze past as an obviously busy and preoccupied young priest, laden as I was with an armful of scrolls and papers.

Hopefully, the garb, the manner and the name of the Cardinal on my lips would serve to open doors. Bluff would have to do the rest. I shaved to a suitable look, waxed what was left of my beard and wore the robes and cap about town for a few days, passing the palace on numerous occasions, where I took the opportunity to nod to guards, bless those who acknowledged me and to always have armfuls of books and parchment. Having effectively familiarised the guards with my persona, I hoped they would recall me as someone familiar without asking awkward questions.

I decided to test this by making an approach to leave a scroll for the High Ambassador. Since my father was not at court and would not pick it up and ask questions, anyway, I simply wrote a note to the effect that I hoped he was well and could make a meeting with the Cardinal's trusted priest, Father Edmund of Gavrey-Le-Vaux. I walked up to one of the officials on the steps. The guards watched me come but made no move to stop me. When I asked the official if I could deliver the scroll, he turned, looked at me as if he had seen me before and then asked if I wished to go in and deliver it myself. I said it was not necessary but, of course, I would be happy to do so if it saved him time.

As expected, he then explained that even a good priest like myself should hand over documents for delivery by the court clerks rather than add to the number of people floating around the court.

I bowed and said that if he did not mind seeing to the matter, that was all the better from my point of view. He took the scroll, I smiled and bowed again and the guards watched me with disinterest as I walked away.

The ground was laid, as far as I was concerned. I waited two days and then watched until the same official and at least one of the same guards were on duty. Approaching with a bundle of parchment and scrolls, I hurried to the official and told him I had to deliver a scroll, which was very inconvenient as I had a meeting in an hour on the other side of the city as well as a service to take and on top of that all these messages and instructions to hand out.

The official once more asked if I had to go inside and I said I did. He then asked for a letter or something to back this up. I began looking and then, of course, dropped all the scrolls and parchment. Guards and officials scrambled to help me as I rushed about picking things up and looking even more hassled, hot under the collar and put upon. The plan worked, perfectly;

"Never mind Father. You'd better hurry on before the Dean of Court leaves. He is due to be at a meeting elsewhere, I happen to know."

The man piled more scrolls into my arms and I made a great show of trying to mop my brow while hanging onto the papers, resulting in more falling on the floor, "Oh dear, oh dear," I muttered, trying to pick them up and spilling several scroll cases, "this isn't my day." Actually, it was very much my day, as I was helped on my way into the court and doors opened for me without challenge.

Clutching the armful of papers and thanking them profusely for their help while apologising for wasting their time, I made off across the court reception with guards and officials shaking their heads and smiling sympathetically. I allowed myself a smile and blessed several people as I passed by. Having reached the door that I knew I had taken to head towards the library, I remembered that last time I had got there, it had been by sneaking up a couple of levels and walking across a link corridor. I had no idea what the official route was. I approached a guard and then thought better of it. I coughed and dropped some scrolls. While the guard helped me recover them along with an earnest faced clerk, I mentioned that I had still to get to the library.

"I could spare a few minutes to assist you, father." I thought it was the clerk, but the voice came from behind me. I straightened and peered over the top of my heaped paper. The face looked vaguely familiar but I couldn't place it. He was around my age and dressed in the garb of a young nobleman.

"Thank you, my son" I said.

"Fine," the door guard said "go straight down the corridor, turn right and speak to the guards on the double doors, there. They will ask the librarian's clerk if the chief librarian is still there and admit you on his say so."

He swung a door open and we were on our way down the cool corridor, footsteps echoing as we forged ahead.

The door closed behind us. Once again, I had penetrated the palace with no authority. It seemed that it was easier than rumour suggested.

My companion marched up to the guards, "The cardinal's envoy and knight commander of the Red Legion to see the Chief Librarian" he said with a brashness that I admired.

I studied him more closely. He had a slightly beaked nose, strong features that I would expect from one of the noble houses and a long, curled wig of red hair over his own.

He wore a thin, slightly curled goatee in a similar colour so I guessed he was actually red-headed. His moustache was also neat and turned up at the tips. He was of average height, quite light framed and wearing a red tabard with gold lines through it, rather affected puffed sleeves with a white ruff and matching white cuffs.

A slim duelling blade hung at his side, which looked like it had been well-used, from the wear on the roughed leather grip and marked guard. Oddly, he also had a longish dagger tucked in a boot sheath, but other than raising an eyebrow, momentarily, I avoided dwelling on this.

In short, he seemed to suggest a young noble who was more than a foppish clothes-horse. I wondered if the blade had only been used in one-to-one arguments or in wider action. I also wondered what he would make of the garb that was hidden beneath my priestly robes, particularly my own blades.

The guards parted with a slight bow, one of them part opening the door, which he turned through and spoke in a low voice to someone we could not see.

The door opened wider and a slim, little man with greying hair dressed in greens and greys and sporting a soft velvet cap in which he wore a feather from some game bird stepped out; "I'm sorry, I don't recall your appointment, gentlemen. The Chief Librarian is a very busy man and not given to patience when it comes to appointments that he has not sanctioned."

I waved my scroll, "I don't have an appointment. I am carrying a personal message from the High Cardinal. It was not planned."

This had a visible effect on the small man who bowed, "I will tell my master, father."

He disappeared from view, again. My companion stroked his moustache with a thoughtful air, "It seems you will gain admittance, anyway."

I inclined my head, "The Cardinal's name does tend to open doors, my son." He smiled. In fact, I could have sworn he was holding back laughter but I pretended I had not noticed, being a sanctimonious, self-centred clergyman of the 'do as I say, not as I do' class. The small man opened the door and looked out. "You may enter, father."

"And my companion, the Knight Commander of our red legion? I assume he may continue to accompany me." The small man coughed and then muttered, "I suppose if he is your guardian, he must." He stepped aside. I looked puzzled at this, momentarily, but then we were inside and the door was closing behind us.

I saw the tall, angular figure of the librarian approaching, stooping as he peered at us over his gold pince nez. At that moment, things took an odd turn, "I don't know who you are after," my companion said to me, "but I recognised you from the guild. You may need to rush on as I'm about to complete my assignment and get out. You wouldn't want the blame to fall on you." He drew the duelling blade and went for the librarian. "Pardon, monsignor but your death is required by one of your fellows."

The librarian raised a hand and started to attempt a spell but I knew he had no chance of beating the thrust of a sword. I threw off my robe and drew two daggers. The librarian's clerk just stood transfixed and then ran for the door.

I sent the first knife on its way at once. It hit the assassin in the back of the head, hurling him forward. Before he could recover, the blow not having penetrated, properly, I was on him. My white handled dagger struck once, a deep, clean stab under the sternum from behind. I pulled the weapon free and stepped back as he swung out with the sword, but he was falling, already. He sprawled, rolling half onto his back.

"Why?" he whispered, "Was I the target?" I said nothing but stood over him. The door swung wide as guards rushed in.

I held up a hand, "The librarian is safe."

"Thanks to you, young man," he dropped his hand and walked up, putting a hand on my shoulder, "you had no reason to save me, either, given what I said at our last meeting."

"Yes, I did. The Von Tacchims may be out of favour but we still support the rule of law and are loyal to the throne."

He inclined his head. The guards surrounded us and I was being ordered to put my weapons aside. The Chief Librarian drew himself up, "That will do, Lieutenant." He ordered, "You can take that away," as he indicated towards the dead man, "and leave us. But keep a better watch on the door. You should have disarmed them both."

"My pardon," the young officer said, "I saw no weapons on the father...um, man who seems to have saved you. The other was a high-ranking officer."

"You mean he was disguised as a high-ranking officer. Status is of no matter. Nobody comes armed into the library. That is a rule passed by the thirteenth Emperor and has been in force ever since."

He turned to me, "As for you, young man, I owe you my thanks and my life so it seems you have an advantage. What did you really want?"

I paused, considering. I had intended to use the library to access the central palace. "To understand why the Emperor would turn his back on my family in favour of a beast from the wilds"

The librarian looked steadily at me and then nodded, "Come with me." He pushed on double doors opposite and led away up a corridor flanked by windows that looked onto two beautifully manicured quadrangles with lawns and borders. The gaps between each window were hung with masterpieces by famed artists from many generations. I looked, left and right, trying to take them in.

"Interested in art?" he asked. "Yes, my lord," I said, "always. Particularly Nuardi. We had one of his paintings in Falkenberg. It was a favourite of mine."

He nodded, "Such life. Nuardi always brought it to his works. He was a great talent. His pupil, Valenci is very good. He shows great promise. You should see what he has produced."

"I will try and do that."

We approached a second pair of doors guarded by men dressed in tall helms with scarlet plumes and scarlet tabards with a white eagle. There were four of them, two with halberds and two with shields and long maces. They stood to attention as the librarian took out a great key and unlocked the doors.

He opened them onto a darkened hall lit only by lanterns beyond its edge. I could make out a great throne in the centre of the room set on an oval dais with three steps leading up. On one step, I could just make out a cloaked figure, small and lithe, sitting in thought. The throne was clearly fashioned of gold and gems, the dais itself, a solid piece of polished semi-precious stone, probably malachite as I could see a green hue even in the nearly dark room.

Corridors ran away and there were other sets of doors. I held my breath. This was the Imperial reception, the second throne of the Emperor, himself. As we entered, the small figure rose and watched us approach, "Ysmelda, here is someone you should know who has questions. This time, you may answer them, I think. I owe him."

He turned to me, "Your father knows the truth. We needed a beast to win a war that we were losing. Drachefauste's command will overturn the Carnossian threat and then he will lead against the Surmey-Karilian alliance. He is the best choice. His elite guard are more than a match for any other force in the world today. We need him and there is no one else who has his unique qualifications."

"Raef could have led. He was a great general. You sacrificed him!" I said, angrily.

"That was unfortunate. We did not anticipate him involving himself as he did. Everyone, nearly everyone," he corrected himself, "thought he would persuade your father to be reasonable and to settle the matter. His death was regrettable."

"Regrettable?" I said, bitterly, "Maybe I should have let that assassin kill you. Is that it? Regrettable. What is regrettable is what you have done. Shameful would be a better word. To let a loyal family suffer at the hands of a creature. Perhaps you should have me taken while you have the chance because I swear I will kill the beast and undo your plans."

"Young man, because you saved me, I will disregard that statement. But I will agree to a pact with you, if you will only be reasonable, unlike your father. Let the beast do our bidding and you may slay him when we are done with him. He is a necessary evil at this time, but this time will pass."

I curled my lip, "So end all tools of the Emperor, I gather. Discarded when of no further value. I understand that is what they term political expediency."

"That is correct. And if you ever wish to rise to the heights that your father has achieved, you should learn that well."

"Perhaps my ambitions do not soar so high and I will find I have to disappoint you."

He looked at me, steadily, again, "I hope not." He turned on his heel and walked away.

All this time, the woman had been watching us. She was wearing a heavy veil of blue and pink silk. Her bodice was of light blue satin and her long, slashed skirt that showed beautiful, shapely legs was also blue with a pink stripe of satin along the line of the slash, just emphasising it. Her dark hair was long but put up in a plait, curled in two layers into a bun in which she wore long decorated sticks with jewelled ends. I noted a dagger strapped to one thigh, half hidden but showing when she moved. There was something very familiar about her.

She put up the veil and I must have gasped, sucking my breath in with shock. "Mother?" She shook her head, "Not so, Edmund Von Tacchim. I am her twin sister, you might say."

"Might say?"

"We were created."

I looked blank. I didn't understand her meaning.

"Both fashioned, from the same original woman by a magus. You don't know what I'm talking about do you? Then let's just say your mother and I are sisters, were taught the same things, asked to do similar jobs and then parted. I haven't seen her for fifteen years or more." She paused and smiled, softly. She was so like my mother in every respect, manner, voice, even the way her mouth crinkled at the edge when she smiled. It was unnerving.

I knelt at her feet, "My lady," I took her hand and kissed it, gently, "your sister, my mother, is dead." my voice wavered as I said it and I bowed my head. She rested a hand on it and stood in silence for a moment. When I looked up, tears were running softly down her cheeks. "But she was still young. I didn't feel anything. We always thought we would know if something happened to the other, but I didn't feel anything. Ah, Edmund, your coming brings clouds. This talk of your family. Was it Drachefauste that slew her?"

"More or less. It was madness that took her after he tortured her. She killed herself after a long illness."

"I'm sorry. I did not realise what our decisions would visit upon you."

"Your decisions?" I felt a cold shiver pass through me.

"I am the Emperor's chief concubine and one of the Imperial Council."

"But the decision was ultimately his?" I argued.

She shook her head, "Edmund, there is something I am going to tell you, because the Chief Librarian said I could entrust you with knowledge, but what I am going to say must never pass your lips. Never, do you understand?"

I nodded, "Alright. What you tell me in confidence will remain a secret."

"Your father keeps this same secret. You came here with a message years ago, I understand. I imagine you wondered then how a librarian could dismiss you and deny your father's request?"

"I realised he was much more than merely the Emperor's librarian."

She smiled and raised me to my feet, "You are so like your father when he was younger. Dashing, charming and dangerous." She eyed me coyly.

I was a little taken back but inclined my head, "My lady is far too generous."

"No, my lady is not. You don't understand, Edmund. My lady has to make choices with great care."

"Of course. To disrespect the Emperor would mean your death."

"To disrespect the Emperor," she laughed, almost gaily and I could not help but smile at her laughing eyes, "Edmund, there has been no Emperor for two generations. It is the best kept secret of this mighty leviathan that we call The Empire. The council has ruled since the death of Nausilus VII, the Mad. He left no heir as he had butchered all his bastards and so many others that the council of the day decided it would be more stable to do without an Emperor."

"But he is seen at public ceremonies--"

She smiled, "A decoy." I stood stunned at the realisation of her words. The Emperor had not made the choice, they had a council of men and women. I had considered in my fits of rage taking my dagger and slaying the Emperor in defiance and to mark my family's revenge for what he had done to us, only to find there was no one person to whom I could attribute this.

"Then who made the decision about Drachefauste?"

"Your father, me, the others."

"My father?"

She looked at me and squeezed my hand, drawing me in. "Oh Edmund. Didn't you realise that your father was on the council? He is High Ambassador, one of most senior posts in the whole organisation.

Drachefauste was his find, his idea, but it went wrong. He expected to be able to manage him to do his bidding. When we had committed to the course, the council voted on it and decided that your father must handle the matter alone as he had promised. The Empire is fragile, its resources limited, its armies more meagre than you imagine.

We could not afford to waste it fighting on our own soil unless it was to defend the Empire from incursions by the warlike neighbours who now threaten our peace. And we have had peace, Edmund. Over a hundred years of peace. Would you toss that away?"

She let me go and stood back, regarding me, her hands holding both my hands, now at arm's length. I remembered what my father said, how my mother was one of the most dangerous assassins in the Empire. I guessed her sister was trained at least as well.

I bowed my head, "No, I suppose I would not, but I would have found a way to enforce a peaceful settlement. Who voted against my father when he proposed a change of policy regarding Drachefauste?"

She watched me as she answered, "The Chief Librarian, The Cardinal, the Imperial Steward, The High Chancellor of Law and me. The Lord Treasurer was the only one who opposed it and your father's vote was taken to be against, of course. I am sorry. We did what we did for the good of the Empire that we seek to preserve. We have to consider the welfare of millions of people. Set against that, we chose not to interfere. The last imperial army to march against the Drachefauste lands was slaughtered. We even lost the last Imperial Steward who was posing as the Emperor at that time. In a short time, Drachefauste will be appointed High Warlord of the Empire and Marshall, responsible for all of our forces, he will receive a Dukedom and will fight our enemies for us, believing he is on his way to a position where he can influence and maybe even usurp the imperial throne.

Because his ambition knows no bounds, he will die when he is finished. It is an agreement we made, long ago. There is no going back Edmund. He has to do this and we have sacrificed too much to change the path we have taken, now.

You must understand this and go home. Talk to your father, talk to your brothers. We will offer a new dukedom and a settlement that will end this war. We sent letters just a few days ago. Drachefauste will get Raga and Rosgovia. You will keep Littesburg and gain Valdaria. It is all agreed."

"I cannot speak with my father," I said, softly, "I do not know where he has gone. Frederick is the Duke now."

"You mean Leopold?"

I creased my brow and shook my head, "No, I mean Frederick. Leopold is younger than Frederick and I."

She put a hand to her mouth. I saw her look. She knew something I did not. Tears sprang into her eyes a second time as she looked up at me, "Edmund, I am so sorry. Your brother Frederick was killed in a battle outside Strasnar last week. Drachefauste decimated your forces. Leopold is the Duke and Rosgovia has fallen. He is retreating to your western territories while Drachefauste completes his sieges of your remaining cities. I thought you knew."

It was as if she had taken her dagger and plunged it into my heart. I felt myself go cold, bitter cold. I shivered and sank to my knees. I was shaking with tears as I cried for my brother, for my friends and for our lands. It was all lost. I was too late and now it was beyond me.

Shadows IV

The heavy oak door opened slowly, framing the lean figure of Master Grey. He was hooded and indicated with a hand; "Your presence is now required."

The four of us rose from the bench where we had been waiting and slowly filed into the council chamber, where the other masters awaited.

"Please be seated on the bench facing the Masters' table" Master Black spoke, in a flat monotone. We all sat, nervously. Facing us from the slightly raised dais across an old and beautifully carved table of dark wood, three masters of the guild sat, hooded and formally dressed, one in the plain robes of Master of Grey, one in the night-dark robe of Master of Black and one in the silver trimmed black and grey of the Master of Shadows.

"We had such high hopes for this pentagon," Master Black begun, "but despite its successes in carrying out missions, there have been obvious conflicts which you have not seemed able to resolve." Nobody spoke. I took a deep breath but then decided to wait.

Master Shadow spoke next, "This enquiry was called, not because one of your number died on the last mission but because two of the remaining four raised concerns about working on the team."

That surprised me. I knew Wanda would have blamed me for Verity's death. It was her way of hitting back against my assertions that she failed to retain discipline when she led and we lost our first member, Zeth, some months earlier.

"The masters have read your notes and heard your individual statements. In the matter of Verity's death, we find Black Finn entirely blameless. He chose a valid exit under very real pressure and, in the opinion of the masters, he saved the pentagon. The presence of a tunnel worm was unfortunate. It could have happened to anyone. There was nothing that any of you could have done. Even had you known the creature was present, you would still have made a decision to run the gauntlet, given the alternatives."

I heaved a sigh of relief. I didn't feel that it had been my error, but the death of a friend and a good team member weighed heavily with me. His death had hurt the group. Master Shadow continued with the judgement.

"The reason for this session has been to understand what it is that has caused this group to behave in a dysfunctional manner. The masters had to decide if it was a problem of leadership or simply clashes of personality and why these rifts grew instead of healing, as the team had to pass through the crucible together. We had two charges to consider. First, Wanda's assertion that Black Finn displays reckless leadership that is liable to get anyone who follows him killed.

The second is Jen's accusation that Wanda has not only worked against the pentagon from the outset, in particular against Black Finn, but is probably the source of three events which have compromised the group. I refer to when targets or others with agendas were aware of operations, leading to dangerous and life-threatening situations that ought not to have occurred, in the course of your normal training. I must impress upon you, that this latter charge is far more serious. If the masters find that Wanda had indeed betrayed the guild and her patronage, the sentence will be death."

He paused and sat back, slightly. Wanda turned quite white, and Cody and Jen both turned to look at her. Master Black scanned the four faces on the bench, probably gauging our reactions, "The masters have heard the evidence and have asked a lot of questions of you all to which you have given answers that demonstrate how you think matters lie. On the first charge, we find Black Finn not guilty of the charges of reckless leadership. Whether he engenders loyalty is perhaps less clear, certainly with all types of people with whom he works.

On the second count, the masters believe there are some grounds to justify a view that someone has worked against this pentagon and in particular, may have targeted Black Finn.

However, the council do not find sufficient evidence that Wanda is the responsible party, and therefore agree she is not guilty of the charge that she has been the source of this.

The council does find, however, that Wanda has been a disruptive influence, blinded by her ambition and drive to lead the pentagon. The council also agrees that this team is unable to work together any further in light of these findings and thus, there is no other recourse but to disband it immediately.

All of you will qualify, but Wanda, you will return home to your lands immediately after receiving your tokens. The guild will not educate or house you, further. Jen will also leave the guild house with immediate effect. It is noted that one brings accusations only with facts to back them up or face the consequences. To bring a case where a colleague could face execution is too serious a matter to overlook. Jen, you may collect your tokens in one week but you will not cross the threshold of the guild again."

Master Black let a few moments pass and then lifted the heavy stone of judgement, banging it down upon a tablet beside him so that sparks flew, "Session dismissed. There is no recourse to appeal. These matters will never be discussed formally again."

We all rose, "Black Finn," Master Black raised a hand "please will you remain." The others stood and left, silently. Only Jen looked back, tears welling in her eyes, her mute expression appealing to me to say something more but I knew I could not. The guild had spoken through a quorum of its masters. I had told her not to take this course of action out of loyalty to me but it seemed she had made an accusation anyway.

Master Grey closed the door behind them and all three put off their hoods, "A tunnel worm seizing Verity like that was most unfortunate, one of those random accidents that occur in life."

"You should not blame yourself or dwell upon it," added Master Black, "we exist and we operate in a dangerous world."

I nodded. "We were laughing and joking about the way we had seemed to disappear from under the noses of all the Krales and their dogs after leaving their feast in such disorder."

"Yes, you did extremely well," Master Grey nodded, "you have been a credit to me, Finn. I can only think of two who are up to your standard and one of them is dead."

I smiled and looked down. "Everyone liked Verity. We were clear and away. We should have come back together in triumph and enjoyed the moment. Even the mercenary bowmen who were seeking us would have been forgotten, despite turning our planned exit into an unexpected retreat."

"Like I said," Master Black spoke softly, "these things happen, who knows why. Move on with your life, lad. You have much to do and much living ahead of you."

"On that subject..." Master Grey drew out a scroll from under his robes. It had a key hanging from the seal.

He put it down in front of me on the table where Master Shadow had placed four small goblets of fortified wine. "All the Masters have conferred and we would like you to stay on as a journeyman of the guild, help to train new apprentices, perhaps, in time.... who knows, maybe rise to master, yourself.

First, should you accept, we have a couple of assignments for you. The Guild will pay you a stipend of three hundred silver crowns each year in three instalments, provide rooms for you here or in Riassa or possibly Saxburg, depending on longer-term plans. You may also claim a free room at any of those when you visit. You will find that your key now admits you to parts of the guild house that are beyond the reach of apprentices.

The offer does not prevent you from working for your family from time to time nor indeed in your own interests. As long as you deliver on your commitments to the guild, you are free to come and go as you please. We will avoid anything involving a conflict of interests. You will also find that most targeted jobs are relatively open ended on when they must be completed. It is rare to be given something that is very tight on time although it does occur from time to time, of course. Will you consider it?"

He pushed the scroll towards me and then a goblet. I looked up. Master Black was smiling.

My own master, Grey, was grinning and yet, I saw something in his eyes that I had not seen before. It was urgent and important to him that I said yes to this offer.

For the first time in our relationship, I felt a chill hand touch my heart. I didn't know why. I picked the scroll up, "May I have until morning?"

"Of course," Master Black patted my shoulder.

Master Grey also touched my arm with a hand, "Say yes, Finn. You won't regret it". I heard the urgency hidden there, behind my master's words. What promise had he made? Did he stand to lose face if I refused or was it something more? I smiled and nodded, using every skill that I had been taught to avoid his eye and yet seem both positive and pleased.

"This is an unexpected honour, masters," I bowed, slightly, "more than I had ever anticipated. I only wish to let it sink in rather than answering on the spur of the moment. I should properly weigh up what it is that you have offered me."

"Quite right. Spoken like an experienced guildsman." Master Black commented. He rose and opened the door.

"We will drink a good bottle to celebrate when you say yes, Finn. I have a 1492 Vitali that I have been saving for such an occasion" my own master smiled broadly, again.

I bowed, once again, but left full of thought. There was something else here but, as Master Hand would say, it was "concealed beneath pretty words."

It was to his door that I went and knocked, softly.

"Come." I entered. Master Hand looked up from a plan that he was studying. He was a tall, lean man with a long face, much creased by experience and having obviously carried a lot more weight at one time that now hung about him in loose folds here and there. His hooked nose was like a fleshy beak in the centre between deep set, reflective eyes. He turned his thoughtful gaze upon me,

"You have questions? This is an unexpected visit, Finn. I assumed it was another apprentice, one who keeps coming with one question or other, one who perhaps doubts his place in the guild."

I paused, trying to decide if he was subtly referring to my own thoughts. "I have one question for you and it is a question that I wish to stay between us."

He put down the map and steepled his hands, then, regarding me more seriously than he had at first. "You have been made an offer, then?"

"I have."

"And did you accept, or are considering doing so?"

"I imagine I will but no, I required time to consider what it entailed."

"Always wise to read what lies in the words, eh?"

I nodded. It was something I had heard him say, often enough. "It is exactly that which gives rise to my question, master."

"I see. Then I cannot promise to answer it fully." He waved a hand for me to proceed. I sat facing him and took a moment to compose my thoughts before I began.

"Which masters, if any, urged for me to be offered the post of journeyman so soon?" He nodded, "That I can answer. As you would expect, your own master pressed for the promotion but he had little persuading to do. Masters Black, Shadow and myself were all of a mind. Master Street has had no dealings with you so was neutral on the matter. Was that all you wanted to know?"

"No. That was a conditional question, you might say."

"I see..."

"Of the jobs carried out by our Pentagon, which masters knew of them all?"

"All?"

"All." I confirmed, very definitively. He waved a hand. "Only your master would know of all your missions, why?"

"I just wondered who was really setting the tests that we were put to. We were an unusual pentagon. I thought perhaps there was another hand in it."

"In some cases, that was true but not in every mission. In the later ones, most of us were in some way involved with the discussion on what we should challenge you with and how we might wield what we had effectively. And now I have answered your question in full, I believe."

I bowed, "Thank you Master Hand, for everything. I have learned much that I will not forget."

He nodded and smiled. I think he took it as it was intended although my thoughts were not merely on what he had taught me in my time as an apprentice. As I walked away, heading for the usual inn where I would meet up with my comrades, I was considering something. The conclusion frightened me. To be sure of this, I would have to travel and to take whatever time was required. Only when I had concluded the matter would I be able to properly celebrate my promotion.

Decisions I

My father had joined the council of his peers whereupon "the emperor" made the decision to recognise Drachefauste as Duke of Rosgovia and Raga and First Warlord of the Empire. The proposal was exactly as Ysmelda had indicated. The Von Tacchims would keep Littesburg and gain the consolation of the Ducal Isles of Valdaria, lately vacated by the death of Duke Torvald Lunneberg, the last of his line.

I knew little of the isles at that time. My father seemed satisfied with the decision, although he and Leopold said little upon their return to Littesburg. I had accompanied them only to shadow their moves in the event that an attempt was made to remove them altogether. I rode back on the edge of their entourage. Neither spoke to me although they spoke very little even to each other. The family convened to hear what my father had to say and now, I was called in and bidden to take a seat at the council table.

My father laid out a map of the Ducal Isles and another of the Empire in a smaller scale.

"Gentlemen, it is time to reveal what part I have played in these last months while you were all at war. I knew Frederick would be a better war leader with Adhils and Pellinore to advise. Sadly, we could not hold back Drachefauste as I had hoped.

I intended to offer a compromise which would have given up what he wanted without the loss of so much of our dearest blood. That it cost the life of my eldest son," he tailed off, choking on the words. It took him several moments to compose himself.

"The empire has run its course. This desperate act, throwing meat to the circling predators in an effort to leash them and turn them into our servants will not succeed. Should Drachefauste win the war against Surmey, Karilia and the Carnossian Empire, he will want the throne and will slaughter any who stand between him and the imperial crown as have other such warlords before him. If he loses, we are no better off, worse, in fact as we will have given up two duchies which will need to be re-conquered and his barbarian horde ejected as well as whatever we lose in the battles with our three neighbours. No, the imperium is a sick body and we cannot hope to find a cure."

He paused and flattened out the map of the islands. "The Ducal Isles are rich in resources. The families that have taken root there are interested in independence. In the last few months, I have spoken with each of the dukes in turn and then gathered them together. We have a new aim.

We will break from the Empire and establish each ducal throne as an independent kingdom, with the smaller islands around divided between the group according to geography.

To retake an island is much harder than marching across the mainland states.

They are far from the imperial throne and there are other enemies to consider, as well as new powers arising in the south and west. The only one of the Dukes who is reticent is Grimwald Devereux, Earl of Asmarish.

His family have small lands in the central empire. The rest of us have notable estates that will be at risk but will also provide further concern to the beleaguered imperial council.

The choice will be a hard one. There are only two warlords that the council will trust. If they send Edmund Beresford, we will intercept him before he even leaves the mainland and worry at his supply line. They will not send Drachefauste. His role in this will soon be over and then he will die. The empire cannot entrust him with an army that would be great enough to seize the pearl throne. His death is assured."

I looked at him and saw it in his eyes. So, my father would be the executioner. How very like him to arrange it all so coldly. He drew himself up and continued his speech,

"I promise you. The dukes of the western isles are made of stern stuff. We will have strong allies."

"And what if the emperor himself takes the field. Will he not use the artefacts of his house and unleash demon lords and creatures upon us all?" I was surprised to hear Adhils sounding worried. He has seemed so dour, stern and unyielding when opposing Drachefauste. I was slightly taken aback.

"The emperor" laughed my father, cynically. "That is one of the many dark and dirty secrets that I have guarded for the good of this ungrateful state. There is no emperor. There has been no emperor in over two generations. Those who have played the part were just that, actors in effect. The council rules and pretends there is an emperor upon the pearl throne. I have been part of that conspiracy for over ten years. There are no wondrous artefacts, no unbreakable sword, no dark mages or animal masked slayers. The imperial throne is weak, nearly bankrupt from defending foreign wars and buying services. All that this war will do is to put a dagger between the ribs of the lingering old man. It will be a mercy."

There was a long silence. Pellinore sat back, stroking his beard. Everyone looked surprised apart from me and interestingly, Herlenbrand.

"No emperor? That is quite a secret that you have carried even amongst your closest family, brother" Adhils said, at length.

"But there must be an emperor" Leopold insisted, "Who signs the decrees? Who attends the public ceremonies? Who sits upon the pearl throne on any day? Surely nothing can work unless one leads."

"In a sense, that is part of the issue for the empire," my father nodded, "although I do believe that a council is more moderate and more able than an often unstable individual.

The emperors of the last age were touched with madness and other traits born of too much interbreeding within a few weak blooded families. As to the artefacts, if there ever were any, they have probably been sold off by councillors before I ever took my seat. I imagine they were only ever stories to bolster the position of the throne. So, now we must plan a new war, one of resistance and defence against whatever retribution is sent against us, for I am sure there will be some, however much debt it loads upon the throne. It will fail, though. All we have to do is to hold back the initial assault and the council will run out of money so fast that they will find nobody prepared to risk more coin for fear of never seeing it returned."

"And if the war does not go so well?" Adhils fixed my father with a long look, "I seem to recall you thought we would hold Drachefauste at bay. You may be politically astute, Vas, but in military matters, it was always Raef who led.

With he and Frederick gone, we are not as replete with war leaders. Pellinore is not as young as he was, Raef's sons are too young," here he nodded across to Rupert who had been invited to sit at council, "apologies, Rupert but it is true at the moment. Edmund here may have some experience and Fulk, though I do not like to take the open field, as you know. So, I say again, where will the leadership come from to manoeuvre our troops, besiege fortifications and win battles?"

Adhils sat back and looked about the table. My father frowned just slightly and then leaned forward, "The alliance of the dukes will provide plenty of capable war leaders. Why do Valdarian troops need to be commanded by Valdarian generals?

They may be led at unit level but the strategy and the overall lead could come from Baruna or Hanneberg, Gwythaor or Northmanay. The Grand Duchy can offer at least five highly experienced leaders who have campaign experience in one command role or another. And there are those who felt that Duke Bardus of Baruna, young though he may be, should have been the one the imperial throne turned to and not Drachefauste. This war may be fought on our own home soil but it is much more likely that the empire will strike at the Grand Duchy and our mainland territories, first. In terms of tactical planning, any war leader opposing us will not want to strike north against Valdaria and Gwythaor, leaving the Grand Duchy, Pharsalia and Baruna at their backs. If those fall then I would accept that we could lose the war, but I doubt any landing will be made that is not hurled back into the sea within weeks. I know what the imperial purse can stretch to, I know the minds of the council and I know the other pressures they are under."

"And what about Littesburg?" Pellinore asked, "Who will defend our mainland territories?"

"We will retain the majority of our forces in Littesburg. The revolt will come from the islands and it will be Leopold who is the rebel duke. The rest of the family will remain neutral at the outset and even make it known that we are available to intercede to try to talk Leopold into withdrawing his support for the rebellion. We will provide funds which are not traceable to the family so that mercenary armies can be assembled and the war paid for in a general sense."

There was a general stir at the table. Adhils shook his head and spoke first, "That will not be believed nor will it prevent the imperial throne striking at Littesburg. We are not well positioned to defend against an imperial assault despite the forts, castles and troops we have in Littesburg."

"If Littesburg stands neutral and the imperial council send out an army against us, do you not think the other central states will rise? The council cannot afford to inflame the nobility and the states upon which they rely to power the empire.

However, if they do come, Convar will march to join us as we will march to their aid if the council decide to strike at the Vas Coburgs. Saxonia will rise at that point and possibly Lander, Cytelia and Cylmarda. I believe the rebellion will be seen as being led and fuelled by the ambitions of the Von Samedes, as closest blood to the imperial throne. They will send their fleet and armies to crush Lothar and his brothers. The Ducal Alliance will meet them head on and we will win."

"I'm glad that you have made this decision on our behalf" Pellinore said, softly and with a little menace. "We lost our lands in Raga before the last war and we did not regain those. Now, you say we should risk Littesburg as well as the token lands we have been given in recompense for Raga and Rosgovia. Your role will be uncovered in this alliance that you have been putting together and vengeance will be directed at us all."

"I intend to 'die', with your hand being suspected of holding the dagger. My disappearance, followed by the rumour that you and Adhils took action to distance yourselves from my error and potentially withdraw the family from the war will throw the imperial council. They are so used to subterfuge, ambition and politics and so unused to loyalty that they will assume it to be true."

There was another silence. I had to admire this move on my father's part. It was unexpected but had a logic to it.

"And what of our allies? How will they feel when the majority of the Von Tacchim house steps aside?"

Adhils leaned forward to face my father directly across the table, "Will Convar march to help us, then, if the empire should send Drachefauste and an avenging horde to burn Littesburg, anyway?"

"It is part of the plan. Convar will also declare its position to be neutral.

So also, will other mainland landholders. One or two will even back the empire and promise some money or help which will come too late or be planted to cause trouble later. This war has been considered with some care."

"But not by the rest of your family. You have assumed too much, Vasely. Why should we go along with your plan? How do you know that the council is not already in possession of all the detail and already have their own considered plans in place? Can you really trust all those that you have spoken with? I don't like this plan. I think it has too many flaws and I think that we will pay dearly in blood for it."

Pellinore sat back, "It does not get my vote."

"Nor mine." Adhils added. "A well-timed rebellion I could support, but only when the imperial council had committed its forces and money and it was obvious that the time was ripe. I believe your judgement in this is flawed. Some of the islands will back the throne at the last moment. When that happens, the rebellion will totter and could fall into ruin. It would not surprise me if the Grand Duchy was really the agent of the council. Lothar Von Samedes would make an obvious choice as a councillor and yes, maybe even an emperor."

"Obviously, I vote for." Leopold said, a little sullen. "I think it's right that we should take vengeance."

"The Duchy of Littesburg votes yes, as well. I'm sorry Uncle Pellinore, Uncle Adhils but I am sure my father would have taken this on." Rupert flushed as the older mens' glowering focus turned to him.

"Two on each side of the argument. I agreed to forego any vote so that just leaves you, Fulk and you, Edmund."

"On what authority does Edmund speak?" Leopold began. My father gave him a hard look and he bit off the rest of his sentence.

"Fulk as a captain-general and I think Edmund has more than earned the right. The Marquess of Navarine, Conderys should also be here as he will also be one of our war leaders, but I have his vote here and he wishes to go ahead. So, Fulk."

"I'm sorry, my lord Duke, I have to go with Adhils and Pellinore." Fulk ran a hand through his short, iron-grey hair.

"It seems you have the casting vote, Edmund." My father watched me from under his brows, weighing my reaction.

"I am inclined to agree with our elder councillors." I began. Rupert looked down and Leopold's face showed a spasm of fury, momentarily, "But nothing is won if nothing is risked and I don't see why we should give up the lands that belong to the family.

Uncle Pellinore, I remember you saying we should have taken up the war in Raga, ourselves, and put together an alliance when the Emperor failed to defeat the barbarian horde.

Had we done so, perhaps we would not have let Drachefauste emerge from that as the leader and to swallow up Marshelyn, Jarlond and Rosgovia the way he has. We owe no allegiance to an imperium that has let us down and, indeed, insulted us with the decision they made. And we owe the beast death on or off the field of war.

Even if we set all those things to one side, there is an opportunity in the islands to play our part in the rise of a new power and to be close to its heart. I know Duke Gwayne and I have met Dukes Bardus and Merador. As for Tancred of Northmanay, I hear he is an independent kind of man and the goblin lords of Dalmania have no love for the Empire. I am thinking back to something that Alvale, Gwayne's cousin, said - that if Lothar wanted the Pearl Throne why did he not involve himself more closely in imperial politics? The Grand Duchy is very rich but pays a lot in taxes and dues. I imagine he is thinking about how rich and powerful he and his brothers would be if that money went into their coffers. So, in my view, like Alvale's, the island rulers have far more to gain through a successful rebellion than switching to support an already ailing and distant imperial throne."

I sat back to a nod from my father. Rupert was grinning. Leopold remained sullenly quiet. Adhils steepled his hands, "The argument is a sound one. Let us hope you are correct."

Pellinore nodded, softly, "War it is, then. I will gather what forces I can. I have no doubt that Parsifal and Uriens will be only too ready to ride to war with Adhgar." He sighed, softly. "I had hoped we had lost enough of our youngest blood."

The die was cast, as they say. If I'd known what a long, hard winter was to come and the shape of the war to follow, I may have been more reticent but that tale will have to keep. The rebellion was still in the future. There were alliances to cement and many months of manoeuvring ahead. The next move in this game was for us to accept the Ducal throne of Valdaria and make it our own.

Arrivals

From the moment that I first beheld Valdaria, I knew I had found the land that I could call my home. Sad though I had been to leave Rosgovia and Raga behind me, there were deep sorrows ploughed like eternal furrows into the face of those lands.

I remember standing at the prow of the cog, listening to the creaking boards and the wind in the sails. It was then that dawn crept from her bed and lit a lantern whose golden light revealed a breath-taking world.

I gazed for the first time on the frost-crowned peaks of Valstra Ghortha and Valstra Velnor and below them, falling into the deep cleft of Ravensfjord, the steep slopes of Thunderfell. Beyond the fells, I could see the spray from Neu-Erbtochfalle, the daughter of the mountains, a deep channel which captures the rainwater from every rill and combe on the west side of the peaks, before storming down in her unrequited passion and flinging herself from Griffon's Edge into the Solsjdammer, which flows out into the fjord just above the tidal watershed. And so onwards, along the waterway to where the rivers called The Three Sisters or Tresyster gush and chatter as they make their way down the gentler slopes of Veglensfell. There, nestling under the shadow of the Hammer Rock lies the small river port of Skyddshamn, with its bastion and tower that jut out into the channel, guarding the entrance to the small natural harbour around which the town is built.

The cog maneuvered, coming around to slide between the fort and the harbour gate tower. Slowly, we crept towards the outstretched arms of the jetties which gathered us in Skyddshamn's embrace. A small crowd had gathered on the waterfront to welcome their new Duke, most curious to see what their lord looked like and to hear what he would say.

My father, as ever, radiated confidence and charisma, stepping onto the gangplank. He waved his guards away, exhibiting not only trust but that he had no fear of any who might await his coming with darker motives. Although he was never a tall man, with his slim frame and short iron-grey hair, he seemed to project an image of a giant among ordinary folk as he strode to meet the town elders and guildsmen. He extended both hands, seizing those of the lead guildsman, Hjarn of Summerfell and heartily shaking hands as if they were old friends reunited. He greeted them all as if each mattered to him personally. It was a skill that I admired in him and knew I would seek to emulate in my latter days.

When he spoke, it was succinct. He promised little other than his effort to be a good lord to the people of the island and to lead them out of darkness - a veiled commitment to continue the bid for independence from the Empire, I thought.

At this, someone jeered but stern looks were cast and the sound died half-heartedly in the throat of the offender. My father said and did nothing to indicate he had even noticed.

No guards were signalled forward to seize the man as they might have been under the old regime. Instead, he spoke of wanting to understand the land he had inherited and of his love for the rugged places. He spoke of hill farms and hard weather, of hardship and care.

In all, his speech lasted perhaps no more than ten minutes but, in that time, he painted a picture of a duke who would be a leader and yet one of them. With those words, he committed us all to Valdaria and set the tone for our governance from that day forward. I wished, then, that my mother had been there to hear those words and to see the faces of the people. She would have read them for us. I wished too, that Finnmeyer had been with us. He would have revelled in those mountains and talked of trapping whatever beasts roamed their highest passes.

But they were not, and neither was Frederick who should, have been heir to this new land. We were less for it, but I made a promise to myself that we would one day regain the strength we took for granted that fateful day in Rosgovia when the beast first crept in to warm itself beside our fireplace.

Stones III

I was back in Riassa because I couldn't resist my curiosity. I had been there pursuing questions, had lingered to spend some time with my old friends, Tu'Lon, Coyle, Rill and Merik and then headed back to Car Duris. I had been back there only for a few days, to find out if the guild had any tasks for me. As they did not, I had decided I would visit Littesburg and find out how my Uncle Pellinore and Raef's family were doing.

There had been a shock wave and much speculation when my father was apparently assassinated. He had disappeared as promised. Pellinore and Adhils had immediately divided the Von Tacchim lands to keep up the facade that they were behind the act. Leopold had received Valdaria, Pellinore took Littesburg and Adhils the rest of our lands, including the title of Duke of Rosgovia, in defiance. Rupert and his brothers were apparently disinherited by the action. In truth, of course, the moves were made to shelter and strengthen positions in readiness for war. I assume Robert of Convar was brought in on the scheme because one minute he was readying men to take back Littesburg for Rupert and the next, he had signed an agreement with my uncles.

But then my interest was aroused by something else. It had begun with a token sent via courier to the inn where I was staying.

I recognised it at once. It was a message from an acquaintance I had made, Jaef. I knew it was from him because there was a chip of tiger's eye stone inside the folded parchment which simply read, "Looking for reliable contractors. Look for me where the blue boar winks." It was a reference to the one-eyed boar sign that hangs from an inn off Riassa's Street of Supplicants. It was not a place frequented by those on pilgrimage.

I was curious. We had only met twice properly since the night when he stepped out of the doorway on the quayside and yet here was a message requesting I came to Riassa to do a job. It had to not only pay well but be something of importance. For a couple of days, I had just kept the scrap in a pocket but I could feel it there, nagging me in quiet moments. When I tried to sit and just have a quiet beer, it whispered questions. In the end, I gave way to my less than idle curiosity. I packed a travelling bag, swung it onto my shoulders and set off for the canal port.

Less than a week later, I was back in Riassa, smoking a pipe and tucked into a suitable corner of the inn in question. A day passed with no contact. I walked a little but returned regularly to my corner. I contacted Rill, Coyle and Tu'lon, of course and they joined me. It was while all four of us were sitting there, drinking, that Jaef appeared, suddenly. I don't quite know how he did it but suddenly, out of nowhere, he was there beside my shoulder.

"I'm glad you responded."

"No others?"

"Most of the others arrived several days ago. I am waiting on two. Are your friends in?"

"We are," Rill spoke first, "although Finn wouldn't tell us what it was about."

Jaef smiled, slightly, "Then I will enlighten you, but not here. We should take a walk to somewhere we can be sure there are no eavesdropping shadows."

"If you can see them." I said, giving him a smile, "You seemed to have the skill to hide in plain sight. Surely others do, too."

"True," he said, "but you have friends who no doubt have ways to actively discourage such rudeness."

Tu'Lon gave a short laugh. "I like your friend, Finn. He reminds me of you."

"As that is a compliment, I shall accept it." Jaef gave a slight bow.

"Who said it was a compliment?" Coyle said dryly, dryly, with a wry smile.

Everyone laughed. We made our way into the street and walked until we were in a square with enough open space to make it difficult for a normal approach to be made. Tu'Lon and Coyle dutifully cast a couple of wardings and scanning around us.

"As far as I can tell," Tu'Lon nodded "we are alone."

"Then I must tell you that this is a serious matter and one I do not expect you to enter into lightly. If you decide against, I will trust to your discretion but will ask you to leave Riassa at once, at least for a few days."

Rill frowned. The other two grinned at this.

"Oh, is that right?" Coyle said, toying with his short blade, "And I suppose if we don't, we'll become targets or something like it?"

"No. I will have to defer or change the plans we have and that would be... awkward."

I nodded and waved a hand, "Let's assume you can rely on us and proceed. I have come a long way for this, unlike these layabouts."

Jaef nodded and dropped his voice. "In three nights, there will be a coup that seizes control of the Thieves Guild here in Riassa. Most of the old masters have become not only corrupt beyond the normal level but take no interest in promoting the guild or its many members. They have turned their backs on the traditions and there are vengeful spirits whispering to the priests of The Brothers about it. We have a great deal of backing from various quarters to act, but have made it all look like just talk until now. Quietly, we have been bringing in those who can be trusted to take direct action. Two of the existing masters and three new will take over the council, with five senior journeymen as the planning council to be their shadows and masters-designate. From there, we can rebuild the structure that served so well."

"And you will be one of these masters, no doubt." Rill asked, a hint of aggression in his question.

"One of the journeymen of the shadow council. My own master will sit in the five."

I nodded. I knew who Jaef referred to, "He'd make a good leader to have."

"Actually, that honour will go to the old head of the guild who is coming out of retirement to set things right before deciding on a successor with the others. Montoroy is a well-known face and adds credence to the new organisation."

"Montoroy, eh?" Coyle nodded thoughtfully, "I remember him. A smooth operator and a man who could keep a sense of perspective. In with some of the nobility and administration, too."

"Indeed, he is and was. He was a great believer in the apprentice to master system. Last year, the council tried to have him killed twice but he eluded the strikes. It is said that the Brotherhood of Executioners and Excruciators were quite put out, but refused a third contract. There was talk that they failed deliberately, but that would imply an agenda and that has never been their role."

A silence followed.

"So, what do you want us to do?" I asked.

"You would be assigned one of the masters. I had expected just you, Finn, but four makes it easier, I think.

Your job is simply to kill him and bring a token to the council in time for the announcement that the five are dead and a new regime is taking control. A full council has been called to coincide with the Night of Wolves, when The Brothers Halcar and Valcor slew all the traitor members of the great guild, here, five hundred years ago. We know there will be enough members there who will welcome the news and we expect to be supported by a show of hands to take control."

"And if not?" asked Tu'Lon softly.

"Then we offer an election by all members. A show of hands or secret ballot as preferred. There will need to be appointments. In the end, the result will be the right one."

"You would leave it up to chance?" Rill asked, surprised.

"If the masters of a guild do not have the blessing of those they lead, then they should not sit at the high table. The great craft guilds know this. They have re-elections every year. Just because our guild has lost its way and forgotten how to conduct business does not mean we should follow the same course as our predecessors."

I nodded. "I am in. There has been too much discord, and what you will achieve is right for the guild and for the future."

I looked at Rill and Coyle. Rill raised his mug.

"I'll say aye to that and I'm in, too. My questions were only to understand how different you might be from what we have now."

"I'm in, too. I wouldn't miss out on this. It's going to be far too interesting." said Coyle.

Tu'Lon paused, "I am not of the thinking that leadership should ever be forcibly removed in this way. I recognise the current regime's shortcomings but I must commune and let my true masters guide me in this. I shall give you an answer on the morrow."

He rose, slowly, "Upon which, I should begin before it gets too late."

Jaef rested a hand on Tu'Lon's arm, "On the morrow then, but should I see you abroad beyond this inn tonight, I will have no choice but to conclude the part you have decided to take."

There was a hush. Tu'Lon withdrew his arm and measured Jaef but then nodded, "I understand the cloak worn by your conspiracy. You need not fear any whisper from me."

He walked away towards the stairs to the rooms.

"He can be trusted." I said, with finality in my tone, "I would trust him with my life."

"And I" added Rill. Coyle nodded assent.

"Then, gentlemen, I will meet you at the western gates to the Empress' Garden tomorrow morning. I will bring a name and details to you of where the individual may be found. It will rest with you, then. I will also bring a retainer. I had calculated on one or perhaps one and an apprentice. The rate we were looking to offer is five thousand."

"It will suffice," I said, "split between us it is still enough, given the incentive."

***

So it was we came to enter the grand hall of the guild on a darkening evening in Autumn, bearing a small bag in which was the head of a master thief. The hall was buzzing with conversation and alive with people moving from group to group. Rumours were obviously rife and the younger members in particular, watched every new entrant with interest. After a while, the double doors at the head of the stairs above opened slowly and just about every conversation died on the lips of the waiting assembly. This was the entrance made each week by the masters but tonight, only one stood on the landing who had been there a week prior.

In the centre, wearing a grand master's robe beneath an open coat of bear fur, was the famed Montmoroy.

On his right were Charley Bates and Vados Gaar, the latter being the one surviving original master.

On his left were Scalvendar Redhand, formerly a senior journeyman and Bragos the Black, a master from the Guild of Crows, said to be the third most powerful guild in the Empire, based out of Ravenak.

These five descended the stairway, followed by the five senior journeymen in new robes of maroon edged dark grey with no fur on the collar or hood.

"Brothers in shadow, brothers in the streets and alleys, brothers in endeavour, pray be seated," intoned Bragos as the steward of the council.

Montmoroy continued, his rich tones rolling across the now silent hall. "Tonight, there have been changes. This is a momentous night and one that will witness a rebirth of this great guild. No more shall the masters reap the reward while those who work complain of having naught but scraps. No more will masters stand aloof when there are apprentices who would benefit from their teaching and guidance. Tonight, we return to the great days, the old days when we stood together as brothers. Tonight, we shall also pay our proper respects to the masters who have gone before, yea, even those who have made way this eve, for others to take their seats. We shall also make proper compensation to our founders and to The Brothers from whom our skills and powers stem.

From this day forward, not one, but two per cent of all declared takings shall be placed in the old treasure room where seats will be set up for the skeletons of our founders to sit, robed and revered overlooking their cut of the spoils.

In time, we shall revert back to one percent, once the council feel we have made good the tribute that others have failed to pay. The spirits have been disquieted and some of you will know of the incidents and visitations which are one of the many reasons for what had to be done."

Reaching the high council table, Montmoroy spread his hands; "Bring forth the heads of the four so all may be sure that they shall not come again to this table."

Around the hall, those of us who had been involved pushed forward and from three of four hemp bags came the severed heads which were taken from us by one of the senior journeymen and held high.

"Behold the traitorous, who have been judged by our founders and sentenced to death. These thieves failed their guild and stole from all. Their skulls will be placed at the founders' feet and there they may learn humility. Kosgorin's head will soon join these."

He turned, arms wide and nodded around. The guild members gathered around their tables. Rill, Tu'Lon, Coyle and I were accorded places on a table not far from the masters. Montmoroy lifted his arms. "Let the founders see that their Guild has been returned to the path." He sat down and the whole hall sat as one.

Chairs scraped, a soft murmur of voices began and Montmoroy lifted his goblet. "To the great Guild of Riassa, mother of them all..."

Then, he choked and clutched at the bolt which seemed to spring from his chest, leaving a red blossom around it.

Suddenly the air was full of the whine of missiles and then the shouting and panic of a hall full of even more deeply shocked young men. I saw Montmoroy topple and then I was diving for cover reaching for my sword. I saw a bolt skim the table top and take Bragos in the lower face, toppling him, instantly. Scalvendar managed to get to his feet and send a dagger spinning towards one of the six or seven men in black hoods, taking him in the heart but more were coming and three knives in sharp succession sent him sprawling across the table.

Men in the black hooded outfits of the Executioners Guild assassins were descending on ropes from above, swarming on the balcony, appearing through doors and amongst them, curling black-purple tendrils of power that seemed to spawn shadowy figures in armour. Behind these, arms folded, a look of triumph on his face was a figure I knew only too well. It was Klavon.

Beside him stood the Necromancer-master Kosgorin. It seemed that the promise of his death might have been a promise made too soon. Through the double doors came a whole troop of armoured skeletons, wielding rusted and hacked up weapons with deadly intent. Beside me, Tu'Lon was chanting and throwing bolts which turned skeletons aside leaving a potential gap for us.

"Come on," he yelled.

We rose. Coyle blasted a man in black and I took another down with a parry and thrust. Rill got a third with a thrown dagger. We came up in a burst and started for the door. Out of the corner of my eye, I saw Rill stagger and realised that he had been hit in the back by a bolt. He turned, reaching out a hand for my shoulder. I tried to support him but a second shot hit him in the side and a third snapped his head jerkily towards me. The expression on his face was surprise before the light in his eyes faded to nothing.

Then a cold darkness fell. I only vaguely remember seeing Klavon and three others picking their way through the fallen. Groups of apprentices huddled in corners.

Everywhere, hooded men in black stood, long blades pointed in a fence of steel corralling the groups in. I stirred and looked around me. One of the men pointed at us.

"What about this lot?"

"Leave them. They were just contracted in and besides that one is one of ours." Klavon waved in my direction. "Did anyone find Jaef or Bates?"

I remember us being hauled up and I remember hearing Klavon announcing that tonight, we had all helped bring together two of Riassa's most powerful guilds.

It was later that I learned how he had used us all to merge the assassins and thieves guilds into one, with Kosgorin as its head and Klavon as the power behind the throne.

It was sometime later that I came to understand the full extent of the change. He had brought together Riassa's main guilds with others as far flung as Jordis. He had even tacit approval and non-intervention agreed from Car Duris. He must have had the broad support of the masters who trained us both. It was as bold as it was decisive but how it had been done left me cold. How Klavon's reach had grown so long, I could not fathom, but it seemed he had continued to grow his power and influence while I had been away from the capital. There were also rumours that his patron was the High Cardinal himself.

Coyle and I took Rill's arms and hauled him between us but we all knew he was gone. The night air was chill that evening.

Beasts and Burdens

We saw to Rill's burial in an old churchyard on the edge of Riassa. On his gravestone we had written simply: "Rill – Adventurer. Died 1488. Our companion in life and death. Friends for eternity."

With a sour taste in our mouths, we then prepared to leave Riassa behind with no intention of returning. We decided to travel for a while, adventuring and living by our means for several months. We told some tales around the fire in the evenings while by day we combined the travel with a few small adventures. We paused for a time in Valkharis, an ancient city that was formerly capital of the city state of Zachia.

There, once again I met up again with the troubadour, Marcabru who was accompanied by another friend from his group, Teiwaz Nuin. Perhaps I will tell more stories at a future time of those adventuring days and of my new companions but suffice to say that Teiwaz was perhaps the most accomplished walker in shadows of anyone I have ever met. She had a strange companion which seemed to be a dragon-horse and acquiesced to being her mount. There seemed to be some deeper link between the two but to this day, I have never learned what that is. Behind her occasionally acerbic tongue and sharp questions, I found Teiwaz to be a good and loyal companion.

In Valkharis, too, we heard stories of Drachefauste. He had led the Imperial army to a great victory over the Carnossians. He had also personally slain the Karilian champion, broken the assault on the border city of Hashmard and was now preparing to make war on Surmey. I cared little for his accomplishments. Raef would have delivered the same with some of us riding at his side, too.

I had contacted Kharr to let him know we were heading back and he joined us outside Riassa in Terass, a small town where we stayed for about a week. We reached Riassa just before midsummer. Marcabru and Teiwaz left me there as they had arranged to meet Ylloelae and others at some celebration. We said goodbye and I asked them to remember me kindly to Ylloelae.

I learned that Drachefauste was staying at the Imperial Palace, where he had been feasted. That presented an opportunity as far as I was concerned. Before I left her, Ysmelda had given me instructions on how to visit her and with it, a key that would admit me to her private gardens. The gardens and her rooms led onto the main wing where all the council members had their chambers. I do not know whether she had considered what she had done as potentially dangerous or whether it was a deliberate act of defiance against the empire that she served. Either way, I had no qualms about using what I had been entrusted with to enter the palace unnoticed.

I had just turned up a narrow walkway with hedges and flower borders on each side when a figure stepped out from somewhere. How he did it, I cannot say, but I was caught out and I heard the rasp of a blade. I went to draw my own swords but saw the man re-seat his blade and approach. He was unkempt, with a scraggly beard that had been allowed to grow wild, long greying hair in similar condition and eyes that you could not read.

When I heard my father's voice, I could only stand in shock.

"Edmund, to what lengths do you go? Did I not teach you better than this?

I can guess what brings you here but Drachefauste is my concern. When it is time, I will do what must be done, as was always agreed. Had I foreseen what would happen when we chose him as our instrument, I would have killed him at that first meeting but now it is too late and what has happened has happened. You cannot call the waters back when they pass from the river to the sea nor can you reverse the events that have befallen."

"Stand aside, father," I spoke with contained rage, "you had your chance and you failed us."

My father's head came up and I saw the hurt in his eyes. His disguise may have fooled anyone else, but there was no mistaking those eyes.

"If you are planning what I suspect, desist, Edmund. You should leave Riassa at once."

"Why?"

"I already told you. It is not the time, and when the time does come, Drachefauste is mine."

"Not so. As hunters trying to bring down the prey, so whoever gets to the beast first gets to spit it."

"There was a time you would have been content to trap rather than to kill."

"Times change."

"Back down, son. I know what I am doing."

"Yes, so do I. Sacrificing your family for your political ambition. I understand now, how you rose so high, but you are just a dog not a master and like a dog you have been kicked.

You are not the man I thought you were. I have lost the mother that I loved, I have seen the man I admired above others and the man I treasured most as a friend all die because of your inaction and cowardice."

For a moment, his eyes flashed and I almost willed him to draw a blade so I could strike him down, so coldly furious was I towards him at that moment.

His expression changed and a sadness came into his eyes.

"I had hoped it was me that you most admired."

I gave a short, barking laugh, "you?" I leaned back on the garden wall and looked down on him as best I could. "You lost my respect a long time ago. You had the chance and supposedly the ability to deal with Drachefauste. But what about Finnmeyer, about mother, Raef and Frederick. Those burdens are all yours to carry." I hurled the last words at him with utter contempt in my voice. His eyes brimmed with tears.

At that moment, I would have loved to see him cry but he hardened. "Had you been the right man to be duke, you would understand the decisions that have to be taken."

"Convenient nonsense. You simply didn't have the guts to do what you knew in your heart was right. You are not my father. He died a long time ago. I don't know what you are, but whatever it is, it deserves only to be despised."

It was deliberately hurtful. It was also somewhat adolescent, but we often lash out and hurt those we love most with words or deeds. I held him to blame for what had happened to Frederick. So, I was abrupt and harsh.

With that, I risked a dangerous thing and turned my back on him, walking away before he could find any words to answer. I could feel his eyes boring into my back but no answer came, only sobs as he broke down. I was right, he was no longer the man he had been but then, after what he had lost, who would be?

I walked on with bitterness in my mouth, angry at him, angry at myself and angry at the world in general. Later, I regretted that parting, but when you are that age and have such self-belief, you can trample on the feelings of others all too easily. I felt cold but in control as I put the key in the lock that would admit me to the palace. Standing on the threshold, I checked behind me to ensure there were no guards or other watching eyes that I could see. When I looked back, my father had gone. I spat, symbolically behind me as if to cast one final insult his way and then stepped inside.

Beyond the encounter with Drachefauste, a meeting I had played over and over in my mind, I had no definite plan. It was still early on a midsummer morning, but the sun had long risen from her slumber and the nobles of the palace would have already broken their fast. The temperature was balmy but the slight bite of pre-dawn still lingered and dew clung to the manicured lawns of the garden where there were still shadows cast. I took a winding path between collections of shrubs, flame lilies and other exotics.

The only eyes that seemed to watch me go by were the dew drops in the centre of lupin leaves and the bright centres of some border flowers. The seductive scent of mock orange and buddleia might, at some times, have brought me calm.

I would have stopped to admire the slow sway of flower-laden stems and of butterflies as they fed upon the offered pollens.

The garden was indeed full of colour and the constant humming of at least a dozen types of bees and flies, of hawk moths flitting between the blooms, whirring like tiny hummingbirds as they sipped nectar with long curling tongues.

Today, however, I was drawn into myself, focused on one task alone. There was just a whisper of noise behind me and I swung about, daggers appearing in both hands as I anticipated having to add an unfortunate death to the price attached to the head of the beast. Kharr looked around the edge of a prickly leaved mahonia.

"Unless you are planning on some impromptu pruning, my friend, I think you are safe to put those away."

I couldn't help grinning. I spun both daggers, theatrically as I sheathed them. There was a soft clapping and Merik and Tu'lon stepped into view, Coyle a pace behind them with a short sword in hand and a black scarf about his head like a stage pirate. He gave me a lop-sided grin, "hadn't got anything better to do when these two suggested a morning stroll."

"I don't suppose there is any way that I can persuade you all to go back to the inn and wait for me there?"

"Not really, no," said Merik. Kharr inspected his falchion as if he had found a speck of dirt on it. He gave the blade a little polish with his sleeve and avoided my gaze. Coyle shrugged again.

"You are all going to get into trouble with the Empire if you are seen helping me get inside the palace."

"Overrated commodity, Imperial gratis" Kharr said, drily.

"Do I look like I would care?" Tu'lon added.

"So many other roads to travel," Coyle gave another grin.

We moved on together. At the outer door to the hallways, I produced the key.

Merik handed me his great sword sheathed in its scabbard decorated with rubies. "Here. Take Clave. He will give you an advantage against Drachefauste if we find him."

I hesitated. I knew something of the sword's power.

"Go on, Finn. It may make the difference."

I nodded and swung the sword onto my back as Merik always did using the long cord attached to the scabbard so it could easily be brought off the shoulder to be drawn.

"Thank you."

"Friends, remember." He gripped my hand, "Clave, look after my friend, Finn."

It took me under thirty seconds to pick the next lock. I suppose that the imperials had got used to reputation keeping people out.

I have to say that I find reputation overrated. I hadn't been stopped once on any of my visits to the great and the good.

Maybe that's one of the reasons they gave up having real Emperors. They were probably far too easy to assassinate.

Predictably, the long gallery was empty anyway. The curtains were all drawn, but by the sunlight I was now admitting, I could see its whole length. There were some shuttlecocks, a set of skittles, plenty of fine paintings and a couple of impressive marble busts on half-pillar stands but no guards. I stepped inside and drew the curtain back across the opened door. I went first, moving silently down the hall to the far door.

Out of nowhere, five ghost-like apparitions materialised. I realised then why the curtains were kept drawn when the gallery was not in use. I drew my falchion and Rill's dagger.

The others surged in around me and we engaged in one of the strangest combats that I have ever been involved in. The wraiths, or whatever they were, had no voices and fought with blades and shields that gave off a chill, while we five were like ballet dancers trying to move, block, riposte, slash and stab whilst remaining as quiet and careful as we could.

Five on five was a one-sided confrontation given the composition of our group. I had barely started to duel with my opponent when Tu'Lon released some kind of wave of light that sent all the ghostly guards backwards as if they had been physically struck.

The contest was brief thereafter. Within a few moments, all that remained as evidence of the encounter was a slight cold edge to the air and five fading shadows on the ground where our enemies had been anchored to this plane of existence.

I tried the door, this time pausing to check first that there were no further traps set, either physical or magical. Best to make no more assumptions, I decided. We went through an ante-room to a second hallway which entered a hall, with a four-sided mezzanine accessed by a staircase at each side of the hall close to the halls that emerged into it. I could see four guards on the lower level and pointed out positions with a series of motions. The upper level was my target. That was where the main dignitaries, including the council, had their chambers and where I hoped and expected to find Drachefauste.

Fate often lends a hand in these things. You may have noticed in your own experience how that happens. Heavy footsteps sounded down the upper hallway and I looked towards the landing. Drachefauste, with some courtiers in tow, was approaching the staircase to my right. I finally had my quarry in sight.

"Drachefauste" I hissed, low under my breath, "it's now or never."

My companions nodded and I broke cover. Sprinting across the hall, I leapt, speaking a single word that enabled the cloak.

My magical leap carried me past the shocked guards to half-way up the staircase.

I was drawing my falchion and a long dagger as I took the steps, two at a time. I was gladdened to see Drachefauste shove the closest courtiers out of his way and draw his own weapon. He came to meet me at the head of the staircase.

Now, everything was in motion. Drachefauste sought to use the advantage of height and better position before I reached the mezzanine, but I bounded onto the landing, dodged his rush and spun about so that we faced one another along the line of the landing rail.

Four guards came for the stairs, two loading crossbows only to find they had unexpected company.

Merik sent the first sprawling with the flat of his blade. Kharr rapped one of the crossbowmen on the back of his head with the hilt of his scimitar, clubbing the archer to the floor where he kicked the poor unfortunate in the groin and used his other foot to send the crossbow sliding away across the polished floor.

Coyle blocked a wild swing in his direction, wagged an admonishing finger at the guardsman concerned and then slid his blade around the pike in a circling riposte that pierced the man's shoulder.

He followed up with an uppercut with the hilt, smashing the man's nose so it gushed blood. The guardsman dropped his weapon and clutched his broken nose in both hands.

The fourth man raised his crossbow but couldn't get a clear shot with Drachefauste and I engaged in combat. Merik tapped him on the shoulder.

When the archer looked around, he was propelled to the ground by a push that was more like the kick of a carthorse. Tu'Lon stood behind the others and stopped several more entrants, frozen on the spot by his commands.

Meanwhile, Drachefauste and I circled one another, warily. He had a long-handled axe in his right fist. "So, boy, you survived the assassins. I should have known I would have to deal with you myself, in the end."

"I don't understand." I said, blocking a blow and scarring his left hand with my dagger as he pulled back, "you had two chances to kill me. Why then, turn to assassins?"

"You didn't matter, then. More use to me alive to taunt your father. Later, I had more important matters to worry about than dealing with you personally, boy."

He was lying. There was something else in his eyes, something I had not seen before. He had aged and put on weight but more than that, I sensed some actual fear. Drachefauste was afraid. I leapt back but his axe caught my dagger, shattering the blade to the hilts.

I threw it down and cast the falchion aside, too. With a thought, I pulled Clave free and the sword flamed into life. The great red gem gripped in the fist of gold that fashioned its pommel glowed and pulsed. Drachefauste took a step back.

"You're a liar as well as a beast, a creature that doesn't deserve to be treated as anything other than vermin," I spat, "you may have killed my uncle and my friend, my mother and my elder brother but they will be avenged and you know it, don't you? That's why you wouldn't face me a third time."

"Insolent pup!" He lunged but my confidence was growing. I was quicker, more experienced than I had been years ago, a veteran of many types of contests and now all those stood me in good stead. I evaded his blow and carved his left hand off at the wrist. Blood poured but only briefly from that wound. As I expected, it staunched quickly. A ripple passed across his face and a vein pulsed at his temples. He scowled deeply as if he was distracted by a thought.

I pressed him hard. He slid the axe in his hand so that it gained a foot or so and then swung again but I was already on the move. It struck the railing of the mezzanine, throwing up sparks as it split metal and stone with a crack that sounded around the hall. My blow was a thrust into the fleshy area above his right knee. I twisted Clave until Drachefauste groaned in pain, the first time I and probably others had heard such a sound from the man. It proved how mortal he was, or had become. I pulled the blade free, letting the flame cauterize the wound. I wasn't done with him, yet.

"That was for Raef," I said.

He grunted and came at me, trying to use a kick and a quick backswing with the axe but once again, I had his measure.

Clave met the haft of the axe and fire burned Drachefauste's face, singeing his hair and licking hungrily about his fleshy visage. I sliced with precision, taking off his left ear.

"For Finnmeyer." I said, watching Drachefauste stumble back, burned and wounded. Suddenly double doors below blasted open and Drachefauste's personal guards rushed in. Somehow, they must have known he was in peril. I realised, then, what he had been straining to do when he looked so far away.

Kharr, Coyle and Merik galvanised into action and a fray broke out as they blocked the Dragon Guards from accessing the stairs backed up by Tu'Lon's enchantments. I concentrated on Drachefauste. He stepped back as I came for him.

"Fool," he threw at me, "my men will kill your pathetic little band and then I will have you to carve my name into before you die, screaming."

"You think so?" I retorted as I saw Coyle yell and point a finger from which leapt a green lightning flash. Three troll-folk fell smoking to the floor. "I think you overrate your chances."

I closed, this time and we met, pushing on one another. He tried to use his superior size and brutish strength to gain an advantage but I had learned to fight big men.

I gave before him, turned him using his own weight and, hooking Clave's cross-hilts under the curved rear blade of his axe, I ripped upwards, tearing it free of his grip.

My blow cut him across the chest from ribs to shoulder and he fell on the marble floor, looking up from all fours.

"That was for my mother." I said, using the blade to tease the wound open as I stood at sword's length.

He gasped as the fire from the blade burned him, again. I guessed, rightly, that it was preventing him from healing as quickly as he normally did.

He knelt up, "Alright boy, you win. After you took your mother home, I met with a magus, a wise elven woman who was supposed to be an oracle. She told me that a bastard, clothed in black like a creature of the night would come for me. I knew, then, I had made a mistake in letting you live or fate had intended that we clash a third and last time but I fear no words from witch women. She screamed all through the long death I gave her." As he said this, he moved swiftly, snatching up the axe and rising to hurl it in a single motion, just as he had the day he slew Raef. It was a manoeuvre I had day-dreamed over a hundred times in imagining our meeting and the axe flew by as I moved to dodge even as he rose.

"And this is for Frederick," I yelled. Clave came around in a fiery arc and took off the beast's head. It rolled across the mezzanine floor while his body stood, fixed in place. Then Clave's flames engulfed it and the charred remains hit the floor in a wreckage of blackened bone and ash. I lifted the head by the hair and faced it towards the remaining guardsmen who were penned in by one of the doorways as my friends pressed them back, step-by-step.

"Behold the head of a traitor, a beast and an abuser of the helpless."

It was then that I saw the imperial guardsmen had returned with an entire troop. At least half a dozen crossbows were pointed in my direction. Drachefauste's guards were all down, now and my friends had turned to face the new threat. Merik just leaned on his blade, smiling as the guards flooded in to level polearms and crossbows at he and the others.

Kharr stood at ease, falchion hanging down at his side, similarly, giving them a smile as if they were just some group of unarmed and untrained peasants protesting about an injustice. Coyle twirled his blade, taking time to inspect his appearance, straightening his headscarf, brushing his shirt down and flouncing the cuffs back up. Tu'Lon although clearly exhausted, raised his long stave with the mace head and it started to glow. I kept hold of the head in one hand and jumped from the balcony. The guards nearest scattered backwards, nervously while two crossbow bolts loosed in reaction whined over my head to strike the mezzanine balcony. I landed heavily but managed to rise, even though my ankles felt like they had been crushed by the force of the landing.

A slow, sarcastic clap sounded from the doorway. The Cardinal was even taller and more imposing than in the paintings I'd seen of him. He towered over many of the guardsmen as well as his own small entourage.

"I am only surprised that it is not your father standing there, but then he would have shown more restraint and removed Drachefauste when the time was right. Seize them."

My friends all lifted their weapons ready to resist but I stepped forward.

"It's me that you want. Let my friends go."

Guards grabbed me roughly. The others closed in, numbers growing steadily as they appeared from every door and the stairs behind us. I looked at my companions as they moved forward to intercept.

"No, stop, don't let it end this way. Put your weapons aside. I've only killed Drachefauste, don't spill innocent blood on my account."

Decisions II

We were dragged down many flights of stairs to a dungeon with little light and chained to the bars. Our equipment was listed and then removed. Needless to say, it was dank, smelly and there were rats that moved about outside the light of the single candle flame we were permitted. At night they came closer, but we ignored them unless they got too bold. Food was brought in although it was a thin gruel that tasted sour. It must have been three days before anyone came to see us.

A face appeared with two guards hanging back in the darkness. It was the austere figure of the Librarian.

"Young man. I thought we had agreed that there would be a right time." He directed the comment at me. I stirred and stretched, moving about so I could face him. The others watched me.

"The right time," I replied, softly and with an air of menace, "was at the beginning when he first crossed our threshold. You should have seen to it before you let him kill one of your number."

"Oh no," the Librarian waved a hand airily, "that was far too good an opportunity to rid ourselves of a pretender whose intentions were to pass himself off as the true emperor, to seize the pearl throne and so overstepped the mark.

It was unfortunate that Drachefauste should fall now. He still had work to do and you, young man, have deprived your empire of a necessary servant. I will not say a loyal servant, but a useful blunt instrument in times of trouble."

"I saved your life once. Let my friends go free."

"I cannot do that. I know that I owe you a debt, but do not ask too much. There is a process to go through. I will ask the head jailor to see to it that you are a little more comfortable so that you can at least face your trial with some dignity."

He rose and left. I hung my head.

"We'll get out of this, don't worry." Coyle grinned. His head scarf had been taken and he had a rough bandage where he had been cut in the fracas that followed. It was soaked with blood.

"They already think I am a Surmeyan spy," Kharr smiled, "hopefully, I can change that belief. I have no intention of going to the block, or whatever they use here."

"And if we don't get out of it, we'll all come back and haunt that Cardinal fellow. Him and Klavon. I'd haunt the pair of them." Tu'Lon grinned but there was fear in his voice, beneath the bravado.

"Let's just see what happens. There's no point in talk unless it has a purpose." Merik growled.

"Why don't you try finding a way out of here?" He asked Coyle, "You and Rill were always the ones for some scheme of how to get in or out of a place."

That evening, or what we judged evening, as far as we could tell from the light that reached down here, we got a slightly better meal.

Our main jailer was called Bail. He seemed a reasonable enough man. After many attempts, we engaged him in a conversation about his family and how he came to be doing the job. After that, we got colder water that tasted fresher, too.

However, the two other jailers, Nod and Cubby came in to give Kharr a beating, accusing him of being Surmeyan scum. He remained calm and tried to tell them he had fought against the Surmeyans for the Empire. They didn't seem to like that answer and knocked some of his teeth out. When the morning came, strangely, I couldn't see any gaps when Kharr gave us a smile and said he was alright. The next evening, they returned and we all got asked questions, aimed to get an answer they could use as an excuse to give another kick or punch. We realised that someone else was there watching in the darkness beyond. We appealed for a chance to be questioned properly. There was no answer other than more punches.

The following morning, Kharr was removed.

He didn't return.

I felt tears sting my eyes when evening came and I guessed he had been executed. The mood in the cell was very subdued that night. We talked about how we might convince the court to let us go free and tried all the bars and floor, seeking anything to work on. At least Nod and Cubby made no further visits.

"I hope Kharr convinced them that he wasn't a spy." Tu'Lon said. "He told me that he had been a captain in the imperial cavalry at one point, a mercenary but still an officer. Sounded like he had a distinguished campaign, too, fighting the Surmeyans."

"He never told me that." I replied.

"Oh, we were just having a drink one evening at one of the times you weren't about. He was visiting Riassa. I think he was hoping to find you there. He found us easily enough, anyway. He's quite a fellow…. was quite a fellow."

The air hung heavy with that sentence. I hung my head again. I had been doing that a lot over the last few days. It was my fault they were here and I felt the burden of it. It twisted my insides until I wanted to yell out or cry.

They took Merik next. The day after, Tu'Lon, then Coyle. I was left alone.

I had plenty of time to reflect. Perhaps the Librarian was right.

It could have waited. Why was I in a rush to get it done?

After all, we had lost everything that really mattered. I think it was because I had completed my training and wanted to move on with life, but until Drachefauste was resolved, I couldn't rest.

Now, I had brought my friends to their deaths, whereas had I waited, the time would have come. It's not as if the beast was interested in Valdaria. He had long forgotten his threat about the duchess with Rosgovia in his hands and my father gone from the scene.

While I was contemplating, Ysmelda appeared brushing between two guards and bringing a sweet scent of roses and some other flower.

"Oh Edmund, what have you done?"

"What you or someone should have done before the pointless war that killed half my family and tore a chunk from the Empire that will bleed like a wound for years to come."

"I did not give you the key to misuse. I gave it to you so you might visit."

"You think I would not have found a better way than the front door?"

"But you only knew of the way in through the gardens because I showed you."

I stayed silent.

"You were told that there would be a right time. Couldn't you wait?"

"No. Drachefauste wasn't winning any wars for anyone but himself. He had designs on the throne and would have removed you all. I heard that the Imperial Steward had been found mangled in a ditch."

"The High Chancellor of Law has also disappeared, believed killed by a very clever and experienced assassin. His residence was supposed to be secure against all sorts of magic and cunning. It was laden with traps and guards. They say only a master could have got to him. There was a black silk hand grasping a dagger found in his bed. I understand that is a message from the guild."

I swallowed hard. I knew that signature. It was from Car Duris. Whoever wanted the Chancellor removed had used our guild. "Who stood to benefit?"

"The Cardinal has assumed control of the courts for the moment. He is moving to try to retain that as well, suggesting we can do without a chancellor on the inner council. He will try to get his man appointed."

"But Drachefauste also might have been moving in."

"Yes, that was the feeling of the council. That Drachefauste knew who to remove. If he got to the Cardinal, Librarian and Treasurer, he would have no opposition.

I certainly wouldn't have tried to resist his rise and made that clear from early on.

Your father was missing - is still missing - perhaps he really has been assassinated by his brothers. I did not think they had it in them. It's possible that it was the same hand that was behind the death of the chancellor and nothing to do with Pellinore or Adhils.

I think the Cardinal was even worried. He would be the only other with such ambition and from my experience, he has tried to ensure there is a full council until most recently."

"Why Car Duris?" I mused, ignoring her mention of my father. I wondered what she would have said if she knew how close he was to the palace. "Of course, because the Cardinal controls the guild here. It wasn't the Cardinal. He'd have asked Klavon to see to it. Although that could be a double bluff, I think he would have moved through his own direct influence. So that points at Drachefauste, but there has never been any suggestion that Drachefauste resorted to assassination as a means to further his own position. Presumably he would be just as prepared as any. But I wasn't aware he had any connections."

"I'm not following completely, Edmund. Car Duris? Klavon?"

"I thought you were a well-connected assassin."

"I was trained. I am not connected as much as I would like to be. My contacts on the streets and in the noble houses have been falling by the wayside over the last years.

Most of us are targeted that way. Usually it is by one another as we try to have the best base for information and influence. I didn't need anyone in your ducal court as your father and I were friends. But the others tried often enough. You may recall a man called Vorne De Haille."

"My father's head of guards and castellan."

"One of the Cardinal's men. He died in the war, didn't he?"

"Yes, Frederick wrote about it."

"He was killed by someone on your side who worked for the Librarian during the battle. These things happen, and opportunity allows removal of pieces from play. Sometimes for political advantage, sometimes it is the old tradition of vendetta, an eye for an eye. Both are expected, the latter allowed under the old laws, of course."

"Is that all it means to you and the others? A bloody game?" I raged, my voice rising.

"If you were a player, you'd understand. The game is deadly."

She rose and smiled sadly, "Goodbye Edmund. I doubt we will talk again like this. I wish it could have been different. I had such hopes that you would do this right and prove an effective weapon for the Empire."

I was about to retort that I'd be damned if I did anything for the empire but bit that back.

If anyone else were listening or Ysmelda reported back my words it might make matters worse.

"I could still be and even more so if you had left my friends alone so I had them as companions on missions and in the field. I wanted to be the next Raef, not an assassin. But now I have a range of skills and I will put them to use if I escape this situation. I would serve you well, my lady, but not as an unwitting piece."

"I cannot free you and you would be too obvious. It is a great pity. You could have been quite…magnificent."

They came for me the next morning. I was cleaned up and allowed to dress in a decent tunic and black leggings. I got my boots back, too and my rings. I was marched between two halberdiers into a courtroom. I was directed to sit on the single chair facing a curved table behind which sat five figures all in shadow. There were guards in numbers.

"Edmund Von Tacchim, Black Finn, you are here because you defied imperial law and entered the palace without authority, began a fracas which ended with the death of an imperial warlord and then tried to justify the attack as the right thing to do. Have you anything more to say before the court discusses and pronounces sentence?"

I considered. Something Ysmelda said came back to me. "I believed I was entitled to enact vendetta, revenge for the killing of my brother and my mother by Drachefauste."

There was a pause. Heads turned towards the figure in the centre. He or she inclined their head.

"Your plea is noted. Have you anything else to add?"

"Drachefauste was moving to seize the throne. The council knew it in their hearts. He had two killed already."

"How do you know that?" the voice was that of the Librarian, I was sure of that.

"He was a man with the strength to twist and mangle the Steward's head. No doubt he exacted information while providing pain and death. Who else would be so crude? It was a message. Then there was the Chancellor. The silk fist is a message from Car Duris. That means a master of that guild committed the deed. Only Drachefauste and the Chancellor stood to gain by it. The Chancellor has control here in Riassa, so the use of Car Duris means it was someone else. Drachefauste must have a contact there."

And then I sat back and a cold realisation passed through me. "Of course," I said aloud, "that explains something else."

"Would you like to explain that last comment?" asked the Cardinal.

"No. It is something I have to deal with or would have done."

"Anything more?"

"No, I believe I have said enough. You should have freed my friends. They were not at fault. They were being loyal followers. We do not execute followers, only leaders. We did the empire a favour, did all of you a favour and we could still have been there to call on again. You have wasted us foolishly. I hope you'll realise that one day."

"The prisoner will now remain silent. If you speak during deliberation, your tongue will be cut out."

I relaxed back in the chair. Only now did I see clearly. The game had been afoot and I had missed something not only vital but right in front of my nose.

A court official moved into the centre, carrying an imperial sceptre. The end of it glowed softly with a magical were-light spell. It was placed in front of the central hooded figure, throwing his features into a sharp silhouette.

"Death or Exile are the options." Intoned the central figure which was obviously the High Cardinal. "I have heard the claims made, which are not necessarily accurate. There are arguments which can be made for leniency but this has cost us a war leader who has put fear into our enemies at a time when we are sorely beset. Furthermore, I do not like the implications that have been aimed at us. I doubt that Edmund Von Tacchim will serve us again and as such is of no further use. My decision is death."

He folded his arms and sat back. The sceptre was passed right.

"I do not like to cast aside a useful resource, but I am inclined to the opinion and argument of my learned friend." Came the voice of a man I did not know. It seemed they had replaced one of their number at least. "Death is the safest course."

"Thank you, Lord Steward," said the middle figure. Once again, the sceptre moved right.

"I will not countenance the execution of a Von Tacchim when they have already paid such a high price. What Edmund did was wrong but I believe he has greatness in him. The Empire needs such men. Exile." Ysmelda spoke with passion.

"Thank you, Chief Concubine. Your connection is well known. I would have expected no less."

The sceptre was carried left of the Cardinal. The next figure was shorter and stouter than the Cardinal. I guessed this was the Lord Treasurer. "I dislike the sound of death for someone capable of heroism. I think we should put our faith in the Von Tacchims. They have served the Empire with distinction. Exile."

My heart was thumping, now. I had been thrown a lifeline. Only the lean figure of the Librarian remained. I wanted to appeal, remind him he owed me his life but I could not afford to speak. I stared mutely at him, wondering if he could see me better than I could see him.

"My inclination is to follow my more learned friends. Edmund Von Tacchim is damaged and unreliable, in my view. I have doubts about him and I worry about his father."

"Death then?" The Cardinal waved for the sceptre to be returned but the librarian put out a hand and held it down.

"I did not complete my thoughts." The librarian pondered for a few moments. "I owe the boy my life. That debt is now settled, irrevocably. We owe one another nothing. Exile it will be."

I breathed out. I couldn't believe it. My bonds were being loosed and I was hauled to my feet as the sceptre was passed back to the High Cardinal. He thumped it end down on the table.

"By the power invested in me by the most high and powerful Emperor of Nordovicia and by the authority of his council, I sentence you, Edmund Von Tacchim to ten years' exile.

You shall not set foot in Nordovic during that time on pain of death, nor shall you stay in any of the imperial states for more than a day at any time for the next five years.

Your companions are subject to the same sentence as you.

You will be granted ten days to leave Nordovic and one month to travel out of Imperial jurisdiction.

At the end of the exile period, you will report to this court to be freed of the sentence, depending upon your actions. During that time, if the empire chooses to call upon your service, it is expected that you will respond in our favour for your own good and that of your friends and your family."

He banged the sceptre down three times and they all stood. The five figures filed out while I was led gently through the doors to an outside cage where my friends were chained in a row under heavy guard. The door was opened and they were set loose.

"I'm sorry" I knelt. "I thought I had got you all executed. We have been exiled for ten years from Nordovic and for five from all other states. We have to leave Riassa and the imperial lands swiftly. We have a month's grace and then we are all outlaws. I'm sorry. This is my fault."

The other four were grinning. They hugged me and each other.

"I always said I thought the Empire was overrated." said Coyle.

"Come, Finn. Look at all the places we can travel. I will show you why the desert lands are so much more beautiful than this crumbling sewer of ambition and greed." Kharr replied.

"I fancied a change, anyway." Tu'Lon added.

Merik offered his hand. "Friends, always, remember. We'll find new lands and adventures, together."

While we were talking, to my surprise and gladness, all our money, weapons and armour were brought and listed from the chests and we were asked if anything was missing. I handed the men five silver each and another small bag which I had them promise to give to Bail.

Ysmelda appeared in a gold silk dress with white flowers and a white flower in her hair. Merik whistled and Coyle gave me a sign behind his back. I scowled at them both.

"Edmund. I couldn't keep to what I said. I wanted to say goodbye properly."

She moved up and offered her hand. I knelt and kissed it.

"My lady. You remain my patron and one day I will reward your faith, though I have not today."

"You did reward my faith today," she said softly, "and did what I knew you would. Fair travels Edmund until we meet again." Then she kissed me, softly on the cheek and stepped back.

I wanted to say more but the words would not come. I bowed, deeply. When I looked up, she was walking away.

Friends IV

We were escorted only as far as the edge of the Noble Quarter and reminded there that we had a ten-day lease, after which we would be arrested for our crimes against the Empire. The captain of the guards spoke with no conviction and bowed his head to us as we lifted our hands and rode away. Clearly, the imperial guardsmen didn't think Drachefauste was a loss, either.

I suppose, looking back, I had been experiencing a kind of fatalism and had no plan beyond putting an end to the beast. Suddenly, here I was, cast back onto the streets and told to leave all the places that I had ever known.

Merik, Tu'Lon, Coyle and I decided that we would take a ship from Riassa to Jordis and from there, I planned to address a few matters that would lead me back to Car Duris. Ultimately, my plan was to sail to Gwythaor and hide there, visiting Valdaria and the other islands if I needed to keep moving. After all, there was a death sentence hanging over us now though it seemed unlikely to pursue us to the further corners of the Empire.

Coyle, Tu'Lon and Merik were thinking about going into business together, based in Car Duris. They had asked me to join them when I could. We would do a little adventuring in the mountain tunnels that were attracting many to the town in search of a quick fortune or artefacts.

It would enable me to continue my work as a guild journeyman and still leave time over. They seemed to have come to the conclusion that once I returned to the guild, I would stay in Car Duris as a journeyman and rise to master. Under the aegis of the guild, I would be immune from prosecution so the imperial ban would not find me there.

Kharr left us for a while after that. He had quite a bit of business and some money tied up in Acondium. He would go and disappear there for a while as Convar was a safe state with no love of imperial decrees. He would meet us in Jordis or in Car Duris in a few months' time. We embraced and he mounted up.

"I have one or two other friends I must introduce you to." Kharr smiled. "You should come and visit my little place in Acondium, Finn. And the rest of you, of course. Be careful and make sure you choose a ship that's not full of holes." He laughed and with the ease of an expert horseman, turned his mount and was away leaving just floating dust. I watched him go a little sadly. I disliked partings, especially when the future remained so uncertain.

Riassa had always been the last port of call on my quest that I had set myself on the day I had accepted the ring of a guild journeyman at the Car Duris house of the Executioners. The answer to the question on which I had pondered for so long left a storm cloud of doubt and of sadness hanging over me.

Although I was pleased that we had survived the encounter with Drachefauste, by my normal standards, I was sullen and withdrawn. But I was not alone. My friends were all affected similarly, so we had little joy from each other's company as we headed for the port where we went seeking berths on a fast ship.

As if reflecting our current luck, there were neither berths nor room on any of the coast-hugging caravels that would have taken us to Jordis in good time. Eventually, we departed Riassa on an armed merchantman, a large cog which would be making a couple of calls in the islands on the way. The chance to see Pharsalia and Baruna seemed as good as anything at that time. The four of us spent some time up on deck, picking up some skills, helping out with the watches and generally keeping busy. None of us really wanted to think about or discuss what had happened in Riassa. We hadn't even been paid for our involvement, which just compounded the loss of our friend.

We were two days out with land in sight when the wind seemed to drop as if it had been called away. Within a few short minutes, the land vanished into a haze which turned into thick banks of chill fog which quickly enveloped us.

For a few moments after, all you could hear were the creaking sounds of the cog's timbers and masts, punctuated by muffled shouts of crewmen as we tried to find the wind and steer the ship safely through. It was then that something appeared out of the fog bank, looming above us like a huge shadow that foretold our doom. Out of the mist, came a weathered skull so huge that it rose above the level of our deck, its dark and empty eye sockets staring ahead, great horns of bone jutting back towards the vast stone body of the vessel. And then, there were hundreds of glittering faerie lights describing towers of black stone with flying walkways upon which small dark shapes could be seen moving about. But these were no fae lights that brought joy to the heart of the beholder but rather, baleful lanterns which brought a rising terror to our hearts.

Death struck in the form of a storm of bolts. From towers and other mountings on the vessel, they came with a whine like the approach of a swarm of angry wasps diving vengefully upon us.

I leapt at Tu'Lon and brought him down. Merik had already taken a defensive posture behind a mast with shield raised and Coyle had dived down behind a barrel, which he now rested his back against while muttering some enchantment half under his breath.

The first volley shredded our mainsail and tore the crow's nest from its mounting, sending a screaming look-out plunging into the sea below.

Men spun and fell as they were impaled, some unable to move through fear or indecision. Others leapt overboard in panic. Now, the sea around us boiled as huge serpents appeared, snapping and feeding in a frenzy that served only to increase the hopelessness of our situation.

There was a crunching of distressed timber and then the dragon serpent skull was ploughing through the deck, ripping the hapless cog in two, sending torn wood and splinters flying in all directions. A second hail of bolts fell from above, accompanied this time by strikes of green lightning. I saw one man draw a blade and run for the dark elven vessel only to be caught by one of the ghostly bolts. His whole skeleton lit up through his skin and when he fell, all that remained was a twisted, blackened corpse, smoking as the burned flesh sloughed away from the frame.

I looked across to Coyle. "Can you get a protective spell around us? We have to make their deck and get under cover. This ship is going down the moment they take what they want from it and we aren't going to stop them. The best thing we can do is to try to hide."

"What do you think I was trying to do?" He snapped back. Tu'Lon stirred and raised his hands also, as he got up, "Ready?" He shouted across to Coyle, "When you are!"

Merik answered for him, moving in behind the mage. With a shout, Tu'Lon invoked Lannos to grant us protection and a shell of blueish light seemed to drop about us. We went for a gap where the railing had been smashed. Half clambering and half sliding, we landed on the deck of the monstrous dark elven ship.

Have you ever seen a dark elven ship? Well, of course, I know you are unlikely to claim to have shared that with me. Few have seen such sights and lived. There is no seagoing vessel that I know of, which one can compare. They are not ships as you and I would think of sailing vessels.

A dark elven ship is like a floating city complete with soaring towers with a multiplicity of eerily lit windows. The levels are all connected by ramps and walkways, arches and spiralling staircases vanishing into the darkness that hangs like a shroud about the heights of the vessel. Occasionally, fell creatures emerge to flap heavily around the towers.

Beneath the deck runs a maze of cavernous corridors inhabited by all manner of things which live alongside their dark elven mistresses, the greatest of whom are witch-priestesses who wield dark and awful magic. It is said that these floating fortresses are built upon a huge magical heartstone from the ancient homes of the Klanaar, the oldest of the dark elven civilisations.

Once, the histories say, the dark elves ruled over mankind and all other races except the highest of the noble elves. The enchanted stone allows the ship to traverse the stormiest of seas and even to crawl across land as if it were calm water. To finish each of these vessels, the forward prow is fashioned from the skull of a gigantic beast, usually a sea drake.

Since dark elven folk can rarely stand direct sunlight, they walk the decks only occasionally and anyway, the creatures that they allow to live and breed below are often so fierce that it is dangerous to remain at the lower levels.

As we slithered down onto the deck, a couple of seamen followed us so by the time we huddled in cover at the foot of one of the large towers, we were eight in number. The four seamen introduced themselves as Glance, Roper, Rud and Vorson. Glance and Roper were obviously guards from our ship as they had scale, crossbows, swords and daggers. The other two had no armour and were equipped only with rough falchions and a dagger apiece.

"Can either of you use a bow?" Merik asked.

"I can but Rud there is a much better shot" Vorson replied. Rud nodded, "I'm one of the ship's archers when we run into any trouble."

"Take this then." Merik swung a light quiver off his back holding an unstringed short, recurved bow and about ten arrows. He found two bowstrings in a pouch and handed them to Rud. "String it as you prefer."

Rud seemed competent enough and did as he was bidden. "Reckon we're all dead anyway, but it's good to be with yers in this." Vorson said, ruefully.

"That's some sword you got there." Rud pointed to the great sword secured, as ever, on Merik's back. I smiled, grimly. I had learned a little of Clave, the blade that Merik used so reluctantly. When I handled it in the fight against Drachefauste, the blade talked to me. I knew what it wanted. It had a dark soul. In the darkness, the great red gem gripped by a golden claw that was the pommel of the weapon seemed to glow ominously. Clave had not been in action for some time. I imagined the sword could sense strong life forces around us and wanted to sate its savage desires.

We watched as our ship went through its final death throes, a groaning, painful end as it rolled and broke, sinking beneath the seething foam and swell. The sea serpents had dived and vanished a few moments earlier, leaving just a group of dark elves who had been plundering the ship to come back aboard using magic to float a trail of crates, boxes and chests behind them, which came along as if they were dogs on leashes.

The dark elven raiding party were grouped together on the prow deck now, concentrating on retrieving what they had taken, which was as well for us, as we had to huddle down even more to avoid being seen.

Two male dark elves were arranging barrels and crates as they arrived on the deck, while a third male seemed to be maintaining the enchantment that was drawing the bobbing line of items to them. A sparkling rainbow of twinkling lights extended from his open arms to the end of the line. A fourth dark elf, a woman dressed in black armour, was supervising, snapping the odd order and pacing impatiently.

I looked around for the others. Vorson was moving up behind Coyle, Tu'Lon and Merik. Rud was on their flank but Glance and Roper seemed to have disappeared. I imagined they had been overcome with fear and hidden. Merik pointed in the direction of the spell caster and spoke to the seamen. "If we have to get into combat, that dark elf in the cloak who's casting the spell is your target."

Rud nodded, moving around the base of the tower, presumably where he could get a clearer view. I loaded my crossbow, trying to stay silent.

"Let's hope it doesn't come to that," whispered Tu'Lon, "it's going to be hard enough as it is to remain undiscovered until we get a chance to make shore."

Merik gave a nod. Coyle remained sitting hard against the tower, his gaze far away. He looked pale. "Are you alright?" I asked him, "You didn't get hit getting off the ship, did you?"

Coyle shook his head. "It's something that's hard to explain Finn. I'm not sure I want to say."

I gave him a quizzical look. He lowered his voice to the barest of whispers. "Years ago, I had an aunt who was supposedly psychic and could read the future albeit in a vague way."

I nodded, "go on."

"When she first met me, I was little more than a toddling babe with my first words on my lips but she took my hands, anyway, and then her eyes rolled so that my mother could see only the whites and was afraid. Apparently, my aunt began to intone in a strange voice and said that I could be a hero or a villain. She said that a great deal of wealth would pass through my hands and only my choices would decide if I held onto it or not, that I would count both the poor and the nobility amongst my friends. Then she let go and shivered and her final pronouncement was that in the end, it would come to naught because the dark faeries would come for me."

He paused, "She terrified the life out of my mother, of course. My father forbade her from ever stepping into the house, again." He put his head back on the stone looking up into the darkness, "But though it seemed at the time like a nonsense story to scare a young child, vague and ridiculous as it was, you have to accept she was speaking true. I can number poor folk and nobles amongst my friends and here we are, metres away from a dark faerie ship." He shuddered.

"Well it can't happen yet," I said, trying to remain light hearted, "where's all this wealth or have you been keeping that secret?"

He half smiled at this. I continued, "Anyway, what happened to this aunt of yours?"

"She was attacked and eaten by a land worm while she was working on her farm."

"Not much of a reader of the future, either, then," I added with a wry smile. Coyle grinned back but the grin quickly faded.

It was then that I looked up and saw Rud with an arrow on his bow, taking aim. My look must have alerted Merik who looked right and started towards Rud, "What in the nine hells do you think you're doing?" But it was all too late. To be fair to Rud, he could use a bow. The arrow sped to its mark, hitting the elven mage squarely between the shoulders so that he fell to his knees with a cry.

We all leapt up and Merik grabbed at him. The dark elves reacted immediately. The two carrying a crate, dropped it on the deck, drew short swords and swung bucklers from their backs, moving to cover the fallen mage. The female leader lifted her shield to cover herself and pulled a strange implement from her belt. Before I could bring up the crossbow and take aim, she had put it to her lips and blown. A high pitched, rattling series of notes carried above the wind followed by a shrill blast. A few seconds passed like a pause for breath. My bolt hit her in the throat and flung her back over the parapet into the heaving sea but the damage was done. An answering blast came from the towers and then three sharp whistles.

At once, dark shapes issued from portals high above us. Three huge manticores leapt into the air. They had bodies like lions, with heavy ball ended tails full of spikes and great leathery wings.

On each sat a rider, clad in glittering black mail marked with silver. Doors opened in the same tower, some ten feet above the deck from which ladders rolled out to the deck. Onto these moved warriors in black and silver. They were all female, lithe and deadly. I counted at least eight as they jumped lightly onto the deck with weapons in hand.

"We can't afford to be flanked!" shouted Merik. I nodded, drawing my two blades. We surged forward to meet the two male warriors who were defending the mage, looking to clear the smaller number first and leaving the others to defend against the newcomers. Coyle pressed his back against the tower, waiting to ambush the first dark elf to pass him by. Rud turned and took aim with the bow again while Vorson drew a falchion and hefted his buckler, waiting to counter the enemy attack. Tu'Lon stayed behind these two, praying to Kenubis as he threw up a shield of light around all three of them which made the approaching dark elves recoil. Merik used our height and weight advantage to launch a savage assault on the hesitant males, battering them backwards and overwhelming them. It was over quickly and we turned to see how the others were faring.

Merik stabbed the dark elf mage before he could rise but even as we swung around, we saw a line of manticores diving towards us.

"We aren't going to survive this unless I use Clave." Merik shouted to me. I nodded, "Do it." He brought the long holster from his back and reached for the hilts. At once, the sword came to his hand, eager to do battle, shedding the belts that held it. The ruby in the pommel pulsed and he charged. I swung my heavy crossbow from my shoulders, loading it with a barbed and poison coated bolt from a small case at my waist. The air was full of noise from the shouts and sounds of the engagement.

Tu'Lon had called upon Lannos, the battle god with the hawk's head, casting a spell that settled around all of us in a sparkling blue and gold, and I felt spurred to action. One of the female dark elves held an arm aloft and similarly invoked her demon goddess, so a purple and green haze surrounded the approaching elven warriors. A second female ducked from the group, flinging an arm out to reveal a green orb clenched in her fist. Green power erupted from it, crackling through the air to strike Tu'Lon who was flung back, with smoke coming from his tunic where he had been struck.

Then, it was Coyle's turn. He slipped from his place against the tower and put a dagger in the neck of the first female warrior to pass his position. Coyle jumped back as his first target fell, narrowly avoiding the wild swing of her blade. He flung a second knife, hitting the mage with the orb who cried out and fell backwards onto the deck.

Four more of them rushed forward. Vorson moved to engage one. I saw another emerge with a sleek but double-barrelled crossbow; the bolts fashioned from a glittering black metal with the same sheen as their armour.

She moved swiftly to the right to find an angle. Vorson hadn't seen her when she loosed the bolts. The first took him in the forehead, snapping his head back. His eyes looked surprised as he toppled to the deck at Merik's feet. The second bolt flew by, not missing Coyle by much. Then Merik was between the first two warriors, fire surrounding him and his sword.

He swung with such speed and fury that even as she raised her sword to block, the first female's head leapt from her shoulders to roll across the deck and a burst of flame charred her falling body. Fire exploded around the second, hurling her across the deck, still burning where clothing under her mail had caught fire. Rud put an arrow in the fourth warrior's right leg, her thrust missing Tu'Lon.

Then, Coyle emerged again, this time sending a bolt of lightning from his outstretched hand, lifting the same warrior off her feet and throwing her against the base of one of the great masts. I had not been idle. Seeing the manticores making their descent, I had picked the first rider off and seen her plummet to the deck where she rolled over, limbs at angles which assured me she would not rise again. Reloading as swiftly as I could without fumbling, I had loosed the barbed bolt into the third manticore and heard it keen as it felt the pain. It pulled away and circled slowly. The other two kept coming.

I tried to yell a warning but there was so much happening, it was hard to get anyone's attention. The first manticore came through, tearing at Tu'Lon, who went down. It glided by, riderless but obviously trained to fight on. The second pulled upwards, allowing its rider to hurl a javelin which went through Rud's left leg so he stumbled and shouted in pain, dropping his bow as he tried to pull the shaft from his leg. The third rider leapt into the open air.

For a moment, I couldn't believe what she had done until I realised that her cloak spread like a single wing under which she seemed to glide effortlessly, turning slightly into a slow spiral as she dropped towards us. Her stricken mount, poisoned by the bolt, sunk from view, trying desperately to fly on wings that were overtaken by the paralysing effect of the venom until they folded and it dropped into the sea.

The gliding warrior drew a hand crossbow, loading it and loosing two shots in quick succession. She knew her business. The first hit Rud in the mouth and he fell sideways, hands still on the javelin he was trying to pull free. The second took Merik just under the heart and I heard him groan. My focus was on the dark elf with the double-barrelled crossbow as she raised it to shoot, again.

My first knife flung in haste, made her dodge so she had to adjust as I had intended. The second hit her crossbow, knocking it sideways so her first bolt went out to sea.

As she swung it back, I leapt at her. A bolt tore across my lower arm and I felt the burning agony of torn flesh but I caught her around the waist and we went down together.

I was the much better brawler, having learned many dirty techniques from the guild. I smashed her kneecap with a kick and, as she writhed, I got astride her and banged her head on the deck. She tried to draw a dagger but I grabbed her arm and twisted her wrist hard until I heard it snap, the dagger falling from her fingers. She screamed. I rose and plunged a dagger down into her heart, using my weight to add to the blow. She rolled sideways; a scream frozen on her lips. I swung about. The gliding dark elven rider had landed as softly as if she had stepped from a doorway. She now used a whistle not unlike the one that gave the alarm, earlier. The loose manticore responded, giving a keening rasp and turned to head for her. Merik moved to block its passage.

"No, Merik!" I yelled.

Six spikes shot from the tail as it swung the ball end around towards him in a whipping motion. Merik looked down at his body armour. The spikes seemed to spring up as if they had been concealed within its weave, two in the stomach, one in the left thigh, one in the chest, one above the right knee and the last in the right ankle.

All six punched through the greaves and heavy leather of his jack so blood welled around them. The manticore kept coming and I saw him raise Clave even though I knew he must be dying from the wounds he had taken.

There was a final arc of fire and he yelled in pain and fury. The sword beheaded the manticore even as it collected him between its front claws. The impetus of its flight carried them both onwards, spinning and tumbling. They hit the stone parapet of the main deck, demolishing it. Merik and the beast fell over the edge and vanished into the heaving waves. Ominously, Clave, flung high by the impact, landed point down with a thud, close to me, standing in the deck as if waiting to be drawn.

I looked around. Coyle was leaning against the tower, drawing a short bolt from his shoulder. Tu'Lon was groaning as he crawled across the floor. Only the female rider and I now stood on the deck. She was loading a hand crossbow, intent on finishing Tu'Lon.

The second manticore and its rider were heading in towards me. I made the decision in an instant. I snatched up Clave and rushed the rider before she could shoot Tu'Lon. She dropped the hand crossbow and drew a short sword in a fluid motion, starting to move into a defensive stance but I burst into green fire that made her take another step back. I slammed her blade aside with Clave and kicked her between the legs. As she started to rise from her doubled-over position, I carved through her shoulder and neck with the great blade. Fire enveloped her.

I could hear the blade talking to me, telling me what it could do for me. I turned on the approaching manticore, but out of nowhere, Coyle leapt out and flung a blast at it. The bolt of lightning spilled the rider over its haunches into the sea.

"I need a bow for this, Clave. Sheathe!" I yelled. I moved the sword towards my belt. It wrenched free and drove itself into the deck at my feet. Snatching up my crossbow, I rolled away as the manticore's spikes whined between us, bouncing off the tower, thudding into masts and skittering away. I came up on one knee as it turned back for another pass. My crossbow bolt found the back of its head and I saw it tumble, crashing amongst the masts, bringing down a heavy crossbeam in its ruin. I pulled Clave from the deck and finished it before it could rise.

I lifted myself up slowly, the pain cutting in as I gazed about me. Tu'Lon was sitting against the base of a mast, trying to press on a wound that was seeping blood. It had spread in a dark stain across his tunic. He was praying softly to Kenubis to grant healing. Coyle leaned, head back, looking up towards the sky, spasms of anguish and pain passing across his face. He had one hand on another bolt in his thigh, summoning the courage to wrench it free. Vorson lay slumped on his side, nearby and Rud beyond the tower. Dark elves were scattered about us and where Merik had fallen, foam spilled through the gaping hole to wash the deck.

I shook myself and moved to the other two. "We need to go before others come to see why nobody has returned."

I started across the deck, picking up items that had fallen. I found Merik's belts that he used to hold Clave. I undid one of the holsters from the dead rider and took one of her hand crossbows as well as her bolt case and the strange cloak.

Finally, I helped myself to the double-barrelled crossbow. It was lighter and much more finely sprung than my weapon. I dropped my old crossbow on the deck near the hole in the parapet. I handed throwing knives to Coyle and we took other items that looked useful, cramming them in pouches or tucked into our belts. We had dumped our packs at the base of the tower when we had come aboard. I went through these as quickly and methodically as I could, collecting bandages, a water bottle, flint, whetstone and fletching kits. The last thing I took was Merik's favourite pipe, which I toyed with, momentarily before handing it to Tu'Lon. "Something to remember him by" I said, softly. Tu'Lon nodded and tucked it into a pouch. He seemed to have succeeded with his prayers. The enchantment settled over us all and the pain of the wounds lessened considerably.

"That didn't feel like a victory" said Coyle

"Some battles don't," I replied, recalling one in particular, "and some hurt worse than others."

"To be honest," Coyle said, pushing himself off the tower wall and walking across the deck, "I thought we were done when those manticore riders appeared."

We moved slowly off, packs in one hand and a weapon in the other. We flung the spare packs overboard to prevent the dark elves working out if any of us were still alive and began searching for somewhere to hide.

"With luck," I said hopefully, "they'll think the manticores got the rest of us. What we need to do is find a way down into the passages where the beasts live. It's the only hope other than spending our days and nights for maybe weeks, dodging patrols. We'll only be able to sleep in snatches."

"If we do that, how will we know if the ship gets close to shore?" Coyle asked.

"We will have to find somewhere where one of us can easily come up and have a look every so often." I replied.

"What about the other two seamen?" asked Tu'Lon. "They must be about somewhere."

"I don't fancy their chances." Coyle replied, "We ought to try to find them and stick together."

"They went off and hid at the first sign of a fight. They might give us away. I still think we should go down." I said.

"I don't know, Finn. The catacombs of a dark elven ship are said to be deadly, full of dark things that most races have forgotten. We might be better taking our chances with the dark elves." Tu'Lon frowned.

I shook my head. "No. The dark elves are intelligent and can call re-enforcements. If we kill a creature and take its lair, we should be left alone."

Coyle nodded, "It makes sense."

Tu'Lon sighed. "Fine. Just don't let me have to say 'I told you so' when we would have had a chance to get ashore instead of spending months on this thing gnawing lizard bones."

We found a worn set of steps that spiralled down and began our descent. We were just coming off the bottom step when Coyle noticed a movement and warned us. We scattered for cover. A crossbow bolt struck the wall close by where I had been standing. Another hit just behind me as I ducked and ran. A long silence followed. I loaded my own crossbow. Tu'Lon stood suddenly and with a word, caused the chamber to fill with soft light. Lurking back in the shadows against the far wall were Glance and Roper. They both had crossbows.

"It's us!" shouted Coyle, "It's alright."

"Stand up and let us see." Roper shouted. Coyle began to rise.

"No," I whispered, "I think they knew it was us."

I stood, slowly, crossbow at my waist loaded and hidden from them.

"It's me, Black Finn."

Two crossbows levelled at me. I ducked down as the bolts flew then rose and loosed my own, catching Roper in the leg. Coyle was up, too.

He hurled a green flash of lightning and they both stumbled backwards. Faced with resistance, they ran for a cave exit, northwards. We pursued them but they had gone into the darkness.

Now we had another threat to be concerned about.

Darkness I

Days became weeks, with sporadic encounters with Glance and Roper punctuating the long pauses in-between. Until one day, coming around a corner I recoiled in horror as I met Roper face to face. His staring eyes and missing left arm said he was dead, hanging suspended in a web that nearly engulfed me. The spider that came to see what had moved the strands was the biggest I'd encountered yet, a huge thing as tall as a horse. It attacked without hesitation. Clave burned the webs and took three of its legs off before Coyle got a short sword thrust between its eyes and it crouched down, bubbling black blood and waving its mandibles and remaining legs ineffectually. We moved in and killed it, then.

Two days or so later, we caught up with Glance. He was shivering from a bite he had taken. He crouched in a corner and tried to use his crossbow. The first shot went well wide. I moved in and grabbed him.

"Why?" I demanded. "What did we ever do to you?"

He laughed but the laugh turned to a cough and blood seeped from his mouth.

"We were paid. But looks like you'll be dead anyway. You'll never get off this ship alive. The things I have seen, they'll find you. They'll find you and they'll eat you alive."

"You survived this long." I said. "I like our chances."

"Who paid you?" Coyle shook him, but his eyes rolled and he slipped slowly backwards.

Tu'Lon tried to revive him, but he had gone. Tu'Lon shook his head and stood. "I suppose they would have killed us while we slept on board the cog. We might never have made land. Who do you think sent them, Finn? Was it the imperials who wanted us dead?"

I pondered and searching the pockets of the dead mercenary and withdrew a small bronze token carved into the form of a hawk. "There are still several possibilities, but I have an idea I need to look closer to home."

***

And then, one day, Tu'Lon had gone. He was taken by a dragon like creature with eight legs, like a blue basilisk that slithered from a shadowy hole and snatched him in its jaws. It had torn half his shoulder and right arm off before we could even launch an attack. Although Coyle and I slew it outright, it was too late for Tu'Lon. The creature must have had a venom on its jaws. He was too weak and delirious to pray and we could not heal his wounds. He died with a last cynical comment that he had told us so, and we were a right pair of fools to come after him.

We carried his body for a while but could find no suitable place to lay him to rest. In the end, we resolved to put him overboard and so made our way back to the main deck. I took Merik's pipe.

Coyle seemed to feel it was a bringer of bad luck. He took Tu'Lon's ring and we divided the other useful items from his pack before hefting our friend's body onto the parapet, the sea soaking us with spray of salty droplets. Standing in the wind helped to blow away some of the dark feelings I had felt were weighing upon my heart as we wandered the endless catacombs below. Perhaps Tu'Lon had been right. We should have stayed on the deck under the sky and the stars.

"Do you want to say anything?" I asked. Coyle shook his head. "Goodbye my friend" he said and hung his head. I considered for a moment. "This circle of friendship has been broken by events we could not have foreseen. But, although our friends have left us, those who remain will honour their memory and they shall never be forgotten."

Coyle looked up and nodded with a smile of approval. Tu'Lon's body vanished into the darkness. The sea had taken another. Now, there were just two of us.

"I don't want to go back into those passages, Finn. I'm not the bold adventurer I always thought I was. I am struggling to even use my powers, down there. It's like being in a waking nightmare." Coyle poured out his feelings with a dejected air. He hung his head, again.

I had felt the same but just hadn't wanted to say it; "Then we'll take our chances up here." I replied and patted his shoulder.

For five days and nights, we slept in snatches, someone always on watch, evading patrols and odd wanderings by creatures from the ship.

Both of us grew tired, our tempers beginning to fray over small matters. On the sixth day after Tu'Lon fell, we got into a fight with a small patrol led by a beast with the upper body of a male dark elf and the lower of a spider with eight legs, each ending in a claw like appendage. It used a blade in one hand and spear in the other as well as wielding magic attacks. We were both wounded but with no healer, could only patch ourselves up and try to rest and recover.

The day after that, we overthrew four dark elves, taking more wounds in the fight. Coyle had been looking pale before that but now he slumped against a tower wall and said he couldn't stand. I hadn't been feeling good either and was hiding the fact that I was shivering. My head felt hot.

The spider warrior's blade must have been poisoned and we had both been growing steadily worse. We searched until we found a high bilge that was dry and slid down into it. We just laid down and tried to rest. I think we were both delirious for a time but after a couple of days, I sat up and stretched. I felt light-headed but my temperature had broken. I moved across to Coyle. He was bathed in sweat. His temperature was running high. I tried to bathe his head with a salt-water soaked cloth and gave him our last healing potion but all to no avail. As daylight came, buying us a few hours of sure safety, he gazed upwards with a smile. "Look Finn, the sun is shining. I think I can see land." And then he died. My last friend from the group that I felt I belonged to lay dead in my arms.

I wept, then. There was nobody to see me and no other's morale to consider, any more. When I had taken what looked of most use and tucked Coyle's magical dagger in my belt, I put on Tu'Lon's ring and got Coyle up onto the edge of the deck wall. I can't even recall in my grief what words I spoke over him. With Coyle gone too, I decided I might as well do what damage I could before I fell as well. I drew Clave and went looking but with the sunlight threatening to break right through the enchantment of mist that hung about the vessel, the deck remained deserted.

It was as I leaned, disconsolate and angry against the deck wall that I heard a distant bell. A ship was caught in the magical fog. There were only two outcomes.

The dark elves would attack and sink the ship or it would break free and run. I hauled up the pack onto my back, secured Clave and turned Tu'Lon's ring as he had shown us. I jumped over the edge. It was further down than I thought and for a moment or two I floundered under the water, thinking I would end it by drowning after all this. Then, I realised I was indeed breathing under water and was fine. I struck out in the direction that I had heard the bell, breaking the surface on and off until a shape loomed above me. I swam up and yelled. There was no answer so I swam around until I found the rope rigging used to climb up and down to row boats. I swung myself out of the water and started to get hold. With Clave weighing on my back, I could barely drag myself out of the water.

"Oi! Oi! you there! There's a bloke climbing out of the water with weapons and stuff." I heard a voice yell. Three heads looked over. Two bowmen pointed weapons in my direction as the number grew to five, seven, more. I lifted a hand. "Help!" I managed. "Help me, quickly! Dark Elves!"

They got some of it and I heard someone above me shout "'Said something about dark elves." I was hauled up and stood, dripping on the deck of a small buccaneer class vessel. I glanced up. It had a Pharsalian flag.

"I need to speak with the master and now!" I rapped, "That would be me, young man" said a voice and an old white-haired officer pushed through the ranks. He had the weathered face of a true old sea-dog.

"Sir," I bowed, slightly, "dark elven ship off your starboard bow. She sunk my ship. Five of us got aboard her but only I survived the fight that followed. There were more of them coming when I heard your bell and jumped for it. You have to steer hard to port. If they see you, they'll attack. They have sea dragons, manticores and other evil things not to mention a bolt thrower in every tower."

He looked at me only for a moment or two, perhaps summing me up then whether he saw something in my expression or decided he could not take a chance, he decided.

"Helmsman, hard port!"

"Commander!" A nearby man snapped to attention, "Get me more sail. We're getting out of here, now!"

Men ran about. I crouched and then sank to my knees. "You alright son?" asked a kindly fellow.
"No…wounded badly in the last fight. I lost my friends, all of my friends." I said, the last almost a whisper. I remember falling sideways onto the deck. My last thought was that the poison must have got me, after all.

Shadows V

Eventually, I was put ashore at Jordis and so reached my destination, albeit by an unexpected route. I heard from the crew of the ship that rescued me that, after I blacked out, their priest-physician treated me for multiple wounds and fractures. At the last moment, the dark eleven ship revealed itself from the mist and started to pursue our vessel but the extra sail which the buccaneer had piled on served it well and the small brig outran the dark elven fortress. They soon gave up the chase and sank back into a cold fog bank with a ghostly green glow. Knowing it was out there, the captain of the brig put the word around and soon the whole port was talking about hugging the coast to avoid the dark elf raider.

When I came up on deck after being treated, I had been slapped on the shoulder and treated like an old colleague for saving the lives of all on board. I left most of the medical kit and ordinary equipment behind with them, taking just enough personal equipment to survive on my own. With a much lighter pack, I headed off to buy a horse for the trip to Car Duris.

Ahead of me, I had another task that I was not looking forward to discharging. I heaved a very heavy sigh. I knew where my next journey would take me.

I would make two stops on the way. First, I had business in Car Duris and then I wanted to find Kharr, before setting sail for Gwythaor to see my friend, Gwayne.

My friends, I thought, bitterly. Being a friend to Black Finn is a dangerous business. I was no good luck talisman.

I had wanted my friends to be beside me when I embarked on the final leg of my current journey. We had discussed it and how, after we were set up in Car Duris, we would visit Littesburg and stay with my cousins. There, we would no doubt be well looked after and would find an opportunity to accumulate some wealth through the feats we would perform together. We even intended to return to my old home in Rosgovia, one day.

But now, they were gone and I was alone on a road that could only lead to one destination, assuming I was successful on my first step. I reached Car Duris three days after disembarking, let the Guild know that I was in the city and that I wished to see my master. I let it be known that I was hoping to have that celebratory drink. My first task, I wrote, was completed and I was taking a well-earned break.

I didn't expect any trouble beforehand, but I remained watchful for the three days leading to my appointment. As far as I knew, there might still be assassins on my trail. My disappearance at sea would have confounded them, I hoped. At least temporarily, my whereabouts would be hard to work out.

The only attempt to get to me since I'd arrived had been in Jordis, where two would-be assassins set off a bar fight as a cover for a strike.

An attempt to assassinate an assassin. It sounded like the plot for a comic play. In such a comedy, the plot would have revealed that I had hired them myself.

Alas, the truth was far starker and was the reason that I needed to speak with my master, alone. He knew of all the attempts to make it look like there had been an accident or unlucky turn of fate on my missions. He had been involved in investigating each of those incidents.

***

It was a warm evening in early summer, so my master invited me to share a good bottle of chilled wine, sitting on his balcony where we could talk over everything I had been doing. The balcony looked out on the inner quadrangle of the guild house. The lawn had been cut so I could smell that fresh scent of grass and crushed meadow flowers. We went out through his quarters, talking about the times when I was an apprentice, about the encounter with the dark elven ship and what had happened there.

"You were indeed fortunate to escape that vessel, Finn. And as a result, you gained some items and quite a lot of money, by the sound of things. I suppose while that was no compensation for the loss of your friends, at least you didn't get thrown up on some foreign shore with nothing."

"No indeed, Master Grey."

"You know, Finn, you can call me by my name, Radjcek. While I am nominally still your master, you are no apprentice any more. In fact, I would say you are no ordinary journeyman either."

He uncorked the wine and poured it into two glasses, turning away to take them to the table on the balcony. I took a seat and reached into a pouch.

"Oh, by the way, Master Radjcek," I said, "I meant to return this to you. You gave it to me a long time ago and I was supposed to bring it back when a particular task was completed."

I placed the token down on the table. It was a small, flat bronze hawk shape, the edges enamelled in grey and marked with a single character which was his sigil or unique marker. My master looked at it, a little surprised, for a moment. He picked it up and pocketed it. "I didn't recall giving you that. I can't even remember which job that was for, either."

I smiled, "You're a busy man with so many assignments, master. It doesn't matter. The task was completed last year, anyway. I just thought you'd want it back and to know it was done.

He nodded although he still looked puzzled, obviously struggling to remember. I turned to another subject. "Master, last time I was here, you said you would show me your old journal from when you were at the guild. I'd love to see it."

His face brightened. "Oh, yes, I know exactly where that is." He rose and went to his bookcase. I switched our goblets around and sat back. He pulled the book, blew dust off it and gave it a brush with the sleeve of his jacket before returning.

"Here we are. Look at this. I haven't opened these pages in years." He chuckled, "Afraid my apprenticing wasn't as interesting as yours, but I had my moments." He steered the book across the table. I turned it around and opened it with reverential care. I lifted my glass. His expression gave away nothing as he reached for his own.

"Your health, master and here's to a great many years working together." I drank. He lifted his own glass and drained it off. I put my own goblet down and pushed back my chair. He watched as I stood and took a couple of steps backwards.

"Are you alright, Finn?" he asked and then fingered his collar. He started to sweat and then to choke. "What?" He tried to say something and to rise, but his legs gave way so he stumbled sideways. Catching the table, he overbalanced it. The table, his chair and the bottle of wine hit the floor. Glass smashed and wine spread in a pool across the polished wood floor.

I looked down at him, struggling on his knees, face nearly purple as his airways closed and the grip on his heart tightened.

"Your acceptance of the token that the assassins were supposed to leave beside me when I was dead was a final proof of what I already knew. I gave you a last chance to refute it, but you recognised your own token. It was you who arranged for my accidental death.

So, having failed through the usual means, you thought you would seal my fate with what you claimed was your favourite wine, one strong enough to conceal the slight bitterness in the poison. That is why I turned down your offer to drink a bottle with you when I first accepted the journeyman's rank. I had to be sure one way or another. When you went for the old journal, it was such a simple thing to switch goblets.

So master, it seems you trained me too well. What I do not understand is why you'd do Drachefauste's bidding. It can't have been for money. You could have what you wanted already so why?"

He choked and his eyes bulged as he tried to spit out an answer. I pushed a piece of parchment at him and offered him a quill.

"You are going to die very shortly, so disclose the answer. It is, after all, guild protocol for such to pass from one master to another."

He spat, bloodily, on the floor. "You will never be a master. You lack the ambition to play the game."

"Not good enough" I said. I took a dagger from my belt and placed it in the soft flesh around his right eye. "You know only too well what I can do to make you feel excruciating pain. After all, you taught me. This blade has a particularly nasty mixture which burns and sends shooting pains into any blood-carrying vessels."

He pushed it away, ineffectually, but dipped the quill in the ink, even though he was dribbling blood and spittle now.

"Brothers" was what he wrote and then under that he added "A game to take control of the Empire." He tried to grin but it was death's grin and it stayed forever on his face. As his bowels released, he slumped over sideways, knocking the ink bottle over so it mixed with the wine. The dark liquid spread like a bloodstain around his body.

I took the parchment. "Thank you master. Now our business is at an end." I unlocked his door. I knew he had silently turned the key, obviously to cover the eventuality that I might try to flee, allowing him to strike at my back.

I returned to my chair and sat, surveying the scene. For a few minutes, I read the journal. Once ready, I rose, satisfied by what I had understood. Stepping out into the long hallway, I shut the door softly behind me and walked towards the stairs down to the ground floor. On a whim, I halted and returned, continuing on past my old master's room until I came to another door. I knocked upon it and waited.

"Who is that?" Master Shadow's voice was always distinctive.

"Black Finn" I answered, evenly. There was a long pause and an exchange between Master Shadow and another person whose voice I could not hear. I hoped I had not caught him in some private moment. The door opened. Master Shadow was dressed, casually in a deep blue silk shirt and dark trews. At the table with a goblet of wine in his hand was Master Black, similarly in off duty garb. They were clearly deep in discussion over something while enjoying a glass or two of wine.

"Finn," Master Black raised his goblet, "come on in."

Master Shadow waved to another seat as he returned to his own chair and a half-filled glass of ruby wine.

"We were just talking about Riassa and the need to create more regular exchanges between the guilds. Klavon has brought the local organisations together and wishes to ensure that we are more than an alliance. He has done well. Master Grey's star apprentice, that young man. We have great hopes that you will do similarly well, Finn."

"You know something of the goings on in Riassa, don't you?" Master Black asked, sipping his wine. Master Shadow found a third goblet and poured one for me, offering it in my direction. I accepted it but didn't drink.

"I do." I nodded. I paused to thank Master Shadow for the wine and then continued,

"But there is another matter that I need to bring to your attention. To save you carrying out any enquiries or asking questions of other guildsmen, I need to tell you that I have just killed Master Grey."

I had to hand it to the two experienced masters of the Car Duris Guild. Neither swore, leapt up or reacted suddenly in any kind of excited or angry manner. Master Black simply raised an eyebrow. Master Shadow nodded sagely. "There was a good reason, I assume?"

"I invoked the right of a guildsman to conduct a vendetta. It was Master Grey who tried to set me up when I was training here and who sent assassins after me in Riassa. He was Drachefauste's half-brother. I read it in his journal. Their ambitions soared too high. He thought he might control the Pearl Throne itself."

I tossed the book down on the table.

"I understand that I can no longer continue as a journeyman. I hope you will not send your trainee assassins after me. I would feel bad about having to kill so many of them."

Master Black started to chuckle. Master Shadow took a long drink from his goblet and then waved a hand airily. "You were entitled to kill him. We always knew that one of the masters had to be complicit in what happened to your pentagon. We were not sure whether it was you or Wanda, or perhaps Verity whom they really wanted to kill and why they left it so much to chance. A kind of extended game, I suppose, to allow the fear to build before the knife finally found its target. So how did you assassinate Radjcek?"

I sat down in the spare seat. "With the glass of wine that he meant for me."

Master Shadow put his goblet down rather deliberately and Master Black started to laugh again.

"Poetic, Finn, poetic. Especially given how many times he must have told the tale of how he used his favourite wine as a way to lull an old rival before he took his life. You realise, of course, that this qualifies you to apply for the vacant master's post."

"I don't wish to be a master in the guild." I said, softly, "Or even a journeyman. A guild that does not look after its own is no guild at all."

"You may think differently in future." Master Black spoke quickly. "This was a matter between you and the one who wished you ill. It was not for the masters to interfere once you and the others had passed from our care as apprentices. We knew it would follow one of you and in so doing, the hand holding the dagger would be revealed. We would have acted once we knew, but we would always prefer that such matters are resolved by the players and not the audience.

For the target, it would be a test which would lead to greater things if they passed it. After all, you survived, didn't you? So, it seems that you passed and thus have now proved to yourself, as well as any others, that you can rise as high as you wish."

"No, I did not die. But I was never able to be idle or unready. Some bribes, some torture and a death or two lie behind on the trail I followed back to Master Radjcek. Don't expect more from me. I mean what I say. I doubt that I shall return to the guild and as of now, I revoke your right to ask me to undertake any further missions on its behalf."

"If you do not return, that will be a pity and your loss as well as ours. But understood. Farewell, then, Finn. I honestly wish you well upon your road." Master Shadow inclined his head.

Master Black steepled his hands. "I shall say farewell until you return, I think. Could you ask Master Hand or Master Streets to join us on your way out? You will find one of them on duty downstairs."

I nodded and raised a black gloved hand. "Fare well then, masters." I closed the door and walked away into the shadows of the long hall.

Shadows of the Past

I wanted to find Kharr, really to let him know that I was leaving and did not know when or if I would be back this way, again.

He had gone on to Acondium after leaving Riassa as expected. There were letters waiting at the guildhouse for me, which I picked up before I left. There were three from Gwythaor. One was from our embassy, a short official note, confirming that Gwayne's father, Duke Gawaine IV had died and Gwayne II had become the new duke of Gwythaor. The second was from Gwayne himself, giving me the same news and confiding how he felt it had come too soon for him. His father had not recovered from the wound he had taken trying to save his eldest son from a giant boar that had gored him. A combination of the wound and the effect of losing his son had caused him to just fade away. The third was from Jeffery about his time with the rangers. He was due to head out on a deep ranging into the mountains with most of his new patrol.

There was also a note from Car Duris. It was from Nick Dance. He had been an apprentice when I was first moved up to the pentagon as a senior. He had just passed out as a journeyman and had an assignment that would take him to the islands. He would leave a note at our embassy wherever he stopped next. He had heard about me leaving the guild in the night and the rumours which followed.

I sat for some considerable time, trying to decide what was best and whether walking away from the guild was wise. I sent the masters a note thanking them for their advice and promising that I would consider returning once I had a chance to wander and to gain some more experience of the larger world. It would be foolish to cut ties with the guild. They could protect and shelter me, provide me with paid work and offer the possibilities of more training, if I needed it.

I found Kharr at an inn near the Acondium quayside, drinking with a man who looked like a burly farmer. Kharr was wearing a scale jack under a travelling cloak in a blue-grey. His open helm with the spiked crest sat on the bar at hand. The man he was with stood well over six and a half feet, in a rough jerkin and leggings of hard-wearing material tucked into heavy boots. A stout quarterstaff of at least seven feet leaned against the wall beside him. He had thick black hair and beard with a voice to match his huge frame, big and booming with a deep, hearty laugh.

I bowed, slightly and offered a black gloved hand. "Black Finn" He grasped my hand in a crushing handshake, "Thunderchild" he replied. I looked at him curiously. It seemed a strange name for a landsman. "Pleased to meet you," I added, "any friend of Kharr's is alright with me."

"So, it doesn't bother you, a noble man, to drink with the serfdom, then?" he asked, jovially.

"We may not be born equal in status." I said, "But we are all born equal as men. For me, it is what you do that matters."

"A refreshing perspective from one of your class."

"I am only half of that class." I said, with a wry smile.

"Kharr said you could be an unusual fellow." He laughed and clapped me on the shoulder so hard that I nearly fell over. "I like him, Kharr. He's just as you said."

Kharr smiled and simply raised his mug of beer. I recovered my composure and supped my own; "I came to tell you that I have to leave my friend," I said to Kharr, "I didn't want to journey without saying farewell and how it has been a privilege to know you."

Kharr put his drink down and frowned. "That sounds awfully serious, Finn. You often travel. This journey implies an end."

I nodded. "If it turns out as I expect, I am unlikely to pass this way again. Assuming I am successful, I am thinking of travelling farther afield. I will be even less welcome in the empire."

The big man watched us, thoughtfully and then asked his own question. "What drives you to this position that seems so extreme? You appear to be a man who takes life as he finds it and, from what Kharr says, one who is rarely disturbed by its course."

I motioned to a table in the corner and there they sat while I told Thunderchild the tale of the beast and all that had gone before. I told him of the likely war between empire and island dukedoms and how my family would one day come back and fight for the lands taken from them. I planned to oppose the empire at every turn. When I was done, the light of the day had long faded. We had drunk several more rounds and eaten, too. At length, Kharr steepled his hands and nodded, softly. "I have been thinking it was time to move on, myself. I think I shall travel with you, at least as far as Jordis."

I smiled and shook his hand, briefly. "I should like that. You would be good company on the road."

"How would you feel about another companion?" the big man asked softly.

I was surprised. "You'd leave your fields?"

"What fields?"

I fell quiet then explained. "I assumed you to be a landsman or forester with responsibilities."

He laughed, "I have responsibilities but not to any land. I range where I will but more often where fate intends I should be."

"Then I would welcome another friend on the road. We could laugh and sing and perhaps forget our burdens awhile."

"Count me in, then." He nodded.

We rose and made for the inn door. As we stepped into the courtyard, I became aware of five or six figures closing around us. It was not an assault, but there was definite intent. The first thing that struck me after their movement was the colourful garb in which all were adorned.

The lead man signalled to them so they all stopped where they were. He was dressed all in mid-blue with a blue and black half helm. His cloak was sewn with peacock feathers. Three more swept back from his hood and the eye of one made a brooch on his chest. Even his knife hilts were multi-coloured, as was the scabbard which held a short sword.

You would have said he was some kind of popinjay or court jester but for the way he moved and stood. Beside him, tall in a white leather jerkin with leggings to match and a white half helm with two egret feathers and a beaked nosepiece emphasised more than standard, was a lean man carrying a two-handed sword, slim bladed with a heavy basked guard. Two hand-axes with black and white grips hung on his belt.

The third, who now leaned on a wagon watching us, wore a cloak of crow feathers, his garb black with a grey-blue half helm and hood.

He was equipped with two slim blades and a belt of flat throwing knives, each with a polished black handle. Again, the half helm was beaked with an ebony piece to make it look more like a bird's beak than a nosepiece.

The other two men stood back on each flank. One was dressed in garb of grey and rusty red-brown, his half helm adorned with the primary flight feathers of birds of prey. His blade was short with a falcon-head hilt and he bore a strange weapon like a claw with three steel talons in the other hand, its round guard giving it the same function as a main-gauche. The other sported mainly grey but his hood was a red-brown and he wore a strange black "bandit mask" over his eyes. His weapons were mostly curved knives but he also sported a scimitar.

"Black Finn," the leader's voice was familiar to me. He turned slightly, letting the light fall on his breastplate which glittered gold and green as iridescent scales caught the sun. "Don't you recognise me?"

I shook my head slightly and then it dawned on me who this strange colourful individual was. "Cody?"

"His name is Peacock now" the lean man said, firmly.

"I left the Guild, Finn, turned mercenary. I serve only rich and powerful employers, these days." He turned to his cohorts. "Gentlemen, this is the man who taught me what I knew, my mentor, inspiration and once my master. A mercenary, warrior and assassin with a justified reputation in many places."

There was something in the way he said this that I found sinister. Kharr and Thunderchild hung back, watchful, observing how matters unfolded.

"You do me too much credit Co…Peacock. You were always capable."

"Yes, but you taught me about style, about planning and how to really use a weapon to disable or kill."

I bowed, slightly. "I am glad that you have found a direction of your own. More showmanship than I would have gone for, but a little drama can certainly add to one's reputation."

Cody nodded. "And now one more thing that will take that reputation to the level where men will fear my name. I shall challenge and defeat the great Black Finn in a knife draw."

I gave my old cohort a hard look. "That will not be necessary."

"You're afraid, ain't ya?" The crow-cloaked individual gave a sly grin and toyed with a knife.

"Hush, Jackdaw. I was always quicker." Cody stated, eyes watching me intently from behind the mask of his half helm.

"There is no need for a contest," I said, "I know you are quicker than me and you may say so. I will not challenge that assertion, if asked."

I went to walk away, but the man in white put out a hand and gripped my arm, blocking my passage. "No, you and Peacock are going to duel and when he kills you, everyone will know who was the better man."

I sighed, shaking him off and stepped back. "That is foolish."

Cody continued, clearly basking in the theatricality of it, "No Finn. Think of it. A glorious end. Two of the greatest knife throwers ever to walk the city streets in a head to head match. When I walk away, the victor, your reputation will live on too. You will be the man that Peacock had to beat to prove he was the best. They will remember you as the old master, our names linked ever after."

"Thanks," I said, "but I'm not all that old and you don't know for certain that you will win. Better to walk away, with your reputation intact, Cody. I'm leaving these shores so you'll have no competition from me."

"Peacock! It's Peacock. Cody is no longer my name." He retorted, with a voice that sounded increasingly fraught and sulky. I looked back at Kharr who shrugged. The big man remained impassive, standing in the shadows of the doorway.

"As you wish." I unbuckled Clave and my falchion and handed them back to Kharr. Cody and I checked our knives were positioned for throwing and the others made space so we could put a little distance between one another. The tall man in white placed his two-handed blade between us on the ground.

"Back off five paces and turn to face one another. I will count to three and then shout. When I do, you may draw and make your throws."

We took our positions and I waited.

When the count reached three, I dropped a hand as if to draw but at the last moment, instead, I flung myself sideways. Cody's blade grazed my upper arm, drawing blood. I rose from one knee and felt the wound.

"You won, Peacock." I said, finding a neckerchief and turning it into a tourniquet to prevent more bleeding, "congratulations. You have proved forevermore you are faster than Black Finn. I wish you luck. I doubt we shall meet again."

Cody shook his head, looking disappointed. "I'm sorry Finn. I'd hoped you would make it easy but if you insist on being difficult. The Wings of Night do not default on a contract."

The other men began to move in, drawing blades. I realised, then, what lay behind this sham contest. I went for my own blade but, of course, I had given it over to Kharr. I whipped out my two remaining knives and went into a crouch. Cody and the man in white moved in but as they did, Kharr's scimitar touched the throat of the one in the crow cloak, "I wouldn't do that" he said. Crow-cloak dropped his daggers. At the same moment, a familiar huge figure, clad in storm grey armour and now bearing a two-handed blade which dwarfed any I had ever seen stepped between me and the two who were closing on me.

The man in white flung down his blade. Cody hesitated and then his hands dropped to his side.

"We have no quarrel with you, Thunderchild. This is between Finn and ourselves."

"I think not." The deep voice was the same but now from behind the great helm, it was even more imposing.

"The contest is not over but it will be resolved. If Peacock wins, then it is done as you desired. If Finn wins, you will treat him as if he is a dead man and bother him no more, else you will feel my wrath as well as that of his other friends. Is that understood?"

There was a general assent from the five over-dressed fellows. I stroked my beard and then nodded. "If that is the only way."

Thunderchild took up a position and levelled his sword. "This time, I shall count and when I raise my blade, you will both go for your knives. If either party breaks the agreement, I have described, I will enforce the penalty."

Silence fell. Kharr sheathed his scimitar and came to stand at my shoulder. "I shall act as Finn's second to bear his arms and if necessary, his body from the field."

"And I, Egret, shall do the same for Peacock" said the man in white. "Shrike, Falcon and Jackdaw will see that fair play is done.

"So be it" Thunderchild nodded. "Egret and Kharr may come forward. The rest of you will stand back and watch. If I see anyone draw a blade or make a move, they will regret it."

The others drew back as they were instructed. It seemed that they feared and respected the big man. I made a mental note to find out more about him when this was done.

"Time to die," spat the man in the crow cloak, directing his words in my direction, "coward."

We took our positions, once more. I adjusted my weighted knives on each hip, lowering the left to just above the knee and waited.

"This is your last chance to walk away, Cody. You don't have to do this." I said.

"He doesn't need your advice anymore." Egret said, curtly, "Just your death."

"Count then, Thunderchild." I said.

Cody was quick but his blade was still in his hand when mine took him just above the heart. Cody half raised his arm, staggered, dropped the blade and looked down at the spreading stain around the hilt of my knife. I couldn't help noticing how it spoiled the look of his garb.

"But you were slower..." Cody sounded surprised. He fell and rolled onto one side and then was still.

Thunderchild stepped between us as the other four started forward and there was a flicker of green lightning down his great blade.

"It is done" he said, his tone giving the statement an air of finality. "As far as you four are concerned, Black Finn is dead. Do I make myself clear? I'm sure you wouldn't wish to take on Finn, Kharr and myself in a fight, would you?"

The four stopped in their tracks. Egret bent and picked up Cody's body in his long arms. "Over, but not forgotten." he said, before. turning and walking away. I watched them go, before I turned to Thunderchild.

"My thanks."

"For what? I did not stop the contest, merely made it a fair one."

I smiled and offered my hand, "Nonetheless."

He gripped my hand and shook it. His grip with a mail gauntlet on was like a vice and I winced, slightly.

"You are undoubtedly a rogue, Finn but I name you my friend."

"And I will treasure this friendship, I am sure."

"What was that really about?" asked Kharr.

"A left over. I find I am thirsty again, let's return to the inn and I can tell you the rest of the story."

We returned to the inn where I washed my wound and bought another drink apiece. I explained about my old master and the contract he had put out on me. Kharr looked grave. "There could be more of them looking for you."

"There could be, but I doubt it."

Thunderchild had resumed his previous look of an ordinary landsman before we even reached the door of the inn.

I learned a little more about him before we headed for the livery stables. As we walked across the street, six men with halberds and a sergeant in chain mail with a large axe intercepted us.

"Hold up there, you three." I heard the sergeant before I saw the men coming up behind us. I turned.

"Can I be of assistance?" I asked. Kharr stopped and spun about, one hand on the hilt of his scimitar.

"There's been a report of a fight and rumour a man was killed."

"The report is correct." Thunderchild turned about to face the men.

"Thunderchild," the sergeant gulped, "I didn't realise you were involved. As an honorary sheriff, I assume justice was done, then."

"It was, sergeant."

***

The next morning, we set out for Jordis. We took a merchantman down the Imperial Canal as far as we could and then went by horse across Valcoria.

There seemed to be rumours of war everywhere we went and, in several villages, people ran and hid when we rode in.

Eventually, we reached Jordis and I set about trying to find a ship that would sail directly to Gwythaor. I had told Thunderchild much about the island and he had decided that it sounded somewhere he would enjoy visiting. I was glad. I wanted to walk in Warvane with Kharr beside me again. Having Thunderchild there would add greatly to it.

I visited our shipping clerk in Jordis and found two despatches waiting. One was from Leopold asking me to contact him about a task that he wanted me to take on. I tore that one up.

I intended to take some time as a free man to do what I wanted. The second was from Viktor. His order was going to rebuild and fortify an old abandoned monastery in The Marish, a neglected island just outside the Imperial borders with no single ruler but a number of warring barbarian clans. They intended to bring the word of Narva to the natives and try to cement alliances to turn the island into a viable state. I smiled at his long narrative covering various events. I didn't know, then, but the order's decision to set down in the Marish was going to lead me on one of the most dangerous of my adventures to date.

I wandered back to the dock, picking up a few pieces of equipment, some powders and liquids from the apothecary and had some repairs made to my armour. By the time I found Kharr and Thunderchild it was mid-afternoon. Kharr looked up and smiled, sadly.

"I'm sorry my friend but I will not be able to join you and Thunderchild. I have received a letter from my sister and must join her."

"Then we'll put off Gwythaor for now and ride with you." I said.

Thunderchild smiled and shook his head. Kharr also smiled, meeting my eye,

"It's just family business. You would feel awkward. It is no matter. I will soon be on my way, again."

"It would be good to meet your folk."

"Another time. It is a small and private matter that we must discuss. It won't take long to resolve matters and then I can take ship for Gwythaor and we can join up again. Look for me as the shadows lengthen, one summer eve in Warvane."

My heart sank. "Then I guess this is farewell for now" I said, clasping his hands in mine.

"All things come to an end, my good friend," Kharr smiled, "but friendship remains."

He shook hands with Thunderchild, "Whatever happens and wherever our paths take us, we will always be friends."

And with that, Kharr walked away towards a big eastern trader with a colourful lateen sail.

Although we heard the odd tale and even when I went seeking him in his own lands, I never saw Kharr again.

Freedom – A short postscript

That wasn't the end of the tale, of course. It was just a beginning. There is simply too much to tell.

In Gwythaor, I renewed old associations and made many more friends before the shadows of war stretched over us and I found myself drawn by ties to family and friendship. I also renewed some old rivalries. There are a host of stories to be told there.

There were some dark times and there were some good times. Best of all was that I met my lady love, the sweet Sylvander. Our adventures together were also many and varied.

I have tried to tell some of those as fireside tales, too, along with stories about my friends, many of which I heard second hand myself.

Who knows, maybe I'll write some of them down one of these days, soon.

Black Finn

About the Author

These words were written by Alun in 2015, I can think of no better way to give you a feeling for him than sharing his own words about why he wanted to be a writer:

"I think I have always wanted to be a published writer since primary school when I started writing a sporadic magazine and untold quests of King Arthur's knights in about twenty volumes of ten to twenty pages apiece.

I imagine like most writers, I have a collection of abandoned novels, mostly just first chapters that I never took further. For thirty years, I worked as a project and programme manager.

In my university years, I was widely published as a poet in magazines that circulated around a certain circle of colleges as well as appearing in a few independent anthologies, local magazines and e-zines. For years, I used my pursuit of a professional career to a senior level as an excuse for not putting the time required into the novels I had in mind.

My full time career was cut short by cancer which today, gladly, is stable although I am realistic about the long term prospects. I read a great deal and have a room dedicated as a library with over twelve hundred books. Other than that, I live in semi-rural Hertfordshire (England), have a wife and two adult children and no dog. I like to walk, think too much and play golf, badly."

***

Sadly, Alun passed away from cancer, aged 59 in 2019. He left behind several unfinished novels, the first of which we are sharing with you now.

Perhaps in time we may share more of these stories, which he longed to see read and enjoyed by people such as yourself.

It took a mammoth series of editing sessions between us, hundreds of cups of tea and the removal of several thousand commas to bring it to you today.

Having said that, we have done our best to preserve his story in his own words, as he intended it to be read. He wouldn't after all, have had it any other way

We are grateful to him for entrusting us with his most cherished character and we hope that through the telling of this story, we do him justice and that you, the reader, can enjoy the story he has to tell.

Anthony & Kirsty (Alun's aforementioned children)

Printed in Great Britain
by Amazon